BEYOND REDRESS

A HARRY BROCK MYSTERY

BEYOND REDRESS

KINLEY ROBY

FIVE STAR
A part of Gale, Cengage Learning

GALE
CENGAGE Learning·

Detroit • New York • San Francisco • New Haven, Conn • Waterville, Maine • London

GALE
CENGAGE Learning®

LIBRARY OF CONGRESS CATALOGING-IN-PUBLICATION DATA

Roby, Kinley E.
    Beyond Redress : a Harry Brock Mystery / Kinley Roby. — First Edition.
        pages cm
    ISBN-13: 978-1-4328-2726-7 (hardcover)
    ISBN-10: 1-4328-2726-X (hardcover)
    1. Brock, Harry (Fictitious character : Roby) —Fiction. 2. Private investigators—Florida—Fiction. 3. Murder—Investigation—Fiction. 4. Gulf Coast (Fla.) —Fiction. I. Title.
PS3618.O3385B49 2013
813'.6—dc23   2013019182

First Edition. First Printing: October 2013
Find us on Facebook– https://www.facebook.com/FiveStarCengage
Visit our website– http://www.gale.cengage.com/fivestar/
Contact Five Star™ Publishing at FiveStar@cengage.com

Printed in Mexico
1 2 3 4 5 6 7 17 16 15 14 13

For Stanley Weintraub
Thank you for your guidance, generous help, and many
kindnesses in those early years.

"For every one of us, living in this world means waiting for our end."

—*Beowulf,* translated by Seamus Heaney

CHAPTER 1

Harry Brock and Tucker LaBeau were sitting in bentwood rockers on Tucker's back stoop, letting the sweat dry after toiling in the Florida sun. They had been clearing Tucker's vegetable garden of wrecked bean frames, shattered corn stalks, shredded tomato plants, and the scattered remains of tree branches and palm fronds that Hurricane Sheila's visit to Florida's southwest coast had left in her wake.

The sour smell of rotting pumpkin vines, tomatoes, peppers, and cucumbers was still in Harry's nostrils, but Tucker's home-brewed ale was dispelling it rapidly. While cooling down, they were reflecting on the hurricane, but Harry suddenly changed the subject.

"What's your take on the concept of evil?" he asked.

Tucker had put down his glass to mop his face with a large blue handkerchief after dropping his ragged straw hat beside the rocker. Tucker was a small man, thin as a rail, bald, with a fringe of soft white hair that lifted with every stir of the air, making it look in certain lights like a halo. But there was nothing angelic about the old farmer.

His china blue eyes sparkled with humor and his tongue was sharp, both qualities gained from his accumulated years, the exact number of which was either a closely guarded secret or something Tucker did not know with certainty. Harry had seldom heard Tucker speak of his childhood, and it was not a subject about which he invited questions. But Harry felt certain his old friend had been casting a shadow at least a decade beyond the biblical number of three score and ten.

"How convinced are you that such a thing exists?" Tucker asked.

"You're dodging."

"Here's another question. Are you trying to cast off the stigma of being a private investigator by taking up seminary studies?"

"Well," Harry said, growing impatient, "if I've now got to justify a simple question by citing a supporting passage in the Constitution, I suppose I'll have to say I read something in the *Banner* that put the question into my head. It's been buzzing around in there ever since, and I'm sick of listening to it."

Harry got up and stretched, to ease a cramp in his back, a residual from having a bullet pass through that area of his body a few years ago. He was a man of medium height and moderately heavy build, most of which was bone and muscle, padded a bit around the middle with the effects of enjoying eating and not running as frequently as he often told himself he fully intended doing just as soon as . . . well, anyway, very soon. His cropped hair, which was retreating from his advancing forehead, was a faded blond, liberally salted with silver. Like nearly everyone in Southwest Florida, he was tanned and, unlike most, moderately fit.

"Am I going to hear about what you read?" Tucker inquired after a period of silence during which Harry stood staring at the dense woods behind the house, rehearsing yet again what the fly was saying and liking it less with every repetition.

"What? Oh, yes. I was thinking about it again and forgot what I was doing."

"Not doing is more accurate," Tucker said. "While you're organizing your mind, let's fill these glasses."

Harry picked up his glass and followed Tucker through the

screen door into a large kitchen, brightly lit by windows trimmed with red and white gingham curtains and furnished with a large, black cookstove, an ancient Shaker table that had long since cast off the restraints of its varnish, and half a dozen spindle chairs. In one corner was an old and battered easy chair with an ottoman on which an extremely large cat lay curled, sleeping.

"Why is Jane Bunting sleeping in the house at mid-morning?" Harry asked. "And where are the kittens?"

"Aurelius and Frederica haven't come back from their nightly hunt," Tucker said, pausing to glance at the cat. "I'm a little concerned about Jane Bunting. She hasn't eaten anything for two days."

"Is it time to call in Heather Parkinson? If Jane Bunting isn't eating, something's seriously wrong."

Harry frowned and walked over for a closer look at the cat. He reached out to stroke her, but Jane Bunting opened one eye and fixed him with a malevolent yellow gaze. Harry snatched his hand out of her reach. As she weighed nearly thirty pounds and struck first and inquired after, Harry had made the right decision. Her kittens were even larger than she, probably because their father, according to Tucker, was a bobcat. But that was not mentioned in her presence because, as Tucker explained, she now regarded the relationship as a moral lapse and wished to put it behind her.

"Whatever's wrong hasn't improved her disposition," Harry said, giving her additional space.

"No it hasn't," Tucker answered, handing Harry a replenished glass and leading the way back to the stoop. "I suspect that has something to do with Frederica and Aurelius' keeping to the woods. Let's hear what you have to tell me."

"It's not good news," Harry said when they were seated. The morning wind off the Gulf had picked up, rattling the dead fronds on the cabbage palms scattered along the edge of the woods, and bringing with it the rich earthy smell of the forest.

"I remain undaunted," Tucker said. "In my experience, good news is usually bad news tarted up. Go ahead."

"Does the name Henrico Perez ring any bells?"

"Isn't he the man who was shot to death about ten days ago?"

Harry confirmed his friend's recollection. Tucker thought a moment and then asked, "Wasn't he largely responsible for shaming the city council into turning that land in East Avola where the old water treatment plant was into a park for that much-neglected part of the city?"

"That's right. More recently, he and his group of community activists jawboned the council into converting several abandoned buildings on the Seminole River into temporary housing for the homeless."

"I remember now," Tucker said. "Arthur Bingley turned them over to the city for unpaid taxes after his boat business collapsed. I believe that experiment's been a success, hasn't it, despite the charges of flagrant socialism brought in by the Tea Party people?"

"That's right, but I've been postponing having to speak about his being murdered because he was shot six times, the last, apparently, through his heart. At least that's my reading of the sequence."

Harry went silent, and Tucker sat rocking slowly, watching him.

"Malice," the old farmer said flatly, breaking the silence.

"Maybe."

"I gather you're not willing to entertain the possibility the killer was just a bad shot."

"No."

"And that's why you asked if I thought there was such a

thing as evil," Tucker said quietly.

"The question has been in my mind," Harry said.

"Apparently for several days," Tucker said.

"Go ahead, be sarcastic, but it's been growing on me."

"I can see that. Well, going directly to your question and leaving the shooting aside for the moment, if evil does exist, I guess it has to be an abstraction, which means it's not connected to any specific thing although you might say the evidence of it is everywhere, as in the murder you've just mentioned."

"Is there an answer coming pretty soon?"

"I'm just laying out some necessary groundwork," Tucker said comfortably, folding his hands across his stomach as if to show that as the rest of the day lay before them, there was no point in hurrying. "Providing a definition for evil is not a simple task," he continued. "I expect our hunter-gatherer ancestors sat out a good many nights, watching the stars, arguing over it."

Harry had been growing increasingly irritated. Although few knew better than he the mayhem created by people against people, Henrico Perez's murder had rattled him, and he knew that Tucker's mental spinning wheel could run on, producing *ifs* and *buts* and *on the other hands,* as long as there was light left to see by.

"Why not just say yes or no and have done with it?"

Tucker looked up at the stoop roof as if seeking guidance and asked, "Who was it said, 'For every complex problem there's always a solution that is clear, simple, and wrong'?"

"Humpty Dumpty."

"Very funny. I think it was H. L. Mencken, who indirectly heard it from Noah. And because you're impatient, I'll act against my own best judgment and say that I think evil is an *omniparens* word and probably not susceptible to definition."

"Are you being deliberately difficult or is it that I'm not paying sufficient attention?"

"I wasn't going to mention it, but you do seem to have developed an attention deficit, worse at some times than others. What's caused this most recent flare-up?"

"I won't dignify that with a response. Then, if it evades precise definition, according to you, it's meaningless?"

"I mean something far more serious. Believing that evil is an entity responsible for the world's Hitlers and Stalins is extremely dangerous."

"How so?"

"It wasn't evil who built the death camps of WWII. They were built by people. It was Stalin who ordered the mass killings of his own citizens and people who carried out the orders. It's all too easy and dishonest to say, 'Hitler and Stalin were evil'—as if that took care of the matter."

"Weren't they?"

"You might want to describe what they did as evil, but calling *them* evil separates *them* from the rest of us—separates us from their crimes, exonerates us, and that's dangerous."

"I can't see you doing what was done to Henrico Perez."

"I hope not, but it was another human being who did do it, not something by the name of *Evil.*"

"I find that very hard to believe."

"Because you can't believe one person could do that to another person?"

"No, because I don't want to."

CHAPTER 2

Harry and Tucker finished their ale, and Harry left, lamenting that he was returning to a long list of unwritten insurance company reports.

"They may be my bread and butter," he complained, "but they're also my ball and chain."

"You're not getting any sympathy from me . . ." Tucker replied, walking Harry out into the yard. "You do less work to earn your living than any other man I know."

"Well, it's not the work I first chose, but now I find I wouldn't want to do anything else. I'm surprised it's grown on me the way it has."

"You've brought a lot of help to a lot of people over the years I've known you," Tucker said seriously in an abrupt change of tone, resting a hand on Harry's shoulder. "See to it you don't do anything foolish and get yourself killed."

"With that encouraging thought, I'll leave," Harry said, not at all surprised by Tucker's warning.

He had been hearing it in one version or another for about twenty years, ever since he moved onto the Hammock. As he started away, a big blue-tick hound and a large black mule, wearing a straw hat, emerged from the woods. Seeing the two men, the animals broke into a trot.

"What have you two been up to?" Harry asked, grasping the dog by the loose skin on his neck and giving him a rough shake, at which the hound bared a serious set of teeth and pushed forward with a rumbling growl to bury his head in Harry's stomach.

"Whoo! Sanchez!" Harry protested, freeing the dog and stepping back from him. "Skunk!"

The mule took advantage of the moment to move forward and lower his head, pressing his nose against Harry's chest and blowing softly in greeting.

"Oh, Brother!" Harry said, grasping the mule's ear with one hand and stroking his glossy neck with the other. "Can't you convince your friend to be more sensible?"

Sanchez, unrepentant in the face of criticism, continued to growl and bare his teeth and wag his tail while looking intently at Harry.

"The thing is," Tucker said in a disgusted tone of voice while regarding Sanchez with a mild frown, "he hasn't gotten it through his head that just because Florinda lives under the back stoop and has managed to patch up some kind of noncombatant relationship with him, he can't walk up to every skunk in the woods and expect a nose bump."

Oh, Brother! pulled up his head, snorted, eyed the dog with a marked expression, and edged away from Harry when Sanchez made another attempt to push his snout into Harry's stomach.

"That's it!" Harry said with a laugh, dodging around the dog. "I'm off."

Twenty minutes later, Harry was approaching his house on the narrow white sand road that he and Tucker shared and that connected Bartram's Hammock to County Road 19. In Southwest Florida a hammock is a heavily wooded low island, a foot or so higher than the surrounding swamp, and was favored by the Indians as a living place because the soaring figs and other hardwoods made hammocks ten degrees cooler than the surrounding mix of water and land.

Harry and Tucker were the sole occupants of Bartram's Hammock. And when several years earlier the state of Florida had added the Hammock to the Stickpen Preserve, Tucker, in exchange for the deed to his property, was allowed to go on living on the farm until he died. At the same time, Harry was appointed a Florida State game warden and had the care of the Hammock as well as the Stickpen Preserve, the huge expanse of water and cypress located on the eastern side of the Hammock. The preserve was bordered on the east by the sprawling expanse of the Everglades.

Just before coming in sight of the house, Harry heard the clatter of the two loose boards on the small hump-backed bridge across the creek that separated the Hammock from the mainland on its western boundary just before merging with Puc Puggy Creek. The creek ran alongside of the sandy road on which Harry was walking.

Visitors, he thought with disgust.

It was not his love of company that had led him to live twenty miles outside of the city of Avola, the source of most of his clients. Making the last turn, he saw a black Jaguar XKR coupe parked under the big live oak on the front corner of his lawn beside his silver Land Rover. With resigned interest he studied the woman who was walking slowly toward her car across the sun-baked and very patchy lawn, gazing about with no obvious interest in what she was seeing.

"Hello," she called, when he was within hailing distance. "Do you know who lives here?"

She was shading her face with her purse as she spoke, and Harry thought it didn't bode well that she lacked the sense to be wearing a hat in this sun.

"I do," he said, leaving the road and walking toward her. "Are you lost?"

She was about his height, dressed in a red sun suit and match-

17

ing sandals. Her thick dark hair, held in a gold circlet and pulled over her left shoulder, fell in long burnished waves over her breast. Her sunglasses made it impossible for him to tell what color her eyes were, but she was tanned and, he thought, clearly at ease in her body.

A tennis player, he told himself, resorting to stereotyping.

"I'm not sure," she told him, lowering the purse and regarding him in frank appraisal.

"Want to look at my teeth?" he asked.

Harry had a history, and none of it had made his relationship with women easy, although he liked them. He liked them a lot, but he had been trying hard for a while now not to think about that.

"No," she said, apparently unfazed, "but if you lost five or six pounds you'd be fairly presentable."

Harry laughed. *What is that accent?* he wondered. Not Irish. "I'm afraid it would take more than that for me to win a ribbon in whatever kind of show you've got in mind."

He was wearing shorts that sun and bleach had stripped of their color, a faded short-sleeved shirt, leather sandals that looked as if they had crossed the Great American Desert, and a Tilley hat that an alligator had once mistaken for an egret.

She laughed. It was a good laugh and Harry lost some of his attitude.

"You ought not to be standing out here without a hat on," he told her. "Come onto the porch and tell me where you're trying to go."

"All right," she said, "but I don't need your advice regarding the sun. I've been coming to Florida off and on for twenty years. Don't you know that down here porches are called lanais?"

"Slow learner," Harry said, holding the screen door to the lanai open for her. "Have a seat. I've got some cold root beer. How does that sound?"

When she stepped past him he caught a breath of her perfume that cut through all of his defenses. For an instant he closed his eyes and breathed it in.

"Are you okay?" she asked, having turned to face him.

"Relatively," he answered, pained at having been caught. "How about that root beer?"

"Got any coffee?"

"I suggest you settle for iced tea. My coffee isn't really potable."

"Okay," she said with a grin. "I didn't know anyone actually drank root beer anymore."

"A saving remnant," Harry said, disappearing into the kitchen and returning after a minute with two glasses of iced tea, sporting some sprigs of mint.

"Salad," she said, pushing her glasses onto her forehead to study the mint, giving Harry the opportunity to see the tiny wrinkles at the corners of her eyes and better assess her age.

"Home grown."

They were still standing and Harry, a bit at a loss, said, "My name's Brock, Harry Brock."

"Then you're the man I'm looking for," she said in a lower, more serious voice. "I'm Gwyneth Benbow."

"That accounts for it," Harry said without thinking.

"Accounts for what?" she asked sharply.

"Let's sit down," Harry said, having noticed that her eyes were a piercing blue. In that tanned face, set off by her dark hair, they were arresting, almost feral, he thought. Benbow of the wolf clan.

Once settled on a white wooden lounge chair, she said more forcefully, "That accounts for what?"

"The blue eyes and the dark hair," he replied.

"You think I look weird."

It was clearly a challenge.

"I certainly do not. I think you have beautiful eyes, but my saying it can't come as a surprise. Tell me what's brought you to this unorganized corner of Tequesta County."

"It's the Welsh heritage and maybe it does, a little. Not everyone agrees with you."

"Gwyneth, the shining girl," Harry said, letting himself go a little.

"You're an odd man. Do you know that? Knowing what Gwyneth means."

"Yes, look where I live."

"But not alone."

"Yes, alone if one can be said to be alone in the midst of this seething life around us."

He gestured toward the screens just as a mixed flock of white and glossy ibis descended in a rush of wings, landing on the banks of the Puc Puggy Creek. The birds spread out, hurried down the bank, and instantly set to work probing the mud with their curved, orange beaks.

"I guess this place *is* special," she said as the flock moved away, "and noisy."

The cicadas and locusts in the surrounding oaks were fiddling in top form, the volume rising and falling like waves, washing over the house and the lanai.

"They will keep going until dark," he said. "Then the colony frogs and the rest of the night choir take over."

"I'd better try to tell you why I'm here," she said suddenly, setting her glass down on the low oak table beside her chair.

Harry wondered where the difficulty came in, but he did not find it surprising. Many of his clients found beginning as daunting as Gwyneth did, and for good reasons. Things long held secret were going to be revealed.

"Have you heard of Henrico Perez?" she asked after a lengthy pause spent staring toward the creek, but seeing, Harry guessed from the drawn look on her face, quite another scene.

"Yes, and I happened to see another piece in this morning's paper."

"I can scarcely bring myself to think about what happened to him, it's so dreadful. Whoever did it must be a monster." She clasped her hands and shuddered.

What, he wondered, could this woman have to do with Perez? They inhabited worlds separated by light years of social distance.

"Were you in some way connected with him?" Harry asked as the silence between them lengthened, finally to the point that he concluded she needed prompting.

"Yes and no," she said, relaxing slightly and swinging her legs off her chair in order to face him.

Harry matched her move and then set his own glass down, giving her his full attention. Every client with whom he had ever held this initial conversation had reached the moment of decision as to whether or not to trust him. This, he was sure, was such a moment for Gwyneth.

"I knew him . . . well. I'm on the board of directors of his organization."

"The Friends of St. Lazarus," he said, wondering why she had paused.

"Yes, patron saint of the poor. I'm not a Catholic. Perhaps I'm not much of anything."

"Raised an Anglican?"

"How did you guess?"

"It goes with the Welsh background—either that or Methodist."

"A dying breed," she said cryptically. "It's the Catholics who are increasing. I left Wales when I was fifteen. My father was an electrical engineer who specialized in radar and sonar. The Raytheon Company in Sudbury, Massachusetts, offered him a job that doubled his U.K. salary, and we emigrated."

"How did you feel about that?"

"Brokenhearted at first, losing my friends, but I soon made new ones. I liked Sudbury. My mother almost fainted with joy when she saw the house my father had bought for us. Five bedrooms, four bathrooms on an acre lot. We had been living in a small semi in Croydon for three years. You can imagine."

"I can't, actually. I've never been to Croydon."

"Most people haven't."

"Most people haven't been to Sudbury either."

"Thank heavens. There are still stone walls along many of the roads and even a few fields where the farmers mow the hay, twice in a good summer."

"Are you aware that you are avoiding telling me what you came here to tell me? I don't mind that, you know. I'm enjoying talking with you, and I'm not in any hurry."

"But you thought you'd call it to my attention."

Harry noted the drop in temperature in her voice, but remained calm.

"No one outside of the police is going to do a damned thing to find Henrico's killer," she continued. "That's why I'm here."

"Have you met Jim Snyder? He's the captain of the Tequesta County Sheriff's Department."

"I know who he is," she said, displaying some uneasiness.

"Okay. The Avola police are not equipped to investigate a major crime of this nature. Very soon—perhaps it's already been done—the assistant district attorney for the 21st district of Florida will pass the investigation along to the sheriff, who will pass it to Jim."

Harry stopped, to give Gwyneth time to ask any questions the information may have given rise to.

"I'm with you so far," she said.

"Good. Jim is a skilled and dedicated policeman. His staff is highly trained and thoroughly professional. Believe me when I tell you that Jim will leave no stone unturned when he and his team launch their investigation."

"I can't tell whether you expect them to form a soccer team or build a wall," she answered, all trace of humor stripped from her voice.

Harry took his time before responding but in the interval had no luck finding the reason for her sudden hostility.

"What do you know that I don't?" he asked, hoping to discover in her answer what had gone wrong.

"I think the real question is, why don't you know it?"

Harry was concerned to see that his question had increased her anger instead of reducing it. There was, he knew, always the risk, when stepping into another person's magic circle, of having your head snatched off. But if his goal was to understand what this volatile woman wanted from him, he decided to risk it.

"To answer that, you will have to tell me what I obviously don't know."

She sat for a while, her blue eyes darkened to violet by whatever was angering her. Harry waited her out.

"I think I'm wasting my time," she said, swept her purse off the table beside her chair, and more or less flew to her feet. Then, back straight and chin up, she strode toward the door.

"How old are you?" Harry asked just as she was reaching for the door handle.

"That's none of your damned business," she barked, spinning on a heel and glaring at him.

"I placed you above eleven," he said in a cheerful voice.

"God knows I am," she said bitterly. "Just as he was leaving, my last husband said I was too old for him."

Harry grasped the opportunity. "How many husbands have you had?"

"Two," she said in a hard voice, "and I have sworn a blood

oath that there won't be a third."

Harry got up and stepped toward her, his hand extended. "Congratulations on your courage," he said. "Like you, I've been married twice, but I tried for a third. When she turned me down, I folded. And I feel compelled to say that while we've shown courage—you especially—neither of us can be accused of possessing much judgment."

It worked. She grinned, and it transformed her face from a thundercloud to a warm spring morning.

"Do you ever eat crullers?" he asked.

"Not since I was eleven," she replied.

"Hot tea, warm milk, sugar, and a plate of crullers. How does that sound?"

"Real tea or tea bags?"

"Earl Grey, real tea."

"Can I make it?"

"At your own risk. I'm very fussy."

"You're on."

They moved to the kitchen. "An electric kettle!" she exclaimed with obvious pleasure on entering the room.

"Rinse it, fill it, and I'll round up the makings."

Preparations made, they sat down at the kitchen table, the plate of crullers, the small pitcher of warm milk, and the sugar bowl, cups and saucers, and spoons between them, to wait while the tea steeped.

"Is it time to talk seriously again?" Gwyneth asked.

"Almost," he said. "I think I need some tea for fortitude."

"This is the real thing," she said, pouring.

Harry added a little warm milk, stirred once, and sipped.

"You're hired," he said, "or if you'd prefer, you could just move in."

"That's the tea talking," Gwyneth said, giving him a weak smile as she dealt with the milk and the sugar.

"Where were we?" he asked, regretting his sally, regretting the possibility she might think he meant it.

Did he? Not on this light snow.

She had, apparently, been following her own thoughts because after tasting her tea and adding more sugar, she said, "A minimum amount of either time or money will be spent searching for Henrico's killer," she said. "You know it. I know it. I don't know why I dumped my anger on you. I'm sorry."

"My name just came up," he said, breaking a cruller in half as though he intended to eat only one of the pieces.

She looked puzzled.

"Ever hear of Charlie Brown?"

"Of course. Oh! Sure, Charlie Brown's in bed and he says, 'Sometimes I lie here and ask, Why me?' and the answer comes back, 'Nothing personal, your name just happened to come up.' Thanks for giving me an out."

He nodded and silently awarded her extra points, then said, "Do you think this because he's Hispanic or because he's been a constant thorn in the city and the county's sides?"

"All of the above."

"Then why are you here?"

"You're not going to admit it, are you?"

"I have known and worked with Jim Snyder for twenty years. He's one of the most upstanding, decent men I know. He is no more a racist than you are."

"I know nothing about Captain Snyder," Gwyneth said. "And whether he's a racist or not is mostly irrelevant."

"But you just . . ."

"At the risk of insulting you," Gwyneth said, "I'm going to suggest that our perspectives are rather different, and I apologize for not having remembered the fact sooner."

"Meaning you're rich, and I'm not," Harry said, stung. "What does your being wealthier than I am have to do with racial prejudice or lack thereof in the Florida legal system?"

Gwyneth leaned back in her chair and regarded Harry with apparent concern. When she spoke, the edge had gone out of her voice. "Harry, I've been clumsy and hurt your feelings. Please accept my apology and let me try again to say what I mean."

While she was preparing to speak, Harry gorilla-ed his anger back into its cage. "I'm listening," he said.

"I've been working on the St. Lazarus Political Outreach Committee for almost eight years," she began, rather tentatively, Harry thought.

"Wade right in," Harry said. "Treat me to total immersion. I won't drown."

Gwyneth looked at him for a while. Harry looked back.

"Okaaay," she said as if accepting a challenge. "In those eight years I've spent as much time in Tallahassee as I have in Avola. What I've seen in both places during that period hasn't strengthened my hopes that we're all going to be living together in a state of equality, harmony, and mutual respect any time soon."

"Should I be surprised?" Harry said.

"Well, if I don't surprise you, why are you telling me that the state, county, and local law enforcement entities are going to make a genuine effort to find Henrico's killers, especially if, as I suspect, the evidence starts leading toward someone or a group of someones who carry a serious amount of political influence—i.e., people loaded with money?"

CHAPTER 3

Harry swallowed a serving of crow and then began his response.

"I can't deny that position and wealth influence the administration of justice in Florida. Like you, I've lived long enough to know"—a bit of payback that wasn't called for and he instantly regretted—"that racial issues still exist in this state and that sometimes these issues take the form of denying justice to people of color."

"But that won't happen in this instance, in this place, at this time," Gwyneth said.

"At least in Florida, Henrico Perez still has name recognition. He was the darling of the media because wherever he walked, he created an uproar, and the investigation of his death is going to be covered by that same media. That is going to be a factor in his favor that makes it very risky for law enforcement to do less than they should be doing."

Harry got up and cleared the table. While he was doing that, Gwyneth sat, staring at his empty chair.

"I'm sick of sitting," he said when he was done. "What about you?"

"Have you just switched off the conversation?" she asked, looking up at him with a frown.

"No, just suggesting a change of venue."

She glanced through the door at the stairs and then at him, her expression darkening.

"There's a real bathroom up there," he said, concealing his

amusement. "If you want to use it, please do. Then I thought we might take a walk. I've got a woman's hat that will fit you."

Gwyneth colored slightly, her frown fading. "Thank you, I'd enjoy a walk. Excuse me."

A graceful woman walking is a thing of beauty, mystery in motion, he thought, briefly watching her progress up the stairs. *It wasn't a mystery you were looking at,* he told himself harshly by way of a warning, and strode off to find the hat. But his mind ignored the lecture and went on remembering her climbing the stairs.

"Do you object to the orange ribbon?" he asked, holding out to her the pale straw hat with its low crown and wide brim, when she came out of the kitchen and onto the lanai.

"A respectable lawn party hat and a very nice one," Gwyneth said, turning it in her hands. "Never mind the orange ribbon. Will anyone but you and I see it?" she asked, setting it on her head at a slightly rakish angle. "Where are we going?"

"Up the road," he said, trying not to think about the woman who had last worn that hat and was now in Seattle. Fully recovered, he hoped, but that was probably wishful thinking and he knew it. "Puc Puggy Creek borders the road for a couple of miles, and the trees provide enough shade to make walking bearable."

They crossed the lawn through the blazing sun and stepped onto the soft white sand of the road and into the live oak's welcome shade, the tree's branches forming a flickering arch of leaves over their heads.

"Do you think the evidence will lead toward money?" he asked.

"Not right away," she said.

"Explain."

"If moneyed interests are behind his death, they will be shielded by multiple intermediaries acting on their behalf."

"How surprised were you to learn about his death?"

"I think you mean was I surprised that he had been killed? No. I'm only surprised he lasted as long as he did."

Harry winced inwardly at the sudden bitterness in her voice. "Have you made up your mind about me?"

"What makes you think I've been evaluating you?" she asked, putting a hand on the crown of her hat as a wayward breeze stirred the air around them, transforming the surface of the creek into a shattered mirror of flashing lights.

"Didn't I tell you? I read minds."

They had reached a place where the Puc Puggy, having swerved away from the road, had swung back and turned again to continue its path beside the grass- and brush-covered embankment. The turn had created widening in the creek and a slow spiraling of its dark water where the creek turned back on itself briefly before hurrying on.

Harry and Gwyneth had stopped to deal with the mind-reading business, and for once Harry was not paying attention to what the rest of the world around him was up to, having given his attention to the results of the wind pressing Gwyneth's sundress against her body. As a consequence, he was surprised when a small deer burst out of the trees, nearly running into him as it bounded across the road.

Gwyneth, positioned to see the deer first, gave a small cry of alarm or astonishment, causing the deer to veer suddenly, breaking its stride and hesitating before leaping from the top of the bank. Having lost some of its momentum, the animal plunged into the middle of the creek instead of clearing it, disappearing for a moment before it surfaced and began swimming hard for the far shore and the expanse of open swamp beyond.

At that moment Harry saw a heavy V-shaped head emerge from the brush at the bottom of the bank below them. The head, driven by a long, thick, dark body, slid swiftly through the water, gaining quickly on the struggling deer.

"Harry!" Gwyneth cried.

Before Harry could reply, the snake had overtaken the deer. Its jaws gaped, struck, and grasped the deer by the neck. In an instant, the rest of the huge snake flung itself onto the bleating deer and forced it down. The water closed over its head, the bleating ceased, the last glistening coil slid from sight. The black water wrinkled briefly, then ran on smoothly and silently.

"Oh, God," Gwyneth said in a fading voice, still staring at the place where the snake had dragged the deer below the surface.

"I'm sorry you had to watch that," Harry said. "It's the first one I've seen on the Hammock."

"What was it?"

"A Burmese python," Harry said, shaking off as fast as he could the revulsion and anger that the snake had stirred in him.

"I didn't think I was squeamish," Gwyneth said, her voice steadying, "but the sight of that thing drowning the deer turned my knees to water. Of course I know they're here. After the news coverage lately, how could anyone living in southern Florida not know? But seeing one is different from seeing pictures."

"Yes it is," Harry agreed, taking her gently by the arm and moving them away from the eddy. "I have to remind myself constantly that what we just witnessed is a part of life here and pretty much anywhere living things exist."

"Do you walk along this road at night?"

"Not in the dark of the moon or not without a good flashlight," he said, releasing her arm. "The sand holds the heat after the sun goes down and, being cold-blooded, snakes like lying on it. It's bad enough thinking about unexpectedly stepping on a six-foot rattlesnake in the dark, but just imagine stepping on a fifteen-foot python."

"I don't want to," Gwyneth said. "I'd rather think about your ability to read my mind."

"I lied. Why did you come looking for me?"

The sun was now almost straight above their heads, and the sand of the road was a kaleidoscope of shifting white and black patches as the Gulf wind stirred the tops of the canopy trees.

"I want to hire you to find out who killed Henrico."

She had stopped walking to tell him that, and when he stopped and turned to face her, he found himself looking straight into her blue eyes. She had pulled off her glasses, apparently to emphasize the seriousness of her request. Masked by her sunglasses, their intensity had been hidden long enough to be startling.

"Harry," she said sternly, "don't make a joke of this. I'm serious."

"I know," he said, regrouping. "That's why I'm having trouble responding. One more question first before I deal with your wanting to hire me. How did you find me?"

"GPS."

"Now who's being funny?"

"Holly Pike recommended you."

"How is she?" Harry asked, surprised and pleased.

"She's fine. Why didn't you two become an item? According to her you walk on water."

"She'd just lost her husband. I was committed elsewhere."

"Too bad. She's still not married."

"I know."

"She'll like hearing you're keeping track of her."

"I'm not, but she went through a very bad time. How's her daughter?"

"Harriet is fine. I think she's in preschool. Spoiled, but I suppose Holly's love has to go somewhere."

Harry nodded and let what might have been a hint slip past him.

"You would be wasting your money by hiring me, Gwyneth," Harry said. "Despite your doubts, Jim and his people are going to turn over every leaf in the woods to find Henrico's killer."

"And if I'm right, and they'll do just enough to keep the press off their backs and then let the investigation fade away?"

"They won't, here's why. If there are in this case, as is obviously true, indications that the victim's civil rights have been violated, the FBI has a door through which to enter the investigation. No state or local police or sheriff's department wants to be steamrollered by the feds. But whether they like it not, if Perez's death gains national attention, they may, at the very least, send in an observer, to make sure a full bore search is under way and to serve as a federal contact person for the local authorities in case they want help."

Gwyneth shook her head. "I've done my homework, Harry," she said. "The FBI is up to its ears in caseloads. The last thing they want is to become involved here if there's any way they can stay out. This thing may turn very nasty. People with powerful connections may become involved. It's my belief, despite the truth of what you've told me, that the local police and the FBI are not going to want to be scorched in the political barbeque that's coming."

"Well," Harry said and meant it, "I'm impressed. But if you have looked at the situation this closely, why don't you know that paying me to chase this fire engine will be as futile as pounding sand in a rat hole?"

She laughed and joined him as he began walking back the way they had come. She appeared to have lost interest in the subject because she began noticing the flowers at the edge of the road and the birds that were moving through the lower branches of the trees.

"Why aren't they singing?" she asked, having confused a tiny gray gnatcatcher, scarcely larger than her thumb, with a hummingbird.

"The breeding season for most of these birds is over," Harry said, "and because singing is principally a function of establishing a territory and attracting a mate, the males are taking a break."

"You ought to give guided tours out here."

"Are you being sarcastic?"

"No, you really should. It's like living in a zoo and aviary combined," she said in an easy voice, stopping to watch a gopher tortoise that looked like half a basketball with legs and a turtle's head plod across the road in front of them, placidly ignoring their presence.

When they got back to her car, Gwyneth took off her hat and passed it to Harry. "This hat," she said with a wry smile, "looks like a hat with a history. I'd like to hear it."

"Just a hat," he lied, having no intention of telling her or anyone else how he came to have it in the downstairs closet. He had closed the chapter on that story and very much wanted it to stay closed.

"Have I convinced you to give up the idea of pursuing your friend's murderer?" he asked.

"No, Harry, you haven't," she answered, looking at him with an expression that made him vaguely uncomfortable but that he could not immediately read. "And since you refuse to take on the task, I'll just have to find someone who will. I'm sorry you won't do it, but I'm not giving up."

She opened the front door on the driver's side and reached inside, grasped her bag, and snapped back as if she'd been stung. The sun had moved enough to have found an opening in the oak's branches and a broad ray of light was bathing the car.

"It's a furnace in there," she gasped.

"Florida," Harry said. "Look, I'm sorry if I've disappointed you."

Instead of replying, she reached into her bag, extracted a card, and passed it to him.

"If you change your mind, this is where you can find me, or," she said with a smile, "if you decide to give nature tours, let me know."

"I'll do that," he said, feeling suddenly bereft.

They stood looking at one another for a moment that stretched a little before she said, putting out her hand, "Good-bye Harry Brock of Bartram's Hammock. Thanks for the tea and the walk. I enjoyed both."

With that she got into the Jaguar, backed expertly onto the road, spun the wheel, and drove away. A few seconds later, he heard the planks thump, and she was gone.

CHAPTER 4

He took no pleasure in her going. In fact, he stood for several minutes with his hands shoved into his shorts pockets, staring glumly at the empty road where the last of the silver cloud of dust, raised in the wake of her glistening black Jaguar, was slowly settling back to earth. He could not have said what he was staring at because his mind was thoroughly occupied reviewing the hour he had spent in her company, recalling fragments of their conversation, but mostly thinking of her and how good he felt just being around her.

While it was distinctly better to be thinking about Gwyneth than not, he finally pulled his hands out of his pockets and walked glumly toward the house, actively dissatisfied with himself, without being able to say why. Then, as he was reaching for the handle on the screen door, he surprised himself into saying to the mockingbird singing in the wisteria vine at the south end of the veranda, "She's going to end up in the hands of some goddamned scammer who will take her money and do nothing for her."

It was a harsh judgment of his colleagues, but Harry knew that her chance of persuading any reputable private investigator to take on the job she wanted done was vanishingly small. Pausing to pull her card out of his shirt pocket and locate her cell number before opening the lanai door, Harry memorized it, then walked into the kitchen and picked up the phone.

"I'll do it," he said when she answered.

There was a loud squeal of tires being stressed, followed an instant later by a blaring horn.

"Whoops!" she said with a rising voice, followed by a happy laugh. "I just did a Uey in front of an oncoming gravel truck and probably scared the bejesus out of him. Well, I suppose he thought he'd have to stand on his brakes to keep from driving right over me."

She laughed again. "Not with this car. I've put a corner between us before he reached the place where I turned. I'll see you in about four minutes. Don't change your mind before I get there."

Harry tried to tell her to be careful coming over the bridge, but she had already hung up. He did not ask himself why he continued to feel so good.

She arrived in a much larger cloud of dust than the one she left in and jumped out of the car grinning.

"What made you change your mind?" she asked.

His heart had not stopped racing from the explosion of sound when the Jaguar hit the loose planks.

"Don't look so worried," she said, obviously pleased with herself. "We flew briefly from the top of the bridge, but we had a soft landing. Tell me. Why did you change your mind?"

"Do you always drive like that?" Harry asked, half angry and half amused.

"Like what?"

"An idiot."

"Of course! They did not build the XKR to be driven at sensible speeds, and I did not buy it to waste time in."

Coming from most people, Harry would have found in that little speech the insolence of entitlement and the bravado of arrogance. But coming from Gwyneth it sounded honest and direct.

The rich are different from you and me . . . Harry thought of that comment and wondered as he had wondered before where the truth was in it. *Is Gwyneth different from me? Praise the Lord, yes! Aside from that. I don't . . .*

"Harry?"

"I'm not sure, and we both may come to regret it."

"I'm willing to risk regret. It's better than not living."

"Still no hat," Harry said. "Let's go inside and try to be sensible for a while—that is, unless you think it might deprive you of the thrill of living."

"Would stepping into the shade be sensible enough?" she asked with a grin. "I really can't stay. I've got a board meeting in fifteen minutes. Can I reach Avola in fifteen minutes?"

"No."

"Okay, you're on. I'll be there in thirteen."

"Not alive."

"Look," she said earnestly, "this car is a wonder on the road. I'll make the meeting alive, Harry. Bet your farm on it."

While listening to the lecture, Harry walked with her into the shade of the live oak, noting that one of the pair of barred owls who lived behind the house was having a nap on a branch above their heads.

"We should move this way a little," he said.

"Why?"

"To avoid being pooped on, big time."

"What is that?" she asked, looking up.

"A barred owl. She and her mate have a nesting tree close by."

"How do you know it's a female?"

"She's bigger than the male."

"That's one advantage to living in town. You don't get pooped on by owls."

"Do you ever eat at Oppenheimer's?"

"You mean the pigeons."

"Ring-necked doves."

"Whatever. Management has put up umbrellas."

"It's about time. What exactly do you want me to do?"

She looked at him a moment without answering, her eyes slightly narrowed. Harry wondered if he'd said something to irritate her.

"There's something I have to tell you. I don't want to, but you're going to find out, and I'd rather you heard it from me first."

"All right."

He doubted that he was going to hear anything that did not involve either money or sex—or both.

"Two years ago, Henrico and I started sleeping together. His wife found out. Somebody told my husband. Henrico patched it up with his wife. My husband was looking for an exit. So was I, and I provided the straw. He abandoned the camel."

For a moment, her expression changed, darkened, and Harry thought before it cleared that something in the memory had pained or frightened her.

"The separation was amicable," she said, having quickly dispatched whatever had been troubling her, "and the divorce settlement partially consoled him for the injury to his male pride, inflicted by having an older woman cuckold him."

"His name?"

"Eric Scartole."

"Just how upset was he?" Harry asked.

"Very," she said, having hesitated briefly and lost her smile. "To be honest, he frightened me until he controlled himself enough to talk rationally about our situation."

"Did he threaten you?"

"Nothing serious," she said with an unconvincing laugh. "Since Henrico's death, I've given the matter of the affair some thought and had, even before this conversation, decided the odds are heavily in favor of its being dragged out again."

"You're right," Harry said, somewhat cheered by her conclusion, even though he was not sure that he was hearing the whole story of the affair and its aftermath or even if what he had heard was altogether true.

"I'm just sorry that Samia, Henrico's wife, has to endure the rehash that's coming. And there's the children," she said.

"Yours?"

"No. Samia's. They're old enough now to have it hurt."

Harry rapidly riffled through his memory for any recollections of scandal involving Perez's name and found a file full.

"Do you have any children?"

Her curt "No" belonged to that category of words meaning, *don't go there*.

"What was the state of your relationship with Perez at the time of his death?"

"I stopped sleeping with him right after Samia learned what was going on."

Harry stood looking toward the house, with a part of his mind listening to the mockingbird run through his collection of other people's songs, and another part trying to decide whether or not the fact of Gwyneth's having ended the affair increased or decreased the possibility that she would become an object of interest in the investigation.

"If you're having some kind of moral moment," she said sharply, "I'm not exactly proud of what I did, especially since it was a calculated act, not a response to either love or passion. On the other hand, you can spare me any critical commentary you may be framing. That's not why I told you about Henrico and me."

"Actually," Harry said, turning to face her, determined to keep his own feelings out of the conversation, "I'm much more concerned about where the CIU are going to place you on their interest list."

"Speak English."

"The Sheriff Department's Criminal Investigation Unit," he said, "is made up of the most experienced people in the department and the most extensively trained in criminal investigation. You become a 'subject of interest' if the detectives assigned to the case decide you are somehow involved in the crime under investigation."

"Are you trying to tell me that I may become a suspect in Henrico's murder?"

"Not *may, will* become a person to be looked at very carefully. How long ago was the affair terminated?"

"Thirteen months ago," she said without hesitation.

Harry wondered a bit about that.

"Who broke it off?"

"I did."

"Can you prove that it was, in fact, over before he died?"

"If I say it was, don't they have to prove it wasn't?"

"No. In the absence of compelling evidence to the contrary, all a prosecutor has to do is convince a jury it's more likely than not that you continued the affair rather than terminated it."

"Harry, are you angry with me or trying to frighten me? Or both?"

"Maybe a little of both"—there went his good resolution—"but I'm not so much trying to frighten you as to prepare you for what is probably coming."

"And the angry part?"

She seemed genuinely concerned.

"I didn't know Perez at all well, but I've heard the stories. You seem too bright to have become another notch in his belt."

"Ouch! That hurt!" she protested.

"I don't like being lied to, Gwyneth. It puts both of us in

harm's way. Samia's finding out you two were sleeping together must have surprised her about as much as waking to another hot day in Avola."

"All right," she said, "I lied about my concern for his wife. But I told you the truth when I said that I launched the affair to get rid of my husband. And even though I wanted it, the divorce cost me a lot of money and a lot of personal pain."

"What kind of personal pain? I'll ask you again, did he threaten you?"

"And as I said, I don't want to go into that, and I won't. It's over."

Listening to her, Harry saw that it wasn't, but he didn't press. If he was patient, he thought they would reach a time when she would tell him. Anyway, there were more pressing issues to deal with.

"Just to clarify," he said, "you chose someone, with enough visibility to attract media attention but not someone whose reputation or marriage would be damaged when the word came out."

"That's right," she answered, giving no indication of remorse or embarrassment, "but it really bit into my husband, who had been living large on me. 'Aging roué replaces hubby.' I gather the ribbing was severe. He finally ran like a rabbit, frightened and furious."

"And you also knew the Perez kids were in private colleges somewhere in the North."

At that she grinned a little. "Right. With any luck they'd never hear about it, and if they did, they'd say, 'So?' Where does that leave us?"

Harry was too deep into the story to let it go. "I suppose you arranged to be caught."

"Henrico and I were coming out of the Canary Island Guest House arm in arm one morning when a reporter for the *Banner*

41

happened to be waiting on the sidewalk."

"Not yet. Why do you care who killed Perez?"

"Good question, Harry," she said in a rush. "I liked Henrico. He was kind, considerate, fun to be with, and a gentle man. I admired him. And I'm very afraid that I may have caused his death . . ."

"Whoa! Didn't you say you thought someone whose toes he had trod on killed him?"

Gwyneth stopped talking and looked at him as if confused. Then she took a deep breath, blew it out, and said, "I may have given someone the cover he was waiting for. And the feeling won't go away. Possibly it's the brazen way I exposed our affair."

"But there's nothing more specific?"

"What do you mean? I just told you . . ."

"I know what you told me, but it's more likely than not your response was triggered by guilt."

"Are you trying to make me sound silly?" she demanded.

"Far from it. You certainly are not silly. It's very common to feel irrationally guilty when someone close to you dies, especially if the death is violent. I'm afraid I see it far too often."

"What if there's really something there but I can't quite see it?"

"Then one way or another, someone will find it. By the way, where is Scartole now?"

"I don't know, and I don't care."

"It might be better if you did," Harry told her, determined to find out where Scartole had fled to and, despite what he had said, chiefly to make her feel better, if there was something other than a guilty conscience making her think she might have caused Perez's death.

CHAPTER 5

Harry was preparing to drive into Avola to talk with Jim Snyder when the wall phone in the kitchen rang.

"Hello, Harry, it's Sarah."

His daughter's voice was so leaden, he felt his heart lurch. "What's wrong?"

"It's Mom. She's dying, Harry."

Harry knew that the moment Sarah called her *Mom*. She had called her Jennifer for years.

"The doctor says that conventional treatment options have been exhausted, and unless she goes onto life support, she will be dead within forty-eight hours. Clive and I have discussed it, and in keeping with her request, we're going to let her go. The doctor read a copy of her advance directive and has agreed to abide by it. The palliative care team is moving into place while we're talking."

"How are you taking it?" Harry said, struggling to stay focused on his daughter but simultaneously reviewing the long months of struggle Jennifer had been through in a fierce effort to stem the cancer's steady advance. "Do you want me there?"

"I'm okay. My brother's a wreck. Now, Harry, I hope you're going to forgive me for saying this, but I don't think it will help her to see you. I know you loved each other once, and it's a terrible thing to say, but . . ."

Sarah broke down for a moment, and Harry waited for the spasm of grief to pass.

When she had blown her nose and collected herself, he said, "It's all right, Sarah. Yes, we were in love once, but it was a very long time ago. You and I made our peace. Of course I won't come. I understand."

It was true, he did understand, and he was not surprised at the flood of bitterness that rose in him like caustic bile, "familiar as an old mistake, and futile as regret." But what did surprise him was the cloak of sadness and mingled regret accompanying it. He thought time had wrung out of him all the grief and sorrow of that ruined marriage.

"Thank you for understanding, Harry," she said, "but I want you to come to the funeral. Clive and his family and I will be moving temporarily into Jennifer's house while we settle the estate, choosing what to keep and what to dispose of. I want you to stay with us for the memorial service and the interment."

It was Harry's turn to take a brief time-out. He left the phone to dangle on its cord and walked to the sink and stared out the window through the tangle of the huge wisteria vine to the sunlight falling on the lawn. Then he mentally pulled his shorts up and went back to the phone.

"I don't think it's wise, Sarah," he said and thought, *her brother is not going to want me there. We haven't spoken since he was seven.*

"Harry, I'm three years older than Clive. I remember when we were all together. And selfish or not, I want us all together again in the house that was my home after Jennifer left you and took us out of Maine. And even though she did her best to crush the last of my love for you out of me, she couldn't do it, and she mellowed a lot over the years."

"You're punishing yourself, Sarah. You don't have to," Harry said, trying hard to keep the pain he was experiencing out of his voice. "It's all over. You and I thrashed that all out several years ago when you came to the Hammock."

"You're talking about us, Harry, but you're thinking about Clive. I'm going to say it again. This is our last chance. The house is going to be sold, the bits and pieces of our lives together scattered; and before it happens, I want you and Clive to stand under the rooftree of this house and shake hands."

"Sarah . . ."

"No, Harry, let me finish. I want you reconciled while Mom's spirit is still with us, and the wrong that's been done erased."

"It's a wonderful thing to wish for," Harry said, "but how will you ever persuade your brother that it would be undoing an old wrong when in his eyes, I was the one responsible for his mother's suffering and his being deprived of a father?"

"I'm willing to try. Will you come?"

"I'll come to the funeral and the committal service. But whether or not I'll agree to stay with you and Clive in your mother's house is a question I want to sleep on."

The city of Avola was crowded onto a wedge-shaped spit of sun-baked sand between the Gulf of Mexico and the Seminole River, giving it only two directions in which to expand, north along the beach or east of the river. The growth began by going north, hugging the wide strip of white sand, the source of most of Avola's wealth. But in the years Harry had lived on the Hammock, it had swelled east of the river and begun its mall march toward the Everglades.

It had also become a wealthy city, but the international airport and I-75 had created in Tequesta County a three-tiered world, made up of those who had a lot of money, those who earned enough to live in the city, and an army of dark-shouldered people, documented and undocumented, who swarmed through the city and over the golf courses and associations in the daytime, cleaning, pruning, riding mowing machines, and sinking from sight with the sun.

"Those are the people who were Henrico Perez's base," Captain Jim Snyder said, throwing the pen he was holding onto the desk as though he was disgusted with both objects. He lifted all six feet four inches of his lean frame onto his feet and began to pace back and forth in front of Harry and Frank Hodges, his sergeant and executive officer, as if he was preparing to deliver a lecture. Harry knew it was only one of the ways Jim had of expressing his frustration with the bureaucracy within which he was obliged to function; the small office with its metal desk, folding chairs, aged green paint, seriously worn tiled floor, and creaking ceiling fan serving as an eloquent metaphor for the larger structure embodied in the Tequesta County Sheriff's Department, Robert C. Fisher, Sheriff.

"You're forgetting his second base, Captain," Frank said, "the one where his heart was . . . well, maybe not his heart but his . . ."

"Don't start, Frank," Jim burst out, his large ears getting red, as they always did when he was angry, "and remember that you're not on a pig hunt."

"Lord," Hodges said, winking at Harry, "I wish I was. Captain, you've got to come along with me one of these days. After one hog hunt, I'll guarantee you'll never want to do anything else."

Hodges and Snyder might have gone on stage. Where Jim was tall, Hodges was shorter. Where Jim was thin with a long, horse-like face, Hodges was thick, square as a refrigerator, and gifted with a cheerful round red face incapable of maintaining a frown.

"I gather you've been told to find Perez's killer," Harry put in, more to head off a wrangle that could easily take up the next half hour than to gain any information.

"As if we didn't have enough to do," Frank said.

"There's more to worry about than that," Jim said, stopping

his pacing to sit on a corner of his desk. "It will be a minor miracle if we don't find the FBI setting up shop right in the middle of the investigation."

"There's something to be grateful for," Frank said, beaming. "They can't do it in this office. It's too damned small."

"Jim," Harry said, cutting off Jim's response, "I've got something to tell you, and it won't make you happy."

Frank loved all stories, regardless of race, creed, or place of origin. He immediately swung around on his chair, causing it to groan dangerously. Jim stayed where he was, but his face grew longer.

"Let's hear it," he said.

"Gwyneth Benbow has hired me to investigate Perez's death."

"She's the chairwoman of the Friends of St. Lazarus's Board of Directors," he said in an accusing voice.

"I didn't know she was their chairwoman," Harry said, taken slightly aback. Why hadn't she told him?

"That ain't all," Hodges broke in loudly. "She's also hell on high heels."

"That's enough, Frank," Jim said, "but I've got to admit that she's taken some hide off me at meetings I've attended with her presiding."

"What would have taken you to the St. Lazarus meetings?" Harry asked, surprised by Jim's remark.

"Over the years," Jim said, rubbing his head as if the memories hurt, "Henrico's efforts to organize the hotel workers in the city have led to confrontations. Some got a little ugly."

"Ha!" Hodges said. "A few were real knockdown drag-outs that ended up with people cooling off for a night in jail. And by God, the women were worse than the men. There was one woman in that Canal Street dust-up who started punching a deputy."

He paused to give a shout of laughter. "It took two deputies to get her into a squad car, and one of them—I think it was Foster—got a black eye. Then Perez's people charged the department with police brutality."

"And the sheriff and I ended up at a meeting of the St. Lazarus board to mend fences," Jim added. "Well, Mrs. Benbow gave us quite a carding. Now, what's this about her hiring you?"

"How did you get so lucky?" Hodges demanded. "She'd give a stone statue a . . ."

"Sergeant!" Jim bellowed. "Zip it up!"

"Right, Captain," Hodges said, attempting to look contrite, an expression his face was not made for.

Harry took the moment of silence following that exchange to marshal his defense. He knew Jim was not going to like the kind of interference and second-guessing that might occur with another investigator shadowing his efforts. And he also knew that their being friends would further complicate the issue.

"I tried to convince her that she was wasting her money," Harry began, but that was as far as he got before Jim broke in, his ears flaming.

"Why didn't you just say no?"

"Well, I did actually, and she said she would just have to hire someone else. I actually let her leave, but then I began to think about the riffraff she might find herself hiring, and I called her and said I'd changed my mind."

"Can't say I blame you," Hodges said with a wide grin.

Jim made a circuit of his desk, then folded himself into his chair.

"I'll give you this much," he said, frowning, "you had reason to be concerned."

"Shark-infested waters," Hodges said.

"With plenty of exceptions," Harry said, trying to recover some ground.

"Granted," Jim agreed, "but what do you think you can do

for her that this entire department can't do?"

Harry was about to list several things, then pulled back from that precipice.

"Give her some peace of mind," he said. "She's convinced that this department and even the FBI, if they become involved, will drop Perez's murder into the nearest dumpster."

"What does she know?" Hodges said, perking up.

"How did the FBI come into the conversation?" Jim asked, his eyes widening.

"In trying to persuade her that your people would do their best to find his killer. After giving that a try, for backup I mentioned that if Perez's civil rights had been violated by his attacker, the FBI had a way into the case."

Hodges groaned and looked as if he had missed a meal.

"Lord, Lord," Jim said, shaking his head and leaning his elbows on his desk, "I hadn't gotten far enough into the case to think of that, and of course you're right. But we won't hear from them unless the murder goes national."

"I heard it mentioned this morning on CNN while I was having breakfast," Hodges put in.

"What did they say?" Jim asked.

"Something about Henrico Perez, widely acclaimed civil rights worker and community organizer, being found shot to death in his driveway. That was about it. You know it's one of the things I don't like about cable news. You get about three seconds of a story, then it's gone."

"I read it in the *Banner*," Harry said.

"Shot six times," Jim said with a sigh.

"What's her interest in the case?" Hodges asked.

"I gather from what she said that she and Perez were good friends, and she wanted his killer caught."

"Excuse me for sounding like Frank," Jim said, getting up again, "but being a female friend of Henrico Perez probably meant only one thing."

"Do you think he was shagging Benbow?" Hodges asked Harry.

Harry paused before answering. Their relationship had been reported, but Jim and Hodges may or may not have caught it. He had forgotten it, and their not knowing, he thought, only gave emphasis to the disheartening fact that Gwyneth's world, even in the small city of Avola, scarcely impinged on the consciousness of the rest of the city's inhabitants.

"It's a matter of record," Harry said.

"Well," Jim said, "between that piece of information and Benbow hiring you to interfere in the sheriff department's investigation, there's sufficient cause for us to take an interest in her."

"There's one more thing," Harry said. "She thinks some of the people Perez had been fighting over the years wanted him dead."

"That's all we need," Jim said, throwing up his hands, "an investigation into the lives of the county's rich and influential."

"Life's little surprises," Hodges said, followed by a wide grin.

"Names?" Jim asked grimly, ignoring the remark.

"Not so far."

The conversation drifted away briefly to the consequences of the recent hurricane's center coming ashore at Port Charlotte north of Fort Myers and the damage done in Avola despite its only being brushed by a wing of the storm.

"It was bad enough for me," Hodges said, "but it didn't hold a candle to Donna. I was just a kid, but every once in a while, I still dream I'm back in it. I can wake up hollering. The wife can't remember it, and she thinks I'm crazy."

"Nineteen-sixty," Jim said, looking grim, "just before the storm hit, my father took me down to the beach to see what was happening. I'll never forget it. There was dry land all the way to the horizon, and when the water came back and the wind with it—of course by then, we were back home with plywood nailed over the windows—it came back all at once and kept coming until the Gulf was all the way to Route 41."

"The Hammock took this one pretty well," Harry said. "Some trees went down, but the oaks around the house only lost a few branches and half their leaves. But just the same there were a few hours when it sounded as if a freight train was passing through the lanai."

"How did Tucker fare?" Hodges asked.

"He lost half a dozen trees in his citrus grove," Harry said, "and his vegetable garden was shredded. I've been helping him with the cleanup. It makes me feel sick to see all that food turned into garbage. But Tucker says, 'It will be composted and returned to the earth. The earth heals itself.' He's calm as a summer pond."

"My grandfather was like that," Hodges said.

The room was quiet for a while, with each of them occupied with his own thoughts. Then Harry stood up.

"Are you going to be all right, Jim, with my working for Gwyneth Benbow?" he asked.

"I want you to promise me something," Jim said. "I want you to check in with me on a regular basis, to keep me abreast of your progress. Unfortunately, I can't promise to do the same for you."

"All right, and will you give me some help from time to time?"

"As long as it doesn't cost the department any money or compromise our confidentiality requirements."

"Fair enough. Here's my first request," Harry said. "I only know what the paper said about the Perez shooting. What can you share with me?"

"Not much," Jim said. "At three a.m., our dispatcher took a

call from a man, informing us that there had been a shooting on Mullet Drive. She dispatched officers and the EMS vehicle to the scene. Mullet is only a short connecter street, but it took the officers a while to find Perez. He was lying in the drive leading up to a house that turned out to be his."

"Was his wife home?"

"Sound asleep," Hodges said, then made a happy face. "And if you need someone to provide armed protection for Benbow, I'm your man."

"That's all I'd need," Jim protested, "is to have someone with a bone to pick find out you were driving her around Avola at the county's expense."

Hodges beamed, having gotten the rise out of Jim that he wanted. "Thanks, Frank," Harry said. "I'll keep that in mind. Jim, have you talked with Mrs. Perez?"

"Only briefly, the night of the murder."

"Do you mind if I speak with her, assuming she's willing to see me?"

"You won't find what you're expecting," Hodges said.

Jim said nothing, and Harry left wondering if Hodges' remark was anything more than another example of his penchant for making the world more interesting than it really is.

CHAPTER 6

Not everyone wants to talk when a private investigator calls, and Harry was accustomed to being told to go away. It wasn't a pleasant experience because he preferred that people like him. Nevertheless, when he called Mrs. Perez, he had braced himself for refusal.

After he had finished introducing himself, expressed his regrets concerning her husband's death, and asked if she was willing to talk with him, she said in a cultivated, slightly accented voice that sounded more French than Spanish, "What do you think I can tell you?"

"Whatever it is," Harry said as gently as he could, "it will help to dispel the fog surrounding your husband's death. Any increase in clarity will increase the likelihood of discovering his killer."

"All right, if you wish, I will talk with you, but I must warn you, ours is a house in mourning."

The Perez house was located in a quiet residential area on the southwest side of the city, five or six blocks from the beach. The houses were fenced and gated, set back from the street and largely hidden behind densely flowering shrubs. The streets were lined with palms and fichus trees. When Harry got out of the Rover, he was greeted by the bubbling calls of ring-necked doves that were nesting in the trees. Their calls, the occasional clatter of their wings, and the soft hum of the Gulf breeze moving through the branches were the only sounds breaking the pervading silence.

A parody of peace, Harry thought, his mood darkened by knowledge of the upcoming interview, enhanced by a glance at the driveway where Perez had been killed. But whatever Harry had been expecting, it was not the woman who opened the door.

"I am Samia Perez and you are Mr. Brock, I think," she said in a strong, contralto voice, her large, dark eyes meeting and holding his as if she was searching for something.

"Harry will do," he said, surprised that he had been able to say anything under such scrutiny.

Where have I seen her before? he asked himself.

"Down the hall, first left," she told him, stepping aside and inviting him in with a graceful gesture.

Harry stepped into a large, cool room with ceiling fans slowly stirring the air. Soft, low furniture was arranged on two matching deep red and cream-colored rugs that Harry saw at once were medallion design and handmade, and probably Persian, and also probably worth more than the house that housed them. He felt oddly disoriented as if he had entered another time or place. The disjunction may have been aided by a delicate and fleeting but pervasive scent that reminded Harry of tangerines, with an elusive something added he couldn't name.

"Your rugs are very beautiful," he said.

She waved him toward a low, wide sofa and said, "Thank you. They have been in my family for generations."

While she was speaking, he sank into the dusty rose cushions, and from his new perspective looked up at the walls, which were a pale green and hung with paintings of designs and subject matter he could not remember having seen before. One was mostly in soft shades of gray, depicting three standing women covered from head to toe in what might have been white robes with hoods. A hint of lavender in the light gray background made the painting hauntingly luminous.

"They are wearing djellabas," Mrs. Perez said. "Do you like the painting?"

"Very much," Harry said, and meant it.

A second depicted a black wire trellis, suggesting a barred window with an arched top on which a flowering vine was twining. Around the trellis and through it were fragments of two women's faces and clothed shoulders in brilliant blue, red, and black, suggesting to Harry restrained passions. But he felt unsure whether such a quick reading could have any validity in judging this work so clearly emerging from a formidably different culture.

"Remarkable," he said, enchanted by the paintings.

"You find them strange," she said.

"Yes, and beautiful," he replied, "especially the abstract behind you, the reds are almost burning the canvas. I have rarely seen such intensity."

"My countrymen have never been accused of lacking intensity."

Harry caught the irony in her voice and brought his attention back to her, seeing her properly, perhaps, for the first time. The additional clarity may have been a result of seeing her in the room surrounded by these beautiful objects. She was slender and small-boned and had arranged her heavy black hair into carefully arranged coils confined in a black net at the nape of her graceful neck. She had curled her feet under her as soon as she sat down, tucking under them the hem of her black silk wrapper, which Harry now saw was very like the djellabas in the painting but lacking a hood and caught at the waist by a gold chain.

Like a cat, Harry thought. His next thought was Nefertiti— with her hair down. That's where he had seen her before.

"What country do you call yours?" he asked, thinking that

the resemblance was quite wonderful.

"This one, of course," she said quickly and a bit sharply, "but Algeria was my place of birth and where I grew up."

"You completed your schooling in Algeria?"

"No. My father sent me to Mount Holyoke, mostly, I think, to get me out of the country."

He thought of Gwyneth and thought also that she and this woman were about the same age. They might have been in college at the same time.

"And these are by Algerian artists?" he asked, looking again at the paintings. He was finding it difficult to keep his eyes off them.

"Yes, these men and woman are famous in their own country and sometimes in Europe, occasionally in New York, perhaps."

"Forgive me," he said, "for not telling you sooner how sorry I am for your loss. I didn't forget, but . . ."

"Thank you," she said, her dark eyes searching his face again. "I suppose you, like the police, find it improbable that I could have slept through the shooting."

"I have no reason to doubt your word. Does it weigh on your mind?"

"My not having heard the shots being fired? No. I wear ear plugs, the ceiling fans emit a soft white noise, the walls of the house are thick, the windows are triple paned. Have you heard the sound of passing cars since you arrived?"

"No," Harry said truthfully.

"It is unlikely you will unless it's garbage collection day."

Harry smiled. "I'm sure you know that everyone in the county owes your husband a debt of gratitude."

"Mmm."

The sound was tentative, Harry thought, carrying more doubt than confirmation.

"At least one person would disagree with you," she said.

One comment too many, he thought, angry with himself for having wakened the need for the bitter response.

"Yes," he said quietly. "Do you have any idea who might have done this?"

The sadness in her face lifted briefly, her eyes narrowing slightly as her body shifted.

"Would you like a list of the names?" she asked.

"Have you memorized it?"

"Not in the sense you mean," she said, the pain, the fury, or whatever it was withdrawing behind the widening eyes. "Years ago, I decided that if I was going to live in a tiger jungle, I would have to make space for the tigers and neither hate nor fear them. Until very recently, I succeeded. Now it is clear that to go unarmed in such a place is reckless or, perhaps, simply stupid."

"I gather Mr. Perez was not carrying a gun the night he was shot."

"There are no guns in this house. As I said, I grew up in Algeria. I have seen enough guns. Here," she looked around, turning her head slowly on her long neck, and raised her hands, "I thought we were free of them." Her shoulders slumped. "I see now that I was deluding myself."

"I'm sorry," Harry said.

"So am I," she said, her eyes flashing at him again, "but as you Americans say, 'It doesn't cut it,' does it?"

"No, no it doesn't. Had Mr. Perez received any threats recently? Would you know if he had?"

"Are you being deliberately insolent?"

"No. I'm sorry. The questions were badly framed. I meant to imply that Mr. Perez might have shielded you from such things, to spare you pain."

"Yes, I see," she said with what Harry thought were the ominous, faint twitches of a smile. "In the beginning he made efforts in that direction but was seldom successful. In the end, he abandoned the charade."

"I see," Harry said, stunned by her frankness and wondering if they were talking about the same thing.

"I doubt that you do," she said, unfolding herself gracefully and rising to her feet. "I'm afraid I haven't been of much help."

"Meeting you has been very helpful."

He was on his feet. "Are your children home now?"

"Briefly."

"Aside from your children, is any of your family in the States?"

"No. My father, who was in the Foreign Service, and my two brothers were killed in the struggles of the nineties. My sister became a missing person. Through the intervention of Egyptian friends, my mother gained permission to leave the country, taking with her what she could."

"Is she living in Egypt?"

"No, she died here ten years ago."

"I'm sorry."

"Don't be, Mr. Brock. She was a traditional Algerian woman. With the framework of her life—husband, home, social position—destroyed, she had nothing to live for. Her life had become meaningless, and her death was deliverance. Shall I accompany you to the door?"

It was a question that required no answer and Harry did not give one.

Harry left Samia Perez's house feeling dissatisfied with the interview and with himself, but not because he had failed to learn anything new about her husband's death. He had been in the company of a remarkable woman and through carelessness had bruised her with his questions and caused her to end their conversation.

Nonetheless, he did not regard it as a waste of time. Her comment about her husband's failed early attempts to be secretive might well have referred to his affairs, or not. Was she a woman in profound mourning? There was room for doubt, but Harry left the question unanswered. Her explanation of why she had not been awakened by the shooting was cool, coherent, and unapologetic. Also convincing? That was difficult to judge.

Once in the Rover, he called Jim. "I just talked with Samia Perez," he said. "She was a total surprise. Do you know anything about her?"

"No, except that she seems to have managed to live a completely separate existence from Perez's public life. I don't recall ever having seen a picture of her or of him with her in it."

It suddenly occurred to Harry that there were no photographs of the family in the room. Why not?

"When it's time to interview her, don't send Millard Jones."

"Why not? Women love him."

"Go yourself. Speak softly. Listen and be very careful how you frame your questions. I'm not sure, but I think she threw me out."

"Why?"

"Insensitivity on my part, probably. Just take your time. Let her talk. Remember, she comes from a place where the police were not her friend. I'm not saying more because I want to compare notes when you've talked with her and had a little time to weigh what you've heard. A question dangles: Did she get up when she heard her husband's car, shoot him, and then go back to bed? Any evidence either way?"

During the next three days, Harry spent most of his time cleaning up the arrears of unfinished insurance reports and completing the surveillance of Mulvane's Lumber Yard, from which boards, plywood, PVC pipe, and other construction material had been vanishing with alarming frequency. He also spent a few of his odd hours recalling his interview with Mrs. Perez, thinking about the fact that Mrs. Perez had not heard the barrage of shots that killed her husband.

But Mulvane's Lumber Yard claimed most of his attention, chiefly because the city police, chronically understaffed, had met with no success. Harry spent a day visiting all the building sites and interviewing the supervisors with the aim of finding out if anyone had been offering lumber for sale at a cut rate.

Having convinced the contractors that no efforts would be made or charges filed if it developed that they had bought the materials and asked no questions, Harry soon had a description of the young man and very quickly had his name.

"I have some good news and some bad," Harry said to Kevin Mulvane, the yard's owner, a tall, powerfully built man who perpetually looked as though he needed a shave. Harry had located Mulvane in the rear of the main building, watching a crew unloading roofing flats from a semi that was pinging and banging and sending up puffs of diesel exhaust that looked like smoke signals.

"Let's have it all," Mulvane said, talking around a toothpick.

Harry knew Mulvane well enough to stick to the script. "I have the thief, and he's your son-in-law."

"Which one?"

"Nora's husband."

Mulvane grunted and pulled a roll of large bills out of his pocket.

"Keep it to yourself," he said around the toothpick, peeling off several hundred dollar bills and passing them to Harry.

"Will do," Harry said.

He folded the money and shoved it into his shirt pocket, gratified that the payment had exceeded the contract.

Mulvane put out his hand. Harry braced himself. When it

was over he felt confident that he knew what it would be like to shake hands with a bear.

"Thanks, Brock," Mulvane said. "Don't worry, I'll take care of him. I've paid for his last fucking high, and he's going to know it. So will his dealer."

Harry left, nursing his hand and rejoicing that he wasn't Nora's husband or the dealer, who, he suspected, might end up in the next foundation Mulvane poured.

CHAPTER 7

The ringing of his phone dragged Harry out of a four fathoms sleep. He grappled with his cell on the bedside table, dropped it, recovered it, and said "Brock" in a voice that suggested the object of a resurrection was speaking.

"It's Jim. There's bad news, Harry. Gwyneth Benbow's been shot."

That put both of Harry's feet on the cool floor at the same time. "Is she dead?"

"She wasn't half an hour ago, but the prognosis is shaky. When I left, she was still in the OR. There are two or three surgeons working on her."

"Is she at the City Hospital?"

"Yes. The manager of the Conservation Club called it in at ten forty-six."

Harry glanced out the window at the moon and set the time as after one a.m. "What do you know so far?"

"She was shot in the club's parking lot."

"How long before she was found?"

"The club manager saw the shooting and called it in. Probably saved her life. I'll know more after I talk to the doctor who's in charge of the OR team working on her."

"Did he see who shot her?"

"May have, but it happened in a downpour. We'll soon know."

"Where are you?"

"Back at the crime scene. Frank just told me the crime scene crew's finishing up. They've done all they can until daylight. Are you going to the hospital?"

"Yes."

There was a pause, but Jim didn't hang up, so Harry said, "Kathleen all right?"

Kathleen was Jim's wife and the county medical examiner. The history of their marriage did not make consistently cheerful reading, and it was a subject on which Jim was very touchy. Harry had learned that times like these when most of Jim's attention was on some pressing work was the safest time to make an inquiry. And there were times Jim needed to talk. Harry was one of the few people he would open up to. It also gave Harry something safe to think about while he dressed.

"Yes, thank the Lord."

"And Clara?"

"At six, she's still Clara. With my luck, she always will be."

"You wouldn't change a hair on head."

"True. I've got to go. I hope Benbow is still with us."

"So do I," Harry replied, bending to open his gun safe.

When Harry reached the hospital, Benbow had been moved from the OR to the ICU.

"No, of course you can't see her," the nurse said, looking at Harry as if he had asked her to undress, which had not occurred to him to ask, but he had noticed that she was disturbingly pretty and was disgusted with himself.

"Is any of her family here?" he asked.

"No, and who are you anyway?"

Her tone of voice had changed from personally offended to intensely suspicious. It may have been the hat.

Harry, who resented being disliked, started to say that he was a pervert who specialized in anal sex and confined his practice to hospitalized women in intensive care. A moment's reflection, however, exposed the shortcomings of that response and he abandoned it. "My name's Harry Brock."

He wondered if he should tell her that he was a private investigator working for Gwyneth, then decided he was low enough in her estimation. In the pause that ensued, a female voice said over his shoulder, "As far as I know, he has no criminal record, and he's not as disreputable as he looks. Reluctantly, I'll vouch for him."

It was not a voice he was likely to forget, and he was startled by the flutter of excitement hearing it again gave him.

"Holly Pike," he said before turning around.

"Hello, Old Timer. Who are you sneaking up on in here?"

"I see you've put on weight, but still, I wouldn't kick you out of bed."

"Dream on, Grandpa."

At that point Holly put her arms around Harry's neck and gave him a very good hug, which he returned. Then for a bit they leaned back and grinned at one another.

"Why is it I never see you, Harry?" she asked.

Holly Pike was a trim, tanned woman in her forties with honey-colored hair, worn short, as Harry knew, so that she would not be troubled by it.

"Because you haven't been looking for me."

"Same for you," she said, still holding him.

"I know. Did you come in to ask after Gwyneth Benbow?"

They slowly released one another, their smiles fading.

"Yes, how is she?"

"She's stable," the nurse said, her frown having vanished. "You look familiar, but I can't place you."

Harry started to say, "The newspaper," but Holly cut him off.

"I'm just one of those people who remind people of someone else. It's been the curse of my life. What more can you tell me about Ms. Benbow?"

"I'm not supposed to say anything else," the nurse answered, "especially not to anyone from the media."

"I remember when people said, 'Not from the press,' " Harry said.

The nurse gave him a funny look and said, "You look familiar too."

"Nurse," Holly said, using the voice Harry recognized as the one she used quieting a fractious horse, calming and controlling. "I'm Gwyneth Benbow's very close friend. You may have noticed that no member of her family is here?"

The nurse said she had.

"I'm filling that role. Now, please find me someone with the authority to give me details about her condition."

"I'm not supposed to . . ."

"Please do it now. We'll wait here for you."

Harry listened with interest, and was not surprised when the nurse left. Holly Pike owned and ran The Oaks, a large horse farm a few miles outside Avola. Four years ago he had spent a lot of time at the stud, trying to find the person who had killed her husband. Before that was accomplished, she had been shot, and Harry came very close to being killed by a Spanish fighting bull.

He thought about that as he watched her dealing with the nurse.

"How's Harriet?" he asked. "I hear she's in preschool."

"Yes, thank God. She's a tartar."

"I wonder where she gets that from?"

"Don't start. What's going on here, Harry?"

"I'm in a tough spot, Holly. I can't answer your question."

"Are you working?"

Harry knew what she meant but pretended to misunderstand, hoping she would get the message. "I'm fairly busy. Summer's always a little quieter. I suppose it's because there are fewer people here than in the winter, but summer or winter people get themselves into trouble."

"Okay, but I know you're not here because you've fallen in love with the nurse—by the way, don't even think of it. She could be your granddaughter."

That stung.

"I was an early starter but I'm not that advanced!" he protested.

The conversation died because the nurse came striding back with a white coat in tow.

"I'm Dr. Ingram," the woman said, then pointed a long finger at Holly. "You're Pike."

She turned to Harry. "You're Brock, and neither of you is part of Ms. Benbow's family. That being so, why are you taking up my time and the time of this nurse?"

Dr. Ingram was tall, half a head taller than Harry, blonde, green-eyed, unsmiling, and, Harry thought, accustomed to dominating conversations. *I would not,* he thought, *want her to slug me.* The blood was rising in Holly's face and Harry saw the beginnings of a real brouhaha. Something had to be done.

"Dr. Ingram," he said, "may I have a few words with you in private? I'm sure we can clarify the situation and bring this to a satisfactory conclusion."

Without waiting for her to answer he stepped forward in such a way that she was going to have to either let him bump into her or turn with him. Looking more bemused than angry, she turned and even let him put his hand on her arm as they stepped away.

"The thing is, doctor," Harry said, maintaining the momentum, "Gwyneth and I have a professional and very private connection that without her permission I can't reveal."

Ingram stopped and Harry stopped with her. He started to

look up and found the brim of his hat got in the way of seeing her eyes, so he pulled it off.

"You've got some sun damage on your scalp that needs attention," she said, frowning at the sight.

"Thank you," he said. "As for Holly Pike, she's a good friend of Gwyneth's and is standing in for the family that Gwyneth doesn't appear to have. Both of us have pressing and legitimate needs for knowing her condition. My need, aside from concern, involves her safety."

"I know who you are, you know," Ingram said, bending slightly toward him and regarding him with an expression of wary amusement. "A private investigator and the hermit of Bartram's Hammock."

"Now that's not funny," Harry protested. "Where did you hear that I'm a hermit? I deny the charge."

"I know Esther Benson."

"This is bad. I'm in serious trouble. Benson views me as mentally challenged, constantly on the verge of being arrested, and a menace to women."

"Really?" Ingram said, looking interested and surprised. "Now that you mention it, she did say women who associate with you keep being shot or worse. Any truth in that?"

"Some, but I'm not usually the reason they get shot."

"Are you the reason for Gwyneth Benbow's being shot?"

"No. Could we talk about her, and catalogue my sins of omission and commission another time?"

"Are you hitting on me?" Ingram asked, showing no alarm.

"Is this Benson's fault?"

"Maybe. When I asked her how you behaved around her, she blushed and changed the subject."

"Did you see anything on the top of my head that suggested I was suicidal?"

Ingram smiled and said, "Call Pike over."

"A half inch closer to her heart, and she wouldn't be with us," Ingram told them both a few seconds later, concluding her summary of Gwyneth's condition and causing Harry to wonder for a moment if the shooter really was a bad shot after all. "But, barring unforeseen complications, there's no reason she shouldn't make a full recovery. Now, you tell me something. Why was she shot?"

"That," Harry said, "is what I intend to find out."

After Ingram had left them, and Harry had watched her until she turned a corner, Holly said, "I wouldn't advise it, Harry. My guess is she's got a lot of scalps hanging from the smoke hole in her teepee."

"Never crossed my mind," Harry said, trying to believe it. "I was wondering if Ingram was right in saying it might be a couple of days before I could ask Gwyneth questions and expect a reliable answer."

That much was true. The delay troubled him.

"What difference does a day or two make?"

"The evidence begins degrading as soon as a murder is committed," Harry said. "The killer gets farther away. Time dulls witnesses' memories. The world moves on."

"I'll back you up on the last part and add that it's picking up speed."

Harry smiled and said, "Tucker says a day is now half as long as it was when he was ten."

"I believe it. Something else, I had some trouble right after I was shot recalling the details of what had happened to me. Of course you and Thahn were there to fill in the blank spots."

As she spoke Harry again saw Holly come onto her feet from behind the fence where they had taken cover from a shooter, firing from the door of one of her stables, and run toward another stable only to be flattened by a bullet. The sight of her going down still sent a chill through him even after four years.

"I do remember you were pretty shaky for a while."

"I still can't remember being hit," she said. "It's strange, as if my mind was protecting me from knowing too much."

"Let's hope Gwyneth doesn't forget who shot her—if she even saw who did it," Harry said. "Have you any idea who might want her dead?"

"Not really. Her bust-up with her ex-husband had some pretty lurid moments, but the last I heard he was in Dallas, living high on her money, a real shit, Harry. I'm certainly not going to say anything against Gwyneth, but when it came to Eric, there was a long time when she seemed to have traded in her brains."

"Was he abusive?"

"No, I don't think so. Selfish, greedy, irresponsible is the short list, but violent? He had too much to lose. Besides, what motive could he have? I don't know the exact amount, but word was around that she set him up for life."

"I've heard rumors that he divorced her."

"Nope, she divorced him, otherwise, why the big settlement?"

Harry wondered why he had come away from his conversation with Gwyneth thinking that Eric Scartole had divorced her in a blowback of hurt pride over her having an affair with Henrico Perez, a man considerably older than he.

"I don't know," Harry said. "I'll have to do some work on that."

He and Holly had restored good feelings between themselves and the nurse and were on their way out of the hospital.

"Are you coming in to see Gwyneth tomorrow?" Holly asked.

"Yes, as early as they will let me. I'm assuming Jim has a deputy posted outside her door, but now that I've mentioned it, I think I'll check before I leave. What about you?"

"I can't. I'm flying to Louisville this afternoon. There's a breeders' meeting I've committed to attend and be one of the presenters. But I'll call and hope she can speak on the phone."

They said goodbye, and Harry went back to check on Gwyneth's room. Sergeant Fred Robbins was perched on a metal folding chair outside, reading a copy of *Sports Afield*. The door to her room was closed, and Harry decided to have a talk with the sergeant.

"Fred, how does it happen that a man of your exalted rank is sitting out here reading when you could be pursuing criminals?"

"Hello, Harry," Robbins said with a grin. "What it is, we're shorthanded and Sergeant Hodges didn't want to trust this to one of the new recruits. What brings you up here? I hope you're not having health problems," he added, his grin fading.

"No, I'm fine. What do you hear about Gwyneth?"

Robbins looked puzzled. Then his brow cleared. "Oh, Mrs. Benbow?" he asked, jerking a thumb at the door.

"That's right."

"Well, the nurses are in and out of there pretty often, and Dr. Ingram's been in twice since I've been here, and they all come and go quiet as mice. But all I got for asking how she is was, 'As well as can be expected.' Whether that's good news or bad, I can't say. Pisses me off not to get a straight answer to a straight question."

"That's about all I got from Dr. Ingram when I asked her half an hour ago. Take care now."

He and Robbins shook hands again, and Harry left, intending to have a talk with Jeff Smolkin.

When Harry first knew him, Jeff Smolkin's law practice consisted almost entirely of people swept into the judicial system because they were somewhere they shouldn't have been and too poor to pay for an attorney. Harry thought about this as he stepped out of his Rover into the parking lot in front of a five-story, cream-colored office building in downtown Avola and stood for a moment, enjoying the breeze off the Gulf and the shifting pattern of light and shadow cast by the huge fichus trees shading the property.

Before he turned to climb the wide marble steps leading to the double glass doors with their shining brass fittings, he glanced up at the top floor, where he was going, and reminded himself with some wonder that the scuttling young lawyer he had first known now owned the building, that his offices occupied the entire top floor, and his name was beginning to be mentioned whenever talk of new judicial appointments surfaced in the county.

Stepping out of the hall into the carpeted reception area, Harry was met by the usual blast of frigid air. It was Harry's conviction that Florida was burdened with two curses, air conditioning and leaf blowers. Because the receptionist was missing from her post behind the huge cherry wood desk, he went through the room toward the hall, wading ankle deep in the rug's pile. Smolkin was easily carried away by decorators.

The hall was the usual sepulchral space, dimly lighted, its runner designed to suppress the clatter of hurrying high heels as Smolkin's paralegals flew about in all their glory, carrying out their Master's bidding. In that office no one served by waiting.

At least, Harry thought rather sadly, that used to be so, noting the quiet instead of the ordered pandemonium that had reigned when Renata Holland had been Smolkin's lady of the smoking sword. The grim truth was, not until Renata had quit in a rage that nearly brought Smolkin's practice to a shuddering halt did he finally break down and take in two partners to pick up the slack, and with tears in his eyes parceled out his paralegals among the three of them. Two of those lovely young women, clutching briefs to their breasts, had passed Harry, wearing a hunted look as if they were a prey species. The second one had just shot by, casting him a smile of desperation, when another female figure emerged from the largest office and confronted him, fists on her hips.

Harry fell back and barely stifled a cry of alarm.

CHAPTER 8

"Well, Brock," the woman said impatiently, "are you going to just stand there?"

"God, Renata," Harry said, striding forward and catching her to him with both arms, "I thought you were a ghost!"

"Oh that I were, but you should be able to tell that I'm not. You certainly aren't."

That comment came with the first smile she'd given him.

"No, you're not, and you don't know how glad that makes me."

"Cut out the bullshit and kiss me."

He did, and they kept it going for a while.

"Well," she said when they came up for air, "that was almost worth going to the West Coast and coming back for."

Reluctantly, Harry allowed her to ease out of his embrace, but still held onto her hands and studied her. There were fine lines at the corners of her eyes that were not laugh lines, but her carefully groomed hair was the same light brown. Her gray eyes had the same ironic glint, and holding her, you knew she was a woman.

"It's good to see you, Renata," Harry said, his eyes stinging a bit from a sudden rush of emotion. His response startled him. "I never thought I would, not inside these walls anyway."

He may have been in love with her briefly, he admitted, but that was a long time ago. A lot of blood spilled.

"Neither did I," she said, watching him closely. "Harry Brock!

Are those tears?"

"I'm old. I cry over road kills."

"Well, I'm still flattered," she said, giving him a quick kiss on the cheek and freeing her hands.

"What are you doing here?" he asked.

"I've got my old job back."

"What about Number One?" he asked.

"I'm over it, Harry. I've been married and divorced since I left here."

"But why come back?"

"Why not?"

And that was all Harry ever got out of Renata on that subject.

"I feel ten years younger, Harry!" Smolkin said, exploding out of his chair when Harry stepped into his office. "Renata's back!"

"More fool her," Harry said.

"I don't care," Smolkin said, rocking back on his heels and plunging his hands into his pockets. "My life just got unbelievably better. In a month, you won't recognize this place. She'll whip those lazy partners of mine into shape. No more two-hour lunches. Any para caught walking and not running between here and the courthouse will find herself cleaning the toilets with a toothbrush. We'll double our caseloads, and the money will pour in."

Harry listened and wondered if Renata had come back to kill Smolkin. Stranger things had happened. Why else would she have come back?

"What brought you into this den of sloth? I haven't seen you for months."

"You've heard about the Henrico Perez shooting," Harry said, abandoning the thought.

"Who above ground hasn't?"

"Right. I'm working for Gwyneth Benbow. Don't ask me, doing what? I need to look at her divorce record."

"Benbow? Wasn't she . . . ?"

"That's right. She was shot, and it was a near thing, but she's recovering and should be all right."

"I've met her at a few fundraisers over time. Very attractive and very smart, but aloof, if that's the word I'm looking for. What's the connection between her and Perez's death?"

"I'm not sure there is one."

"Okay, the record is open to the public. Why ask me, or Benbow for that matter?"

"The court sealed it, and I don't want her to know I'm snooping. So keep this conversation between us."

"Okay. You've checked the *Banner*'s account of it?"

"It didn't tell me the two things I need to know: who made the initial filing and how much money did Scartole walk away with."

"Now I remember the name. Flashy guy with too much oil in his hair."

"That's the one."

"Which firms represented the parties?"

"Both went to Miami. Allworth, etc., represented Scartole. Gothrow, et al., stood up for Benbow."

Smolkin grinned appreciatively. "I can hear the chiming of cash registers," he said.

"She's got a deep handbag."

"What about Scartole?"

"She shared her handbag. I want to know how much he took out."

Smolkin rocked on his heels for a while, staring out one of the windows at the Gulf dancing beyond the coconut palms and red tile roofs.

"Any day now," Harry said impatiently.

Smolkin pointed at the chairs in front of his desk, and the

two men sat down. "It's come back to me," he said, losing some of his cheerfulness. "Benbow and Perez were photographed coming out of the Canary Island Guest House at a little after daylight. Benbow and Scartole split, but I don't remember which of them filed or the terms of the settlement."

"That's because it wasn't reported and nobody was interested enough in the event to go looking for the answers. I've made enough calls to convince myself that I'll need your help to find the answer."

"And Benbow won't tell you?"

"She told me that he filed. Holly Pike told me that she filed, but I'd like to know for certain. As for the settlement, Gwyneth said it was a large number but not as much as if she'd done the filing."

"And that's not good enough."

"No."

"Where's Jim Snyder on her case?" Smolkin asked, drifting away from Harry's admission that he needed help.

"Barely begun."

"And Perez?" He paused and scowled. "I used to know all these things when Renata was here." He broke into a wide smile. "Now I will again."

"Lucky you. The Perez investigation is in the complaining stage, which always happens when a new case lands on Jim's desk, especially one like Perez's murder."

"Have they eliminated robbery as the motive?"

"From the way he was reacting with me, I think he has, but at this point everyone in the department is being very tight-lipped."

"Then I think that he and everyone, including our intrepid assistant state's attorney, has reason to be very concerned."

"That's what Benbow keeps telling me, but I can't yet see Harley Dillon missing a tee time over this."

Smolkin looked as if he'd bitten into a crab apple.

"Is Benbow still on the Friends of St. Lazarus Board of Directors?" he asked.

"Chairperson. Are you and Harley still on the outs?"

"We don't agree on a lot if that's what you mean," Smolkin replied, showing some edge.

"I hate to see politics separate people who ought to be friends."

Smolkin waved his hand dismissively. "Over the last five or so years, the Lazarus board has not done a very good job of reining in Perez's public attacks on the developers and their cozy relationships with county government. Oh, and the other business interests in the county," he continued.

"And I'm inclined to say, 'Good.' "

"Maybe," Smolkin said, "but you'd get a lot of blowback on that, especially from the construction companies, their suppliers, and the building trades in Avola. They've all been burned by Perez's largely successful efforts to convert large acreage properties that have come onto the market in Avola in recent years into parks, playgrounds, low-cost housing, and green areas. Developers in this part of Florida aren't accustomed to losing to anyone. There's resentment."

"Don't forget, Benbow, Scartole, and the long line of husbands whose wives Perez has shagged over the years," Harry added quickly.

"Right, but I can't connect Scartole to Perez."

"How about Benbow?" Harry asked.

"Why would he want her dead after walking away with a settlement he must have agreed to?"

"That's what I would like to know."

"Then you think he shot her," Smolkin said with obvious doubt.

"I've got to begin somewhere."

That afternoon, Harry went to see Gwyneth. In the mornings, she was too busy with therapists to have visitors, and aside from Holly, Harry had learned from the nurse that she had no other regular visitors.

"Just when I thought the trials of the day had ended," she said cheerfully when Harry came into the room.

She was sitting on the edge of the bed, dressed in a pair of blue silk pajamas. Her left arm was still in a sling, but otherwise she looked and sounded fine.

"Are you allowed to walk around this place?" Harry asked when his efforts to look hurt got nothing but a wider grin.

"Only if there's coffee in it for me."

"I'm buying, but just so you know, the cafeteria coffee is worse than mine."

"I know, Holly brought me some yesterday, but I'm so bored I would drink anything just to get out of this room."

She had slid to the floor while she was talking, and now her pajama pants were slipping down. She caught them with her free hand and said, "Don't just stand there, tie the strings."

When he fumbled trying to tie a bow knot from the front, she turned her back to him and said, "Reach around and do it. God, I hate not being able to do things for myself."

Harry did as he was told, and they got under way with Gwyneth still complaining. She started off at a good pace, but before they reached the elevator, she suddenly sagged, and he had to slip his arm around her to keep her from falling.

"Whoops," she said after he steadied her, "I think I have to go more slowly. My knees just sort of folded—strange sensation."

"Are you sure you should be doing this?" Harry had been shot three times and knew how easy it was to misjudge one's degree of recovery.

"No, but I want to risk it. If I faint, stick me in a chair and wheel me back to bed," she said, slipping her free arm through his and moving toward the elevator. "Punch the button."

"Feeble but still in control," Harry said.

"Believe it."

Once in the cafeteria, Harry got her into a chair and then brought their coffee.

"Have you talked with the police?" he asked, knowing she had but thinking it would be an easy way of bringing up the subject of the shooting.

"Briefly," she said. "Alice Ingram booted them out before we had talked long. Actually, I was still so woozy that I don't remember much about the interview, but there was one man I recall. There was something about him, what . . . ? Oh, yes."

She grew pink and smiled, then caught herself.

"That would have been Lieutenant Millard Jones," Harry said, amused and jealous at the same time.

"Do you know him?" she asked.

"I've heard that women find him attractive."

"Do they?" she asked, glancing away, her blush deepening. "I can't think why."

"It will come to you," Harry said, beginning to enjoy himself.

"Enough," she said, spluttering with laughter. "Change the subject."

"Okay, tell me what happened."

"Nothing!" she said. "The room was full of people. I was half out of it."

"Your johnny?"

"Harry!"

"Tell me about the shooting," he said.

"I can't. I can tell you where I was before it happened and fragments of the lead-up to my being shot, but then there's nothing until I woke up in here."

"Where were you?"

"In the parking lot of the Tequesta County Conservation Club. There had just been a heavy thunderstorm. The storm had knocked out the electricity. Only the emergency lighting was functioning. That's what ended the meeting. It was still raining, and the lot was streaming with water. Except from the emergency lights on the building, which weren't much use in the parking area, the place was black as pitch."

"What time was it?"

"About ten-thirty. I have two clear memories of the moment. I was worried about ruining my shoes and swearing because I couldn't find the penlight I usually carry in my bag."

"Had you reached your car?"

"Yes. I was digging in my bag for the keyless entry."

"Were there any other people near you?"

"I could hear some people talking somewhere, but I don't think they were close. I really wasn't paying attention."

"Keep going."

"Then someone said, 'Gwyneth.' I looked up, saw a shadow darker than the ambient dark on the same side of the car with me. I turned to face whoever had spoken, saw a flash of light, and then nothing."

Harry knew she would not be able to go on much longer and wanted every scrap of information he could get. "Tell me where exactly you were parked."

"The club faces the river and has parking lots on both sides of the building. I was on the west side in one of the spaces facing the building about midway along."

"Was the person between you and the building?"

"Yes. I turned toward the front of the car."

"Did you recognize the voice?"

"No."

"Male or female?"

"I don't know, and I feel wrung out."

"One more question. Whom does Scartole know in Dallas?"

"I think his mother lives there."

"Her name?"

"Isabel. Can we stop?"

"Yes. Want some more coffee?"

"Is that what we've been drinking?"

"No."

CHAPTER 9

The following morning, Harry made a call. A familiar voice answered.

"Hello, Thahn," Harry said.

"Harry! It is good to hear you. It has been a long time."

"Too long. How are you and your wife?"

"No cause for complaint, but the years accumulate."

"Fortunately," Harry said, eliciting a chuckle.

"Are you well?" Thahn asked.

"I think so. Is Holly at home?"

"Yes. Just a moment. I will connect you. If you are planning a visit, please don't leave without seeing me."

"I wouldn't think of it."

"Hello, Harry," Holly said in that good, strong voice he liked so well. "When are you coming to see me?"

"How about in half an hour."

"Perfect. I'll have Aisha and Scotsman saddled and waiting."

"Great," Harry said, his heart sinking. He had nothing against horses, but he was very glad that he lived in the age of the internal combustion engine.

The Oaks was a sprawling horse farm, which took its name from an extensive stand of ancient live oaks that had been opened on the south side to make room for a large, cream-colored stone house, fronted by a curved, crushed-stone drive and a sweeping view of pastures and woods.

Thahn, the Vietnamese butler, accompanied by a very large

Rottweiler, was waiting for Harry in the parking area at the side of the house. The dog rushed at Harry when he got out of the Rover as if he meant to tear him apart.

"Nip!" Harry shouted, bracing himself for the hurtling animal's arrival.

Nip braked just before reaching Harry, reducing the impact of his powerful body as he threw his shoulder into Harry's midsection, forcing Harry to grasp the dog in both arms to stay on his feet, which seemed to be what Nip wanted because he was wriggling with pleasure and trying to lick Harry's face by the time Harry had caught his balance.

Thahn approached Harry at a slower speed and, having reached him, spoke quietly to the dog, who gave Harry's face a final lick and sat down on his feet.

"I guess he remembered me," Harry said, reaching out to shake Thahn's hand.

"He forgets very little," Thahn replied, his thin, weathered face losing its smile.

"Tuck," Harry said quietly as both men stared down at the dog.

At the sound of the name, Nip looked around sharply and whined.

"He still goes most days to lie on his friend's burial mound for a quarter of an hour and comes away subdued."

Four years earlier, Tuck, Nip's brother, had been gored and killed by a bull that was charging Harry, which the two dogs had tackled and distracted long enough for Harry to shoot it.

"A faithful friend," Harry said, stroking the dog's head. "Those were tough days."

"Indeed. Well, I must return to the house. Mrs. Pike is at Barn One. Nip will lead you if you've forgotten the way."

"I haven't."

With Nip leading anyway, Harry walked along the shaded

path to the horse barns.

Holly Pike, booted and spurred, wearing jodhpurs and a crisp white blouse, was tightening the cinch on the taller of the two horses being held by a groom. Looking up, she saw Harry and smiled broadly.

"Only ten minutes late," she said, stepping away from the horse to hug Harry.

"I was talking with Thahn," Harry said.

"You're forgiven. We have missed you."

"When did you adopt the royal plural?"

"Thahn, Nip, and I, smartass," she said. "Struggle onto Aisha and sit facing forward."

Her response pleased Harry. She gave as good as she got and took no prisoners. In that bad time he had mentioned while talking with Thahn, Holly Pike's husband, Brandon, had ridden into a wire stretched across a riding path and been decapitated. In the course of Harry's search to find whoever strung the wire, Holly, pregnant at the time, was badly wounded in a botched attempt to kill her, and one of the horse barns had been burned to the ground, taking a brood mare with it. Through it all, Harry remembered, Holly had been unmovable in her determination to see her husband's assassin brought to justice.

Scotsman, Holly's mount, a tall gray gelding, irascible at the best of times and impatient with the wait, had decided to become even more of a nuisance by crowding Aisha and trying to bite her.

"Let me have him," Holly said to the groom, snatching Scotsman's reins out of his hand. She pulled the horse away from Aisha, and in a single swift movement swung herself into the saddle while the horse danced and squealed. Holly reined him in sharply but trotted him around the yard to settle him down.

"Want some help with that stirrup, Harry?" the groom asked with a grin.

"God, Buster," Harry said, ashamed of himself, "I was too busy dreading this to even look at you. How are you?"

The two men shook hands and went on talking while Buster held the stirrup until Harry managed to put his foot in it and boost himself onto Aisha's back. The horse watched the performance with cocked ears and what Harry thought was thinly veiled amusement.

"You're head groom now, congratulations," Harry said, settled in the saddle as well as he was going to be.

"Three years," Buster said with a grin. "Remember, anything happen, you grab that pommel and hang on like it was the last stick floating."

"That's a big help, Buster," Harry said but didn't say anything more because Buster slapped Aisha on the rump and away they went, with Harry trying to remember what he did with the reins.

"A light gallop," Holly said with rich sarcasm, riding up beside Harry, holding Scotsman in with one hand and resting the other on the back of her saddle so that she could look at Harry more easily, while the gelding pranced and pretended to buck.

"Laugh all you want," Harry said in an unsteady voice as he bounced awkwardly in the saddle. "You won't laugh when the bill comes in."

Holly grinned.

"Let me run this idiot for a few minutes and give him some fun. Then we can talk." With that, she put her heels into the big animal's sides, loosened the reins, and said, "Go!"

He went, sending up clots of dirt like a shower of comets as he raced away, his hooves thundering impressively. Aisha went on at her gentle pace and Harry gradually relaxed into the rhythm of her body, taking a little weight off his seat. By the time Holly came back with Scotsman blowing happily and ready to stay with Aisha, Harry was enjoying his ride.

"This isn't as bad as I remembered," he said.

"Unless there's another Andalusian bull on the loose," Holly said, grinning.

The last time they had ridden together, a black Spanish fighting bull had charged them, but Aisha dodged his horns and the beast had kept going in a failed pursuit of Scotsman and Holly.

"Bad few minutes," Harry said. "I want to talk with you about Gwyneth."

"Damn! I thought you'd come out here to see me."

"That was my real reason. My good reason is to ask about Gwyneth."

"Good save, but I don't really know much about her."

The horses had slowed to a walk and they were moving along a ride, twisting through an overgrown area of what had once been a pine woods but was now carpeted with saw palmettos and taller shrubs and saplings, full of sunlight and birdsong.

"She said you were her best friend."

"That's flattering, but Gwyneth's idea of a good friend is someone you talk with once a week, lunch with once a month, and meet at charity events."

"I'd forgotten," Harry said, "your penchant for drama."

"No comment. What do you want to know about her?"

"Whatever you know. Her getting herself shot is a major mystery."

"What do you mean, she got herself shot?" Holly demanded. "How was it her fault?"

"No idea," Harry said, "but until something convinces me that I'm wrong, I'm saying there's a connection between the Perez shooting and hers."

"You think the same person shot Henrico and Gwyneth?" Holly asked, her voice rising in obvious doubt.

"Maybe, but not necessarily. What can you tell me about their relationship?"

"Don't you read the paper?" she asked stiffly.

"Anything you say to me about Gwyneth will never be attributed to you or divulged in a way that would enable her to know its source."

"Harry . . ." she began, but he stopped her.

"I got off on the wrong foot. Let me start over. Gwyneth told me that she and Perez had an affair, and that she had entered into it to give her husband cause to divorce her."

"So?"

Holly was clearly still put out.

"How close to the truth do you think that account is?"

They came around a twist in the ride and encountered a barbed-wire fence with a heavy gate, fitted with a digital lock. Beyond the gate was a wide expanse of green pasture. A hundred yards to the west, a large herd of Aberdeen Angus cattle was grazing peacefully.

"Speaking of dramatic," Holly said, ignoring the question. "Want to say hello to Thor?"

"The charming herd bull," Harry said without enthusiasm.

"It will give me a chance to check him and the cows. They're looked at every couple of days, but I like to do it myself when I can."

"This is one of the few times I'm glad to be on a horse," Harry said as the enormous creature trotted toward them, his dewlap swinging, a deep rumble like distant thunder rolling in his chest.

Scotsman did not conceal his distaste for the bull, and Holly had to hold him on a short rein, but even then he danced and pivoted like a ballerina when the bull stopped only a few feet from him. Reaching into a saddlebag, Holly took out an apple and tossed it to the bull. Thor quickly lowered his massive head and began chomping on the apple.

"Since being weaned and except for occasional treats of

apples or dried corn," Holly said, tossing the bull two more apples, "he's never eaten anything but grass. Neither have the cows."

"Premium grass-fed beef," Harry said, dividing his attention between the bull and Aisha, who had taken advantage of their pause to graze.

He would have been much happier if she had been watching Thor, whose company he would have preferred as steaks.

"Yes, but they're a major nuisance," Holly said with a sigh, having managed to defeat Scotsman's attempt to bolt. "I don't know why I keep them."

Harry started to say, "I do," then checked himself.

The herd had been her husband's gift to her. The fact she kept them seemed to Harry strong evidence that Brandon's memory remained strong, and he liked her too much to waken that old pain.

"That's about all of his company I need for one day," she said grimly, lifting the reins against Scotsman's neck. The horse needed no more encouragement and turned away in a single leap.

"Come on, Aisha," Harry said, tugging on the reins.

Still chewing a mouthful of grass, the mare raised her head. Seeing the bull moving toward them and Scotsman trotting away, she snorted quietly as if in comment and broke at once into a gentle gallop, very nearly unseating Harry.

"I wasn't exaggerating," Holly said once they were through the gate and looking relieved to be out of the pasture, "Gwyneth is pretty much a mystery to me. I didn't know about her affair until it was in the papers. And because she never mentioned it to me, not even during the brief flurry that photo caused, I never mentioned it."

"Does her account of the business sound right to you?"

"I suppose it does. If she had ever loved Eric, it's been over for a while. She didn't say much to me about their relationship, but she did tell me that she had been an idiot to marry him."

They rode in silence for a few minutes. Harry was sorting through what he had been told and was nearly at the point of saying that none of what Holly had said was much help, when she brought Scotsman to a stop.

"Aisha, stand!" she said.

The horse stopped, pricked her ears, and looked around as if expecting something surprising. Satisfied there were no bulls in the mix, she began grazing, pulling Harry into the pommel when she dropped her head.

"Really, Harry," Holly said, looking at him with mingled irritation and pity, as one might look at a slow child.

"This is all your fault," Harry said, and she burst into laughter.

"What I've decided to tell you is more serious," Holly said. "I've had a struggle getting this far, and I only hope I'm doing the right thing. But I suppose, at least I want to suppose, that you would unearth it yourself in time. Perhaps I should let you."

She paused and stared into the woods as if spellbound by the raucous calling of a pileated woodpecker that between blasts of sound was hammering chunks of bark off a slash pine. Scotsman snorted and stamped in apparent impatience, bringing her attention back to the moment.

"I'm not going to risk it, however. Too much might be at stake."

"This is beginning to sound like one of Hamlet's soliloquies," Harry said, still in a bad mood from his bump in the stomach and being laughed at.

"You're very thinned-skinned for a man in your line of work," Holly told him, which didn't help. "Gwyneth's marriage to Eric Scartole was not her first," she continued.

Another pause.

"Go on," Harry said, while she was dealing with Scotsman.

"This animal is trying my patience," Holly said. "Let's walk on. Perhaps he'll behave better."

Harry tugged Aisha's head out of the grass, and Holly watched the process with a frown.

"Next time," she said, "tighten the reins and say, 'walk on.' She'll do the rest."

"If I'm lucky," Harry said, his face burning, "there won't be a next time."

"Oh, my," Holly said, "aren't we in a state."

"Just finish the story."

"All right," Holly continued, "but when she was twenty-three, and in her fourth year at Smith, she had an affair with Morrison Perkins, a man ten years or so older than she was, working in the Northhampton branch of a large multinational, headquartered in Boston. Then comes the strange part; they were married, and a few months later he was dead."

"Is that why you were in such a twist before telling me this story?"

"Well, I can't explain why, but I think there's something she's trying to bury, Harry. And if she is, and if she becomes a suspect in Henrico's murder, it might come back to haunt her. That's why I've told you. But now that I have, it doesn't sound at all important."

"She is a suspect, Holly," Harry said. "Have you ever questioned her about Perkins' death?"

"No, I had the strong impression that the subject was closed."

"Why did she open it with you in the first place?"

"I'm not sure, but it was the day after Henrico was killed, and she was very upset."

"She's had a bad time," Harry said, "what with ending an affair, going through a divorce, and being hit with Perez's violent death."

"The day you met her, did she strike you as a woman seriously stressed?" Holly asked.

"No," Harry said, noting the coolness in Holly's voice. "She struck me as a woman very much in control of herself. Of course, I wasn't looking for signs of stress. I was too busy trying to get to know her and find out why she wanted to hire me."

They reached the barns, and Harry gave Aisha to Buster. But once on the ground, he was reluctant to let her go and stood stroking her neck and talking to her.

"Aisha grows on you, doesn't she?" Holly asked, dropping off the big gelding and landing light as a butterfly.

"You make dismounting look easy," Harry said, giving the horse's neck a final slap, "and yes, I do like this lady."

Holly passed Scotsman's reins to Buster and said as the big gelding was led away, "You'd make a good horseman, Harry, given some time and work."

"Next time around, maybe," Harry said, mentally crossing his fingers.

The sun was blazingly hot in the open yard, and they moved quickly toward the house and the shade of the big oaks. When they stepped out of the sun, the sound of the locusts in the trees was loud enough to make them raise their voices to talk.

"Come in and have some iced tea," Holly said. "I think you've earned it."

"Thanks, but I've got to get ahead of this job I've taken on or else it's going to roll right over me."

"Well, promise me you'll make some time to come out here again," Holly said, linking arms with him. "I want you to meet Harriet. She's a peach, and saying no is not an option."

"Then I'll say yes," Harry said. "Give me a day or two and I'll call."

They had reached the portico, but Holly still held his arm and said, "Honor bright? The last time you left here, I didn't see you again for four years."

"Four days on the outside, sooner if it works for us."

"I used to wonder if it might work for us, Harry," she said, releasing his arm. "What do you think?"

Harry's first response was, *I'm not touching that with a ten-foot pole.* But instead, he said, "Be careful what you ask for."

CHAPTER 10

Harry left The Oaks, wondering how serious Holly was in asking him what he thought of their getting together. He was not proud of his answer, and although her smile had stayed in place and she had waved as he was leaving, he regretted the snappy response.

It did not occupy his mind just then because he was already planning what he would say when he called her that would undo the damage, even though there might not have been any. But in those very early morning hours, lying awake with the moon for company, Harry often found himself reviewing without pleasure things from the past he had said or not said that gave him cause for regret.

Harry's intention upon leaving The Oaks was to go to the Tequesta County Conservation Club, but a promise he had been slow in keeping caused him to turn off the highway onto a smaller sandy road that wound through a mixed stand of cabbage palms, slash pine, and saw palmettos. He drove slowly on the narrow road, knowing from past experience that box turtles had made the area their own and when the spirit moved them would simply step out of the ferns and into the road as if they were immortal.

Also, it was a good place to find a timber rattler taking a sunbath on the warm sand of the road. Harry had no dislike of snakes, although to come on a big one suddenly still gave him the response that he always associated with Emily Dickinson's lines, ". . . a tighter breathing / And zero at the bone." But there were no snakes or gray foxes either although they liked the saw palmettos, which provided low cover under which to dig a burrow or expand one belonging to an offended box turtle, evicted into the heat of day.

The road ended at a deserted turnaround opening onto an equally deserted beach with the blue and green Gulf glinting beyond the back dune, populated with beach plums and sea oats growing out of the white sand. After gazing at the view for a few minutes, Harry took out his phone and called Sarah.

"Have you made up your mind?" she asked him without preliminaries.

"Yes, but I'm not sure it's the right decision," he replied in a somewhat critical voice.

"Then you'll stay with us?"

"Reluctantly and with the proviso that if shooting breaks out, I'll leave."

"It's a deal."

"Good. Where are you?"

"With Jennifer. She's sleeping. She's been taken off all the medications except those the new team says are necessary to her comfort and peace of mind."

"Then she is comfortable?" Harry asked, somewhat doubtful.

"Oh, yes. She's also become much more alert since the palliative care team took over. Her nausea has gone. The irritability has declined. From what I can tell, she's feeling better than she has for weeks."

"How are you holding up?"

"Better now. These people are wonderful. Even my mother smiles and chats with them when she's awake. If I hadn't seen it, I wouldn't have believed it. Hello. She's waking and looking at me. I'd better go."

Harry closed the phone and watched the sea again. He

couldn't decide how he should be feeling and was uncomfortable with the degree of calm that had spread through him as he talked with Sarah. It had something to do, he thought, with the change in Sarah herself, her increased ease of mind, perhaps, and apparent adjustment to the new regimen. With a sigh, partly of resignation and something of relief, he turned the Rover and drove to the Tequesta County Conservation Club.

The lot was empty, and when he got out of the Rover, he was welcomed by a stiff breeze from the river that was rattling the fronds in the Canary Island palms surrounding the club and foresting the islands in the parking lot. He had parked beside the space where Gwyneth's car had been sitting, the lot's surface feeling spongy with midday heat. Shredded bits of the yellow crime scene tape still hung from the bushes along the building's foundation.

There were no traces of blood on the tarmac where she had been lying, which, as Gwyneth described it, was awash in water from the downpour. Harry wondered if the club had power-washed the area despite the rain. While he thought idly about that, he looked around, but saw absolutely nothing that would increase his knowledge of what had happened that night.

Nevertheless, he walked entirely around the building, examining the largely composted mulch in the beds as he went. He found nothing, no footprints, no cigarette butts, no gum wrappers, nothing. He continued walking until he was in front of the building again and followed the boardwalk down to the dock. Two white inboards, their brass gleaming, were moored to anchor buoys forty or fifty feet in front of the dock and two white dinghies were turned bottom up on the dock itself.

Because of the flatness of the land, the Seminole River was tidal for miles from its mouth, and a glance at the river told Harry the tide was ebbing. Looking at the dock's ladder, it occurred to him that the killer might have come and left by boat.

He heard footsteps behind him on the dock, and turned to see a thick-set man in white shorts, sandals, and a white short-sleeved shirt with a tan pith helmet on his head striding toward him, gripping a cell phone in his right hand.

"You looking for somebody?" he asked in a rasping, aggressive voice.

"Just looking. The name's Brock. Harry Brock."

"This here is Conservation Club property. Didn't you read the sign?"

"And you are?"

"Manager of the club. You'd better leave."

"Were you on duty the night Gwyneth Benbow was shot in your parking lot?" Harry asked.

"Are you a reporter? Because if you are . . ."

"No, I'm a private investigator. Do you know Ms. Benbow?"

"I know she's one of the club's leading members. Leave, now, or I call the police."

Harry took a card from his pocket and passed it to the man, whose face was growing dangerously red. "There's a number written on the back," he said calmly. "It's the City Hospital where Ms. Benbow is recuperating. Punch it in and ask to speak with her. Tell her I'm asking questions. Then we'll discuss my leaving."

The man was obviously surprised and stood for a moment, staring at Harry. Then he looked at both sides of the card.

"You'll be glad you did," Harry said quietly. "There's no downside to it."

"Well . . . okay."

He opened his phone and began pacing back and forth on the dock as he made the call. "Ms. Benbow," he said in that same rasping voice. "This is Marlow. I found a Harry Brock on the club dock, and he began asking questions."

He listened.

While that went on, Harry studied the manager more closely. The hem on his shorts was frayed. His sandals had been patched with fish line, his shirt had an iron burn on the back right shoulder, and the gray hair sticking out from under his hat needed cutting.

A single man approaching middle age and hanging on without a nickel to spare, Harry thought and wondered if he looked like that to strangers. It was not a pleasant thought.

"If that's what you want. All right. How are you? Good. Thank you." The man dropped his phone in his pocket and said as he approached Harry, "She told me to go ahead and answer your questions and to help you if I could. I'm Marlow Tremple."

They shook hands.

"You were here the night of the shooting," Harry said.

"I called it in. It was one of the worst moments of my life. I thought for sure she was dead. God, she was dumping blood like a drain pipe. As soon as I'd called 911, I pulled off my shirt, which was soaked, of course—it was really bucketing down—wrung it out, and pressed it down on the wound and prayed. I'm not a man given to prayer, but I prayed that night."

"You probably saved her life," Harry said. "How did you happen to find her?"

"As I told the sheriff's people, we've had some car break-ins during our meetings, and I was making a circuit of the parking areas. I'd just come around that corner when I heard the shot and saw the muzzle blast."

Harry thought a moment.

"So you were within forty or fifty feet of where the shooting took place. What else did you see?"

"Very little. I didn't know Ms. Benbow was down until I came around her car and stumbled over her. I was so busy pointing my flashlight around, looking for the shooter that I didn't see her."

"How much did you see of the shooter?"

"Very little. I saw a dark figure moving away from her, but he was soon lost in the rain, and once I saw the blood, all I thought about was getting help for her."

Harry thought that had the ring of truth.

"Are you certain it was a man?"

"Lord, no, it was raining too hard. I might as well have been waving a stick for all the good that flashlight was doing. I didn't even see a shadow."

"Your waving that flashlight when you came around the corner probably scared off the shooter. It looks to me as if you saved her twice. Did you hear anyone running or see a car drive away?"

"I didn't hear anyone running. The rain was drumming too loud for that, but the meeting had broken up and people were coming out and running for their cars. Ms. Benbow must have been one of the first to reach this side of the building. But by the time I reached her, several cars, near the door but none close to hers, had their headlights on and were driving away."

"Do you know of anyone who might want Ms. Benbow dead?"

"She kept her own counsel, but so far as I know everyone liked her. I did. She always found something friendly to say to me."

Said like a man who couldn't count on that from everyone in his life. Harry whipped his mind away from that thought as quickly as he could.

"Just one more question. Who do I see about getting a list of the people at the meeting that night?"

"Julia Alterno, the Club's assistant secretary. She could probably help you, maybe."

He gave Harry a number.

"Thanks for your help, Marlow," Harry said, amused by the fact that while listening to Tremple he had gradually forgotten about the man's buzz-saw voice. "If you think of anything you haven't told me, please give me a call."

"I'll do that," Tremple said cheerfully, sticking Harry's card into his shirt pocket. "It's not going to do our attendance at meetings any kind of good to have one of our members gunned down in the parking lot. Dampens people's enthusiasm for coming out in the evening, if you take my meaning."

"I think I do," Harry said, managing to keep his face straight.

Harry left the Conservation Club in good spirits, thanks to Marlow Tremple, and despite not having learned anything that was going to help either him or Jim Snyder find whoever shot Gwyneth and having to fight off the invidious self-portrait he had drawn from looking at Tremple too closely. Before driving out of the parking lot, he did call the club's secretary.

"Julia Alterno," the woman said.

The voice, Harry thought, did not hold out hope for a brighter tomorrow, or the day after. If the face matched the voice, he decided, seeing it wreathed in smiles would be postponed well beyond the first skating party in hell.

"I'm Harry Brock," he said, hoping to elaborate on that, but was cut off.

"Do I know you?"

"No."

"If you're calling me about the Conservation Club, the office is closed. It will open at ten o'clock in the morning."

"I've just been talking with Marlow Tremple."

"Lucky you."

"Bad day?" Harry asked.

"Average," Alterno said. "What do you want?"

"A list of the people who attended the Conservation Club meeting the night Gwyneth Benbow was shot."

"I said if you want to do club business, call in the morning."

"This isn't, technically speaking, club business," Harry said.

"Is that what you're doing?"

"What?"

"Speaking technically?"

A flicker of humor? The stirrings of rage? Tremple's *maybe* took on more vibrant meaning.

"If it involves the Gwyneth Benbow shooting, the answer is yes," Harry said, hoping for neutrality.

"What's your name again?"

"Harry Brock."

"You with the sheriff's department?"

"No, I'm a private investigator, working for Ms. Benbow."

"How is she?"

"As well as can be expected."

"Okay, that's six. Try for twenty-five."

"The doctors expect her to live. She's propped up, eating, talking, sleeping but still intubated. I've talked with her. She doesn't know who shot her."

"You can count and talk at the same time. That's a beginning. Stop by the office tomorrow morning after nine. I'll either have the list or you don't get it."

She hung up.

"I used to think New Englanders were weird," Harry said aloud, "but this place beats the Northeast all hollow."

Julia Alterno looked like somebody's aunt, except that she was wearing a caftan that made Joseph's coat look as if it came off a Puritan's clothesline. And her hair, a henna red, was piled on top of her head in an unsteady tower. Harry approached her desk with resigned trepidation, struggling to keep his gaze off her hair.

"How's the day shaping up?" he asked.

She looked away from the computer screen, turning slowly

toward him, eyes narrowing behind the pink-rimmed glasses.

"Harry Brock, Pain I.T.A," she said.

"I've been called worse," he said with relief, grateful for escaping with only flesh wounds. "Has word come down from on high regarding the list?"

She picked up an envelope from the clutter on her desk and passed it to him. "Here it is and good luck. There are seventy some names on that list. You ought to get through the interviews by Christmas if you start as soon as that door closes behind you."

Harry felt his heart sinking into black water.

"On the other hand," she said, "you might glance through it, to see if anything catches your attention."

"Or you could help me," he said.

Alterno reached across the desk and snapped the envelope out of his hand, flipped up the flap, and extracted the enclosure, then handed him the opened sheet.

"Second column, item eleven," she said.

"Jack O'Lanton," Harry read aloud. "Is this part of some ongoing joke?"

"My guess? No."

"Were you there that night?"

"Yes, because the secretary was going to be held up. Then I stayed after filling him in on what he'd missed."

"Who is the secretary?"

"Peter Rahn."

"Rahn, Williams & Brawne?"

"The same."

"Would you recognize Jack O'Lanton if you saw him?"

"No, and as far as I can remember there was no one in that room who looked out of place. As I said, there were seventy people in the audience. Of that number, I would estimate there were fifteen I didn't recognize. I've checked their names."

"And none of them looked out of place."

Alterno sighed and stuck the pencil she had been holding into her hair as if she was skewering a living thing, which, Harry admitted, that pile of hair might be. If so, it was now mortally wounded.

"They looked pretty much like the rest of the scruffy bunch that turns out for these things. The people who do the work mostly don't come. Busman's holiday, that sort of thing."

"What was the subject?"

"Gazelle Plimpton, a state biologist, gave a talk on the monitor lizard invasion on this coast."

"Cape Coral is infested with them."

"That's right. I gather they're a nasty piece of work."

"Indeed they are. Is there anything more about the list you want to tell me?"

"You might want to talk with Peter. He knows Gwyneth better than most of the board, but don't tell him I sent you. As I said, I've checked the names I don't recognize. Good luck with your search. Some of the people on that list ought to be shot, but Gwyneth Benbow isn't one of them."

"No," Harry said, "but it seems to be how it goes."

CHAPTER 11

Harry found Gwyneth sitting on the edge of her bed, wearing a pair of blue slacks and flat-heeled sandals. Her sling had been taken off at least temporarily because she was wearing an orange blouse and a paler orange cardigan, but the sling was rigged again.

"I got up here all by myself," she said proudly, sliding to the floor, her dark eyes dancing.

"Congratulations," Harry told her, his spirits buoyed by her enthusiasm, "and you look like an Indian princess."

He had spoken on impulse and now regretted it. Whoever was taking care of her hair had parted it in the middle and plaited it into a long thick braid. Added to the thinning of her face from loss of appetite and pain, the braid, tightening the skin on her face, made her look years younger. But he thought she might not consider the comparison flattering.

"Harry!" she cried, finishing with a broad smile that removed his concern. "A compliment. How wonderful!"

"You've been in here too long," he said, feeling his face burn.

"Wait." She grasped his arm with her free hand. "No, don't pull away."

She kissed him on the cheek.

"Thank you," he said, startled by her gesture.

"You're welcome," she said, tilting her head and looking at him with an expression he couldn't read.

"Coffee?" he asked.

"Has Quaker meeting begun?" she replied with a Mona Lisa smile.

"I suppose so. There are things I should discuss with you."

"Okay, but let's skip the cafeteria uncoffee."

"The last walk we took, you had to lean on my arm most of the way. This time, you walked alone," he said when they were seated in a carpeted alcove with a curved bay window at the end of the fifth floor corridor.

"All good things come to an end," she said with an unconvincing smile.

"We have to come to an agreement," Harry said, leaning forward, elbows on his knees.

"I thought we had."

"Not quite. We've got to agree to be truthful with one another."

"I haven't lied to you," Gwyneth protested, shaking her head as she spoke, her eyes widening.

"No, but you haven't been altogether truthful, either."

"About what?"

"I don't know, and that's the trouble."

"You've found out from Holly about my first marriage, haven't you?"

The color was bleached out of her voice. The alteration almost weakened his resolve on the matter, but he braced himself and went on.

"I didn't hear from her anything approaching a full account, and there was no malice or failure of friendship involved, either. Holly was afraid that there was something you were trying to bury, and that it might come back to hurt you. Was she right?"

Gwyneth got up while Harry was speaking and walked to the window, keeping her back toward him. Harry thought Holly's suspicion concerning the marriage may have been well founded. He also doubted that Gwyneth was actually looking at the glittering bend in the Seminole River that dominated the view.

"Is it something that's too stressful for you to revisit right now? Do you want some time to think?"

He had gotten up, preparing to leave. But she surprised him.

"No," she said, turning away from the window. "Holly may be right. I doubt that I'm a reliable judge."

"About what?" Harry asked, carefully observing Gwyneth's drawn features and dull voice and prepared to end the inquisition.

"In my junior year at Smith," she said in a strained voice, "I met Morrison Perkins. He was ten years older than I and in advance of me by more years than that when it came to maturity. He proposed in August of that year, and I accepted. My parents were adamantly opposed to the marriage, but the excitement of the affair and the sense of power it had given me to be wanted by this handsome, successful, older man overrode whatever my parents were trying to tell me."

"This can wait, Gwyneth," Harry said, fearing that the obvious stress tightening her voice might be increased by whatever she was setting out to tell him.

She left the window and sat down on the rose-colored love seat across the small coffee table from Harry. He came around the table and sat down beside her.

"You don't have to go on with this and probably shouldn't," he said.

She gave him a cold smile and shook her head. "We both know this has to be done, and if you don't, you soon will."

Harry felt slightly encouraged by her flinty tone, but he was far from convinced. Holly's abbreviated comments had not promised a happy ending.

"All right," he said, "but I'm going to sit here and close the curtain if you become upset. You've just been through a nasty experience, and whether or not you know it, it's taken its toll."

"Aren't Indian princesses supposed to be tough?" she asked, blinking at him in mock innocence.

"Only beautiful," Harry said. "Talk."

"It's a miserable story," she said seriously. "But such as it is, here it is. Morrison worked for Grail Enterprises, an electronics company specializing in missile systems. It was headquartered in Boston with a laboratory in Northampton. Morrison was in charge of one of the Northampton divisions and clearly on the way up in the company."

"Had he been married?" he asked.

"He never said so, and I hadn't asked, but, yes, he had. In fact, after the interment service, I stayed beside the grave for a few moments, to say goodbye."

Harry decided not to press her for the answer as to how Perkins died.

"I had a brief exchange with my parents," she continues, "over whether or not it was wise of me to be alone just then. Fortunately, their illusions about my still being their little girl had been shattered by my marrying Morrison, and they gave in fairly quickly and went back to the car. When I had said my goodbyes and turned to leave, there was a woman, waiting to speak with me, with a uniformed man—I assumed it was her chauffeur—standing a few yards behind her, listening and observing. I was a little uneasy but soon forgot him.

" 'Morrison and I were married for eight years,' she said by way of introducing herself. 'I hope you don't regard my speaking to you an intrusion.'

"I said that I didn't, but what she had told me came as a shock. She went on speaking, but I was too stunned to listen carefully and didn't hear much of what she said. She appeared to recognize that I wasn't listening and paused. I had by then brought my mind to bear on her and actually saw her.

"She was striking-looking, perhaps ten years older than I,

wearing a black beret, which covered her hair, a black woolen coat, black leather gloves, black boots, and a deep purple scarf. She would not have been remarkable on a Boston street, but in a Northampton graveyard, she was an arresting figure.

"I found I wanted to see her eyes, but I couldn't. She was wearing black-framed sunglasses, although it was one of those gray, lowering winter days, a New England specialty, designed to crush the spirits."

"What did she want?" Harry asked.

"I never found out. 'You are Gwyneth, and I am Rachel,' she said in a high, clear voice as if she was christening something. I put out my hand, but she didn't take it. 'Two very fortunate women,' she said then, in the same emphatic voice.

" 'Because Morrison is dead?' I demanded, angry and confused. 'Of course not,' she said, going stiff. 'Fortunate to have been married to such a remarkable man.' "

"Unstable?" Harry asked.

"I never found that out, either. The chauffeur stepped forward and took her by the elbow. He said to her, in a low but firm voice, 'Excuse me, Madam. It is time to go. Rosamund will worry.' At that point, after a brief hesitation, she turned her back on me and with the chauffeur at her side, strode out of the cemetery. He helped her into the backseat of a very large car, and then drove away."

"And the color of the car?"

"Black, of course."

"And you said she was in her thirties?"

"Yes."

"Who is Rosamund?"

"I've no idea. Why do you care?"

"Names are important. Please go on."

"All right, but what comes next doesn't have any dark, elegant, mysterious women to tickle your imagination."

"Not true. I have the narrator."

"Harry, take a good look, then give me a break."

"Okay. You're still dark, mysterious, and elegant—on the inside, anyway."

"God! Mr. Rogers." She paused and then asked, "Did I say that I receive an unsigned sympathy card every year, on the date of Morrison's death?"

"No. Rachel?"

"I don't know," she said with a shrug, and took up her story again. "Either just before or just after we were married, I became pregnant and when I discovered the fact, I didn't tell Morrison."

"He hadn't noticed when you missed your periods?"

"No. As I said, he was a man with a lot on his mind, and he put serious planning and genuine hard work into making the most of his opportunities. I didn't think it then, but looking back, aside from slotting me into his plans for promotion and making love to me, I don't think he gave me much thought at all."

"You told him you were pregnant, and the honeymoon ended," Harry said.

"How did you guess?"

Sarcasm, Harry thought, became her.

"You gave me all the clues," he said.

"I was well into my third month when I broke the news, expecting him to be delighted. Instead, he became furious."

"He must have been reading Bacon?"

"What are you talking about?"

"Francis Bacon said, 'He who takes wife and child gives hostages to Fortune.' "

"Perhaps, but I never saw him read anything other than electrical engineering journals and the *Wall Street Journal*."

"I suppose he wanted you to end your pregnancy."

"That's right, and for the first time in our relationship, I said no."

"What happened?"

"He went icy cold and said it was the wrong time for us to have a child. In the remainder of the year I had to complete my degree as well as learn how to help him advance by convincing his superiors and their wives at Grail that I was a young but stable, socially skilled wife, who could be counted on to support him as he moved up the company ladder."

Gwyneth stopped and turned to face Harry, her eyes narrowed. Harry thought perhaps she might offload her anger on him and tried to deflect it. "What was your reaction?"

"Later, I realized that was the moment our relationship was destroyed. But then, I thought only about what he was asking me to do and hated him for it while at the same time desperately wanting this not to be happening. I remember saying that there was no reason I couldn't do the things he wanted me to do and still have the baby."

Gwyneth shivered suddenly, but immediately pulled herself together and said, "He said it was impossible, that his next promotion would probably be under consideration at about the time I was completing my studies, that we would be posted overseas, possibly to India, and that the people vetting him would regard the presence of baby in the mix of pros and cons to be a very strong impediment."

"That's enough," Harry said, putting his hand on her shoulder. She had begun shaking again. "You can tell me the rest another time. Let's get you back to your room."

Harry wondered if even now she had any idea that Morrison probably thought he had walked into a trap that had been deliberately set for him, not that it had been a trap. But at that moment, to a man as driven as he was painted as being, the thought would have surfaced, and, accurate assessment or not, he probably saw his gleaming future turning into dust and ashes.

"I'm all right, Harry," she said, catching his hand in hers. "Let's get this over with."

"You're sure?"

"Absolutely."

He turned his hand over and caught hers. "Even princesses deserve down time," he said.

"Later," she said. She squeezed his hand briefly and with a stiffening of her back, picked up the narrative.

"I lost courage at hearing that and begged for some time to think about what he had told me. What I really wanted was to end the conversation. We then entered into a month of silent warfare. Mostly, we were civil to one another, except when Morrison raised the issue. Then we would go back and forth, with him trying to make me understand why the abortion had to happen and I would dodge and weave, trying to get out of the confrontation.

"We were approaching the holidays, and there were company parties every weekend, most hosted by the senior members of the staff, but occasionally by the lower orders. It was following such a party, this one given by one of Morrison's friends, a person, I knew, who was competing with Morrison for the upcoming promotion, that the top blew off the kettle.

"For some reason there were none of the Grail grandees at the party, and Morrison—in a total departure from his usual practice—drank way too much. I was not drinking by then, and when it came time to go home, Morrison insisted on driving. Several of his friends tried without success to dissuade him. I did not because I knew him well enough by then to know that once his mind was made up, drunk or sober, Morrison did what he wanted to do.

"At first, he refused to speak to me. We were riding in a miserable silence when suddenly he attacked me. Verbally. It was a foul night, cold and pouring with rain. The road, like most of the roads in the area, was narrow and twisting. He should have been giving all his attention to getting us home safely because there was a fair amount of traffic, but the angrier he became, the faster he drove, and the more he looked away from the road to shout at me.

"It was our first real fight, and I wasn't prepared for it. My parents didn't even argue, at least not in front of me, and I had never before had genuine anger directed at me, not to mention by someone who supposedly loved me. He began by saying he wished to God he had never met me, and it went downhill from there. I won't rehash it. It was too awful.

"To be brief, the car skidded on a corner, he lost control, we bounced over a ditch, climbed a low stone wall, caromed off a huge oak, and flipped. Morrison was not wearing his seatbelt. I was. Both front doors flew open. He was thrown from the car onto the wall, and the car rolled over him, crushing him. The car pitched back over the wall and landed on its roof in the ditch."

Gwyneth stopped talking and sat staring blankly down the corridor until Harry broke into her reverie, then said, "I remember going off the road very clearly. I learned what followed later."

"And you?" he asked.

"The medics found me unconscious, hanging in the seatbelt. Sometime that night in the hospital, I miscarried."

"I'm sorry."

She nodded without looking at Harry, clearly lost in very painful recollections.

"Why were you so reluctant to tell me?"

"It wasn't the accident that I was hiding. It was what followed."

CHAPTER 12

"Those were the last words she spoke before she fainted," Harry said, pausing in his task of setting out tomato plants in Tucker's recently raked and harrowed garden. "I assume the description of the accident itself came from the police and insurance reports."

"Talk and work at the same time," Tucker said.

He was on knees in the soft dirt, pushing a three-foot stake into the soil beside the tomato plant he had just planted. He sat back on his heels to survey his work.

"Push the stakes in deep as you can," he said, glancing at Harry, "they're going to have considerable weight on them once these begin to bear fruit."

"I'll remember," Harry said. "Do you want to hear this or not?"

"Only if you can keep working. I don't want to be setting out tomato plants when I should be eating lunch. It's going to rain this afternoon, and I want them to have the benefit of it."

"You'd try the patience of a saint," Harry said, going back to work.

"Then you needn't be troubled," Tucker said calmly, reaching for another tomato plant with one hand and troweling a hole for it with the other.

"And sarcastic," Harry said.

"Go on with your story. I won't get any peace until I've heard it."

Harry knew that was as close as Tucker would come to saying he was interested. He picked up where he had stopped.

"I'm surprised my hair didn't turn white before I found a nurse and a gurney," Harry said, "Then my troubles weren't over because the nurse who reached us first was twice as big as me and from what I saw at least that much stronger, because she reached down and in a single swoop lifted Gwyneth off the floor and laid her light as a feather on that gurney."

"You've stopped working again," Tucker said.

"I know," Harry said, shuffling on his knees to the next set, pulling the basket with the plants in it after him. "I was frightened enough by what had happened to Gwyneth. But when that nurse finished telling me all the things she was going to do to me if Gwyneth had suffered a setback, I was ready to go out the window even if we were five stories up."

"Since you're still walking on your own," Tucker said, "I gather the Benbow woman is all right."

"She is. Dr. Ingram was visiting patients on the floor and was with Gwyneth only minutes after she had been lifted into her bed. Gwyneth had revived by then and Ingram checked her vital signs, examined the wound, and pronounced her in good order.

" 'You're lying in this bed for an hour,' she said. 'Then I'll come back and look at you again. No, you can't get out of bed, but if Mr. Brock can stay, there's no reason not to continue your conversation.'

"I was waiting outside Gwyneth's room and heard all that, and the valkyrie glared at me when she left, but she was outranked and that saved my bacon. When Ingram came out, she stopped long enough to tell me that I could go in but not to upset her patient. She asked me what we were talking about when Gwyneth fainted. I told her she'd been describing an auto accident she had several years ago. A person in the car with her died."

"Morrison Perkins," Tucker said.

"Right. I spent yesterday afternoon in *The Boston Globe*'s archives finding all I could about him and the accident."

"Was it productive?"

Oh, Brother! and Sanchez were resting in the shade of a large oleander, covered with pink blossoms, watching the men work. Harry noticed that Oh, Brother! appeared to be taking an interest in what was being said, but Sanchez was sprawled in the grass, looking as if he had completed life's journey.

"Considering that Morrison Perkins lived in Northampton, his death attracted a lot of notice," Harry said, determined not to look at Oh, Brother! and be forced to speculate as to whether or not the mule was actually listening. He felt that he had to set limits on behaving as if Tucker's animals really did understand human speech. "Although Gwyneth hadn't mentioned it, her husband was one of the heirs to the Alonzo Perkins fortune."

"Wasn't he the hotel tycoon?" Tucker asked.

"Boston, New York, Philadelphia," Harry said.

"I stayed once in the New York Perkins," Tucker said.

"A little pricey for you, wasn't it?" Harry asked, surprised by the glimpse into Tucker's past, something his old friend seldom mentioned.

"Oh, I wasn't paying for it."

"Who was?"

"I've forgotten. Are we to assume his death left Benbow a wealthy woman?"

Harry wasn't surprised that Tucker hadn't answered his question.

"It looks that way. I don't know, however, whether or not her parents are still living. I wasn't satisfied with what I learned from Gwyneth about the aftermath of the accident. If she had intended to be forthcoming on the subject before she fainted, she'd changed her mind by the time I was allowed back into her room." Harry paused to wonder what else Gwyneth had not told him. "But I think the *Globe* gave me all I need to know to understand her reticence."

"Was it suggested that she might have killed him?"

"For whatever reasons, the paper didn't make that clear. What was clear was that Perkins' friends in the company took every opportunity offered to trash her. After learning about the pregnancy, he seems to have told several of his colleagues that Gwyneth had known from the beginning of their relationship that he did not want to start a family and the reasons for his reluctance.

"Over and over in the interviews reported in the paper, those same people, men and women alike, told the same story, accusing her of deceiving him by keeping from him the knowledge that she was pregnant. Somewhere about here in my reading, I learned that the Perkins estate went to court to prevent Gwyneth from inheriting. The effort was quashed."

"Fortunately for her. Any truth in the accusations?" Tucker asked.

"Perkins may have thought so. He knew her parents had opposed their marriage."

"Aside from the ones ascribed to her, what motive would she have had in keeping the information from him?" Tucker asked.

"In several pieces, the *Globe* either implied or said outright that Perkins' friends believed it was done to keep him in Northampton and herself close to her parents. The same individuals asserted that Perkins had frequently complained that she was emotionally immature and still very dependent on her parents."

"Did the police ever get involved?" Tucker asked and then added, "Don't slack off now. We're almost finished, and I hear that chicken salad I made this morning calling. It ought to be chilled to perfection."

"I haven't slacked off. I was just thinking about the coverage that accident got." Harry pushed another stake into the ground. "She was what—twenty-two or three? The shock of the whole thing must have been terrific. Losing her husband and the child were bad enough, but being pilloried the way she was for indirectly causing his death and doing nothing to prevent him from driving, then being smeared as selfish, manipulative, and irresponsible must have been terrible."

They went on working, neither man speaking again until Tucker got to his feet, brushed the dirt off his knees, and said, "Well done. I'm obliged for the help. Let's have some lunch."

"You're welcome," Harry replied, looking at the neatly laid-out bed of young tomato plants. "By the way, when these plants start bearing, you're going to have enough tomatoes to feed the county."

"I'll give most of them to that big food pantry in Immokalee," Tucker said. "Let's get these tools and the extra stakes into the barn."

Before long they were seated in the shade of the back stoop with beaded glasses of lemonade, to compensate for their dehydration, and a jug of Tucker's homemade ale chilling in the refrigerator. "In anticipation of lunch," Tucker had said while decanting it.

"I suppose this will all be raked over again," he observed, "if she becomes an 'object of interest' to the police."

"It's in the stars," Harry said grimly. "She's wealthy. She was having an affair with Perez. But the thing that really bothers me is what else she knows about Perkins' death and hasn't told me."

"Would it be a good time for her to go on a cruise of the fjords?" Tucker asked.

"The answer depends on how *interested* Jim's people become in her," Harry said.

When lunch was over and Harry was drying the last of the dishes, Tucker said, "Have you got another half hour to spare?"

"Yes, what's on your mind?"

"Hang up the towel. I want to show you something."

With Sanchez in the lead and Oh, Brother! covering their backs, the two men walked down to the road. Harry finally asked where they were going.

"Have you been past Willard Trachey's cabin recently?" Tucker asked.

"No, what took you there?"

"Checking on the blackberries. The yard's pretty well grown up to blackberry canes. Some of them are nearly ten feet high, and if the bears and possums don't eat them first, I'm looking forward to a large harvest and some fine-tasting jelly."

"The last time I saw it," Harry said, "the roof had finally collapsed under the weight of the big lignum vitae that fell on it last winter."

It was approaching the hottest part of the day, and the insect orchestras in the upper canopy were performing at full volume, making it difficult for the two men to hear one another without raising their voices. Conversation more or less stopped when they pushed their way into what had once been a clearing where the cabin stood. In addition to the blackberry canes, it was rapidly being reclaimed by weeds, wire grass, blooming Spanish sword, and head-high stopper bushes, which would soon be shaded by the seedling palms and hardwoods struggling upward toward the sun.

"Walking becomes a little more difficult here," Tucker said, pausing. "I'll ask Oh, Brother! to go ahead and notify the snakes of our arrival."

Tucker turned toward the mule, motioning him forward. The

big animal threw up his head and snorted.

"Yes, I was talking to you. Now go ahead. You know snake bite doesn't bother you—well, yes, it does hurt but only for a minute."

Sanchez was sitting in the sand, looking up at Oh, Brother! and grinning. The mule took a long step toward the dog and Sanchez swallowed his grin.

"Never mind him," Tucker said, stroking the mule's neck. "Move on."

A bit hesitantly, Oh, Brother! stepped between Tucker and Harry and pushed into the tangle. Sanchez followed in the mule's wake. Tucker gave them a few seconds' start and then moved ahead, saying over his shoulder, "Just giving the snakes a little extra time to slither away."

The thought of five feet of timber rattler "slithering away" gave Harry the willies, but he followed Tucker, wondering if he had taken a wrong turn in his life when he moved onto the Hammock and made friends with a man who talked with animals. *And so far as I know, he doesn't even own a ring,* Harry told himself for his own amusement.

Once through the thickest part of the new growth, the bushes thinned, and coming to the place near the crumpled cabin that had served as a parking area, the men stepped onto a sandy space, free from undergrowth.

"There it is," Tucker said, coming to a stop and pushing his hands into his overalls' pockets. "Sanchez found it yesterday. The kill's not more than a day old. It was still leaking blood when I got to it."

Harry said nothing at first as he stared at the blood-soaked sand and the ripped and shredded remains of what had once been a large deer.

"A panther didn't do that," Tucker said quietly, "and neither did coyotes."

Oh, Brother! refused to go any closer to the dead animal than the edge of the clearing, and the hair was standing up in a ridge on Sanchez's back, a low steady growl rumbling in his chest as he kept turning and staring into the surrounding bushes.

"A bear?" Harry suggested with little conviction.

"Did you ever see a bear kill where the bones were crushed and bitten through like this? Whatever did this bit right through that deer's backbone and two of its leg bones."

Harry experienced a brief chill as if a cold wind had passed over him.

"No," he said with a mixture of regret and anger, "it wasn't a bear that did this. It was a Nile monitor lizard. They've finally found us."

"Well," Tucker said, "I don't know much about them, but this one must have jaws like a rock crusher. I suggest we hunt it down and kill it."

"You're not too far off about the jaws," Harry said. "Nile monitors grow to be eight or nine feet in length. Along with claws and powerful jaws, they can run, swim, and climb trees. You can see how this one ripped the deer's body apart."

"Not much left but the bones. It even broke through the skull and ate the brains."

"They're always hungry and very aggressive. I wouldn't know how to begin to hunt the wretched thing. At home on land or in the water, it can submerge and hold its breath for an hour. That's just the beginning."

Harry paused to look around. "On this dry ground, we won't find much more than a few claw marks and possibly some drag lines from the tail."

"You don't sound very inspired by my suggestion that we rid the Hammock of this pestilential beast," Tucker said.

"So far, none of the areas where they've shown up has been able to exterminate them," Harry said, "and foot for foot, they're more dangerous than alligators. But I'm willing to try. Maybe Sanchez can help us."

Sanchez had finally stopped his circling and positioned himself under Oh, Brother!, who was standing with his head up and his ears cocked, scanning the bushes attentively. At the sound of his name, the big hound gave a sharp bark.

"Great Scott!" Tucker burst out, "you can run rings around this lizard. So brace up and stop behaving like a puppy."

Sanchez gave a final growl and set off for home. Oh, Brother! looked at Tucker.

"Yes, go ahead. See if you can buck him up."

The mule turned and trotted after the dog.

"Hurt pride," Tucker said. "I spoke to him a little too harshly. I'll give him some extra biscuits when we get back. When he's had time to think it over, and if Oh, Brother! agrees to go with us, I think he'll cooperate."

"Good," Harry said, not knowing what else to say.

His mind really wasn't on Sanchez but on Tucker. Harry did not like at all the prospect of Tucker, even armed with his twelve gauge, coming anywhere near that killing machine.

"Would you call this big lizard evil?" he asked.

"No," Tucker said without hesitation, "I'd say, borrowing from another context, that our Nile monitor lizard is an inconvenient truth."

CHAPTER 13

Harry begged off immediately launching a hunt for the monitor, and dissuaded Tucker from going alone.

"There's no hurry here," he said as they walked back to the road. "That thing will probably stay around for a while. There's fish in the creek. If it was a cougar kill, the monitor will know that, especially if it took the deer away from her, and may decide to go looking for her when he gets hungry again."

"I hope she and the coyotes have the sense not to dispute the loss of a kill with it."

"So do I," Harry said. "They're no match for that creature."

"Where are you going from here?" Tucker asked.

"Jim's office. I've got things to discuss with him."

"Will you tell him what you've found concerning Morrison Perkins?"

"I'm going to think about that on the way to town."

While he was thinking, he recalled that in his search through the *Globe* archives, he had neglected Perkins' obituary. The mysterious Rachel should be identified there."

But before haring after Rachel, he wanted to learn whether or not Eric Scartole really was in Dallas and how long he had been there.

Thanks to online search engines, he soon had the address and telephone number of Elizabeth Scartole, the only one in Dallas. And with some further effort, he knew what the house and the neighborhood in which she lived looked like. Checking his watch and deducting an hour for the central time zone location, Harry was satisfied that interrupting Mrs. Scartole's lunch was the extent of the disturbance his calling was likely to cause her.

Nevertheless, he made certain he knew exactly what he wanted to ask her and how he was going to do it without setting off alarm bells. Over time he had learned that there were always risks in calling someone connected to a person who has attracted the attention of the police, especially if there's a murder involved.

When a woman answered and said, "This is Elizabeth Scartole speaking. I don't recognize your number. Who's calling, please?" Harry knew he was in Texas.

"Hello, Mrs. Scartole, my name is Harry Brock. I'm calling from Avola, Florida."

"Oh, Avola, what a beautiful little city. My son lived there until recently, and I visited with him and his wife a few times. The beaches are wonderful and the shopping, for such an end-of-the-road location, is fine. But the prices! Lord above! They are breathtaking. And I found the humidity very trying. Does it bother you at all?"

"Yes, it does, Mrs. Scartole," Harry said quickly. The temptation to imitate her accent was so powerful, he wondered if it was contagious. "I'm actually calling Eric. Is he at home?"

Harry had gambled that if he was staying with her, it was unlikely he would be spending much time in the house. From what he had seen online, he judged it to be a small, single-level bungalow in a residential section of the city that was either going up or down but definitely not where Scartole would now want to live.

"No, Mr. Brock, Eric has his own place. He was here for a week or so when he and Gwyneth broke up. Do you know

Gwyneth? I'm sorry to say she proved to be a heavy disappointment, and their separating a painful experience for Eric. He was quite unhappy at the time. Now, I'm glad to say, he's much recovered."

I'll bet he is, Harry thought but said, "You're talking about their divorce, I take it."

"Yes, are you a friend of Eric's?"

"More an acquaintance, but I've lost touch with him and have some information I would like to give him. Does he have a number where I could call him?"

"Yes, he does, but perhaps you could tell me and I could pass it along. Eric becomes cross with me when I give out his number."

Harry did not want this to become two people on a rope trying to go in opposite directions. "It's of a personal nature, Mrs. Scartole, and I would prefer to say it myself. Do you think he would object to my writing to him?"

There was a brief pause. Harry wished he could see her face, which might have told him what she was thinking.

"I don't see what harm that could do," she answered a little hesitantly.

"Fine, do you have his address?"

"No, but I ought to be able to tell the name of his apartment building. It's an odd name, something like ostrich. Oh, yes. It's the Austrikand Towers—that's with an *au* instead of an *o*. I hope it's not bad news."

"Just something of interest to him, I'd say. You have my name and number?"

"Well, the phone has it, but I'd rather write it down. I don't trust these mechanical devices. There, I've got your name and your number."

"Thank you, Mrs. Scartole; it's been a pleasure talking with you."

123

But Harry failed in his effort to escape. In fact, it was nearly ten minutes before a fictitious incoming call set him free.

Holly Pike had called Harry, to tell him that her new stallion had arrived and invite him to take a look.

"If he's half as good as he looks," she said, pride shining through every word, "he's going to put this farm on the map, big time."

She had just dismounted from Scotsman, dark with sweat, and passed the reins to Buster when Harry walked into the yard at Barn One with Nip in the lead, displaying by his heads-up trot that he had a prize visitor in tow.

"Buster's going to walk Scotsman, to cool him down, and that's what you're going to do with me," she called by way of greeting, pulling off her hat and passing that to Buster as well.

Scotsman may have just had a hard run, but just in case his handler thought he had no juice left, he decided to walk around on his hind legs for a while.

"You want to ride him, Harry?" Buster asked, keeping his face straight while dancing around with the horse, indulging him.

"Not today, Buster."

Harry's sorry horsemanship had been a source of merriment in the stables for some time.

"Buster," Holly said, "pull the idiot down, hose him then walk him dry."

Buster gave the reins a stout yank and said, "Stand." The big animal came down with a solid thump and allowed himself to be unsaddled without more fuss.

While that was going forward, Holly pulled off her gloves and shoved them into a back pocket of her jodhpurs, then took Harry's arm. "Walk me down to the home paddock," she said. "I wasn't fooling about needing to be cooled down. I hate it, but I find if I don't stretch my legs after a hard ride, I limp around the next day like a candidate for extended care."

"Just wait," he said. "If I'm anything to go by, when you're my age, you can walk all you want, but you'll limp anyway."

"How come you're feeling so cheerful?"

"My work's not going well. Have you seen Gwyneth recently?"

"She's getting restless. So I guess that means she's healing. What about you?"

"I think she's coming along all right. By the way, you were right about which of them filed for the divorce. It was Gwyneth."

"I think I told you she was a very private person."

Emerging from The Oaks, they crossed the lawn to the paddock, a rectangle of white plank fence enclosing an acre of grass with a beautiful chestnut stallion grazing peacefully. At their approach, the horse raised his head, watched them for a moment with pricked ears, and returned to dealing with the grass.

"Are you going to go on riding Jack?" Harry asked, leaning against the plank fence, one foot on the bottom rail, watching the horse.

"No, I'm too fond of the old devil," Holly said, pulling a large, white, man's handkerchief out of a jodhpur pocket and wiping her face, still rosy from her recent exertion. "I'm sweating like a pig."

"Sorry," Harry said, trying to sound cheerful, "pigs don't sweat, at least not the way we do."

"Nonsense. You'd better get upwind of me," she said, grinning.

"Never mind, women glow, men perspire, and horses sweat. What's wrong with him?"

"Reduced sperm motility. We've had three vets look at him, and they said it can't be reversed."

"How old is he?"

"Twelve and still in love with mares, but the percentage of service failures are edging up. Also, lowered motility can mean less than top of the line foals. Something like that can ruin a stud's reputation. I decided to retire him from the breeding shed before it happened."

"What will you do with him?"

"We have half a dozen mares whose colts make fine riding horses, and there's a waiting list for their offspring. We'll turn Jack out with them and see what happens. If he can't keep them pregnant, we'll just pasture him. He's earned his rest."

"He still looks like a winner."

"That's right, want to see his replacement?"

"Yes," Harry replied and started to turn away, but Holly put her hand on his arm to stop him.

"What's wrong, Harry?" she asked. "You're not feeling half as good as you'd like me to think."

He started to say that he was fine, then changed his mind. What would be the point of lying to her? "I've had some bad news. My daughter, Sarah, called to say her mother is dying. Jennifer was my first wife. We were separated when the children were very young. Although she divorced me, she blamed me for the breakup."

Harry stopped.

"Want to change the subject?" Holly asked.

She had left her hand on his arm, and Harry was very aware of its warmth. It had been a long time since a woman touched him that way.

"No, unless you don't want to hear this, and I wouldn't blame you if you didn't."

"I wouldn't have asked if I didn't."

"Okay. We were living in a small, very rural community in western Maine," he said. "I had completed my game warden training two years before and was assigned to a remote part of western Maine in the Rangeley Lakes district. I was away long days, patrolling the area where I had jurisdiction. We lived on a beautiful lake, and the kids took to it like a couple of beaver cubs. Spending the days with nothing to do but care for the kids and prepare our food, do the housework, and read or take walks left Jennifer bored and dissatisfied.

"She'd been brought up in Portland, loved the coast, and hated the woods. She had nothing in common with the few women in the settlement and felt we should not be trying to raise a family in a wilderness. She had a point. But to advance in the profession, I had to take remote assignments for a few years."

"Did you consider doing something else?"

"Not right away. Probably, I should have seen the seriousness of the problem sooner, but I didn't. Then a man who had killed a deer out of season decided to stop me from arresting him by shooting at me. I fired back, intending to knock him down, but the bullet hit a hip bone. A piece of the lead tore upward through his diaphragm, penetrated his heart, and killed him."

"God, Harry, what bad luck."

"Back then, wardens were not popular people in the Maine woods, and I was charged with murder. The jury set me free, but Jennifer filed for divorce and custody of the children. The court awarded her both. My career in the department was fatally crippled, and I resigned. Eventually I came to rest on the Hammock. The greatest irony is that Florida made me a warden as well as a private investigator."

"And Jennifer's dying has brought all of this back," she said.

"Yes, plus the fact that I have a married son, whom I haven't seen since he was seven years old. He does not want to see me, but his sister insists that we are going to come together at the funeral, and we are going to be reunited. She's not taking no for an answer."

Holly gave a brief laugh at that. Then she pulled him around until he was facing her and hugged him. There really didn't seem to be anything to do but hug her back, which he did. He began to feel considerably better, especially when she lifted her head off his shoulder and gave him a robust kiss on the mouth before releasing him.

Harry, at a loss, stood there for a long moment, looking at her, and then said, "Thank you."

"If you could see the look on your face," she said, wearing a slightly mocking smile.

She took his hand, and turned toward the barns. "Let's go look at that new stallion."

I'm glad she didn't know what I was thinking, he told himself, very aware of the woman beside him, then immediately wondered if that could have been why she smiled.

"What do you think of him?" Holly asked.

They were in Barn Three, a single-story building almost entirely given over to the stallion's needs. Buster and an assistant had gone into the stall, snapped leads onto his halter, and led the big horse into the gangway, allowing Holly and Harry to walk around him.

"He is a fine-looking animal," Harry said. "He's a bay isn't he?"

"Yes," she said, "that brown coat and black tail and mane are the markers."

The stallion had danced a little while being led into the gangway, but now he was showing a bit more spirit, tossing his head, squealing, and becoming light on his front feet.

"Hold him down, Buster, Rocky," Holly said sharply, when the horse made a serious attempt to rear. "Let's start him out as we mean to go on. I don't want another hellion like Jack on my hands."

"What's his name?" Harry asked.

"Sunday River," Holly said. "Do you like it?"

"Yes. It fits him somehow."

"Okay, Buster, put him back. He's getting a little too rambunctious."

They left the barn and Harry said, "Good luck with him, Holly."

"Thanks, and it's a gamble, despite his pedigree and his record, which is sterling. We'll have to see what his foals do. It's a long, expensive wait."

They walked back to the house with Nip leading them. They were quiet, and Harry found it a comfortable silence. His thoughts returned to their talk at Jack's paddock. They were still under the over-arching live oaks lining the white gravel track. Doves were calling somewhere in the branches. The sun cast shifting patterns of shadow and light around their feet as a breeze stirred the leaves.

"I was serious when I thanked you for kissing me, Holly," Harry said. "It mattered to me that you cared enough to do it. And it helped. So, I'll say it again, thank you."

They had stopped and were facing one another.

"Grateful. Was that all you felt?" she asked.

"No, Holly, it wasn't."

CHAPTER 14

Harry caught up with Jim on the Marco Island road, a wide berm bordered by mangroves and intervals of open tidewater. Three sheriff's cruisers, two state police cars, and a Derek Motors tow truck were parked at odd angles in the eastbound lane. A sheriff's department deputy was directing the sparse traffic around the gathering.

Getting out of the Rover, Harry glanced up at the man-of-war birds with their deeply forked tails drifting over the road. *Bad weather's brought them in from the open ocean,* he thought briefly. Then he looked higher and saw half a dozen turkey vultures slowly circling. *Cleanup committee.*

Once out of the SUV and walking up the line of police vehicles, Harry saw the reason for the tow truck, which was backed partway down the steep bank. Some twenty feet away from the bottom of the bank, the rear half of an aged Ford pickup was sticking out of the water.

"Nasty business," Frank Hodges said, extricating himself from the small crowd of uniformed officers gathered on the top of the bank like a group of supervisors. He pulled a large red bandana out of a trouser pocket, lifted his hat, and mopped his face. "Hot," he said, closing his eyes until he had replaced his hat.

"What happened?"

"Picture this," Hodges said, shaking his head as if bewildered. "Two idiots drove out to Marco and robbed a grocery store, then shot the clerk and fled with about three hundred dollars. This is a place, remember, with only one access road."

"And someone called the state police and someone else called the sheriff's department," Harry said.

"That's it," Hodges replied, "and if the poor bastards weren't both dead, it would be slap-your-knee funny."

"They went off the road and died in the crash?"

"Nope. Even dumber. A trooper was out there on 41 and took the call. He got to about here and met the two jillpokes barreling toward him going at least ninety. He let them go, pulled over, and put in a general call for help. Then he turned the cruiser across the road and got out of the car, freeing his revolver as he did."

"I'm beginning to get the picture."

"All right, now this road is pretty straight and our two outlaws looked down it a ways and saw police cars barricading the road. The car won't swim, so they turn around and come flying back. Now the trooper's waiting for them. When they get within range, he pops out from behind his vehicle and shoots their front tires out."

"The car goes into the mangroves."

"Right. Now, there's a line of troopers and deputies blasting after them. They get a pretty soft landing in the swamp, which ain't got more than a foot of water in it because the tide's pretty well out. By now the trooper who shot out their tires is standing off the side of the road pointing a gun at them when they crawl out of the car.

"Their transportation's gone. Beyond the mangroves there's open water. In the next thirty seconds there's half a dozen lawmen lined up on that bank, weapons drawn, telling them to get their hands up. Guess what they do."

"I'm afraid I know."

"That's right. They pull their guns and start shooting. The

next instant, they're Swiss cheese."

"Did they hit anyone?"

"Nicked one of the troopers. The EMS crew have him patched up."

"How old were they?"

"Twenty something," Jim said, emerging from the crowd at the back of the EMS ambulance. "It's a pathetic waste of two lives."

Harry saw that the shootings had disturbed Jim. Beneath its tan, his face was drawn and almost haggard. Not for the first time, Harry wondered how Jim had ever taken up law work and remembered Hodges once saying to him, "The Captain really should have taken up preaching and running a still weekdays like his father."

Harry thought there was some truth in what Hodges had said, but he also thought that Jim was one of the best lawmen he had ever known. And perhaps his pained response to human violence and folly had played an important part in his success.

"What's brought you out here?" he asked Harry and slapped a mosquito on his neck. "Let's get into my squad car before they've picked my bones. Saltwater mosquitoes were created to remind us that we live in a fallen world."

"No argument from me," Harry responded, being more than ready to escape.

"Can you take care of things from here, Sergeant?" Jim asked Hodges.

"As long as the OFF holds out," Hodges said with a grin, shaking the spray can at Harry.

Once in Jim's car, with the windows shut, the AC on, and the mosquitoes that had come in with them exterminated, Jim said, "Have you ever asked yourself how to distinguish between viciousness and ignorance?"

Harry asked, "Are you willing to talk about the Perez case?"

"No, I'm talking about those two fools we just shot to death and then fished out of that mangrove swamp. What in God's name did they think they were doing? First driving to Marco Island to rob a grocery store, then, according to first reports, shoot a clerk who probably hadn't so much as said 'boo' to them."

"A few days ago I asked Tucker a similar question, only I asked if there was such a thing as evil abroad in the world. But of course, you'd have more luck getting a straight answer out of the Cumaean Sibyl than out of Tucker. I think your *viciousness* and my *evil* are pretty much alike."

"What prompted your question?"

"The Perez murder. Shooting a man six times at close range seems a little excessive. When I told Tucker several of the wounds were close to the heart and one through it, he said, 'Maybe the killer was a poor shot.' What are you going to do with an answer like that?"

Jim grinned, which surprised Harry because he didn't often find jokes about shootings funny.

"I'd say he was pulling your leg. Is that what you're doing with this rigmarole about Tucker, pulling my leg?"

"Avoiding answering your question would be closer to the truth," Harry said, making a sour face. "Tucker did come close to an answer, I suppose, when he said that it was people who committed the acts that people call evil. And I think he would say that what your two did was vicious and that they probably were stupid."

"Enough! What did you want to talk to me about?"

"The Perez case."

"All right, but first a question: What have you learned so far about Gwyneth Benbow?"

"Not a lot. Do you know that Eric Scartole was her second husband?"

"No," he said, lifting off his hat and sliding it between the seat and the door, then rubbing his head as if trying to clear his mind of some unpleasantness.

"She was in her early twenties," Harry said, still trying to decide how much of their conversation he was professionally obliged to tell Jim. "She was a senior at Smith College and married a man about fifteen years older than she was."

"Name?"

"Morrison Perkins."

"No, I don't recognize the name. Does the marriage have any bearing on the Perez murder or her being shot?"

"I don't think so," Harry said uncomfortably, wondering if what he had said was strictly true. "But it has the potential to draw a lot of unwelcome attention to her if the press gets hold of it."

"How hard is it going to be to pry this story out of you?" Jim asked, frowning at Harry.

"That's what I'm trying to decide, and while I'm working on it, how about your people? Anything new?"

"We know the caliber of the gun that killed Perez, and the caliber of the gun that was used to shoot Gwyneth Benbow. They're not a match."

"It doesn't mean it wasn't the same person who did the shootings."

"No, it doesn't," Jim agreed without emphasis, "but it casts doubt. Do you think now there's any possibility she killed Perez?"

"Well, we both know she didn't shoot herself, but the fact she's been shot doesn't mean she didn't shoot Perez. But what would she have gained? So far, I don't see any motive."

"I guess your answer is that you don't. But to echo you, just because we don't know the motive doesn't mean there isn't one. What is it about the marriage you haven't told me?"

Harry groaned silently. "Can I tell you something that I don't want you to have to read in the papers, but I also don't want you doing anything about until it does come out?"

"Is it material that would advance the inquiry into either or both of the shootings?"

"As of now, I would say no. Later there might be a connection, but it would be a long reach, and I don't think it's there."

"Okay," Jim said, sighing like a man much put upon, "let's hear it."

"They were married in mid-September, and either before the ceremony or soon after, she became pregnant. Possibly because she knew he very much did not want to start a family, as he was coming up for a promotion to a position that would have meant his immediate transfer to India or another southeastern country in that region, she waited three months before telling him."

"Was she still in school?"

"Yes, she was in her final year."

"What month was it when she told him?"

"December, just before Christmas."

"It was going to be a photo finish."

"She would have finished her course work by the middle of May."

"Go ahead."

"Perkins was furious. He demanded she have an abortion. She refused. Things became tense between them. Shortly after their first quarrel over the issue, they went to a faculty Christmas party, and Perkins got drunk and insisted on driving home. It was raining. He lost control of the car and ran onto a stone wall, hit a tree, and rolled over, throwing him out of the car. He wasn't wearing a seatbelt. The car rolled over him and killed him. Gwyneth was wearing a seatbelt and survived."

"The child?"

"She lost it."

"Very sad, but why were you so hesitant about telling me?"

"Perkins was an heir to the Alonzo Perkins fortune. The estate contested her right to inherit. The court found in her favor because the estate failed to prove that she knew she was pregnant before marrying Perkins."

"She told you all of this?"

"No, I went into the archives of *The Boston Globe* and found there that Perkins was an heir on his father's side. Gwyneth had not told me that, nor that Morrison's friends told anyone who would listen that she had not tried to stop him from driving the night he was killed, that Gwyneth was pregnant before the wedding and trapped him into marrying her. What I read was pretty nasty."

"Her concern," Jim said, "is that the story will surface and she will be characterized again as manipulative and dangerously self-serving, thereby increasing police scrutiny regarding the Perez killing."

"You could be right."

"What do you want me to do with this information?"

"First, how important do you think it is?"

"It's too soon to say," Jim said. "The cynical or, perhaps, pragmatic way to go is to leak it to the press, then sit back and wait while they go through the trash. Once that's published, I might be able to come to a conclusion as to whether or not they've found something worth investigating further."

"What do you think our assistant state's attorney would do with what I've told you?" Harry asked.

"As the state's prosecuting attorney, Harley Dillon's always a hard read," Jim said with a grim smile. "He's a political wolf, wearing a lawman's sheepskin."

"I think there's a responsible legal mind in there somewhere," Harry said, surprised by the harshness in Jim's response.

"Don't mistake me," Jim said quickly, "I like and respect

Harley. Essentially, he's a good man and a good attorney, but he lives and dies drawing the breath of state politics. Gwyneth Benbow has a public face, and she swims with the big fish. He exposes her to pain at considerable risk, but if he does and makes a charge against her stick, he walks away with the gold ring."

"By the way, I've talked with Elizabeth Scartole. Her son is in Dallas. From what she said, I gather he's been there since the divorce. I don't know exactly when he arrived because asking her too many questions would have shut her down. As it was, when I asked for his phone number, she balked. Then I asked for his address, and she told me he had moved to the Austrikand Towers in downtown Dallas. I looked it up. It's a fancy place and wouldn't confirm or deny that an Eric Scartole was living there."

"But with the name of the place, you got confirmation from a white pages search."

"Right, he's there, number 1014."

"We're not ready to talk with him, Harry," Jim said, frowning. "Our investigation of the Benbow shooting is barely off the ground."

"Do you want me to back off?"

"What are you going to ask him?"

"If he knows Gwyneth has been shot, and if that goes well, I'll find out how long he's been in Dallas. Knowing that, I can make a search to discover whether or not he's flown from Dallas to Florida since then."

"Can you do this without his knowing what you're up to?"

"That's my hope."

"Then may the Force be with you," Jim said.

Harry's jaw dropped.

"It's from Clara," Jim said defensively, his ears turning red. "She's begun watching reruns of *Star Wars.*"

CHAPTER 15

The following morning Harry went back to the *Globe*'s archives and found the Perkins obituary, which opened briskly with, "On December 15, 1991, Morrison Vining Perkins of Northampton, Massachusetts, died tragically in an automobile accident, having been married slightly more than three months."

Continuing to read, he soon found the information he was seeking: "On February 14, 1978, Morrison married Rachel Hansel Whittaker of Kennebunkport, Maine. They were divorced in 1986. He married Gwyneth Benbow on September 18, 1991.

"He is survived by his wife, Gwyneth Benbow Perkins, and a daughter from his first marriage, Rosamund Whittaker Fairbrother of Lexington, Massachusetts."

Harry turned away from the screen, considering how he was going to go about talking with Rachel Whittaker. Recalling Gwyneth's description of her, he did not think making contact was going to be either easy or necessarily productive.

Nothing ventured, he told himself, immediately discouraged by the banality of the thought. Then he cheered up by arriving at the idea that he might improve his chances with Whittaker by approaching her through her daughter. He immediately turned back to the computer and summoned the white pages, quickly locating the Fairbrothers' Lexington address and phone number as well as the names of Robert, Hedley, and Jackson. She must, he thought, have two children.

Harry dialed the number.

"Dr. Fairbrother speaking." It appeared to be a woman's voice, although pitched low.

"Hello, is it Dr. Rosamund Fairbrother?"

"Yes. Who's calling, please?"

"Harry Brock. I'm a private investigator, located in Avola, Florida."

A dog began barking. The phone went silent for a moment. Harry guessed she was dealing with the dog.

"Excuse the interruption. You were saying?"

"What's your dog's name?"

"Jackson," Fairbrother replied in a much colder voice.

"Really, never mind. Do you recognize the name Gwyneth Benbow?"

"Yes. Where is this going?"

"Nowhere without your cooperation and help. Ms. Benbow has been shot in a failed attempt to kill her. Aside from the person who shot her, neither Ms. Benbow, the police, nor I has any idea who shot her or why anyone would want her dead."

"Why are you telling me this?"

"I'll assume you do know that in 1976 Ms. Benbow married your father, and that he died in an automobile accident a few months later. Ms. Benbow was injured in the accident, survived, but lost the child she was carrying."

Harry waited before going on until Fairbrother finally gave what Harry thought was a very reluctant, "Yes."

"Because, so far as anyone involved in investigating the shooting knows, there is no one in her current circle of friends, acquaintances, and business associates who would want to harm her, it seems reasonable to cast a wider net."

"You're referring to the court case following my father's death."

"And the reported hostility toward her by your father's

Northampton colleagues at Grail Enterprises."

"Yes, I recall Mother's being very upset by the media coverage."

There was a pause, during which Harry created odds both for and against her deciding to tell him not to call her again. But she chose a third option.

"I have a patient to see at McLean in less than forty-five minutes. And I want to discuss this with my husband and, possibly, my attorney." He heard the unmistakable sound of pages being flipped. "If you can call me at eight-thirty tomorrow morning, I can give you thirty minutes if I decide to continue this conversation. If I don't, I or my attorney will say so then. Goodbye, Mr. Brock."

As soon as she ended the call, Harry turned to the computer and went in search of McLean. What he found was a world-class psychiatric hospital in Belmont, Massachusetts, associated with the Harvard Medical School, and listing a medical staff of about one hundred and fifty.

"So, Dr. Rosamund Whittaker Fairbrother is the real thing," he said aloud.

Good, he thought, *if she'll talk with me, I'll learn something. Whether she will let me anywhere near her mother is another kettle of fish.* He smiled, recollecting that he had learned that expression in Maine from a French-Canadian lumberjack, who had picked up his English from a Scotsman and sounded like a full-fledged Highlander with a Quebec French accent, adding color to the brogue.

While Harry was thinking about whether or not to have another cup of coffee, the phone rang. It was Renata Holland. "How are you and the alligators?" she asked.

"Getting along as well as can be expected. How many paras have you flogged this morning?"

"Only one, it's been a quiet start to the day. Number One's got something for you."

"Gwyneth Benbow's divorce record?"

"He didn't say, and I haven't looked at it. If it's for you, how interesting can it be? Are you going to pick it up or do I waste the time of one of our Honey Bunch Team, faxing it to you?"

"I'm going in to see Gwyneth. I'll stop by."

"Be still my heart," Renata said and hung up.

To Harry's surprise, Jeff Smolkin actually came down the hall to Renata's office to greet him, carrying a very official-looking legal-sized envelope. Renata had rushed off, to respond to raised voices in the witness preparation room.

"Someone has not treated Conchita like the top banana," she had snapped and left at a run.

"Who is Conchita?" Harry asked Smolkin.

"Renata's demeaning name for Consuela Barasca, one of my paras, whom she is breaking to the saddle and enjoying every minute of it."

He passed Harry the envelope. "Here it is," he said. "Scartole is one lucky young man. Benbow must really have wanted to dump him."

"Who filed?" Harry asked.

"It's all in there," Smolkin said, tapping the envelope, "but she did. Didn't you tell me Scartole did?"

"Probably. I'm finding that my client has a problem sticking to the truth—telling me the truth, anyway."

"Don't tell anyone, especially Benbow and Jim, you have seen this," Smolkin said, shrugging off Harry's comment.

"Done," he said, "and thanks," knowing now why Renata hadn't looked at it.

"How's Benbow coming along?"

"Good, I hope. I'm on my way to see her. By the way, Scartole is currently living in an upper six-figure condo in Dallas."

"Doesn't surprise me. Is he still on your suspect list?"

"No, but he could have flown up here, done the job, and flown back. I'll be trying to establish whether or not that's what he did."

Smolkin shoved his hands into his trouser pockets and rocked back on his heels, frowning, possibly at his thoughts.

"I can't see it," he said.

"What?"

"Scartole as the one who shot Benbow. It makes no sense at all. Wait until you read the agreement. You'll see what I mean. Got to go."

With that he lost his scowl, shook Harry's hand, and hurried back up the hall.

"To fresh woods and pastures new," Harry quoted to himself, watching Smolkin's retreat.

Gwyneth was sitting in a lounge chair reading when Harry arrived.

"New furniture, I see. You've been throwing your weight around," Harry said.

"The food in here, against all stereotypes of hospitals," she said, "is wonderful, and my ass *is* flourishing like the green bay tree, if that's what you're referring to."

Still unable to put any weight on her left arm, she struggled awkwardly out of the chair, warding off Harry's attempts to assist her.

"I was not making an oblique reference to the size of your derriere," he protested, shaken by her sudden reference to her bottom, which he had not expected to be discussing with her, "and I have not been making a before and after study of it."

She turned away and bent sharply over the bed, causing her wrapper to stretch tight across her rear end. Yes, Harry looked.

"What do you think?" she asked, trying to turn her head to see him.

"It looks perfectly fine to me," he said, seriously flustered and wanting very much to laugh.

"Harry!" she said with sudden urgency, "Quick! Help me up! Oh, shit! My arm!"

Her left arm was straight down at her side, but when she turned her head, she had thrown her weight onto her left shoulder and the pressure was causing grief in all the stitches on that side of her body. Without thinking, he stepped forward and leaned over her, thrusting his left arm under her waist and gripping her right shoulder with his other hand to pull her up, presenting an image that might have led a casual observer, coming upon them unexpectedly, to say, "Oh, excuse me," and go somewhere else in a hurry.

Brunhilda, who did come into the room at just that moment, did not excuse herself. Instead, she bellowed, "What's going on here?"

"Just a minute," Harry said, struggling to pull Gwyneth upright, "I've almost . . ."

He never finished the sentence. The next moment he was flung aside, crashing into the bedside stand and barely saving himself from going all the way to the floor, doing damage to an elbow in the process. Of course, Gwyneth, who had been lifted part of the way up, now fell back. Her left shoulder hit the bed first, eliciting a loud yelp of pain.

She had a strong voice, and it carried, bringing two more nurses running into the room, crowding aside Sergeant Fred Robbins who had just burst through the door with his gun drawn. Once the nurses had Gwyneth upright, things began to settle down. The two nurses and Brunhilda, who despite the evidence of her eyes was not yet entirely sure Gwyneth had not been ravished and out of fear was denying it, eased Gwyneth onto her lounge, having first checked to be sure none of the stitches had torn loose.

By now, the pain in her shoulder had subsided enough to allow her to laugh, which Harry, recovering his balance and rubbing his elbow, suspected she had been wanting to do all along. Robbins, holstering his gun, began easing the red-haired nurse out the door, talking animatedly as they went. Brunhilda, red-faced but with her chin up, swept out of the room like a tall ship with all her sails set.

The remaining nurse, who bore a striking resemblance to Lily Tomlin, finished straightening the bed, pointed at Gwyneth in her lounge chair, and turning a mordant gaze on Harry, said with a deadpan expression on her way out of the room, "Naughty, naughty."

Gwyneth was sitting in her lounge chair, dabbing at her eyes with tissues.

"Why are you crying?" Harry asked.

"I'm not," she said, choking back another explosion of laughter. "My eyes always water when I laugh. It's a damned nuisance."

Harry dragged the straight-backed, hospital room chair out of the corner and placed it where he could sit and talk with Gwyneth. He thought as he did it that it was the kind of chair you might be shackled to if you were being interrogated under a very bright light.

"By the way," she said. "What did you think of it?"

"What do you mean?"

"My ass, of course. You were pretty close to it there for a while before the morals squad found us. Are you going to give me an evaluation?"

"You better have your meds checked," Harry said, his face burning.

"Come on, be a good sport. Tell me."

"If I tell you, can we change the subject?"

"Absolutely."

"I think it's perfect."

"Honor bright?"

"Yes."

"Thank you, but it isn't."

"Beauty is in the eye of the beholder."

"It is, isn't it?" she said, giving him another of those looks he could never decipher to his satisfaction.

"My turn to ask a question," Harry said, anxious to move on. "When you were married to Scartole, what did he do to fill his days?"

"He played golf and hung out with that bunch of good-for-nothings at his club, and he spent quite a lot of time sailing."

"The name of the club?"

"The Seaside. Do you know it?"

"Yes. Do you know the names of any of his friends?"

"I doubt they were friends. Do stoats have friends?"

"We call them weasels."

"A stoat by any other name," she said grimly.

Her retort pleased Harry immensely. *More here than money and pretty eyes,* he thought.

"Do these stoats have names?"

"The two most obnoxious are Hands Brownback and Pencil Pellegrino. Why would you want to know?"

"Curiosity. Did your husband have a boat?"

"No, I wouldn't buy him one, so he leased a twenty-eight-foot C&C 29."

"Where was it docked?"

"I got the bills for the lease and the docking fees, plus the upkeep, from Mulvane's Boats."

"Kevin Mulvane?"

"I think that was the name on the bills. Why are you asking

all these questions about what Eric did with his days? Are the nights coming next?"

"I need to know as much as I can about everyone who's been close to you in the recent past."

He did not say anything about the more distant past, thinking that might only worry her or cause her pain. She had enough to deal with.

"Harry," she said after a moment's pause and in a much quieter voice, "Does the fact that there's an armed officer sitting outside my door day and night mean that someone is still trying to kill me, or is it simply a protocol of police procedure?"

"Standard procedure," Harry lied. "Now, are you up to answering some questions?"

"Let's find out."

"The manager of the Conservation Club . . ."

"Marlow Tremple," she said.

"That's right. Has Jim or anyone else talked with you about this?"

"No, it's the first time anyone's mentioned his name."

"Well, I think you have a right to know most of what I know to be fact. Marlow Tremple came around the corner of the building closest to you just moments before you were shot. Tremple was carrying a flashlight. The person who shot you saw it and ran."

"How does that tie in with my having an armed guard out there?" She pointed at the hall.

"I'm not saying there is any connection between the two events, but if there is any connection between the Perez murder and your being shot, then, yes, the man who shot you, if it was a man, may have been frightened off before he'd finished his job."

When Harry stopped speaking, the silence in the room was profound. He allowed it to extend itself, thinking that she should be given as much time as she needed to process the information. Gwyneth sat back in the green lounge chair, resting her head against its back. She sat that way without, as far as Harry could discern, any expression that might give him a hint as to how she was feeling.

At last, she crossed one ankle over the other and said, "Then until whoever shot me is found and imprisoned, I am living in constant danger of being killed by this maniac."

"Except, Gwyneth, that whoever did this may be as sane as you or I."

"I don't accept that. Why would anyone want to kill me?" she exploded. "I can't think of a single person who would have any reason to harm me."

"Someone can."

CHAPTER 16

At eight-thirty sharp the next morning, Harry called Rosamund Fairbrother.

"Thank you for being prompt, Mr. Brock," she said. "I regard being on time for appointments as a positive indicator of character."

"And tardiness a character disorder?" Harry asked, possibly a result of drinking a second cup of his own coffee.

There was no jolly laugh from the other end of the connection.

"More presentation and evaluation would be necessary before reaching that conclusion," she said seriously.

"Certainly," Harry said, wondering if she was humorless or if his attempt at humor had failed. "Are you willing to talk with me about your father's marriage to Ms. Benbow and its aftermath?"

"Yes, with the understanding that I will terminate the discussion any time I choose, without explanation to or protest from you."

"Of course. Do you recall your mother's response to the news that your father was remarrying?"

"I was in my first year at Choate when he married again. Are you familiar with the school?"

"I know it's located in Wallingford, Connecticut." He stopped himself from saying that the place had *Big Bucks* written all over it.

"Yes, well, as you may well imagine, I was completely caught up in the demanding tasks of adjusting to boarding school life and developing my goals and strategies for achieving the first and executing the second. As a result, I don't recall learning about the marriage until I went home for the Christmas holidays."

"You were told by your mother?"

"Yes. Unfortunately, the effect on Mother had been almost entirely negative."

The silence lengthened and Harry took a chance.

"Did your mother mention to you that she attended your father's interment ceremony and spoke to Ms. Benbow?"

"What did she say?" Fairbrother asked, her voice tightening.

"Ms. Benbow was standing, as she thought, alone at the graveside after the ceremony was concluded. Your mother spoke to her, introduced herself, and said something to the effect that she and Ms. Benbow were very fortunate women. Ms. Benbow, still somewhat preoccupied by her own thoughts and emotions, asked if she meant they were fortunate because he was dead. Your mother appeared to be upset and said, 'Of course not. Because we have been married to such a great man.' "

"Was there any further conversation?"

"No. Ms. Benbow had the impression that your mother was angry with her, but the chauffeur, who was standing close by, told your mother it was time to leave and escorted her back to the car and drove away. Does your mother still consider Morrison Perkins to have been a great man?"

"I'm considering whether to answer your question or to sever the connection," she said in a calm voice.

Harry checked himself again and did not say, "Take your time."

After the silence had begun to sound permanent, Harry looked at his watch just as the dog began to bark.

"Excuse me for a moment, Mr. Brock," she said. "It is time for Jackson's morning walk, and I must explain to him that the routine will be disrupted this morning and the walk delayed."

Harry listened for some time to the muffled sound of her voice, interrupted repeatedly by Jackson's whining and yelping. When Fairbrother picked up the phone, she was breathing heavily.

"I'm sorry to have taken so long, but I consider it essential that animals as well as people when faced with disappointment be given a full explanation of why it has occurred. Finally, to shut him up, I gave him a Doggy Delight. I realize," she continued, "it would be better had he accepted the delay without having to be given a Doggy Delight, but I am sure you have observed, Mr. Brock, that with animals and people as with the weather, we seldom get exactly what we want. How does that make you feel?"

"Frequently, irritated," Harry said quickly, surprised at his save.

"Perhaps we will come back to that later. Mother," she continued in a much calmer voice, "was devastated by the divorce. I was, as I said, thirteen, and, of course, saw everything from a somewhat precocious child's perspective. But I believe I recognized then and came to understand more fully later that losing my father's love was for her a severely disorganizing loss from which she has never recovered."

"Then is it possible that in marrying your father Mrs. Whittaker came to regard Gwyneth as an interloper?"

"I think it's reasonable to say she thought that Father, in marrying a woman so much younger than he, was the victim of a sexual obsession and had, in all probability, fallen into the clutches of a Siren."

"Do you think it would be possible for me to talk with your mother?"

"No. Considering how long ago my father died, I consider it an unreasonable stretch to think that my mother could have any connection to Ms. Benbow's shooting."

"I assure you, Dr. Fairbrother, it is not. Some individuals brood a very long time before acting."

"In this case, it is impossible."

Harry avoided the confrontation brewing. "Would it be accurate to say that your mother is a very wealthy woman?"

"You mean stinking rich."

"Your words, Dr. Fairbrother." Harry was swearing silently and steadily at himself for having been trapped.

"I'm sure Ms. Benbow has already told you that my mother is unstable."

"No, she has not. I was the one who suggested it."

"She is both rich and unstable. Her going to the interment was an unscheduled event. Although it comes belatedly, please extend my apologies to Ms. Benbow if my mother's appearance caused her any more pain than she was already enduring."

Harry thought the apology sincere and told Fairbrother that he would convey the regrets to Ms. Benbow. "Are you saying that your mother has been under some sort of supervision since her divorce?"

"Yes, Mr. Brock," Fairbrother said, her voice freighted with an old burden, "that is the case."

"I'm sorry to hear it. Very sorry. You must be aware that I'm not more than a few steps ahead of the police in the pursuit of leads, and you're right, of course. I should have said so at the outset."

"It was obvious, Mr. Brock. You're exploring the possibility that my mother was holding Ms. Benbow responsible for Morrison Perkins' death in an automobile accident and has only now arranged to have her killed in revenge."

"Assuming that she read the various write-ups in the *Boston*

Globe, yes," Harry said.

"Perfectly reasonable, except that my mother is incapable of making that sort of arrangement."

"She 'arranged' to visit the interment."

"Yes, she has access to certain sources of money, goes shopping with the chauffeur accompanying her, ostensibly to carry her packages but in reality to extricate her from situations that go beyond her capacity to negotiate unaided. He was suborned and is no longer with us."

"How seriously diminished in capacity is she?"

"Sufficiently to be absolutely incapable of doing what you apparently suspect her of having done. If compelled, I will produce the medical records to support the assertion."

"I won't ask for them. The police may. Thank you for your time and patience, Dr. Fairbrother. Again, I'm sorry about your mother."

"Thank you, Mr. Brock, and just so you know, I don't share my mother's delusion that Morrison Perkins was a great man. He was a self-aggrandizing bully, consumed with ambition. Oh, yes, I didn't arrange to have him killed. He died for me many years before that car crash finished the job."

"Goodbye, Doctor. Give Jackson an extra Doggy Delight for me."

What am I going to do about Rosamund? Harry asked himself when he had finished mopping the kitchen floor and was pouring the rinse water from his favorite redwood bucket around the thick and twisted base of the wisteria, which drank like the proverbial pig.

Of course, at one level it was a rhetorical question, to which he already knew the answer. But at another level, it was his way of trying to resolve the conflict between his ongoing curiosity and the part of his mind that told him to forget about Rachel

Whittaker. Her daughter had said she was mentally incapable of planning a murder and could prove it. What more needed saying?

Nevertheless, that less emotional, less trusting part of his mind insisted that nothing had been proved. It was, very likely, a case of the daughter protecting the mother—a very bright daughter with the professional credentials to lend weight to her assertions about her mother's condition. Harry did not like that fool killer part of his mind, but it had probably made him a successful private investigator and kept him alive.

All right, he thought, going back into the house and putting the bucket into its closet, *I'll let it rest for the moment and go on looking.* There was probably not sufficient evidence at the moment to ask Jim to pry out of the telephone company's records a list of calls to and from the Whittaker house for the past three or four months.

He would let the Whittaker issue gather a little dust and move on, which meant driving into town for his appointment to talk with Peter Rahn, secretary of the Conservation Club and a full partner in Rahn, Williams & Brawne, Inc.

The developer's central office differed considerably from the architect's shack with an air conditioner unit stuck in one of the windows run up on the construction site. This was a steel-framed, stucco-clad, four-story building standing in a double lot, beautifully landscaped, and located on Bollard Street just two blocks from the town pier. It protruded into a very staid section of the city that had, a hundred plus years ago, been the city's center. It had not been a city then and scarcely a town, but there had been the pier and eventually a railroad station. From it Avola residents traveled to Tampa and further north and sailed regularly to Key West, Miami, and Cuba on business.

There had been a very loud outcry at the company's incursion into the area, but developer interest prevailed and the office building on Bollard Street went up. It was a handsome building, clad with a very subdued rose stucco, gleaming brass-fitted doors, marble floors and fitted with large windows of tinted glass, and hung on the inside with feather-light drapes, to exclude the fiery rays of the sun but give the occupants a very charming view of their section of Old Avola.

"I'm Carolina, Mr. Rahn's executive secretary," said a tall young woman in a blue silk business suit and spike heels, collecting Harry and leading him deeper into the building, then sweeping open Rahn's office door and saying, "Mr. Rahn, Mr. Brock to see you."

Rahn, taller than his secretary and a lot taller than Harry, came striding around his desk, which was half the size of a king-size bed, his hand outstretched.

"Hello, Harry, call me Peter," Rahn said in that softened southern accent of Virginia that, Harry thought, eases northerners into the Southland, aiding the transition and making the change seem temporarily less radical than it really is.

Harry watched him coming and asked himself, *Why don't I just leave now and save myself some time?*

Continuing to grip his hand, Rahn led Harry to one of the green leather chairs deployed in front of the gleaming desk, and released him as soon as he sat down.

Carolina withdrew. The door sighed softly as she closed it. *I know how you feel,* Harry thought.

"I understand that you want to talk with me about Gwyneth Benbow's shooting," Rahn said, sprawling comfortably in the chair beside Harry, regarding his guest with the smiling interest Stanley might have displayed, having come upon Livingstone. "What a terrible thing. Terrible. Have the police made any progress on it? I'm right in thinking that you are working for Ms. Benbow?"

Harry had taken the opportunity to do some looking of his

own and gather some sense of who he was dealing with. From what he had learned over the years, men, and women for that matter, in the developer line of business were rough, very rough, in their dealings, accustomed to having their own way, and ruthless with those who tried to thwart them.

He did not expect Rahn, soft-spoken and smooth-faced and smiling, as he was, to be any exception. Brilliantly polished black shoes, black stockings, navy blue suit with a hairline stripe, white shirt, and quiet red and black tie, a heavy handicap no doubt to go with his tan, and perfect teeth and dark, perfectly trimmed hair, all confirmed for Harry his guess that he was dealing with the genuine *Canis lupus*.

It was not encouraging, but he was here and something had to be done.

"I was very surprised to learn that you are the secretary of the Conservation Club," he said in an open, friendly voice.

"Why surprised?" Rahn asked, his smile remaining but his eyes narrowing slightly.

"I would have thought the interests of Rahn, Williams & Brawne would generally be running against the current of the Conservation Club's agenda."

Rahn pushed himself up in his chair, stared at the carpet between his feet, and shook his head in a display of patient weariness. "It's a burden that never leaves us," he said, looking up with a pained expression on his face. "If it wasn't privileged information, I would tell you, starting with the CP, how much money this company contributed last year to green causes of one kind and another. I think you would be impressed."

"When it comes to money," Harry said, "it doesn't take much to impress me."

"You know," Rahn said, his smile turning into a grin, "there is another reason for being active in the Conservation Club. I think it was a Chinaman who said it best, 'Keep your friends close to you and your enemies closer.' "

Rahn leaned back in his chair like one of the good old boys, clapped his hands onto his knees, and gave an excellent imitation of laughter.

"Machiavelli, not Sun Tzu, said it," Harry replied.

For a moment something other than good fellowship looked out of Rahn's cold, gray eyes.

"How can I help you, Harry?" he said.

"On the night Ms. Benbow was shot, were you sitting at the table in front of the audience?"

"Yes. I was a bit late getting there, but then I took over from Julia Alterno, and during the business part of the meeting, Gwyneth sat between me and the guest speaker. When the brief business was disposed of, she introduced Gazelle Plimpton, the state biologist, who spoke on the Nile monitor lizard. I don't imagine I have to explain to you what that is."

"No and soon, unfortunately, not to anyone in this part of the state."

"Yes," Rahn answered somberly, "I guess you're safe in saying that."

"Did you look at the audience at all after the meeting began?"

"I expect you want to know if I saw anyone who looked seriously out of place and might call himself Jack O'Lanton?" he asked with a brighter expression.

"That and whether or not you saw anyone leave early?"

"When the intros were over, Gwyneth left the podium to sit in a seat that had been kept for her toward the rear of the hall. I stayed at the table and turned my chair to the right. There were few vacant seats that I could see. Some people were standing in the rear of the room."

Rahn remained quiet for a moment, apparently thinking.

"About five minutes before the presentation ended, some guy

left. I wouldn't have noticed except that he must have caught his foot on the leg of his chair as he turned to go up the aisle and tipped it over. He set it upright again, then hurried out."

"Would you recognize him if you saw him again?"

"No, the lights had been turned down when Plimpton started speaking."

"What did he look like, as close as you recall?"

"Medium height, wearing a baseball cap. I remember thinking that it was unusual to see a working man at one of these events."

"How did you know he was a laborer?"

"From the dungarees and long-sleeved shirt, buttoned at the cuff. Also, he was carrying a sack of some kind in one hand. I glanced away from the speaker to him when the chair went over. This all happened in a few seconds. He set the chair up and left. I had turned back to listen to Plimpton before the door clicked shut."

"One more question. Was he sitting in that chair before the talk began?"

"I don't think so. If I'm remembering accurately, he took the chair just as the lights were going down."

Harry heard the door open behind him and Carolina said, "Excuse me, Mr. Rahn. Three minutes till your meeting with Mr. Hawksbill."

Rahn looked at her, nodded, and Harry heard the door sigh again.

"The governor's message boy," Rahn said, flashing his teeth at Harry.

"One more question," Harry said, picking up the folder he had set on the floor and taking from it a list of names. "These are the people who were at the meeting that night." He passed Rahn the list. "Is there anyone on the list you know who was sitting near the man who left?"

"I don't think so," Rahn said, glancing through the names as he stood up. "The lights were very dim, but I'll give it some thought. You're thinking the man might have gone out early to get to where he planned to shoot Gwyneth?"

"Possibly. Thank you for your time," Harry said, already thinking of the best way to persuade Jim to assign his staff, to help in making some phone calls.

"Stay in touch, Harry," Rahn said, escorting him to the door. "I think a lot of Gwyneth Benbow, and I'd like very much to see whoever did this to her strapped into Old Sparky. Too bad the state has a new one that won't set fire to his hair," he added.

Harry thought the grin had become more wolfish. Carolina, waiting at the door, took his arm, beginning a stately and silent walk through the waiting area toward the burnished doors, giving Harry the distinct impression that he was being expelled from Paradise.

Perhaps he was. It did pass through his mind as he stood blinking in the fiery sun on the hot side of the doors that in this outer world there was a distinct shortage of Carolinas.

CHAPTER 17

"You're looking a little pale around the gills, Harry," Hodges said, dropping a heavy hand on Harry's shoulder. "Are you eating all right?"

Always a serious consideration for Hodges. It was beyond his capacities to conceive of a person's not sleeping well.

"Have you lost weight?" Jim inquired from his side of the desk.

Harry had just walked into Jim's office, and was not enjoying the scrutiny.

"Sarah called me the other day, to say that Jennifer has exhausted her medical options and has opted for palliative care."

"I'm sorry to hear it," Jim said. "I know she's been ill a long time, but just the same . . ."

"How long has she got?" Hodges asked, "and what's pal . . . whatever care?"

Harry told him.

"Well, it's a hell of a thing by any road. I'm sorry," he said loudly, reaching out and grasping Harry's shoulder.

"Thank you," Harry said, touched by their concern.

"How long have you and Jennifer been separated?" Jim asked.

"A long time."

"You going to the funeral?" Hodges asked.

"Yes."

"I don't envy you that," Hodges said. "God, I hate funerals. Did I ever tell you about my brother Jake's funeral? It was in

July and hotter'n the hinges of Hell. It was an open casket and
. . ."

"Not now, Frank," Jim barked, his ears getting red. "This
isn't the time for one of your stories."

"All right, Captain, but I was only going to say that the wax
melted and . . ."

"No!" Jim shouted. "Harry doesn't want to hear it, and neither do I."

"I've got something to tell you and something to ask," Harry
said, rallying.

"What?" Jim asked, losing interest in his sergeant's funeral
story.

"I've been talking with Peter Rahn."

"Damn, Captain!" Hodges broke out, "he's gotten to him
ahead of us."

"Never mind that," Jim replied sharply, waving Hodges down.
"Harry, what did you learn?"

"He saw the man who shot Gwyneth."

"Don't stop," Jim said, coming around his desk to lean
against it, all the while keeping his gaze fixed on Harry.

"You recall our talking about Marlow Tremple, the manager
at the Conservation Club?"

"He's pretty sure he saw the shooter run off but couldn't tell
us a thing about him," Hodges said, already caught up by what
Harry was saying.

"Keep going," Jim said, hitching himself onto a corner of the
desk and giving Harry his full attention.

"You'll remember that Rahn is the club's secretary. The president had conducted a brief business meeting that night before
introducing the speaker. He was seated between Rahn and the
guest speaker and stayed there when the speaker went to the
lectern, to begin her presentation. Gwyneth was probably seated
near the back because according to Marlow Tremple she was

one of the first out when the program ended."

"Sounds right," Jim said. "I don't think she remembers where she was sitting. Did anyone even ask her?" he said, looking from Harry to Hodges.

"Nope," Hodges said. "It's not in Jones' report."

"Now," Harry said, "here's the good part. When the speaker was nearly finished, someone toward the back on the right-hand side of the seats got up, caught his foot on the chair, and nearly kicked it over, causing enough disturbance for Rahn, seated at the table, which was placed on the raised platform, to turn away from the speaker and toward the source of the interruption."

Harry paused, caught up for the moment in his mental picture of what had happened and the fact that the lights had been turned too low for Rahn to be able to identify the man. "It's got to be checked," Harry said.

"Did this person leave the hall ahead of everyone else?" Jim demanded.

"Yes, but . . ."

"Harry," Jim said, interrupting, "did Rahn see the person?"

Harry said he had, then repeated Rahn's description of the man.

"Can he identify him?" Hodges asked.

"Not beyond saying he was pretty sure he was a working man, but he said the lights in the hall had been turned down too low to make an identification possible."

"Black, white, Hispanic?" Jim asked.

"I don't think he knows, but we'd better corroborate his claim that there wasn't enough light for a more detailed description." Harry did not say that he was also going to ask Gwyneth if she heard the disturbance and saw the man.

"Right," Jim said, "and we'll do it before Jones talks with him. Good work, Harry." He spoke with obvious satisfaction, pushing up from the desk. "Now, what is it you want?"

Harry took the list of people who had been in the hall that night and passed it to Jim. "These people should be called, to find out if anyone else saw the man get out of his seat and leave, hopefully someone seated closer to him than Rahn."

"Lord, Lord," Jim groaned, gazing down at the list.

"I've got more good news," Harry said. "I had a talk with Rosamund Whittaker Fairbrother."

"I thought that woman's name was Rachel Whittaker Perkins," Hodges said.

"Rachel's her mother," Harry said.

"The one who turned up at Perkins' burial?" Jim asked.

"Yes, and Rosamund says she had slipped her leash with her chauffeur's help. They replaced the chauffeur and began again. For what it's worth, I think Dr. Fairbrother told me the truth. Rachel Perkins is mentally and/or emotionally damaged, badly enough to make it very unlikely that she could have planned a murder."

Jim rubbed his head and began hiking around his office, practically having to step over Harry and Hodges in his peregrinations. "I can't just take Fairbrother's word for it," he complained.

"She claims to have the necessary medical evidence."

"I hope so. Otherwise, I'll be spending a fortune establishing Mrs. Perkins' whereabouts the night Ms. Benbow was shot, recovering telephone records on the Perkins' house for two or three years back, flying Millard up there to interview her—it makes me groan just thinking about it."

"Pull your pants up, Captain," Hodges said in an encouraging voice. "You haven't written any chits yet, and maybe Harry's right."

"I'm pretty sure I am," Harry said. "In fact I'm going to start looking elsewhere."

"Where would that be?" Jim asked, coming to a stop behind

his desk and dropping into his chair.

"I want to know where Perez had been the night he was killed. His wife either doesn't know or won't say, but someone does."

Gwyneth had been released from the hospital when Harry called. He tried her cell.

"Harry," she said, sounding pleased. "I'm glad to hear from you."

"Congratulations on your release," he said. "I need to talk with you."

"Come over. I've just had a shower and a massage. I feel like a new woman."

"Are the wounds still giving you pain?"

"Yes, I'm sore, especially where the bullet came out; it looks ghastly. I'm just glad I wasn't shot in the back."

"All is vanity," Harry said.

"Easy for you to say. I'm not an automobile. I don't come with a spare. Think of what I would have had to go through during the reconstruction."

"I'm only teasing," Harry said with a laugh. "What has to be done with your back?"

"Skin grafts, for sure, and muscle repair. I don't know what else."

"Are you certain you don't want the luxury of being alone?"

"No, I'm not a hermit like some people."

"It's your nickel."

Harry had read the divorce record and it had weakened his knees when he saw the settlement bestowed on Scartole. In all, it came to about three quarters of a million dollars. And he thought about it again as he drove south through Avola, past the old part of the city and gradually deeper into the section where the shops end and the gated mansions begin.

Gwyneth's house was located on Goodnight Drive. The name

amused Harry, but seeing her house removed the smile. It was set behind a tall, black wrought-iron fence and approached through double iron gates. Harry pressed the voice button on the communication box. A woman with a Hispanic accent answered. Harry gave her his name and said Ms. Benbow was expecting him.

"Oh, yes, Mr. Brock. We are having work done on the house. Please excuse the cars and trucks in the parking area."

The gates swung open, and Harry followed the white, crushed rock drive as it wound through alternating flowering shrubs, palm trees, and emerald lawn and finally passed under a stone and tile portico. There were, as the housekeeper had said, trucks and vans crowding the parking area. Stepping out of the Rover, Harry heard the sound of a tile saw zinging somewhere out of sight. He looked up the stone front of the two-story building and saw ropes dangling from the roof.

Roof tile work, Harry guessed as he stepped into the welcome shade of the portico and took his time climbing the wide marble stairs, taking a good look at the black granite landing with thick, polished stone columns marking the sides and very large double doors with brass fittings facing him. He pressed a button and chimes rang distantly. A young, dark-haired woman dressed in a black skirt and white blouse opened the door, welcoming him with a smile.

"Please come in, Mr. Brock," she said. "Ms. Benbow is expecting you."

A second woman stepped out of a side room that appeared to be an office and also welcomed Harry with a smile. She was dressed in a black business suit and frilled blouse. Older than the maid who had responded to the door chimes but equally dark, she wore her hair pulled back in a perfectly arranged chignon. She came forward and shook Harry's hand with a firm grip.

"I am Gabrielle, Ms. Benbow's secretary," she said in a strong, clear voice, tinged with a Hispanic accent, "and this is Margarita. Ms. Benbow is in the upstairs study. If you will follow me, please, I'll take you to her."

After saying something very quietly in rapid Spanish to Margarita, who hurried away, Gabrielle set off with a purposeful stride toward the pale marble staircase that curved up to the left. "Did you have any trouble parking your car?" she asked over her shoulder.

When Harry, putting on some extra speed to keep up with her, replied that he hadn't, she said, "Good, we are still dealing here with the ravages of Sheila. The roof was damaged and we lost three windows on the ocean side of the house, not from wind but from wind-borne palm fronds traveling like spears that went through them, carrying away glass, frames and all."

"Did the water come in and do any damage?" he asked, trying to conceal the fact that he was breathing a little heavily and only halfway up the stairs.

"Two rugs had to be taken away to be cleaned. But we kept most of the water mopped up. How did you fare?"

"I lost two oaks behind the house, and the wisteria, which is decades old, on the south end of the lanai lost most of its leaves and all its blossoms, but new leaves are already sprouting. Quite remarkable, really."

"Down here, things grow with astonishing vigor," she said, pausing at the top of the stairs and turning to smile impishly at Harry. "I walk these stairs at least a dozen times a day, unlike most of the people in Southwest Florida, who seem to live on one level and, of course, never climb a hill."

Harry laughed, in part at her cheerful manner and also ruefully because of his burning leg muscles. She was, he thought, a remarkably attractive woman. Perhaps it was those dark eyes that danced with good humor and reminded him of light glinting on black water.

"This way, Mr. Brock. Let's take you to Ms. Benbow before she comes in search of you and accuses me of having talked too much, a perennial complaint, possibly justified. Here we are. Please go in. It was a pleasure meeting you."

She shook hands with him again and then took his arm and urged him through the door.

"What do you think of Gabrielle?" Gwyneth asked, coming out from behind her desk to greet him.

"Is she married?" Harry asked.

"Rascal!" she said and broke into laughter, then shook a finger at him, "No, she's not, but don't you dare. She's mine."

"I didn't know you swung east and west," he said.

"Don't tell anyone," she said with a grin.

"How is the transition from the hospital to home going?"

He thought she probably sounded better than she actually felt, recalling his own experiences. And he didn't think her show of good spirits was supported by the way she was carrying herself. There was pain there somewhere.

"Pretty well, but I don't know from one minute to the next how I'm going to feel, emotionally or physically. It's trying."

"Of course it is and a lot worse than having your house broken into."

"A different kind of violation, you mean?"

"Yes. Do you find yourself suddenly becoming angry over trifles?"

"I do, and then I'll be just as irrationally terrified with no obvious cause."

"Are you talking to anyone about it?"

"Alice Ingram urged me to do it," she said. "I tried, but the experience was unsatisfactory."

Harry thought he understood why. She was, temperamentally at least, very like his second wife. Katherine never responded well to probing questions concerning her feelings.

"I've got a name. It's Gloria Holinshed. She's in the book. After my youngest daughter Minna was assaulted, Holinshed worked with her and with her mother and me. Holinshed is very sharp, very tough, and you'll want to strangle her, but if you stick with her, she will help you clean the trash out of your attic."

Gwyneth turned back to the desk and wrote down the name.

"It's either that or a length of rope," she said and tried to laugh but couldn't.

"She makes a difference," Harry said. He wanted to give her a hug but didn't, uncertain about both his motives and her re-action.

"Do you feel up to talking about business?" he asked. "Saying you're not is absolutely an option and probably the one I would take in your place."

CHAPTER 18

"Let's start, and if I begin feeling bad, we can stop," Gwyneth said, leading them to a pair of chairs in one of the two bay windows overlooking the grounds at the front of the house. "The trucks and whatnot spoil the view," she said, making a face, "and the racket of pounding, sawing, and supporting activities dispels the tranquility, but what the hell. The repairs are needed."

"I'll try to bear up," Harry said, sinking into the chair's soft embrace with a sigh he made no effort to suppress.

"I feel I should eat some crow here," Gwyneth said with sudden intensity.

"All right," Harry said.

"Do you remember my saying that I thought Henrico's murder was the work of the developers in Tequesta County?"

"I recall your saying there was money behind it."

"If the same person shot both of us, my accusation has to be false."

"How so?"

"I know and know well every last person in that pack of scoundrels, and not one of them has any reason to kill me. It's impossible."

"It's not impossible, Gwyneth, and you can't be certain you were wrong," Harry said. "But I do agree that it would be a very long reach, and I don't believe it happened."

"Then who?"

Harry heard the anguish in her question and felt very sorry he couldn't dispel it. "Let's go on trying to find the answer."

She slumped back in her chair and said quietly, "I hate it."

"I'll get the hardest bit over with right now. As soon as the doctors cut you loose, I think you should leave Florida and, preferably, the country. Captain Snyder told me that now you're out of the hospital, the department can't give you adequate protection. You're not safe here, Gwyneth. Whoever went after you will try again. It's only a question of time."

At that point Gwyneth pointed her right hand at him as if she was aiming a gun.

"Stop right there," she said in a breaking voice. "The answer is absolutely not. Do you hear me? No."

She was white with either anger or shock; her hand was shaking. Swearing at himself for being an idiot, Harry struggled out of his chair and crossed the space separating them as fast as he could, grabbing a box of tissues off the corner of her desk and holding it out to her as if he was offering a bouquet.

"Don't touch me," she cried and knocked the box out of his hand.

"Good," Harry said, "stay mad. Think of what you'd like to do to me."

While he was talking he was picking up the box of tissues from the floor.

"Keep swearing," he said. "You were doing just fine."

Turning around to face her, he found her watching him and grinning with the tears still spilling over.

"I think we've pretty well exhausted that subject," he said. "What do you say?"

This time she accepted the tissues and thanked him.

"Am I right in thinking you don't want to leave Avola?" Harry asked while she blew her nose and wiped her eyes, dropping the used tissues onto the floor as if the whole room was a wastebasket.

"Sorry about that," she said at last, disposing of the final tissue with more brio than Harry had expected.

He sank back into his chair.

"Is there something else you want to tell me?" she asked with a straight face.

"Do you know how spoiled you are?" he asked, looking out the window into the sun-dappled world of trees and palms, stirring gently in the breeze from the Gulf.

" 'Let me count the ways,' " she responded in a voice rich in irony. So, at least, it sounded to Harry.

"Elizabeth Barrett Browning," he said lightly, "would not have been amused."

"Who's joking?" she said.

"Very edgy. Why did you lie to me about your divorce?"

"For the same reason my attorneys, acting on my behalf, persuaded the judge to seal the divorce record, which you seem to have violated. Care to tell me how you did it?"

"My question first."

"Does it matter why I lied about the filing? I assume that's what you're referring to."

"Yes, and it goes to the issue of possible motive."

"If you think Eric tried to kill me, you are smoking some bad shit," she said, leaning forward in her chair and glaring at Harry.

"Who inherits if you die?" he asked, ignoring the flare-up.

"Not Eric."

"How do I know there isn't something outside the divorce record that gives him a piece of your estate in the event you die before he does?"

It was Gwyneth's turn to look out the window.

"How can I prove a negative?" she asked in a low voice.

"How was the number seven hundred and fifty thousand dollars chosen and who chose it?"

She gave him back her attention. "Harry, how can you seriously believe that Eric Scartole would want to kill me? I made him richer than he ever dreamed possible. He was a masseur when I married him, scraping out a living working in the Beach Club and half a dozen other clubs and spas in Avola and living in two rooms on Blue Street."

Blue Street, Harry knew, was the street address of the poorest black and white working people in Avola. No one lived there who didn't have to.

"Rough area. There's at least one killing a month in the neighborhood, and that's in a good year. Was he a failure as a masseur?"

Harry was hoping to prod her into breaking out of that protective shell she lived in, but her response disappointed him.

"He was a failure at everything except sex. I'm pretty sure that's what I married him for. No, that's not wholly true. Actually, I don't remember why I did it. Maybe I was just sick of living alone. But it didn't take me long to find out that I'd made a mistake."

"Seven years doesn't sound a short time to me," Harry said.

"I felt responsible for him. It was like having a troubled kid, not that I would know. But that's how I saw it."

"What made you decide to cut him loose?"

"Henrico. Being with him made me see how much I was missing in my marriage."

"Which brings us back to the divorce. Why three quarters of a million dollars?"

She got out of her chair and walked to her desk and back, lost in her own thoughts, and came to a stop beside Harry. He leaned back in his chair and looked up at her.

"I cut him loose for thoroughly selfish reasons," she began, returning his gaze. "And I gave him the money to soothe my conscience."

Harry didn't say anything.

"Well, open up your mind, Harry. He was little more than a kid when I married him. Then he was in his thirties. He had no skills, aside from his minimal qualifications as a masseur, only a high school education, with no more qualifications than when I married him. So don't look at me as if I was a moral degenerate. I gave him the money to keep him off Blue Street."

"And that was it. He has no present or future claim on your estate."

"No."

Harry did not believe her, but he let it go.

"Then I have my answer," he said and got up, aware that he had been treating her with more severity than her level of recovery made acceptable, and he felt guilty about it.

"Are you leaving?" she asked, sounding disappointed.

"Are you too tired to confront another question?"

"Of course not."

"This will be quick. What can you remember of the program the night you were shot?"

"The meeting or the speaker?"

"Anything at all."

"Not much. I think I remember being at the back of the hall."

"Do you recall any disturbance?"

There was a pause.

"Vaguely," Gwyneth said with a frown. "Oh! Yes! Someone was leaving and tipped a chair over."

"Do you know the person?" Harry asked, trying not to convey increased interest.

"No. It was just a middle-aged man, nothing special about him except he was dressed in work clothes and a long-sleeved shirt. You don't see that much except in offices. Not down here, anyway."

"Did you see his face?"

"I don't think so. If I did, I don't remember."

"It's not important. Did you recognize anyone sitting near you?" Harry asked.

"I don't think so. If I'm remembering correctly, everything was dim. The lights must have been lowered."

"That's right," Harry said cheerfully. "And I've leaned on you long and hard enough. And as for your being a moral degenerate, Gwyneth, I think you're someone very different. Giving Eric Scartole that money may have been partially done to salve a guilty conscience, but you gave that young man a second chance at life not many of us ever get."

"Thank you, Harry," she said. "I didn't think . . . Well, it doesn't matter what I thought."

"Are you satisfied with what you've done?"

"Mostly, I guess."

"Try for a yes if it comes up again." He turned to leave, stopped, and said, "If you ever find a motive without a splash of selfishness in it, shoot it and have it mounted. It will be unique."

Harry went home somewhat dispirited. The investigation, he felt, had gone nowhere. He was no closer to knowing who had shot Gwyneth than when he started. And after his conversation with her this afternoon, he thought there was a better than even chance that Scartole had not shot Gwyneth. That left him with Rachel Whittaker and her daughter, Rosamund, two extremely unlikely candidates for the office of stealth killer. Oh, yes, there was Jack O'Lanton, who Hodges was supposedly pursuing—when he wasn't attending to domestic disturbances, hit and run incidents, and bank robberies on dead-end roads.

When he reached his house, there was an unfamiliar car

parked under the live oak at the corner of his lawn A tall, powerfully built man with dark hair, tied back in a ponytail, leaned back against the car, arms folded, watching Harry's approach.

Somebody's unhappy, he thought as he got out of the Rover and checked the car's tag. A rental car, probably from the airport. Since the man did not speak as Harry approached him, Harry decided to wait. He did not have to wait long.

"You Harry Brock?" the man asked, pushing away from the car and dropping his arms.

"That's right," Harry said.

If he had not clenched his fist before launching the strike, Harry might have been flattened. But Harry saw the balled fist and was stepping back to his left as his assailant lunged forward and drove his right at where Harry's head had been.

Harry caught the fist with his right hand and continued to step back, pulling the man off balance, forcing him to take another step forward. Then Harry shoved his arm down and, stepping past the man, grabbed a handful of hair, pulled his head back hard, and twisted his fist up between his shoulders. At the same time he drove the side of his right foot into the bend of the man's knee on his back leg and brought him down on his back hard. Stepping around the fallen man, Harry snapped the CZ out of its holster, and as the man struggled to get up, pushed the gun's barrel hard against his forehead, forcing him back onto the ground.

"Now," Harry said, "who the hell are you?"

"Eric Scartole," he said, screwing his eyes shut and baring his teeth. He had fallen on his arm and Harry knew it was hurting him.

"Get up," Harry said, stepping back from him but keeping the gun pointed at his middle.

Scartole made heavy work of getting to his feet, rubbing his sore arm, grimacing with pain. "You didn't have to be so goddamned rough," he complained.

"I could have killed you with a lot less effort. You should be grateful."

Harry almost laughed at the look of outrage on Scartole's face. "You almost dislocated my shoulder," Scartole protested.

"Yes, I intended to slow you down, give you time to think. Now, can I put this gun away without having you try to punch me in the head again?"

"I suppose so," Scartole mumbled, looking at his arm and trying to bend it.

Apparently that hurt because he let it hang loose. Harry slid the pistol under the back of his shirt and into its holster. "Why did you try to hit me? I don't even know you."

"You called my mother and asked a lot of questions about me," Scartole said accusingly.

"She and I had a pleasant conversation. Why does that anger you?"

"I don't like it that a private investigator starts bothering my mother and sniffing around, asking questions about where I live and that shit. It's none of your fucking business."

"So you decided to come all the way from Dallas to punch me out. Or were you already in Avola?"

"See?" Scartole said, his voice rising and his face growing darker. "You're doing it again. It's no fucking business of yours where I am."

Harry saw this was going to be boring and wearisome and said, "Let's go inside. I don't know about you, but I find the sun too hot."

"Fuck the sun," Scartole said.

"Ahab tried that and got into a lot of trouble." He pointed at the house and said, "Go."

Grumbling, Scartole went.

Worse than a kid, Harry thought, following him toward the lanai.

The conversation that followed was not one Harry would have chosen, but he did manage to pry out of Scartole that he had been in Dallas when both Perez and Gwyneth were shot and could provide verification. He got that information without, he was reasonably sure, allowing Scartole to suspect that Harry thought he might have been the person who shot Perez.

"As I've said," he told Scartole after explaining that Gwyneth had hired him originally to keep track of the police investigation of Perez's murder, "Ms. Benbow's being shot meant I have to talk with everyone who knew her in order to prevent any suspicion attaching itself to them. You'll probably be questioned by the police as well. I'm surprised they haven't already done it."

"Perez!" Scartole sneered, his face darkening. "He got just what was coming to him. No, that's not quite right. I should have punched him out first."

"Said that way," Harry said with forced amusement, "it sounds as if you killed him."

"Yeah? Well, I didn't, but I had plenty of reason that I'm not getting into."

"Okay, but I wouldn't say those things to the police. They might think you did kill him."

"Don't matter. I was in Dallas and can prove it."

"Good," Harry said, bringing the conversation to a close by asking if Scartole kept up his Avola contacts or had he decided to make a clean break.

"I fly over now and then," he said, making it sound as if he was a world traveler. "I've still got a boat here. My friends at the club keep calling me to join them for a game, especially if there's a tournament on. I'm a good golfer."

He was sitting in one of the lounge chairs and stretched, managing to get his right arm over his head without wincing and seeming to have forgotten about what had happened on the lawn.

"I considered becoming a pro for one of the associations in the area," he said, having completed his stretch with a loud yawn, "but decided it meant taking too much crap from the old geezers you've got to deal with."

Harry watched him drive away a little while later and asked himself how in the world Gwyneth could have lived with the man for seven years.

Scartole's visit had done very little to improve Harry's views on the progress of his investigation, but neither had it led him to eliminate Scartole as a suspect. The man clearly had a temper and a broad streak of violence in him as well. If the punch had landed, what would have happened next? Kicked his ribs in? His head? Possibly. The man was capable of violence, however incompetent in its execution. Also, what was he really feeling about being taken down by a man smaller than he was and twenty years older?

Harry left the questions unanswered, but the encounter led him to renew his interest in Scartole's friends Hands Brownback and Pencil Pellegrino.

The Seaside Club fulfilled the promise of its name. The hotel was on the beach and its golf facilities across the narrow but heavily travelled street running along that stretch of Gulf shoreline. The club had a restaurant with screened windows opening directly onto the beach and The Merlot, a more formal inner room, specializing in seafood dinners.

The Seaside's barroom also faced the water but at an angle, and its mahogany bar, slowly turning fans, and very subdued lighting gave it an air of contemplative repose that went well with the beer, wine, and spirits that bubbled gaily from its springs. It was at the bar that Harry found two men he assumed were Brownback and Pellegrino, elbows on the polished wood, beer bottles in front of them, eyes glued to a baseball game replay on the television mounted on the wall behind the bar.

"Gentlemen," Harry said, "am I right in thinking you both know Eric Scartole?"

"Who wants to know?" one of them asked. He was very thin, narrow-shouldered, wearing a Red Sox cap. He made a half-turn on his stool as he spoke, squinting at Harry through pink-rimmed sunglasses with a broken bow that had been repaired with adhesive tape. He had not shaved that morning and maybe not yesterday morning, either. It was not, Harry thought, a fashion statement.

"You must be Pencil Pellegrino," Harry said in his best impersonation of a salesman and extended his hand. "Eric mentioned that you and he had played golf together."

"Not since he picked his ex-wife's bones in that divorce, he ain't," the other man said.

Harry took back his hand before someone mistook him for a panhandler. "And I'm going to guess that you're Hands Brown-back," he said to the second man.

Brownback pushed his sunglasses up onto a very tanned brow and ran his eyes up and down Harry as if deciding whether or not to hit him up for a loan. He was a big man, heavily muscled, a look of permanent aggression furrowing his brow.

"What do you want with Pencil and me?" he demanded. "You a process server or something?"

Harry took the precaution of stepping back from the two a bit, just in case they decided to jump him. They looked to be in their late forties and well into the years of reason, but you never could tell. So it was best to be careful.

"I'd fall into the 'something' category," Harry said, letting the bonhomie drop out of his voice. "Can I buy you a drink?"

"In exchange for what?" Pencil asked, obviously suspicious

but interested.

Harry guessed that free beers did not come all that often and an offer of one was not to be lightly dismissed. "A few minutes of your time, and what you tell me will not be used for attribution."

"What?" Hands asked, his scowl deepening as if he thought he might have been insulted.

"What you tell me will never be traced back to you. My name is Harry Brock. I'm a private investigator and I want to ask a few questions about Eric Scartole. What about you calling the bartender and putting in your orders? I'll drink what you're drinking. Then let's get a table over there where we won't be disturbed." Harry pointed back into a corner away from the door and the scattering of customers at the other tables.

Pencil looked at Hands and got a nod. Then he spun back facing the bar and waved his empty at the bartender watching another television screen.

"Three," Pencil said loudly.

The beer came as soon as the men were seated. "That will be twelve," the barman said, making it clear to anyone listening that Pencil and company ran no tab at the Seaside Bar.

Harry paid. Pencil and Hands lifted their bottles to Harry and drank off half of the contents in one go, lowering the bottles with long sighs of contentment.

"There's another where they came from," Harry said, taking a swallow of his beer and wiping his mouth with the back of his hand to make a good impression.

"That shithead got himself in trouble?" Hands asked, then belched loudly.

Pencil's attention was drifting back to the television.

"That's what I'm trying find out," Harry said. "Scartole told me he flew over here fairly often to play golf with you guys, but that doesn't seem to be so from what you tell me."

"Naw," Pencil said, "we ain't seen nothin' of him since the divorce. We heard he really cleaned up, that so?"

"He seems to be living pretty well," Harry said.

"We heard Dallas," Hands said.

"That's right. I heard you guys rode him pretty hard when his wife got caught banging somebody else."

"Henrico Perez," Pencil blurted and gave a sour laugh. "Rico was really pissed. The guy was damned near old enough to be his old man."

"Rico?" Harry asked.

"That's what we called Scartole," Hands said. "You must be some dick if you don't know who was screwing his wife. It was in the papers."

"Pictures of them coming out of the Canary Island arm in arm, big as life. Hands cut it out and had it laminated and stuck it up on the bar mirror. When he saw it, Rico damned near shit himself."

Pencil and Hands shared a laugh and finished their beers. Harry waved his arm. The bartender's motion sensor registered the movement and more beer arrived. Harry paid again.

"I hear Scartole's got a temper. That so?"

"That's right," Pencil said, becoming more animated. "He leaped over the bar and snatched that picture down, swearing like a pirate."

"Wasn't he mad at you guys?"

"I guess so," Hands said with a mirthless grin.

"You know, Hands," Pencil said, sounding serious, "we might've piled it on a little too thick."

"Shit," Hands said dismissively and took a swallow of beer, "he had it coming, always bragging about how good he had it made. Pencil, what was that he'd call himself when he got going?"

"Alpha male. Hands here started calling him Alfalfa, and that ended that shit."

"He must have been really pissed with Perez," Harry said.

"Believe it," Pencil said with a confirming nod.

"And the wife," Hands added. "Maybe even more. There was a while there I thought he might wring her neck, but he calmed down after he filed."

"For divorce?" Harry said. "Did he say he filed?"

"That's it," Pencil agreed, "said he was going to skin her."

CHAPTER 19

Harry left the bar with two thoughts competing for his attention. The first was the admission that Gwyneth had made just after Harry had agreed to work for her, to the effect that she had been frightened by her husband's anger when he learned about her infidelity. The second was a kind of creeping pity for Scartole.

Imagine, Harry thought with a sinking heart as he was getting into the Rover, being married to Gwyneth Benbow and having Hands Brownback and Pencil Pellegrino for friends. The poor fool even told them he had filed for divorce. Pathetic. What kind of fractured life was that for Gwyneth? Well, he reminded himself, he was not being paid to be a marriage counselor, but the admonition did nothing to assuage his feelings.

The following morning, Harry got out of bed resigned to responding to Tucker's repeated requests that they find and shoot that big Nile monitor lizard. Unless he did it, Tucker would try to do it on his own. Harry could not let that happen.

Oh, Brother! and Sanchez met Harry at the end of the farm road as they always did and escorted him to the house.

"You're wearing long pants," Tucker said in surprise when he stepped onto the stoop to greet Harry.

"Where we're going," Harry said, "we're likely to get wet to the waist. The bug repellent will wash off, and I'll get chewed on if I'm wearing shorts."

"I'm glad you're coming to terms with reality," Tucker said. "What are we going to do with this beast when we've killed it?"

"Well, this is a big one, so it's probably a male. If it's fully grown, it will weigh between a hundred and fifty and two hundred pounds. I estimated from its tracks and its tail drag that it is seven or eight feet long. Over a short distance, it can easily run down a human, however fast that person is. I suggest we kill it first and dispose of its body second."

"Do I detect some reluctance in you regarding our pursuit of this thing?" Tucker asked, obviously wanting to laugh.

"You do. Foot for foot, this lizard is more dangerous than an alligator. In fact, it seems likely to me that it has been killing and eating alligators its own size ever since it came out of the egg."

"Don't frighten yourself, Harry," Tucker said, patting him on the shoulder in a comforting gesture. "I think we'll prove to be a match for it. Come along now." He broke open his double-barreled twelve gauge and checked the shells. Satisfied, he snapped it shut, set the safety, stepped off the stoop, and asked, "Where do you suggest we start looking?"

"It could be anywhere," Harry said, "but my guess is that it will either be near water or trailing the panther, looking for another free meal."

"I'm worried about her," Tucker said. "She's pregnant again, and you know how she gets when she's in that condition. Furthermore, she needs her kills to thrive. I'm not sure she won't get mad and tackle the damned thing."

The big cat had moved onto the Hammock six years ago, and after one or two Mexican standoffs when she thought harm was coming to her cubs, she had reached an understanding with Harry and Tucker that involved both sides minding their own business.

"Then let's go have a look," Harry said.

They started off with Sanchez leading and Oh, Brother! covering their backs. For a few minutes Harry and Tucker talked, but then they gradually grew quiet. The heavy forest, with its cool, damp smell of earth and growing things, canopy trees, trailing lianas, and shadowed middle story, had that effect on nearly everyone who entered it. There was something about the place that dampened talk. To Harry and Tucker it had become second nature to slip into silence once they were under way.

In speaking of it, Tucker had once expressed the experience in a way that had stuck with Harry, and he recalled it now as he began the familiar transition into increasing awareness of the place and a diminishing preoccupation with his own thoughts.

"This forest is not just a collection of trees," Tucker had said. "It's a sentient being. I don't think it's at all like us or even knows we exist, but it is a living presence. Once you are in it, you begin to feel it drawing you in. If you let yourself go, you will become part of it. The letting go can become either a transcendent or terrifying experience."

They had been walking for half an hour along a game trail that Harry often walked when making his periodic checks on the Hammock, and were entering the northwest corner of the Hammock, an area the panther had staked out as her birthing place, when Sanchez—who had been moving steadily forward, refusing to be distracted by flushed birds and the occasional bouncing rabbit—stopped, head up, testing the air, a soft growl rumbling in his chest.

Tucker stepped up beside Harry. The two men stood watching the dog until he stopped turning his head back and forth and settled on a direction to the left of the path. Sanchez whined, the hair on his shoulders rising.

"Too bad he can't tell us what it is," Harry said in a low voice, staring in the same direction as the dog, looking for any sign of an animal moving through the low growth peppering the ground between the canopy trees.

They had entered a section of the woods where the hurricane had taken down a few of the oldest trees, allowing the sun to reach ground, something that probably hadn't happened for the past forty years or so. First-growth rye-like grasses had leapt up and were rapidly being overtaken by the sun-seeking shoots of stopper and other bushes. Those, mingled with the waist-high ferns that would not survive long in the increased heat and light, gave excellent cover to anything moving through the clearings but not wishing to be seen.

"It's not a skunk, possum, armadillo, or raccoon," Tucker replied, "or else his back hair wouldn't be rising. At least we're downwind of it, giving us some advantage."

Just then Oh, Brother! stepped up beside Harry, moving with surprising silence for an animal so large, his ears pricked and his gaze following that of the men and Sanchez. A moment later he blew softly and gave every indication of having seen something.

"I'd like to be on his back right now," Harry said. "Hold on, I can see the ferns shaking. It's coming toward us."

"The panther," Tucker said, watching the spot they were all focused on.

"Sure enough," Harry said, as the pale-gold coated cat was suddenly there in an open space, looking at them with her tail switching tensely, showing no indication of being pleased.

Head lowered, she snarled, just in case her state of mind had been misinterpreted.

"Look how heavy she is," Tucker said with obvious pleasure, showing no concern. "I wouldn't be surprised if she had triplets."

Sanchez glanced back quickly at Tucker, and the old farmer said, "Don't you even think of it. I don't want her run up a tree by you, and you don't want to have happen what will if she decides to give you a lesson in panther etiquette."

"At least, we know she's all right," Harry said, "But something's got her riled up, and I don't think it's us. She's pretty sure we won't trouble her. So what's all this display about?"

Harry felt the wind shift slightly, and at that instant both the mule and the dog grew more alert, taking their eyes away from the panther to her right. The hair on Sanchez's back that had begun to drop was now at full attention and the dog was growling again.

"Another country heard from," Tucker said.

The cat had taken note of their shift of attention, and took the opportunity to vanish into the ferns.

"Shall we go over there and have a look?" Harry asked.

"Yes," Tucker said, "but if it's what I think it is, we go carefully. That means you," he added, dropping a hand on the dog's shoulders and giving him a shake that did not move him but made him look up at Tucker and whine.

"I think, if we're going into those ferns and stopper bushes," Harry said quietly, "we'd do well to have Oh, Brother! in front of us. Would he do that?"

"Oh, Brother!" Tucker said. "Walk on. Be careful."

The big mule stepped out, but not fast enough to make it difficult for the two men to keep up. Not to be demoted, Sanchez trotted up beside him. The two led off. Although the two men took turns checking on their back trail, to be sure they had been right about the cat's intentions, they saw no indication that the panther was following them.

The men had only just entered the ferns and tall grass when Oh, Brother! stopped, fully alert. Sanchez also halted. Neither Harry nor Tucker moved but stood listening intently. At first Harry could hear nothing other than the cicadas in the trees around them and the crickets in the tall grass, but then other sounds broke through, the chomping and tearing sounds of a large animal ripping into flesh.

"Now what?" Tucker asked in an undertone.

What happened next might have been called a strategic re-treat. Whatever had been doing the chewing suddenly came charging through the ferns and scrub straight at its unwelcome visitors. Unable to see what it was, Harry and Tucker wisely backed into more open ground and separated, to make it impossible for their assailant to tackle them both at once.

Oh, Brother!, able at his height to see what was coming, also moved back to where he had room to maneuver if the need arose. Sanchez, finding himself alone, quickly turned and trotted to where Tucker was standing, the stock of his shotgun pressed against his shoulder and its barrel slightly raised, and spun around just in time to see the monitor, its heavy body twisting like a snake's, come barreling out of the brush.

"Stay!" Harry shouted as Sanchez went for the charging lizard.

It was too late. The dog was launched. What occurred next happened almost too fast to follow. The monitor had slowed, his eyes on Oh, Brother!, and Sanchez was almost on the creature before it noticed the dog. It rose higher on its front legs and sent its tail crashing into the leaping dog, knocking Sanchez end over end into the bushes.

It then turned its attention to Harry, who had been rapidly closing the distance between himself and the monitor, and charged. Harry and Tucker opened fire on the lizard, and the double charges of buckshot blew its head to pieces. Oh, Brother! had started for the big reptile when Sanchez went down, but plowed to a halt when the firing began and stood snorting and stamping as the dead monitor's body writhed and thrashed in its death throes.

"I'm afraid there'll be more," Harry said when the lizard stopped thrashing, and the smell of cordite had blown away.

"But this one's depredations are over," Tucker said, breaking open his shotgun and ejecting the spent shells. "Let's have a look at Sanchez."

When they found him, resting on a bed of flattened green ferns, the dog was just beginning to come back from wherever he had been catapulted by the blow from the monitor's tail. Harry helped him onto his feet while Tucker was running his hands over the dog. Oh, Brother! stood with his nose as close to the dog as the men's arms would allow. Standing on his own, Sanchez tried to give himself a shake and yelped with pain.

"I thought so," Tucker said, getting to his feet. "He's got a couple of cracked ribs and is going to be sore for a while."

"That was some whack he got," Harry agreed. "I never saw anything like it. He was lucky it wasn't his head or the blow would have snapped his neck like a dead twig."

Sanchez whined pitifully.

"Don't start that," Tucker said. "You're going to walk home and not be carried."

Now that space allowed, Oh, Brother! put his nose against Sanchez's head and blew softly, a gesture that caused the dog to whine again.

"Don't encourage him," Tucker said sharply to the mule. "He's going to be hard enough to live with without your sympathizing with him."

Harry watched the little drama and thought, *No one would believe this.* "I want to know what the lizard was eating," he said and plowed off through the tangle.

A moment or two later, he was back.

"A deer," he said, "or the little that's left of it. I expect it belonged to the panther and our friend took it away from her. At least we know what had upset her. She'll have to go hunting again. There's not enough left of the carcass to interest a crow."

"I say we leave our green dragon to the vultures," Tucker

said. "They'll eat it when it softens up, and I'm pretty sure our cat won't touch it, at least I hope she won't."

"No, she won't," Harry agreed, reloading his pump gun and checking the safety.

The little safari formed and started home. Once on the path, Harry turned back for a last look at the place where they had first seen the cat.

"There she is," Harry said, not really surprised to see her but pleased to find her there.

Tucker looked back.

"Sitting in the sun, pretty as a picture," he said with a chuckle. He stood watching her for a moment as if he was listening, then said, "You're welcome," and, turning, set out along the path.

Harry lingered, noting that the cat had vanished as soon as Tucker turned away.

"King Solomon had a ring," Harry said.

"Affectation," Tucker replied.

CHAPTER 20

That evening, Harry took Holly Pike to Pallister's in Candle Village. The restaurant was one of Harry's favorites, and as it turned out, one Holly did not know. Probably, Harry had thought, because the menu wasn't handwritten.

But she had surprised him by saying, "Oh, good," without her usual edge and sounding genuinely pleased by the invitation and their destination. "Let's go a little early so that we can walk along the canals. I love watching the light flickering on the water."

Candle Village was located a block from the Gulf on what had in the pre-conservation past been a piece of tidal swamp that was stripped of its mangroves and its water shunted through dredged canals between cement walls, and the raised land built on and landscaped into a warren of shops, mid-rise condominiums, and several restaurants.

Pallister's was built one side flush with a cement containing wall, bringing the slowly moving water directly under the windows. The surrounding lights from the building danced quietly on its surface, occasionally disturbed by dolphins making a scenic detour from their fishing grounds or the quiet passage of shallow draft boats either leaving for the Gulf or returning from a sunset cruise. Holly and Harry were just seated when a female dolphin and her baby, not more than three feet long, surfaced briefly under their window, the lights gleaming briefly on their wet backs.

"Did you arrange this, Harry?" Holly asked when she had watched the dolphins pass below her.

Harry was so intent on admiring Holly in her ivory dress that he didn't answer at once.

"Are you with me?" she asked.

"Yes, to both questions. It's part of the tour, and may I add that you clean up beautifully?"

"Thank you. You'll notice that I also scraped the horse manure off my shoes before pulling them on." She was smiling, but her tone of voice was a trifle acidic.

"Could I do this again?" Harry asked.

"There's room for improvement."

"Holly, you look stunning. I've wanted to say it since I saw you coming down the stairs."

"That's more like it," she said with some enthusiasm. "Why the delay?"

"I wasn't sure how you'd take it. I'm used to the woman in jodhpurs and riding boots and no makeup. I'll be honest and say I find you a bit daunting."

"Am I wearing too much jewelry?"

"Not as far as I'm concerned."

Their gin and tonics arrived. Holly picked up her glass and said, "May I ask a favor of you, Harry?"

"Of course."

"Will you please get over being daunted right now, and instead look at me as if you wanted to dive headfirst into my décolletage?"

"I was hoping you hadn't noticed," Harry said, aware his face was burning.

"Try again," she said, eyes dancing. "I didn't say, 'Stop looking.' I said, 'Begin looking.' "

"I am! Now, stop talking about it before I do something that gets us thrown out of here."

"You're quite handsome when you blush."

"It's much better than having you grow pale at the thought of my fiddling around in there."

"That's the first time I've had my breasts mistaken for musical instruments."

"Music hath charms . . . and so on."

She lifted her glass. "Here's to us and the music of the spheres."

"You're good, Holly, very good," he told her, delighted with her response and her company and watching the shifting play of candlelight on her face and hair.

A bit later their conversation turned to Gwyneth.

"Our friend is not happy, and that's a severe understatement," Holly said, dealing with her salad. "Have you any idea what's wrong there? I couldn't get anything helpful out of her."

"She's been very seriously knocked around," Harry said. "Being shot and coming as close to dying as she did rips up more than flesh and bone. It does serious damage to your mind as well."

"Been there, done that! Have you been shot?" she said.

"Yes, three times, but never as seriously as she was. Nevertheless, it took me a while to get over the shock of it. She's looking forward to restorative surgery on the back. The exit wound is large, and I think she dreads going through the ordeal."

"I'm not doubting you, but I don't think I understand why she wouldn't be feeling relief at the progress of her recovery," Holly said.

"If her experience has been anything like mine," Harry said, putting down his fork.

He had never articulated how he had felt about being shot. Now he felt a genuine need to put the experience into words, as much for himself as for Holly. "Gwyneth can't get the fact of having been shot out of her mind," he continued, working his way carefully into the explanation. "She's undoubtedly feeling violated and very vulnerable. It's not only that she's in fear of being shot again—although she does know she's still in danger—it's also knowing that she can be. Until someone shoots you, you just don't know how fragile you are or how dangerous this world really is."

"I never thought of it that way," Holly said, her interest obviously aroused by his comments. "I don't recall how I felt about the experience. In fact, I can scarcely remember anything about it. I wonder why?"

"You were focused on getting back to The Oaks from the instant you regained consciousness. I'm guessing that had a lot to do with it."

"I was worried about leaving the horses," she said. "What were you going to say about Gwyneth?"

"Strangely enough, she may still be wrestling with guilt over the divorce. I thought I had to get several things about the divorce cleared up, and her responses led me to think that she hasn't come fully to terms with having separating herself from Scartole."

"Smartest thing she ever did," Holly said flatly.

"I agree. Then there's Perez. Just between us, I think she may have been at least a little in love with him. Whether she knows that or not, I have no idea, but I think she's grieving his death."

"What makes you think so?"

"When she speaks of him, her voice and her expression change. It's not so much what she says about him as how she says it."

"Then you don't think she killed him."

"Not a chance."

"Interesting. You notice a lot for a man in your line of work," she said, looking at him as if he'd just sat down. "Just don't get too interested in Benbow."

Then their food arrived. They ate, their conversation flowing elsewhere.

As their coffee was being poured, she said, "Have you heard from Sarah recently?" Then she added quickly, "I'm assuming Jennifer is still alive because if she wasn't you would have told me."

"You have an excellent memory for names," he answered. "You can't have heard me mention them more than once."

"I remember your account of the breakup. That helped me to recall the names. Then she is still alive?"

"Yes, she is. Sarah told me that as soon as she was taken off the medications and whatnot that were presumably keeping her alive, she grew more alert, her vital signs improved, and she's talking to Sarah and the nurses. The only medications she's taking now control the pain and regulate her bowels."

"But she is still dying, if that's not too bald a way of putting it?"

"It's not. She's dying, but as Sarah put it, she's dying at her own speed. I'm not sure I know what that means, if anything, but Sarah says Jennifer is feeling much better."

"I don't recall your saying anything about going to see her. Do you want to go?"

The question surprised Harry, and he was not sure how to answer it.

"I mentioned going, but Sarah said she didn't think it would be something her mother wanted." He paused again, finding his response did not satisfy him.

"She's the gatekeeper," Holly said.

A short while later they were standing outside the restaurant, and Holly had slipped her hand under his arm. "Another stroll along the wall?" she asked.

"Whither thou goest . . ." Harry said as they set off. "What

194

did you mean by 'gatekeeper'?"

"Do you hold Bible classes out there for the crickets?" she asked, spluttering with laughter.

"Does my quoting things bother you?"

"Not at all, but most of the time I don't know what you're talking about. The 'thou goest' gave me a clue this time. Now, about the gatekeeper. There's always one when a member of a family is dying. It's the person who decides who gets to see the one who's dying and who doesn't."

They were strolling beside the canal now, stopping occasionally to watch the bloom of phosphorescence in the wake of a passing boat or the play of light falling on the water from the lamps set at intervals along the walk.

"Are you suggesting Sarah ought not be making these decisions for Jennifer?" Harry felt a little ruffled.

"It depends. Ask yourself this. If you were in Jennifer's position and had command of your mental faculties, would you want to be deciding whom you wanted to see?"

"Well, yes," Harry said, feeling increasingly uncomfortable and wanting to be angry, but unable to decide what he wanted to be angry about.

"Have you asked yourself what you want to do?"

Worse and worse, and just when he had washed the problem off his hands and given it to Sarah. "Probably," Harry said with less reluctance than he had expected, "if it were left to me, I'd go up and see her."

He stopped walking, very surprised to find that he was glad to have said it and gradually becoming aware that he had been wanting to say that for some time and had repressed it.

"Why?" he asked after a moment of silence in which Holly had been looking at him with a speculative expression.

"The good reason," Holly said in a cheerful tone of voice while pulling him into motion, "is that Sarah told you not to come, but the real reason is that it was the path of least resistance."

"That's not very flattering."

"No, it isn't, is it?"

"I'll have to think about it."

"Yes, do. But don't think too long. Now, I think I know where there's a very cold bottle of excellent wine. Let's go see if we can find it."

Oddly enough, they found it at Holly's house, and as it was so late when they had finished drinking it, they agreed that Harry ought not to drive home or she sit in her room waiting for a call, saying he had reached home safely, but do something else.

Which they did and found the activity they hit on to be a significant improvement over either waiting or driving and much more vigorous, accompanied by heavy breathing, and a medley of sighs and moans, punctuated by the occasional wild yell. Altogether, a thoroughly satisfactory conclusion to a pleasant evening.

The next morning Harry reached home to find a message on his answering machine from Samia Perez, asking him to call her. He could not judge from her voice or the verbal content of the brief message the emotional force behind it.

Rather than wasting his time speculating, he called her. A young man answered, and when Harry identified himself, he said, "Oh, Mr. Brock. Thank you for returning my mother's call. She's not here, but I have been asked to give you a message. It's a request, actually. Can you come to the house this morning? Mother would like to talk with you. As usual, she did not tell me why," he added with a pleasant laugh.

"Yes," Harry said, "and I'm very sorry about your father."

"Thank you. There doesn't seem to be much progress toward

finding his killer."

"I wish I could say you're wrong. Please don't hesitate to refuse, but would you be willing to answer a few questions?"

There was a click on the line, followed by a swift verbal exchange Harry could not understand, then a woman said, "If you don't mind, Mr. Brock, I'd like to take part in this conversation. I'm Basma. My idiot brother has probably not introduced himself. His name is Alex. I'm the older, more intelligent, more responsible sibling. What do you want to know?"

"Is this all right with you, Alex?" Harry asked.

"Sure."

"Thank you. Where do you go to school?"

"MIT."

"Congratulations," Harry said. "I'm impressed."

"Don't be," Basma said. "Admissions lost his application and covered their asses by admitting him and also giving him a scholarship, screwing someone who deserves it. I'm astonished he's lasted this long without being kicked out."

"Have you always been this rough on your brother, Basma?" Harry asked, smiling with pleasure at how much she sounded like his stepdaughter, Minna, harassing her younger brother to cover up how much she loved him.

"My earliest memory is of her empting my Pablum bowl over my head," Alex interrupted. "I never got a full night's sleep until I left home for college. My body was never free from black and blue marks where she had pinched me. She made my life a living hell. I still have nightmares over it."

Basma gave a snort of half-smothered laughter.

"He's right. I was rough on him. I was three when he was born and very jealous. So I tormented him to get even. I loved it when I made him yell."

"Basma, where are you enrolled?"

"The Pritzker School of Medicine at the University of Chi-

197

cago. Psychiatry is my area of specialization. I'm trying to find out what's wrong with my brother's brain. Whatever it is, I doubt it can be corrected."

Every family deals with grief in its own way. It was clear to Harry how these two were dealing with their father's death. He wondered to what extent Samia participated in the game.

"Question," Harry said. "Have either of you any idea why your father was shot?"

The silence that flowed in when he stopped speaking was vibrant. He waited, guessing it would be Alex who broke it, and he was right.

"Our father lived a complex and intense life with more than its share of drama," the young man said in a tight voice that Harry thought was carrying a significant burden of anger. "He made a lot of enemies, some of whom are powerful and potentially dangerous people."

"Anyone in particular come to mind?" Harry asked mildly.

"No names, Alex," Basma put in.

"Have you two talked about this?" Harry asked.

"Since we were old enough to talk sensibly about anything," Basma said.

"And with your mother?" Harry asked.

"No," Alex replied. "Our mother does not believe that such things should be discussed with one's children."

"Not even now?"

"Not ever," Basma said with distinct emphasis.

"It was one of the reasons why for years while we were growing up we referred to home as the Gulag," Alex said. "It's no mystery to us why North Africa and the Near East are overrun with assassins."

"Also suicide bombers," Basma added.

"I can't wait to hear your mother's side of this story."

"You never will. Family matters are never discussed outside

the family," Basma said.

"Have you thought of taking this show on the road?" Harry asked.

"At the moment, we're only giving private performances," Basma said. "How would you rate it on a scale of one to ten?"

"Well, I'm certainly glad I asked to talk with both of you—if that's any help."

"We're as in the dark as you are, Mr. Brock," Alex said in a much more adult voice. "It's been a horror, and we're not through it yet."

And you won't be for a very long time, Harry thought but did not say it.

"I just pray whoever killed our father can be found and punished," Basma said. "He is a monster and ought not to be left free to kill someone else, because he almost certainly will."

Interesting, Harry thought, *she assumes it's a male monster that did the shooting.* What would Tucker say to her?

"If it's any consolation, there's a good chance your father's killer will be found," Harry said.

"I hope so," Alex said, then added. "Mother's just come in and wants to speak with you. Goodbye, Mr. Brock."

There was a quick three-way exchange in Arabic and then Samia said, "Thank you for responding to my call, Mr. Brock."

"You're welcome. Your son and your daughter are delightful. You must be very proud of them."

There was a moment's silence.

"What have they been telling you?" she asked, her voice rich in suspicion.

"I'm not sure I should tell you."

"I was afraid that you might say that. It would be best if you tried to forget as much of it as you can. I must be frank with you and say that, embarrassing as it is, I do not understand much of what they are talking about and haven't since they entered secondary school."

Harry allowed himself to laugh. "That's because they are extremely verbal, intelligent, and great teasers. But mostly it's because they are American, and American parents are not supposed to understand their children. I have five, and can only say to you, 'Join the group.' "

"Can you come this afternoon at two?" she asked abruptly as if abandoning a pleasant distraction for the grim reality of her situation. "I do not wish to talk on the telephone."

"Yes, and talking with your children gave me a great deal of pleasure."

Chapter 21

Harry decided to drive to Avola, using the time to think about the case. He did manage to decide that he must have another talk with Kevin Mulvane, this time about Eric Scartole's boat and how often he was using it.

But that done, his mind drifted to his evening with Holly and how it ended. Image after image from dinner to breakfast drifted through his mind, all of them pleasant, some exciting, others much quieter but in their varying ways equally delightful. There were no moments in all of those hours that Harry would have changed or expunged, not a single one.

It was their perfection that frightened Harry. He could find no reason not to go on seeing her, and unless he had seriously misread her—and he did not think he had—she too had enjoyed their time together. Then what was the problem? He knew what it was but kept shying away from it, closing his mind to its implications.

However, there was no effective way of going on avoiding it, and before he turned off County Road 19 onto the feeder road from I-75 into the city, he had confronted the problem. Briefly put, there were two lost marriages, an agonizingly failed love affair on his scorecard that had left unhealed wounds, and an overflowing dumpster filled with shattered hopes.

The accumulated failures had broken his confidence that he could sustain a lasting relationship with a woman. And yet here he was again, setting out on another romantic journey to hell.

How much more suffering did he need before putting an end to these wretched experiences? And it wasn't only himself being run through the wringer. The women involved in these emotional train wrecks had endured more than their share of pain and disillusionment.

Somewhere on a dark back porch of his mind, someone was knocking on the door, calling to him. Very vaguely and unwillingly, he heard the voice urging him to end this litany of misery and reminding him that he was not married to Holly. Further, he had no reason to believe she loved him or wanted to marry him. Just before reaching the Perez house, he wondered if he should call Holly and on the specious argument that it was too early decided not to.

"Sometimes," Samia said, with a wry smile, having thanked him for coming and settling him where he had sat on his first visit, "I think my experience as a mother has been a failure of Koranic proportions—may Allah forgive me."

She was still dressed in the black wrapper, but today she had freed her hair to fall down her back, and for a fleeting instant he saw Gwyneth. Two strikingly elegant women, he thought, wondering briefly if they would like one another.

Harry wasn't sure whether she was asking forgiveness for her failure as a parent or for having referred to the Koran in a secular context, but decided not to ask, although he wanted to.

"Parents who claim to hold the key to perfect parenting," Harry said, "are rowing downstream on the St. Lawrence and ignoring the increasingly ominous roaring coming from somewhere ahead of them."

"You have an interesting mind, Mr. Brock," she said. "If I were not in mourning, I would allow myself to laugh."

Harry smiled, pleased by her comment. "Not any more interesting than yours, Mrs. Perez."

"I hope I have not offended you," she said quickly.

"I've taken it as a compliment. If it's not, please don't disabuse me."

"You are quite right. It was a compliment and thank you for returning it. Shall we turn to less pleasant things?"

"One of life's requirements."

"Are you a philosopher, Mr. Brock?"

"A skeptic—lowercase variety."

That took a moment of thought, and then her slight frown was replaced by a smile. "Ah, yes," she said. "I'm afraid I have not been truthful. You see, I know or I am reasonably sure I know where my husband was on the evening he was killed."

Harry's first response was concern for her. He had seen this happen too often to be surprised. "Have the sheriff's people questioned you?"

"Yes, several times, and yes, I lied to them as well."

"Why have you been hiding the information?"

Samia had been leaning against some brightly colored cushions with her feet tucked under her, but at his question, she snapped them onto the rug and sat up, her hands folded in her lap, her back straight.

"Because, Mr. Brock, I was ashamed and angry and . . ." Here she stumbled and, to Harry's consternation, her eyes filled, but she continued to face him as though she was looking into the eyes of a hanging judge. ". . . and hurt, humiliated. Does this surprise you, Mr. Brock?" she demanded, tears glistening on her cheeks.

"Have you ever spoken to anyone about your husband's infidelities?" Harry asked the question as an alternative, which he quickly rejected, of moving to her side and putting an arm around her.

"Never."

"So telling me or the detectives who questioned you would have removed the last barrier separating you from . . . is it your

203

own or the world's harsh gaze?"

"Both, Mr. Brock."

"Of course. Unfortunately, you've got to tell the police. It might make it easier for you to tell me first and learn how to do it in a way that causes you the least pain."

Quite suddenly, Samia leaned toward her knees, clapped her hands over her face, and began to sob without restraint.

"Forgive me," she gasped in a choked voice and, leaping up, fled from the room.

Harry stood up, not feeling as though he should be sitting in that room without her there. On this second visit he felt more strongly than the first time that this was her private space, which did not make sense until she was in it.

What should I do, he wondered, *if she comes back having decided not to tell me where Perez was that night?* It wasn't a pleasant question, and his mind was pulled back to that insight he had experienced when she broke down and began sobbing. He had seen in an all-encompassing instant her isolation, how completely alone she had been in her anguish over her husband's philandering.

That insight was followed by a thought possessing less clarity but possibly more penetration. Perhaps she was not weeping over Henrico's infidelities but over the insults to her pride to which his philandering had exposed her. She was, after all, a stranger in a strange land. She was also a beautiful woman. The suffering imposed on her by these repeated rejections must have been intense.

That thought gave rise to another. Was it possible that she had murdered her husband? "Ridiculous!" he said aloud, shoving his hands into his pockets in angry rejection.

"I see that you are upset, Mr. Brock," Samia said, sweeping into the room, the skirt of her wrapper billowing behind her as she advanced, all evidence of tears erased from her face.

She came to a stop in front of him, her large, dark eyes bravely fixed on his. "Please forgive me. My outburst was inexcusable and extremely embarrassing for you. Also, you are right, but my behavior was worse than *ridiculous*. It was vulgar. I am deeply ashamed."

Harry decided to shoot the moon. "Mrs. Perez," he said, having guiltily yanked his hands out of his pockets, "I was not the least embarrassed by your tears, but I was deeply moved by them. They evoked sympathy and sorrow. I doubt that you are capable of being vulgar, and when I said, *'ridiculous'* with such emphasis, I was thinking of something"—here he was stretching it—"that had nothing to do with you or your situation. As for the tears, considering what you have been through, why shouldn't you cry?"

"Mr. Brock," she said, her shoulders sagging slightly, the harshness drained from her voice, "thank you from the depth of my soul, and I do not care that you are a shocking liar. Sit down, and I will tell you who my husband was with. Her name is Olivia Karapis. She is a minor official in the Greek consulate in Miami."

Harry left the Perez house without seeing Basma and Alex, which was probably just as well. Because if he had encountered them, he might have knocked their heads together and told them to stop being so goddamned selfish and begin showing their mother some love and sympathy. Of course, he didn't really know that they weren't being as supportive as they might have been, but he wanted to be angry with someone. Samia Perez had plucked the blood-red chord in Harry that was strung between women in pain and his heart.

On his way to find Kevin Mulvane, he allowed himself to return to the idea that he had, initially, so forcefully rejected and ask himself if there was any possibility that she might have killed her husband. He was forced to admit to himself that, yes, she might have. She had motive and opportunity in the prosecutor's trinity, lacking only means. And because the house had not been searched, it was possible that she did possess a gun.

He turned the Rover into Mulvane's lumberyard and parked. He found Mulvane behind the big storage shed in the milling section of his operation, scaling a truckload of oak logs. When Mulvane was finished, he told the driver where to unload and turned his attention to Harry.

"Hello, Brock," he growled. "You back here for the scenery?" His grin was not the endearing sort, but Harry knew the man well enough not to start running.

"Mr. Mulvane," Harry said, steeling himself as he reached out to grasp the proffered hand. He didn't say anything more until Mulvane released him.

"I've got a favor to ask," he said when he trusted himself to speak, leaving his hand to just hang for a while. "Do you know the name Eric Scartole?"

"That little prick," Mulvane said around his toothpick, scowling as he spoke. "What's he done now?"

"I don't know that he's done anything, but I heard he was storing a boat with you."

"Yes, he is. You heard about his divorce from that society woman that got herself shot? Think he might have done it?"

"Probably not, but I'm working for Gwyneth Benbow, his ex-wife, and I'd like to talk to the man who's in charge at your boat operation, and I'd like very much to have this conversation stay between us."

"You know that little job you did for me?" Mulvane asked.

Harry said he did.

"That's worked out pretty well so far, in part because you've kept your mouth shut about it. It wouldn't've been much help to my business if rumors got out about one of my son-in-laws being a thief and a druggie. Whatever you say to me will stay with me."

"Well, thank you. What I'd like to do is talk with your boat man about how often Scartole used his boat and who he's been taking out recently."

"This got anything to do with Benbow's shooting?"

"Maybe, but I won't know for sure until I've had some questions answered."

"Hank Tolliver is the man you'll want to talk to. He's run that boathouse for the last twenty years, and he's run it damned good. You can talk to him and know you're not being lied to."

"Then it's all right with you if I have a talk with him? That is, if he's willing."

"Sure. I'll call and tell him you're coming," Mulvane said, his grin returning. "He's one of the Virginia mountain Tollivers that drifted down here during the big war and was brought up to be suspicious of people who ain't named Tolliver."

Mulvane stopped and looked pensive for moment, then said, looking at Harry with a changed expression, "I guess I should tell you that he's in a hard place and has been for a while. It's his wife. She's dying and needs a liver transplant. First year costs for one run over three hundred thousand dollars, and that's just the beginning."

"No insurance."

"He's got insurance, but it don't begin to meet the need, and because he's working, Medicaid won't touch him."

"And not a veteran."

"Nope, he's up shit's creek and no mistake. Somebody told him to quit his job, stop paying his bills, stop making mortgage payments on that henhouse they're living in, and declare himself a pauper. That way, Medicaid would take him. But his wife won't let him do it. 'I'd rather die,' is what she said."

"Sounds as though that might happen," Harry said, an old

anger stirring.

"Yes, it does, and it's a goddamned shame, if you ask me."

A man wearing a welding mask shoved up from his face stepped into the door from inside one of the sheds off to their right, looked in their direction, and gave a shrill whistle. Mulvane turned his head toward the sound.

"More trouble," he muttered. "Good luck with Tolliver and remember what I told you."

Mulvane's boathouse was located on the east side of the Seminole River a couple of hundred yards below the Route 40 bridge and something over a mile from Snook Pass where the Seminole emptied into the Gulf. The east bank in that area was crowded with buildings servicing or storing boats and others offering everything for sale from snorkeling gear to computer-aided marine navigation systems. The west bank was given over to the city's public docking facilities and restaurants.

Harry had never shed his inlander's distrust of the ocean. All that water made him uneasy. Even Moosehead Lake when he first saw it had seemed excessively large. His preference when he was in a boat was to be on a body of water where he could see at least two shorelines.

Hank Tolliver was a lanky man, dressed in a tattered gray T-shirt and ancient dungarees, cut off halfway between his knees and his ankles. His feet, no doubt because they were constantly wet, were housed in a pair of grimy, rubber-soled sneakers.

Harry took in these details, along with the straw-colored hair shot through with white and the long, weathered, unsmiling face lined beyond the man's years. Because of his appearance and something unsettling in his worn face, Harry found he did not want to pursue this interview with Tolliver and nearly said he'd made a mistake as a preliminary to leaving. But Tolliver hung the coil of rope he was carrying on a peg drilled into a heavy, unpainted upright support timber, turned to Harry, and said, "Are you Mr. Brock?" in a quiet but firm voice.

"That's right, and you're Mr. Tolliver, I take it," Harry answered, putting out his hand. "And Harry will do for me."

"Mr. Mulvane said you was coming. What can I do for you?"

The boathouse was an open building with boats suspended from structures extending from the river water, forming the building's floor, and extending a full two stories to the roof. Harry and Tolliver were standing on one of the dozen or so wooden catwalks, giving access to the boats, running at intervals across the boathouse and made accessible by slanting, narrow stairs with strung roping for handrails. Over their heads were what Harry's quick count estimated to be thirty-five or forty boats, mostly inboard/outboard powered, all with cabins of varying sizes.

"I guess those in here for longest storage are at the top," Harry said, staring up at the strange sight.

"That's right. Electric-powered winches raise them up and down and to the right and left when that's needed," Tolliver told him with a fraction more life in his voice than was there when he greeted Harry. He was looking up as he talked and pointing to the chains and pulleys that made the operations possible.

"Thanks for the explanation," Harry said when Tolliver was finished. "I understand you've worked here a long time."

"I've been here some while. What is it you want to ask me?"

If Harry had not been forewarned by Mulvane, he might have felt offended by Tolliver's brusqueness, but instead, he noted it with interest and moved on.

"Before I get to that," Harry said, "Mr. Mulvane told me your wife is ill. I'm sorry to hear it."

"Yes, well, we're looking for an improvement soon."

Given what Mulvane had told him, Harry thought that was

unlikely and concluded the comment was intended to end the discussion rather than convey factual information about the woman's health. He decided not to follow up on Tolliver's statement. "What I want to ask you is whether or not Eric Scartole is keeping a boat here."

Tolliver's expression went from resistance to one of hostile suspicion. "What business is that of yours?" he demanded.

"Didn't Mr. Mulvane tell you I planned to ask you some questions about Scartole?" Harry asked, keeping his voice calm.

"Why are you asking questions about Scartole?" Tolliver demanded a second time, his long jaw thrust toward Harry.

Two can do this, Harry thought. "Are you going to answer my questions or not?"

"Can you swim?"

Harry decided to accept this situation as a puzzle that needed solving and not as a threat to his ego. Reminding himself of what the man was enduring, he said, "Not well. Mr. Tolliver, I'm a private investigator. Recently, Scartole's ex-wife was shot, and, according to the surgeon who worked on her, escaped dying by an inch. Someone wanted her dead. Have the sheriff's department people talked with you yet?"

"No, what would they want from me?"

The belligerence was still audible, but Tolliver's narrowed eyes, which Harry had been watching carefully, began to show increased suspicion. Harry decided to be creative.

"Gwyneth Benbow was shot outside the Conservation Club. There's a large dock in front of the club, and the crime scene crew think the shooter may have come to the club by boat and left the same way. Ms. Benbow was married to Scartole for about seven years before they broke up. The sheriff's people know Scartole owned a boat and kept it with this boathouse."

"And the sheriff's people think Scartole shot this Benbow woman?"

"I don't think so. But in an investigation like this one, they often have to eliminate suspects as part of the process of finding out who the likely suspects are."

"Well, if Scartole done it," Tolliver said quickly, "he sure didn't use his boat. There ain't nobody used it since Scartole left for Dallas."

"I guess you've given me the answers I was looking for. Where's the boat now?"

"Up there," Scartole said, pointing at the roof.

"Which one?"

Without hesitation, Tolliver indicated a boat almost directly over their heads.

"That one. There are four boats under it, all long-term storage."

"How long has it been since it was last taken down?"

Tolliver frowned and appeared to be thinking about the answer, but Harry suspected he knew exactly how long it had been up there. "I'd say six or eight months ago."

"And that would have been about the time Scartole left for Dallas?"

"No idea."

Harry began to thank Tolliver for talking with him, then interrupted himself to ask if Scartole had been in the habit of taking a lot of people out sailing the boat with him.

"As far as I know, aside from them bottom feeders from the Seaside Club, he never took anybody with him."

"Not even his wife?"

"Not from here, but every third house between here and the Gulf has got a dock in front of it. He might have taken her or half of Avola on board from any one of them, for all I know or care."

"That's true. Do you ever hear from him?"

"I'd have no reason to."

"No. Thanks for your time."

CHAPTER 22

Harry left the dock area thinking that Kevin Mulvane had underestimated Tolliver's distrust of outsiders. He also decided he had no reason, aside from disliking the man, to think he had been lying. What did he have to gain? Nothing Harry could see beyond the satisfaction of doing it because he didn't like having to answer questions from someone he didn't know.

"Not likely," Harry said and wrote off the interview as a waste of time except for having caught Scartole in a lie about returning to Avola from Dallas. Another thought crowded out that one before Harry turned his mind to something more pressing. What did Tolliver and his very ill wife find in their lives of sufficient value to be worth her dying for? Her husband's pride? Family honor?

Probably something close to that. From what Mulvane had said, they didn't have much else.

Harry dropped the question and his mind instantly reverted to the fact that it was pushing noon and he still hadn't called Holly, and he knew he was swiftly approaching the time line separating the insensitive from the despicable. As soon as he had re-crossed the Route 40 Bridge, he pulled off the street into a Dairy Maid parking lot and with a deep sigh called Holly.

"And the excuse is?" she said by way of a greeting. Then, before he could sweat out a response, "If this weren't Southwest Florida, I'd guess cold feet."

"Holly, I enjoyed being with you last night in more ways than

I can begin to say."

"But it seemed too much to you like finding yourself in Commitment Alley and you . . ."

"Hold that thought," Harry said, interrupting her. "Do you like crab cakes?"

"Harry . . ."

"No, do you like crab cakes?"

"Yes."

"Have you eaten lunch yet?"

"No, but . . ."

"Good. I know where they serve the best crab cakes this side of paradise. I'll pick you up in twenty minutes. Wear something really light, and spray your legs and ankles with insect repellent."

"Oh, good! Is this the prelude to something kinky?"

"Maybe, after the crab cakes."

Harry knew that the strategy was not earning him points with heaven, but desperate situations called for desperate measures. Or was it simply that his desire to see Holly again had overridden his flight impulse?

Fred's Chickee Hut was located on a small sand island overgrown with wire grass, wild oats, Spanish sword, beach grapes, buttonwood, white mangrove, and scattered clumps of saw palmetto. It was linked to the Marco Island road by a narrow sand road, subject to submergence in the spring and fall tides or the random tropical depressions and their big brothers and sisters, which from time to time clear the island of its encumbrances, leaving Fred's to start over.

The building bearing the name was not roofed with palm fronds like the genuine article, but wore a shiny new tin roof that had been added since Harry was last there. Four unfinished oak logs, set on large blocks of roughly poured cement, supported the roof, and the walls consisted of light wooden framing covered with back porch screening, greened in patches with algae.

"Lord have mercy," Holly breathed when she climbed down from the Rover, "you've brought me to eat at the Second Little Pig's house. Where's the Big Bad Wolf?"

"It usually but not always comes from the southwest," Harry said as they walked toward the screened-in shack with its rickety bar and scantily clad and raucous clientele crowding the wooden picnic tables with attached benches.

"Looks like the crew of the Good Ship Venus got here ahead of us," Holly said, stepping past Harry and the warped screen door with a rusted spring and into the teeming interior.

"How many?" demanded a bronzed and hefty waitress, wearing an inadequate bikini and sun-dried hair of no specific color, gripping a clutch of menus that looked as if a dog had been chewing them.

Holly looked around as if surprised by the question and said, "I make it two. What's your count?"

"I'll go with your number, honey. Follow me." Several parts of her person became active as she strode into the crowded scene ahead of them.

"Are you looking?" Holly asked Harry over her shoulder.

"At what?" he answered.

The noise around them was such that they had to converse just under a shout. "It's a moveable feast."

Harry laughed but no one heard him. As soon as they were seated, he ordered beer and then pulled a can of Deep Woods Off out of his shoulder bag and passed it to Holly. "Start with your feet and spray everything up to where you can't go any farther."

"Why am I doing this?" she asked.

"Mosquitoes, no-see-ums, sand fleas, ticks, and assorted bit-

215

ing critters," Harry said. "You may have noticed there are cracks between the floorboards wide enough to let you watch the gopher tortoises on their way to and from."

"Where?" Holly asked, having sprayed a small puddle of liquid into her hand and begun applying it to her legs vigorously.

"No one knows," Harry said, glancing at the menu, "but they're always going somewhere or coming back."

The waitress came jingling back. "What'll it be?" she asked, setting their opened bottles on the table.

"You order for me," Holly said, sitting down again.

"Crab cakes and whatever," Harry said.

"Got it."

Then she spoke to Holly. "Honey," she said, turning her back, "spray some of that on me, will you?"

"Where?" Holly asked.

"Begin with my ass, then use your imagination. It don't do anything for the customers' appetites to have me scratching here and there while I'm waiting to take their order."

"It was a large canvas to work on," Holly remarked to Harry after the waitress had given her a gold-speckled grin and thanked her before hurrying off.

"She seems to like you," Harry said. "Are you thinking about coming back and working something out?"

"It's an option if other things fizzle."

Harry had sprayed himself, and now the two were sitting, forearms on the table between them, leaning toward one another to make it easier to talk.

"Do you think they will?" he asked.

"Just how scared are you?" she asked.

"Answer my question first."

"I can't until you've answered mine."

They had maintained their light and bantering tone, but Harry knew the conversation had just become serious. But answering her was not going to be easy.

"Okay, I'm not sure I know," Harry said.

"Despite what you may think, Harry," she said, placing a hand over his on the table, "this is not a test, neither is it a trap. It's just Holly researching Harry, hopefully, to help both of us make good decisions."

"Fair enough," Harry said, coming to a decision of his own. "I'm older than you are, Holly. I have two failed marriages and a serious relationship that broke on a reef in my past, plus five children on my resume. Three women have left me. I think it's possible that I'm incapable of maintaining a lasting relationship."

"Not a great record," Holly agreed, leaning back to let the waitress put down her tray and unload their plates.

"There's some flame in these side dishes," she told them as she worked. "How about more beer?"

"Yes," Holly said.

"Good choice, honey," and, turning to Harry, she said, "What about you, sweetheart?"

"Put me on the list," he said, unable to suppress his smile.

She winked at Holly and said, "He's a keeper," and strode away.

"Maybe you'll be the one to come back," Holly said, scanning the huge, heaped plate in front of her.

"I've already asked her to put me on her list."

They began to eat and made a desultory effort at talking. But once Holly reached the crab cakes, her attention ceased to be distracted by such nonessentials as conversation about a conjectural future. Harry watched her with pleasure but was soon occupied with eating.

"Those have got to be the best crab cakes on earth," Holly said in a reverent tone when she finally fell back from the fray, having finished the last of her beer, "and that chili, the hottest.

Thank you, God," she said more loudly, "for having let me live long enough to eat this meal, which, yes, I understand may be my last."

Gradually, they gathered the strength of purpose to make their way back to the Rover.

"My vision's still impaired from eating that chili," Holly said, fastening her safety belt.

"Is that what it is," Harry said, turning onto the sandy track, causing the Rover to rock like a boat lifting and falling on the waves. "I thought it was fog. By the way, you were commenting on my past failures."

"So I was, but I want to veer off slightly. How much is Jennifer's dying contributing to your anxiety about this fledgling affair of ours?"

"I haven't thought about it," Harry replied, puzzled by the question and a bit irritated. "I don't see why there should be any connection at all."

"It's worth considering," she said. "After all, there was a time when you and she were in love, and you still have the children. Isn't that true?"

"It is, but what we had has been dead and buried for a very long time," Harry said with increased uneasiness.

"But you do want to see her again while she still knows who you are."

"Yes. Look, Holly, I don't want you occupying the same space in my mind as Jennifer inhabits."

"Why not?"

"Because I was about Sarah's age now when Jennifer and I crashed. It was a horrible time for me and probably for her too. Christ, Holly, I just want to get through this and have it over without doing any more damage to Sarah and Clive than we've done already."

"Harry," Holly said quietly, "you're driving too fast, and

you're gripping that steering wheel as if you wanted to tear it out of its socket."

They were rapidly approaching the Marco Island road. Harry pulled his foot off the accelerator and braked in time for them to come off the sand and onto the tarmac without leaving the ground. To keep from skidding across the road and diving into the water, Harry had to make a turn. Swearing silently and fervently, he cranked the wheel to the left. The Rover groaned as it slid sideways on the tarmac with a loud squeal of smoking rubber and leaned heavily toward the south before slamming back to an even keel.

"Good driving," Holly said coolly, pulling herself away from the door and regaining her seat. "Too bad there wasn't a car coming to add to the excitement."

"My apologies," Harry said. "That was a damned fool thing I just did. I guess I'm more rattled by what's happening to Jennifer than I was willing to admit."

He pulled off the road and turned to face Holly.

"I guess," she said with cold emphasis, "it was also partly my fault for mentioning Jennifer in the first place. You're right. She doesn't belong in the conversation we were having, and I don't think this is the time to renew it."

"I've made you angry," he said, turning the Rover back into the road. "That was not my intention. I'm sorry."

Harry did not resent having to apologize, but he was disgusted with himself for having put himself in the position of a supplicant seeking forgiveness.

"Maybe a time-out is what we both need." She said this with a clipped incisiveness that Harry knew only too well from past experience. It meant that Quaker meeting had begun and forfeits were open-ended. They rode back to The Oaks without Harry making any racetrack turns, and their conversation was marked by civility and not much else. They did not shake hands when she got out of the Rover, but their parting kiss was polite and completed with minimum bodily contact.

"Shit," Harry said as he drove away.

Harry got home to find Sanchez lying under one of the live oaks closest to the house. The dog trotted up to him as soon as he left the Rover and pushed his head into Harry's stomach, his greeting of preference.

"Have you got something for me?" he asked.

Sanchez pulled back from Harry's grasp and barked, then turned and set off for the lanai, looking back to see if Harry was following.

"I know the drill," Harry called after him, "water and biscuits."

While the dog was eating, Harry untied the red bandana Sanchez wore for a collar and unrolled it until he found the message he expected to find. It was from Tucker, asking him to come over when he could.

"Shall we walk or ride?" Harry asked, tying the bandana around the dog's neck when he had finished his biscuits and slaked his thirst.

By way of an answer the big hound pushed past Harry and onto the lanai, stopping to wait for Harry to join him. As soon as he had, the dog shouldered open the screen door and loped over to the Rover and sat down, grinning back at Harry, his tongue lolling.

"All right," Harry said, "we'll ride."

He opened the back door for Sanchez, and before backing onto the road, opened both back windows to let the dog stick his head out and feel the wind on his face, something that seemed to please him.

They found Tucker turning over one of his compost piles, which the old farmer treated with the care and reverence usu-

ally restricted to religious shrines. Oh, Brother! had been waiting for Harry and Sanchez at the top of the drive, and after
pressing his nose against Harry's chest and blowing softly by
way of greeting, led them to where Tucker was laboring.

"Sprinkle a little water on the pile while I'm forking it over,"
Tucker said, not pausing for a more formal greeting.

Harry picked up the sprinkling can and began adding water
to the tumbling mass of disintegrating contents of the pile.

"Shall I spell you on that fork?" Harry asked, knowing what
the answer would be.

"No, thanks," Tucker said, huffing a little. "I'm about done.
That's enough water."

Harry set down the can and Tucker straightened up from his
work. This pile was in a three-sided, wooden pen about four
and half feet square with no top or bottom.

"That's got about another week," Tucker said, mopping his
face with his handkerchief. "Then it's going onto the garden,
and it's almost as good as cow manure."

"I know it's all chemistry," Harry said, eying the pile with interest, "but there's something almost magical about the way all
that grass and weeds and leaves turns into something looking
like soil."

"Yes," Tucker said, leaning on his fork, "it's the process of
slow burning that returns everything to the earth. If we came
back tomorrow and thrust our hands up to our elbows in that
pile, we would find it warm as the sun on our skin, cooking
away in a mystery of its own making."

Both men stood staring at the pile, but Harry was contem-
plating another mystery, the one concerning him and Holly and
what they were cooking.

"Soot and ashes," he said before he thought.

"Where did that come from?" Tucker asked.

"The mystery of life," Harry said with a painful cynicism.

"What has brought me out here?"

They were standing in the thin shade of a stand of Dahoon hollies behind the henhouse, and they could hear the quiet communion of the rooster's harem and his more authoritative gurgling, indicating that all was well.

Not everything, Harry thought, pulling his mind back to Tucker.

"I think there's another monitor lizard on the Hammock," Tucker answered.

"What makes you think so?" Harry asked.

"I'll show you."

With Sanchez leading and Oh, Brother! covering their backs, Tucker led Harry down through the citrus grove to a shady patch of ripped-up ground at the base of a large lignum vitae tree.

"Up until a couple of days ago," Tucker said, his voice heavy with disgust, "a burrowing owl had a nest of young ones under those roots."

"Until something dug them out," Harry said, sharing in Tucker's disgust. "You sure the coyotes didn't do this?"

"I've never seen them bother. You could set two of those chicks in a teacup. The mother's not that much bigger."

"Whatever did the digging was certainly bigger than a teacup," Harry agreed. "Look at those torn roots and how far it flung the sand."

"And the claw marks," Tucker added.

"No bear would have taken the trouble," Harry said, "and only a starving panther would have gone to such an effort."

"With the creek full of gar and pan fish, why would the lizard have done it?" Tucker asked.

"I think because they eat whatever's in front of them, and they're so strong that ripping open that shallow den would have been a moment's work."

Harry looked around, feeling suddenly that living was useless. There was no way he and Holly were going to grow what they had planted. There was no way to stop the spread of these monitors. They were going to strip the Hammock of every creature they could find, even their own hatchlings that didn't get out of their way fast enough.

"Do you suppose that chain-link fence on the hen run will stop it?" Tucker asked, breaking into Harry's dark reflections.

"I think so," Harry said, glad for the distraction. "But you might want to make sure there are no weak places in the henhouse itself."

"I'll clad it with tin roofing if I have to," Tucker said with a grim frown.

All the time the two men were talking, Sanchez had been walking around the place stiff-legged with the hair on his shoulders and back flared. Oh, Brother!, ears cocked, had been keeping a close watch on the surrounding woods.

"Are we finished here?" Harry asked.

"It looks that way," Tucker said. "Let's go back and try a glass of lemonade, unless you want something stronger."

"Lemonade will do just fine," Harry answered.

Neither man had suggested another hunt. Thinking about it later, Harry concluded they both were too depressed by what they had seen to think anything they could do would slow the spread of the dreaded lizards.

On their way back to the house Tucker asked Harry how the investigations were going, and over their lemonade Harry brought Tucker up to date, glossing over, so he thought, his troubles with Holly.

"I knew Hank Tolliver's father and Hank as well when he was a boy," Tucker said. "The father's name was Jeb. If I'm not mistaken, Hank's wife has been very ill. I don't have the details."

"Kevin Mulvane says she needs a liver transplant," Harry said, "and they can't afford it."

"We lost our way somewhere back there, and now the richest country in the history of the world can't take care of its own people," Tucker said, then added after a brief pause, "Well, it's too bad, but you and I can't cure the problem, at least not today.

"Getting back to Jeb Tolliver, I worked with him fifty-odd years ago on a freighter called the *Mary Jane*. Miami was her home port, but she worked all the ports from Havana to Key West to Mobile, Alabama. As I recall, possibly through a rosy haze, he and I had a couple of good years on the *Mary Jane*, working our way up through several promotions and getting to know a lot of men and women."

Tucker paused to rock quietly, sipping his lemonade and staring out into the sun-drenched woods. Harry waited for him to return to the story, or not. Tucker sometimes just left his stories hanging. Harry had long ago stopped asking him why because the answer was always the same: "I've forgotten."

This time Tucker went on with it as if he hadn't paused. "Someone once said, 'A sailor can go around the world without leaving home.' That's true enough as far as it goes, but Jeb had only recently come to Florida from southwestern Virginia with a young wife and two children, along with a brother and his wife, to start a small cattle and hog ranch out toward Immokalee. I think they had all come from the same clan, and he missed them. He'd get back to see them every month or so, but even though the money was good for those times and steady, he threw it up and went back to farming."

Tucker fell silent, but Harry was impatient to know more and he said, "How long did you stay with the *Mary Jane*?"

"Not long. I'm easily bored. That's probably why I never developed a profession. Once I learned how to do something, I soon tired of it."

"Good Lord," Harry protested, "you've been on this farm for thirty years."

"Longer," Tucker replied with an innocent smile, "but here no two days are ever the same."

"Tucker! You can't expect me to take that seriously."

"But I do," was the reply. "You see, Harry, I don't work here. I live here, that's an important difference. I'm surprised I've had to point that out to you."

"I give up."

"You're much too young for that option. Instead, why don't you tell me what's troubling you. Perhaps between us we can do something about it."

Of course, Harry told him about Holly, and while Tucker listened, he said very little beyond extending the occasional word of comfort. When Harry finished describing the lunch with Holly at Fred's Chickee Hut and the revival of the Jennifer issue, along with its unpleasant aftermath, Tucker put down his lemonade glass and gripped the arms on his rocker as if expecting it to take flight.

"Are you at all clear in your mind as to what feelings if any you have toward Holly Pike?" he asked, a slight frown creasing his forehead and his voice acquiring a little edge.

"I like her a great deal. I thought that was obvious."

"In matters of the affections nothing is obvious. And how does she feel about you?"

"Up until I almost drove us into the Gulf, she gave every indication of wanting us to go on seeing one another . . . Well, actually, we'd gotten a little farther than that."

"But the issue of Jennifer's funeral got between you, and now she doesn't want anything more to do with you. Is that it?"

"Yes."

"All right, now, although you know how reluctant I am to

give anyone, especially you, advice on such matters, I think I'm going to make an exception in this case."

The first part of Tucker's statement about not giving Harry advice was such an outrageous, knee-weakening canard that Harry's mouth fell open in astonishment.

"No, keep your comments to yourself for the moment," Tucker said quickly. "I want to get this over with, and I want you to listen to me. You managed to give her the impression that you had reservations about entering into an extended relationship with her because of the bad experiences you've had with other women. Is that about it?"

"Well, yes."

"That should put you in the top ten percent in any assembly of idiots that I can imagine, but let's not dwell on that. It probably didn't occur to you that when you said that, you immediately relegated her to the sisterhood of difficult women."

Harry thought that was grossly unfair and started to say so, but Tucker went on talking.

"Before the sun goes down, you round up all the roses in Avola, and you get yourself out to The Oaks. And don't you leave there until you've convinced Holly Pike you'd walk barefoot over broken bottles to convince her she's the best thing that's happened to you since your mother brought you into this world."

"What if she wants a demonstration?" Harry asked, on the verge of laughter.

"Prepare to shed some blood. Believe me, Harry. She's the real McCoy. Don't screw this up."

CHAPTER 23

"Harry," Thahn said in surprise when he opened the door to find Harry standing there with an enormous bunch of roses under each arm. He seemed momentarily at a loss, then continued quickly, "Please, come in. Is Mrs. Pike expecting you?"

"I wouldn't think so, Thahn," Harry said, his heart beginning to thump uncomfortably, causing him to wonder if he was having a heart attack.

"Who is it, Thahn?" Holly called, having come partway down the stairs.

Thahn looked at Harry, and Harry looked at Thahn. Both men looked worried.

Thahn recovered first. "It's Mr. Brock," he said. "I believe he wishes to speak with you."

"Well, I don't want to speak with him," she said and turned to go back up the stairs.

"Holly!" Harry called after her, stepping past Thahn and looking up at her.

She stopped.

"Would you like to buy some roses?" he asked. "The money is going toward the establishment of a home for brokenhearted idiots. I've already qualified for admission."

That brought a snort of laughter from Holly, who tried to cover it with a cough.

"What should I do with him, Thahn?" Holly asked, reversing position on the stairs and looking down at Harry.

"I don't know, but I suggest that you abandon your original plan to crucify him," Thahn said.

"I'll think about it. Please send Fiela up with two vases. Have Mr. Brock bring the roses up to my study. I'll write a check."

"Yes, Mrs. Pike. Will there be anything else?"

"Hold my calls."

She turned again and marched up the stairs.

"Mr. Brock," Thahn said, "please follow Mrs. Pike."

"Thank you, Thahn," Harry said. "If I don't survive this, it's been good knowing you."

Thahn made a slight bow. "If Mrs. Pike becomes agitated," he said in a low voice, "and pulls open the center drawer of her desk, you might want to go out the nearest window."

His heart was still giving him trouble when he walked into Holly's study. She closed the door behind him.

There was a knock on the door soon after; Fiela, no doubt, with the requested vases, though Harry had other things to tend to at the time. Later, he would retain no more than a vague memory of something being set down out in the hall and light footsteps hurrying away.

The door remained closed until sometime after the sun had set. When it was opened, Holly stepped through it, saying over her shoulder, "I'm starved. What about you?"

In the morning Harry telephoned the Greek consulate in Miami and asked to speak to Olivia Karapis. After being passed from one official to another like the proverbial hot potato, a woman with a rich contralto voice, said, "Wolenski," which surprised Harry in several ways.

She listened to his request in silence. Then, when he had finished, said, "Why?"

"Does it matter?" Harry asked.

"Perhaps not to me, but it presents problems."

It was Harry's turn to ask, "Why?"

"Mrs. Karapis is in Greece."

"When is she returning to Miami?"

"It's unlikely she will."

"Has the Avola Sheriff's Department been trying to reach her?"

"Does it matter?" Wolenski asked.

"Not to me, it doesn't, but it presents problems."

Wolenski laughed. "I have enjoyed talking with you, Mr. Brock," she said, "but the work is not doing itself."

"No. Is there a number where I can reach Mrs. Karapis in Greece?"

"She is on medical leave and is traveling for her health. No cell."

"Therefore, no problem," Harry said.

Wolenski laughed again. "What problem?" she asked.

"The dead man with six bullets in him, as you well know, Wolenski."

"It is Celestyna, Mr. Brock."

"What?"

"My Christian name is Celestyna. You like it?"

"Very much. Mine is Harry. How do you happen to be working in a Greek consulate?"

"Is a long story, Harry. I have a call I must take. Goodbye and have a nearly nice day."

"The same to you."

That was the most pleasant being gotten rid of I've experienced in a long time, he thought, hanging up the phone. Then he called Jim.

"I've got some things to go over with you," he said, and then Jim asked if Harry had called the Greek consulate in Miami.

"Yes. Olivia Karapis has taken wing. How much effort are

you going to make to track her down?"

"I doubt Harley Dillon will spend a penny on the effort," Jim said.

"I don't think there's anything there, do you?"

"No, unless you want to drive to Miami and interview Wolenski."

"You're at risk of losing your reputation for seriousness."

"Undeserved anyway, are you coming in?"

"I'll be there in twenty minutes."

Harry stopped the Rover on the bridge and got out to watch the creek for a few minutes in hopes of seeing the otter that had a den under the bridge, and her four-month-old pups, but they were not in sight. Then, watching the dark water swirl under the bridge, he began thinking about Holly. Had Tucker been right? Probably, but Harry was still not sure, even with their reconciliation still very fresh in his mind, if he wanted to risk another marriage. Wasn't he just setting himself up for another life-threatening calamity?

At that instant, something slammed him against the bridge railing, kicking his feet out from under him as a searing pain burned through his right leg. The fall probably saved his life because as he lay on the planks, looking up at the wooden railings where he had been leaning an instant before, bullets smacked into the wood, spraying splinters, followed by the sharp reports of a handgun.

Despite the pain, Harry slithered under the lowest railing and plunged into the creek. Surfacing long enough to take a deep breath, he went under and began breast stroking with the current, kicking with his left leg, and counting on the dark water to shield him from the shooter's eyes if he had, as Harry guessed he would do, run up onto the bridge to finish the job. Moments later, his guess was confirmed by the wet, chugging sound of bullets surging through the water, trailing bubbles. He glimpsed three slugs zipping past his head. Then the dull thumping of the gun stopped.

The pain in his leg was bad enough to make it difficult for Harry to think clearly. But when his chest began burning, he steered toward the right bank, and when his head bumped into the cattail stems, he fought his way into them as far as he could and slowly raised his head until he broke the surface, coughing up swallowed water. Grasping the thick stalks of the cattails to keep the current from pulling him out into the center of the creek, he listened but could hear no sound of anyone crashing along the brush-lined bank above him.

Intending to put as much distance as possible between himself and the bridge, Harry took another deep breath and slid back under the water. Making sure to stay as far below the surface as possible, he gave all the help he could to the current bearing him away. He found it a struggle to judge how far he had traveled, but when he was forced to come ashore again he found himself in a large stand of bulrushes. There he rested, trying to find the courage to actually drag himself onto the bank.

While he was resting, he turned onto his back and raised himself enough to look down at his right leg. Through the murky water, Harry could see a dark, wavering ribbon of blood flowing away from the wound. The pain was so dispersed through his upper leg that he could not locate the wound and only hoped it was not too high for him to put on a tourniquet. But for the moment, his chief concern was staying away from whoever was trying to kill him.

After dragging himself up the bank far enough to be out of the immediate reach of any big alligators frequenting that stretch of the creek that might be following his blood trail to its source, Harry pulled his CZ out of its holster, shook the water out of it and worked the action, sliding a shell into the chamber. Then he lay still for a bit, waiting for the pain to subside enough for his vision to clear before taking on the daunting task of crawling to the road, which he knew from the stand of bulrushes was not more than ten yards from the top of the bank.

Harry had just begun pulling himself through the reeds when he heard a car pull to a stop on the road, and a moment later the sound of someone crashing through the bushes. Harry sank down until only his face was visible and waited. Whoever it was walked back and forth along the top of the bank for a very long four minutes, then crashed his way back to the road. Harry heard a door slam and a car pull away.

He never could remember much of the crawl, lost as he was through most of it in a fog of pain and increasing confusion. His last clear memory was dragging himself onto the tarmac and hoping its surface was not hot enough to burn his face, and realizing that tying a tourniquet was far, far beyond him. Then nothing.

His return to consciousness was not auspicious. He was lying on his back, naked save for the corner of a white sheet thrown across his left hip and more or less covering his privates, or so it seemed from his awkward perspective of staring down the length of his body. He thought of *The Dying Gaul* and wanted to laugh, then checked himself. *Medication,* he told himself, adding that from the foot of the bed the view was going to be radically different and less edifying. He attempted to sit up and found himself constrained by a canvas strap crossing his chest.

"If you turn out to be as much of a nuisance awake as you were unconscious," someone behind him said in a loud, judgmental voice, "then you're in for an education."

Harry screwed his eyes shut. The voice was unmistakable. Brunhilda! And nowhere to hide. Maybe he'd died and this was Hell.

"Stop pretending you're not awake, and cover yourself. What do you think you're doing?"

Harry opened his eyes. A large person loomed beside him as he ineffectually struggled to reach the sheet. "Lie still," she said, tossing the sheet over him. "I've got to work on you, and keep your hands to yourself."

"What's your name?" Harry asked, struggling against despair.

"Martha Vickery."

"Mine is Harry Brock. How did you get here?"

"I work here. Don't you recognize me?"

"Am I dead?" he asked, having decided to face the answer now rather than later.

"No. It's the medication."

She thrust a needle into his arm. To his surprise, he felt scarcely a prick. Was it possible she was telling the truth? He was having increasing trouble keeping his mind on anything. He was very tired. She bent over him, and he found himself looking into her eyes. They were gray. He could not recall ever seeing eyes that color before.

"You have remarkable eyes," he said just before drifting away in a warm river in which breathing was not necessary.

"You are a piece of work, Harry Brock," she said, staring down at him and shaking her head.

"Mr. Brock," Alice Ingram said, placing her hand on his forehead. "Wake up."

"I am awake," Harry said, having reluctantly left his river.

Ingram straightened up and draped her stethoscope around her neck. "How are you feeling?"

"Nothing hurts," he said. "I was shot in the leg."

"That's right and someone up there likes you. A driver of a gravel truck found you lying in the road and called for an ambulance. Twenty minutes later and it would have been the county M.E. operating on you instead of me. You lowered our blood supply significantly making up for the deficit."

"Good save. How long before I can be unstrapped?"

"What? Oh, Vickery," she said and laughed, unfastening the straps. "She thinks you're the victim of satyriasis. Is she right?"

As she bent over Harry, he was reminded that she was a woman and said, "In your case I might be."

"Thank you," she said, smiling at him as she straightened up. "It's always nice to be appreciated."

"You're welcome. How's the leg?"

"Remarkably, aside from tissue damage and muscle trauma and considering what happened to you, you're in good shape. The bullet missed the bone and the CFA, although some of the minor branches were shredded, hence the bleeding."

"What's the CFA?"

"Common femoral artery. Our sciences have become infested with acronyms."

"When can I leave?" He was getting that going-away feeling again.

"I think I'll keep you around for a few days. Just watch yourself with Vickery." With that she placed her hand on his forehead for a moment, then said, "Sleep."

He watched her turn away but was gone before she was out of the room.

Nurse Vickery, glaring and bloodied but unbowed, let Jim and Frank Hodges into Harry's room, but only after Mr. Braithwaite came down in person from Administrative Olympus and told her either to let them in or clear out her locker.

"I thought I was going to have to draw my weapon to get in here," Hodges boomed, bursting through the door.

"I haven't figured out whether she's my protector or my jailer," Harry said. At Ingram's orders, he was now sitting up. And the tubes and drips were gone.

"Lord, Harry," Jim said, folding his long frame into the chair Hodges had pulled up to the bed for him. "Unless it was deliberate, whoever shot you had seriously bad aim. We've been out there and located where the shooter was hunkered down in the weeds. It's not more than fifty feet from where you were standing. That was easy enough to locate. There was blood on the planks where you'd been."

"I went down as soon as I was hit," Harry said, "and the next shots went over me as I was clawing my way through the water."

"Three shots," Hodges said. "We've recovered two casings and a couple of cigarette butts. One shell was caught between the planks, and we located another in the weeds. It looks like he picked up the rest."

"He fired some into the water," Harry said. "I didn't keep count."

"Scartole was in Dallas when you were shot," Jim said. "Rachel Whittaker, Rosamund Fairbrother, and Samia Perez are all accounted for. Oh, yes, the Greek embassy said Olivia Karapis is still in Greece, 'travelling for her health.' That leaves us empty."

"You've been busy," Harry said. "Of course it's guesswork to say whoever shot me also shot Perez and Gwyneth."

"We've got casings from yours and the Perez shooting," Hodges said.

"And we might look to old Occam for guidance on this," Jim said. "The least complicated way to look at these shootings is to assume it's the work of one person. And until I get evidence that it's not, I'm going to continue looking in that direction."

"The only way to do that," Hodges said, "is to find somebody who wants Perez, Benbow, and Harry dead."

Harry broke the ensuing silence.

"What if that person is a hired killer?" he asked.

CHAPTER 24

Two days later Ingram and Vickery gave Harry back to the world.

"No woman will be safe," Vickery said to Ingram as he was being wheeled toward the entrance, but even as she spoke, she fished a tissue out of a side pocket and dabbed her eyes.

Ingram pretended not to notice but slipped an arm as far as she could around Vickery's waist and gave her a quick squeeze.

Coming home after an absence of even a few days was a complex experience for Harry. While the Hammock was the only place that meant home for him, the empty house, echoing to his footsteps as he hitched his way up the stairs, shaded his relief at being back on the Hammock with melancholy.

The price, he reflected sourly, of becoming attached to anyone. Of course, he was thinking about Holly, who, along with Gwyneth, had arrived at the hospital and filled his room with flowers, which Vickery threw down the trash chute as soon as they left.

"Why did you do that?" Harry demanded.

"I'm allergic to the nasty things," she said, refusing to look at him. Harry suspected she had not even come close to telling the truth but wisely avoided challenging her.

Aside from the one step at a time routine on the stairs, Harry found he was able to get along well. Driving was a bit awkward, but doable, and once home and settled, he began almost at once reestablishing his routines. That evening, he was just starting his dinner when Sarah called. Noting the caller's name, he prepared himself to be told Jennifer was dead, but that was not her message.

"Hello, Harry," she said in her usual voice. "How are you?"

"Recovering from being shot in the leg. In fact, I was discharged from the hospital this afternoon. Are you okay?"

"Are you on the Hammock all alone?" she demanded, her voice rising.

"Don't upset yourself," he said. "I'm all right. It was only a flesh wound, but Dr. Ingram kept me for two days because they had to patch me up a little."

Sarah was not deceived. "You are there all alone, aren't you? Where's Holly?"

"Home, I guess."

"Does she know you've been discharged? No, you haven't told her, have you? Of all the dumb, stubborn people I've ever met, you win the medal. No wonder Jennifer divorced you. If I'd been old enough, I'd have wrung your neck."

"Stop!" Harry said. "I'm all right. I've been living alone a long time. How's Jennifer?"

"Never mind Jennifer. She'll live to be a hundred. Why didn't you tell Holly? Have you two quarreled?"

"No, but we're in a 'let's go easy' phase."

"*Phase!* You're getting cold feet, aren't you?"

"Children aren't supposed to become involved in their parents' personal affairs."

"*Parent!* Harry, come off it. You were my parent for about my first seven years. After that you were 'roamin' in the gloamin' as I remember."

"Have you been watching very old movies—'come off it,' 'roaming in the gloaming'?"

"Just trying to make you feel comfortable while talking to someone much younger."

"A hit! A palpable hit."

"Two can play at that game. I'll mention the swift approach of Time's winged chariot."

"You've been reading in odd places."

"Yes, I caught the disease from you that summer I spent on the Hammock. But don't change the subject. Are you really all right?"

"As rain, my love. I'm fine. Now tell me about your mother."

"It's most strange. Ever since she went into palliative care, she's been getting better. No, wait! I don't mean that. She's not any 'better.' Not in the sense of reversing her illness. That is progressing as predicted, according to the doctor, but she's not deteriorating the way she was. She feels much better. She seems to be at peace with herself. She's out of pain, thanks to the medication. She's no longer being urged to fight what's killing her and has turned her remaining energies to just living. She's reading again, watches a little television, takes an interest in the people around her, and has stopped fighting with me—a miracle in itself. I would even go so far as to say that she's given up worrying about Clive."

"I'm glad to hear it," Harry said and almost told her that he was going to visit Jennifer. But he did not force the thought into action. It would, he decided, only upset Sarah to no purpose.

"Would she see me if I were to come up?" he asked instead, testing the waters.

"Oh, Harry, don't think of it. She's comfortable, finally. Why would you want to disturb her? It would be so selfish."

Harry almost asked, *Who's being selfish here, you or I?* And then wondered if, indeed, he was being irresponsible in thinking of appearing at his ex-wife's deathbed and imposing himself on her now after all these years of mutual avoidance.

"Sarah, my coming or not and the consequences either way are not your responsibility," Harry said. "You have enough to deal with as it is."

Sarah appeared to understand the gentle rebuke in the message because her reply was cooler in tone than earlier.

"I'll try to remember that, Harry," she said. "One more question, do you have any idea who shot you and why?"

"Unfortunately, not a clue."

"Then whoever it is might try again?"

"Frankly, I don't think it was a very serious try. Don't add that to your worries."

"If you say so, but I think you're bullshitting me. Please behave as if you're still in danger. I don't want to have to arrange another funeral in the near future."

"There's some news," Hodges said, accepting the glass of diet Pepsi, which was the closest to a diet that he was ever likely to get. Harry had already placed an open box of crullers at his elbow.

He and Harry were seated on the lanai. The sun had burned away the morning fog from the creek and the last of the flocks of wading birds, calling excitedly to one another, were on the way to their feeding grounds in the swamps and along the rivers and beaches.

"Good or bad?" Harry asked, sitting down.

"Depends," Hodges replied, doing a poor job of brushing the powdered sugar from his chin. "The lab report says the gun that shot Perez was used on you. We can't tell about Benbow—no slug, no spent cartridge."

He paused to fish another cruller out of the box. Harry thought with amusement that his crullers were probably the deciding factor in Hodges' decision to bring the news in person rather than using the phone. Hodges beamed at Harry, having added more sugar to his large face.

"Now, that is interesting," Harry replied. "What was Jim's response?"

"That brought him partway over to where you were the other day when you said the shooter might be a hired killer, but if he is, he's surely not a pro—that last bit's my opinion."

"Why not all the way?"

"He says there's no proof that the person doing the shooting isn't the one carrying out this vender-something or other."

"Vendetta," Harry said, weighing Jim's argument.

"What?" Hodges asked, interrupting his preparations to take another bite of cruller.

"Vendetta," Harry said, still absorbed in his own thoughts. "It's an Italian word that drifted into English a few centuries ago. It means a blood feud."

Hodges still looked puzzled.

"Like the shooting feuds between families in the Southern mountains."

"Oh," Hodges said, finally getting to take the bite he had put on hold.

"Whether Jim's right or not," Harry said, "we still don't know who the shooter is, no good suspect at all."

"Then we'd better haul up our pants and look harder," Hodges said around the last of the cruller as he got to his feet, dusting his hands and making a small, white cloud of powdered sugar.

"Are you convinced yet?" Gwyneth asked Harry, wearing an "I told you so" expression. She had surprised him by driving to the Hammock to talk with him instead of calling.

"About what?" he asked.

He was not in his best frame of mind, although Gwyneth's arrival had proved to be a welcome break in his solitude.

"Is this white powder around my chair something for the

ants?" she asked suspiciously. "If so, they're eating it."

"No," he said. "It's the remains of Hodges' attack on my box of crullers. I haven't gotten around to sweep. Some of us have to do the housework instead of having it done for us."

"Poor baby," she told him, reaching over and giving his shoulder a shake. "Have you been off this porch this morning?"

"It's a lanai. No, I haven't."

"I'm with Humpty Dumpty on this," she said, pushing up from the chair. "If I say it's a porch, then it's a porch. Get up. I'm tired of sitting. Let's take a walk."

"In case you haven't noticed . . ." Harry began, but she waved a finger in a "cancel that" gesture.

"Up," she said. "You're supposed to be working that leg. On your feet."

Looking at her and listening to her ordering him around like one of her house staff, Harry was reminded of both Sarah and Holly.

"Do you know my life is infested with bossy women?" he demanded. Even as he was speaking, however, he was struggling to his feet. Gwyneth watched him critically but made no attempt to help him.

"You could have at least offered me a hand," he complained.

"Nope," she replied with no shred of apparent guilt, "this is your karma. Deal with it. And, speaking of deficits, you still owe me an answer to my question. Are you convinced yet that the authorities are not going to pursue Henrico's death with any vigor?"

"Get our hats, or I'm not going out," he told her. His hat was on the kitchen table and visible from where Gwyneth was standing.

"God," she said in a disgusted voice, "and you accused me of being spoiled!"

"Thanks for getting me out of that lounge chair," he said,

taking the hat from her and making a point of not thanking her for it as well.

Once they were on the white road and in the shade, Harry took a deep breath and closed his eyes for a moment, to feel the Hammock closing itself around him. It was a feeling that never failed to raise his spirits. "You're right that the FBI have been conspicuously absent, and I think that in this case so far they wouldn't have been much use at all."

"But you think Captain Snyder's people have been doing all that could be done?" she asked without obvious sarcasm. "Oh, look! What's that thing?"

A small, scuttling animal was crossing the road in front of them, raising little puffs of dust in its rush to get out of sight.

"That's an armadillo," Harry said. "It's unusual to see them in the daytime. Something must have rousted it out of its den. Around here, they're mostly nocturnal."

His comment brought to mind the monitor. What else would dig an armadillo out of its burrow?

"It's the first one I've seen that hasn't been run over."

Harry pushed the thought away and said, "Do you know why so many are killed on the roads?"

"They don't look both ways before crossing?"

"Mostly because they commit suicide."

"Oh, what a fib!" she protested.

"It's true. When something startles them, they jump straight into the air. If the car is passing over them just then, of course they're struck by the undercarriage of the car and killed. But since they have no other predators, it does help to control their numbers."

"I've heard they carry leprosy. Is that true?"

"Yes. Some armadillo populations are infected. There have been quite a few cases in Louisiana and Texas of people being infected by diseased armadillos. I don't know of any cases in

Florida, but that doesn't mean there aren't any."

"Ghastly," Gwyneth said with a scowl as she watched the animal scramble into the ferns.

"Don't be too hard on the little critter. In North America his kind contracted it from humans."

"That doesn't make me feel any better about them."

"That's all right. I want to raise an uncomfortable subject. I'm sorry, but I need the information."

"Fire away."

"When Scartole confronted you over your infidelity, how did he handle it?"

"Two questions," she said. "The first, how did he react to my *infidelity* as you call it, a very judgmental term. The second, what form did his response take. Which do you want me to answer?"

"Both."

With the armadillo out of sight, they resumed their walk, which was for Harry a kind of "Peg Leg Pete" progress, but one which, to his own surprise, was frustratingly slow but not painful. For her part, Gwyneth had removed the hat with the orange ribbon that Harry had put out for her. Holding it in her hands, behind her back, she was strolling beside Harry and looking attentively at the world around her.

"Just when I was enjoying myself," she grumbled.

"Sorry, it's your karma," Harry said. "Get on with it."

"Stinker," she said. "I'll give you one answer that will close out both questions. He reacted as I thought he would—with red-faced rage."

"Go on," Harry said.

"He threw a six hundred dollar Terrance Chino pot across the room, smashing it to bits and seriously damaging a U Lun Gywe ocean scene that I had recently bought and had hung. Are you getting the picture, no pun intended?"

"I think so. Where were you?"

"I was backed up against the side table where he had found the pueblo pot, trying to feel grateful that it wasn't my head being tossed around the room."

"Was he threatening you verbally?"

"That has such a clean, clinical sound. Actually, he was loudly associating me unfavorably with a series of female dogs he had humped in the past—at least I think his repeated use of the phrase *fucking bitches* was intended to convey that meaning.

"When that part of the program was over, he spun me around, slammed my head down onto the top of the table, ripped my skirt up the back, tore off my panties, and opted for anal sex, but he couldn't maintain his erection and failed to cross the finish line. But it went on long enough to satisfy my curiosity about the experience."

Harry had tried twice to stop her, but once launched she refused to be checked. By the time she finished the part about the anal sex, tears were streaming down her face, and Harry reached out and caught her in his arms.

"Gwyneth, Gwyneth," he said, holding her against him and speaking quietly, but steadily repeating her name until she sagged against him, threw her arms around him, and gave in to the tears. He thought it likely it was the first time since the assault she had allowed herself the release.

"Harry," she said when the storm of grief and, probably, anger had subsided, "I'm very sorry about this. I had no idea . . ."

She was standing with her forehead pressed against his shoulder, not, he guessed, wanting to look at him.

"No apologies, and take all the time you want."

"Have you a handkerchief?"

They didn't have even a tissue between them. He thought of Tucker and Hodges and the fact that they would have been prepared for such an emergency. That made him want to laugh, but he checked that impulse.

"Here, wait," he said, releasing her. He pulled his T-shirt over his head and passed it to her. "Use this—you may want to hold your breath."

To his relief, she laughed and looked up, taking the shirt and rubbing her face.

"You might want to blow your nose," he said.

"Thanks," she said in a muffled voice and blew her nose vigorously.

By this time, both of their hats were lying in the dust of the road, and a gathering of red ants appeared to be trying to drag the straw hat by its orange ribbons back to their nest, having, he thought, mistaken it for an outsized insect. His Tilley hat lay alone and neglected, which slightly annoyed Harry. He picked it up and beat it unnecessarily hard against his good leg. Then he shook the ants off the ribbons and passed the straw to Gwyneth, who was watching him and grinning.

"If thy hat offend thee . . ." she began.

"Don't you dare," he said. "How are you feeling?"

"Oddly, very good, Dr. Brock. Thanks for the treatment, but I think I've said all I want to say about Eric's and my discussion of my extramarital relationship."

"You are an ironist, Gwyneth Benbow," Harry told her, taking back the damp T-hirt and hanging it from the fork in his crutch. "Did he threaten to harm either you or Perez?"

"Aside from saying several times he intended to, 'kill the son-of-a-bitch and you along with him,' he spoke quite reasonably about the possibility of castration in Henrico's case and tearing off my tits, although what he had against my tits I don't know. So far as I know, none of what happened was their fault."

"Gwyneth, no," Harry said, "don't. I had to ask, but please let it go now. You've had enough reality show for one day."

He did not ask her why she hadn't told him about this at the very beginning because he thought he knew and was glad that she had finally trusted him enough to tell him as much as she had. He thought it unlikely that she had told anyone else. But he also knew her outburst was the beginning, not the end, of the overdue healing process. And she hadn't even begun to cope with the anger.

CHAPTER 25

"Why didn't she have the sucker charged with sexual assault?" Hodges asked in an angry voice, his face turning from red to crimson.

"That was going to be my first question," Jim said in rare agreement with his sergeant.

"I didn't ask," Harry said, "but I think she may, understandably, have wanted to get away from him as fast as she could."

The three men were standing together in the shade of a huge fichus tree, one of a dozen lining Dolphin Avenue in a southwest corner of Avola. They were facing Snook Pass, where the Seminole River entered the Gulf. Behind them were a dozen large houses, fronted by a canal. Each of the houses had its own boat landing, and all were equipped with electric-powered lifts that raised the boats from the water to the level of the broad, manicured lawns.

There had been a theft of one of the boats, a thirty-four-and-a-half-foot Catalina, *Tall Rig*. Someone, as Hodges put it, "had the *cojones* to sneak in after dark, bypass the alarm system, engage the lift, lower the boat into the canal, and 'putt-putt' right out into the Gulf. Probably approaching Havana where she'll get a makeover and a load of Mary Jane."

"Ms. Benbow may not have wanted to expose herself to the publicity that would go along with such a trial," Jim put in, "and I don't see how such a case could be settled without going to a jury."

"Maybe she was too shit-scared to do it," Hodges added, bringing a protest from Jim about swearing in the office or at any time when on duty.

"I'm sorry, Captain," Hodges said, "but when I think what that piece of road apples did to her, I just want to wring his neck."

As that exchange progressed, Harry began thinking about Hodges' comment. Was it fear and not guilt that accounted for the size of the settlement? Had she been threatened into changing her will in Scartole's favor—which might account for that semi-hysterical outburst about her breasts?

Harry couldn't decide whether Hodges' lurid view of her motivation should be taken seriously or not, considering the fact that Hodges never saw a story he couldn't adapt for the rags.

Nevertheless.

"Harry," Jim said sharply, "Come back. What were you saying about the settlement? What settlement?"

"Her divorce settlement," Harry said. "It was huge. She said she just wanted to get away from Scartole and was also feeling guilty for having manipulated him the way she did. But I'm not so sure."

"About what?" Jim demanded. "Add a bit to what I said about the humiliation and embarrassment that would accompany such a trial, and I think you've got as much motive as you need."

"You're probably right," Harry agreed, wanting to have time to think some more about the ramifications of Hodges' suggestion. "Have you made any progress toward identifying the man who left the lecture at the Conservation Club?"

"No, and it seems odd," Jim said. "All those people around the man, and no one we've reached so far can remember anything other than the fact he was wearing work clothes and carrying a sack."

"And I doubt the last three rows of people in that lecture hall conspired to have Benbow shot," Hodges said. "And that makes the whole thing even harder to understand."

"Aside from the brief disturbance caused by the chair going over, there was no interest factor at play," Harry said.

"Meaning?" Jim asked.

"Picture it," Harry said. "The lights had been dimmed for the duration of the talk. By all reports the speaker was interesting, and her subject matter, the spread of Nile monitor lizards in our area, was riveting in itself. Toward the end of the lecture, someone at the end of one of the back rows gets up and accidently knocks over a chair. You look around just long enough to see the shadowy figure of a man with a sack in one hand, dressed in work clothes, set the chair on its legs and leave. There's nothing to fix your attention. Your glance may have lasted three seconds, more likely two, and you're back listening to the speaker. You probably didn't miss a word of what was being said."

"But what about those sitting closer to him?" Hodges demanded.

"It's not an attractive explanation, but it's probably what happened: How many day laborers were in that room?"

"I would have thought none," Jim said with a puzzled expression.

"There'd have been a lot, if the lecture had been about hunting and killing those lizards," Hodges put in and laughed loudly.

"Frank's probably right," Harry said, "but it wasn't. If he really was dressed in worn dungarees and a none-too-clean, long-sleeved shirt, and if Peter Rahn is right and the man came in just as the lights were dimming, nobody got a good look at him. As for the nasty part, here it is: My guess is that after the first quick glance, the rest of those seated near him deliberately avoided looking at him."

Jim and Hodges sat staring at Harry for a while until Jim said in a quiet voice, "I remember reading once in school a poem by one of those bygone English writers that had something in it about being ashamed of how people don't do the right thing to one another."

"Was it this one?" Harry asked. " 'And much it grieved my heart to think What man has made of man.' "

"That was it," Jim said. "The feeling that came over me when I first heard it has stayed with me. Do you remember the name of it?"

"Lines Written in Early Spring," Harry said. "Wordsworth."

"Kind of sad, ain't it?" Hodges asked as if he was risking something by asking the question.

"That's right, Frank," Harry said quickly.

"I don't remember much about school," Hodges said. "I never quite figured out why I was there."

"Well," Jim said, shifting his feet and looking around as if wondering where he was, "I guess Frank and I had better be getting back to the office. Plenty there almost every day to make you ashamed of our fellow men. Thanks for the report, Harry. Don't lose heart. We'll solve this yet."

As Harry drove away, he suspected, with a slump in his spirits, that Jim's encouragement was aimed chiefly at himself. This "case," as he had called it, was going nowhere.

Harry found a heavy, pearl-white envelope in his mailbox addressed to Mr. Henry Brock and almost dropped it in surprise. When he worked up the courage to open it, he found inside a heavy, blue-edged card with a dragonfly engraved on the upper left corner, bearing a message in beautiful penmanship that looked as if the scribe had been using a quill pen.

Dear Mr. Brock,
  Please excuse the brevity of this note. It has been brought to my attention that over the last several months, Mother has been

making telephone calls to the residence of Ms. Gwyneth Benbow and to a series of call boxes in Avola. Because she feigns ignorance of the calls and denies having made them, I have been unable to ascertain either their purpose or their contents.

I feel compelled to alert you to the facts. Whether or not they have any bearing on your investigations, I am not competent to say. For reasons I presented to you earlier, my mother will not be available for interrogation on this or any other subject.

Please do not hesitate to call me if you deem it necessary.

Sincerely yours,
Rosamund Whittaker Fairbrother, M.D., Ph.D., M.A.

Harry stood in front of his mailbox, staring at the note for several minutes, alternately feeling puzzled and amused. Then he walked quickly back to the Rover, turned it around, and drove back to Avola. On the way he called Gwyneth and asked if he could talk with her.

"Harry," Gwyneth said when they met, handing him the card back, "the gal is goofy as a Gooney bird. What can I tell you?"

"First, tell me why you kept these calls secret,"

"Harry!" she protested, dropping her feet to the floor, "I wasn't keeping them secret! They were nonsense. And sit down, rest that leg."

She was sitting behind her desk and had leaned back in her office chair with her feet propped on the edge of the desk, legs crossed at the ankles. Harry was still on his feet, looking down at her.

"The leg will bear up," he said. "How am I supposed to function without your full cooperation—and don't say I've scarcely functioned at all."

"That's not what Holly tells me," she replied, avoiding his eyes.

"Way out of bounds!" Harry protested, his face burning.

"Maybe, but I found out what I wanted to know."

"I didn't say . . ."

"No, neither did she, but one look at your face was all I needed. Congratulations."

Harry felt as if he'd been skewered, and Gwyneth still hadn't met his gaze.

"Shit," she said.

"What's the matter?"

"I'm jealous."

"And I'm the Pope's son. Could we stop fooling around?"

"Stop? We haven't even begun, and if you think Holly is hot . . ."

"No more!" Harry said, staggering to a chair. "We've got serious business to discuss."

Gwyneth came around the desk and pulled a chair close to Harry's, reversed it, and sat down facing him. She had combed her hair out to its full length and caught it at the base of her neck with a ribbon that matched her sundress, a shade of blue slightly darker than her eyes.

Lord, Harry thought, *if only Rossetti had painted you.*

"What's wrong?" she said sharply, looking down at herself.

"Nothing," he heard himself saying, "you're as near to perfect as it gets."

"Harry! What a delightful thing to say," she told him, beaming.

"You're welcome. Look, Rachel Whittaker may be slightly loony, but it's possible she arranged to have you killed. In addition to you, she's also been making calls to various call boxes in Avola as the note tells you."

"Who on earth uses call boxes anymore?"

"Rachel Whittaker, for one and others so far unknown for two and three and four," Harry answered.

"Why, after all this time, would she want to kill me? And supposing by some immense stretch of the imagination that was her intention, how would a woman like her get in touch with a gun-for-hire? They don't advertise in the yellow pages."

"If you want it, and if you have enough money, you can get it."

"Well . . . probably, but I still don't see . . ."

"Let's stick to the script," Harry said. "The trigger may have been an anniversary of either her marriage or her separation. Equally likely, your affair with Perez having reached the national news may have attracted her attention. It's possible she's been keeping track of you ever since your husband's death."

"She's bizarre and seriously detached from reality, but I don't think she's that crazy."

"You may be right, but I'm not willing to bet your life on it."

"What about yourself, Harry? It was no love bite that put you into Puc Puggy Creek."

Harry leaned back in his chair with a sigh and shifted his injured leg to ease the ache. "The problem with my theory about Rachel Whittaker is that if it's right, someone else must have shot me."

"Not necessarily," Gwyneth said. "If her nuttiness has gone this far in the direction you think it has, she might want to wipe out as much connected with me as possible."

A light popped on in Harry's brain. "How much does Scartole know about your first marriage?" he asked.

"Do we have to dig around in that bone pile again?" Gwyneth demanded, anger sharpening in her voice.

"Yes. I don't have the dates yet on Rachel Whittaker's calls to Avola, but if some of them were made between the time your marriage collapsed and Scartole left for Dallas, it's possible she was talking to him, at least on some of the calls."

"I suppose I may have mentioned Rachel's name. That grave-side chat we had has stayed with me."

"Can you recall whether or not Scartole showed any interest in her?"

"My husband was interested in me slash money and himself."

"And he never mentioned her after the breakup."

"I don't think so."

Harry got up.

"I've got to talk to Fairbrother, to see if I can get the dates of those calls her mother made. I'm also curious about how she came to learn of them. Fairbrother's almost as strange as her mother, and she may decide she doesn't want to tell me. Nevertheless, I'm going to try. And, Gwyneth, try to remember whether or not Scartole talked to you at all about Rachel Whittaker."

It took patience, but Harry finally succeeded in making phone contact with Fairbrother.

"This is time, Mr. Brock," she told him, "that I usually devote to reflection and meditation. Action and freedom from action are essential to good mental and emotional health. However, because I wrote to you and gave you permission to call me if need arose, I will allot fifty minutes to assisting you in any way I feel appropriate."

"Thank you, Dr. Fairbrother," Harry said, keeping all traces of comic relief out of his response. "I would like to ask you some questions about the telephone calls you refer to in your most gracious note." He paused in alarm and struggled against his almost overpowering impulse to go on mimicking her.

"Thank you, Mr. Brock, what were your responses to the note?"

"I'm very interested in your mother's telephone calls."

"Oh? Why is that?"

"Have you discussed them at all with your mother?"

"Given my mother's degree of impairment, why would anything she had to say interest you?"

"Dr. Fairbrother, may I be frank?"

"Certainly."

"Thank you. If you go on treating this as a therapy session, I'm not going to have any of my questions answered."

"How do you feel about that?"

"Very funny, Doctor."

Whittaker made an odd sound that might have been either a snicker or a choking noise. Just then Jackson began to bark hysterically.

"Please excuse me, Mr. Brock," she said in her normal voice, "I have an emergency to cope with."

A moment later Harry heard the squall of a very unhappy cat rising above the yelping of the dog. That was followed by the muffled sound of things falling to the floor, and a swishing, thumping sound Harry couldn't identify. Then a door slammed twice, and all sounds stopped together.

"I'm sorry, Mr. Brock," Fairbrother said, still breathing heavily from some sort of strenuous effort, "the goddamned dog chased the cat onto the top of the refrigerator, which is very much off limits, and I was obliged to use the broom to dislodge her, causing a certain degree of damage to things that had, hitherto, lodged on that surface. Both animals are now having a time-out in the cellar, where, with the aid of the broom and my right foot, I deposited them in a most unceremonious manner. I apologize for the interruption in our session. Please, let us begin again."

"Quite all right," Harry said, still astonished by the heartfelt *goddamned*. "You wrote that you had discussed the telephone calls with your mother."

"She refuses to admit she made them."

"Are you aware of any contact, aside from these phone calls, between your mother and anyone in Avola?"

"No."

"Has your mother shown any interest in Gwyneth Benbow over the years since Morrison Perkins' death?"

Harry was aware that the silence suggested more than a thoughtful pause.

"Amongst her memorabilia devoted to my father's memory, there is an album tracing the main events in Ms. Benbow's life. These items are, necessarily, almost entirely newspaper clippings."

Harry waited a moment to be sure his voice would be free of any of the excitement he was experiencing and said, "Why would your mother have wished to record the life of your father's second wife—especially since she was so intimately involved in the events of his death?"

"That is easily explained by the nature of her delusions. As you know, she has come to believe that my father was a great man, worthy of adoration. It naturally follows for her that in marrying him she was given a great gift, as was Ms. Benbow."

Harry digested that comment and said, "Would it also follow that your mother would see any failure on Gwyneth's part to live up to the role to which she had been committed by marrying your father as an insult to his memory?"

"Very likely, Mr. Brock, and I see where you are going with this. It is also, at a minimum, three bridges too far, to attempt to connect my mother with the death of Mr. Perez," Fairbrother responded with marked huffiness.

"I understand, Dr. Fairbrother. I am simply trying to understand your mother's state of mind."

"You may as well try to grasp St. Elmo's fire, Mr. Brock."

Harry felt certain she was smiling.

"Were we to enter her mind, which we cannot," she continued, "we would find ourselves in an unmapped land where everything is strange."

"Alice," he said.

"Perhaps, but less interesting."

"Could you look in your mother's Benbow album and find out whether or not there are any clippings or anything else referring to Ms. Benbow's affair with Henrico Perez and her subsequent divorce?"

"I will look."

"Thank you. Is there any possibility of my being given the dates of those phone calls?" Harry asked, thinking it odd that she would think her mother's mind boring.

"I think so. Knowledge of them came to us from the telephone company. I will make inquiries."

"Thank you. What brought them to your attention?"

"I'm afraid that our time is up. Perhaps you will want to visit this again at our next session."

CHAPTER 26

"It's a good thing we weren't making love," Harry told the wall as he hung up the phone, then burst out laughing.

The risk attendant on laughing out loud when one is alone is that it quickly develops a hollow sound. Laughter, like sex, is usually better shared with at least one other person. Harry knew the risk and when the laugh impulse had spent itself, he turned his attention to something else before being forced to confront the silence that reclaimed the spaces from which it had been briefly evicted.

When he stepped into the front yard, he found the shadows of the live oaks reaching across the creek to its eastern bank and decided to fill the remaining time until dinner with a visit to Tucker. There were several things he wanted to talk over with him and one or two he didn't.

Sanchez and Oh, Brother! met him as they always did where the farm road met the Hammock road, and Harry walked between them with one hand on the mule's glossy black shoulder and the other on Sanchez's head. He asked them about their day and gave them the highlights of his, including his talk with Fairbrother.

"I wonder how much of what I say you understand?" he said when he had finished.

They had reached the garden by then, and both animals stopped and looked at him. Oh, Brother! was wearing his straw hat with a white egret feather in the band and Sanchez, his red bandana collar.

"What?" Harry asked, feeling a bit uneasy.

Oh, Brother!, who had thrown up his head when he stopped and was staring down at Harry, dropped his head and gave Harry a push in the chest with his nose, shoving him back a full step. Sanchez, who was also staring hard at Harry, barked sharply.

"I'm sorry," Harry said, feeling both embarrassed and foolish, whereupon Oh, Brother! dropped his head again and this time pressed his nose against Harry and blew softly, and Sanchez, not to be outdone, pushed his nose into Harry's crotch.

"And I like you too," Harry said, extricating the dog's head from his personal equipment, and then stroking the mule's neck.

"What did you do to offend Sanchez?" Tucker asked when the little parade reached the back stoop.

"I made the mistake of speaking before thinking," Harry replied.

"The cause of much of the world's unhappiness," Tucker said, getting up from his rocker. "You've arrived just in time to help me to take the bung out of that keg of cider I was telling you about the other day."

"Is it the one with the dash of lemon juice in it?"

"Yes, it's in the barn. I didn't dare keep it in the house."

"You mean you were afraid it would explode?" he asked with a laugh.

"No, it gets too hot in the house. The day temperature in the barn is always six or eight degrees cooler. And I've got it located so the air can move around it, which also helps."

Tucker kept the roof of the old barn with its mortise and tenon-pegged construction well shingled, but with the exception of Oh, Brother's box stall, with its windows fitted with wooden shutters, the rest of the structure he left open to the elements, to give free access to the on-and offshore winds.

"There it is," Tucker said, having stopped in the tool shed to arm Harry with a small crowbar and a crack hammer, which Harry said looked like a small sledgehammer.

"Just the thing for driving bungs," Tucker told him, picking up the gallon jug and the bucket containing two glass mugs that he had set down to choose the tools. "When the bung gives," he warned Harry, "the cider's going to be right behind it. That's where the pail comes in. Then, when we tip the keg upright, which we'll do as fast as we can, we can drive in the spigot."

"Sounds simple enough," Harry said, looking at the large keg in its frame. "How much does it weigh?"

"Hmm," Tucker said, rubbing his chin. "Let's see, that's a big keg. It's about half a hogshead in volume. I'd say it will run about two hundred and fifty pounds, plus the oak barrel."

"We should try not to drop it on a foot," Harry said, rapidly losing enthusiasm for what lay ahead.

"There are several things we shouldn't do with it," Tucker replied, "chief of which is not let it fall on the floor, because if we do, it will burst like a ripe watermelon, and there goes a whole summer of drinking cider. Not a prospect that pleases."

"No, how do we go about this?"

"You see that bung in this end of the barrel? We're going to start that with the crowbar. Then, when it blows—and it will blow because of the fermentation left in the cider when I drove the bung in—we're going to heave this end of it up and let it slide down the planks I've put back there. When it stops, you'll drive in the spigot with the crack hammer. Then while you're holding this end of the planks, I'll pull away the rack it was lying in, and you'll lower the barrel into the frame.

"Oh, one thing," Tucker continued, "Don't be standing in front of that bung when it blows. Getting shot once a year is enough."

"I'm beginning to understand why I'm carrying the crowbar," Harry said.

"You'll be fine," Tucker said. "By the way, did you walk over?"

"Yes, why?"

"Just curious."

Harry doubted that but set to work. The bung came out in an explosion of cider, flew across the barn like a missile, and struck the wall with a loud crack. The bung missed Harry, but the cider didn't.

"You asked me if I'd walked over because you didn't want me driving home soaked with cider, that's it, isn't it?" Harry asked when he had driven in the spigot and was pulling off his shirt in order to wring it out.

"Yes and no," Tucker said. "I wasn't really prepared for that much cider doing what it did. The bucket turned out to be a failure. We lost most of what squirted out, which is too bad. Let's get this barrel laid down so that we can draw a couple of mugs and find out what we've got here."

They secured the barrel in its new rack and Tucker drew a couple of inches in each of the mugs. "Leave the tools," he said. "Try this."

Harry was astonished by how good it tasted. "Tucker," he said, "it was worth losing the Garden to get this."

"Sacrilegious, but thank you, I think you're right. We'll have better testing after I draw a gallon and get it into the refrigerator to chill and settle. It's pretty wild right now."

Using Tucker's shower, Harry washed most of the cider out of his hair, and with a towel tied around his waist went back to the stoop to sit down, encouraged to find his eyelids were no longer sticking together. Tucker had placed a tall glass of lemonade beside his chair.

"The flies were beginning to take an interest in you," Tucker said as Harry sat down and gratefully took a sip of his lemonade.

"I've got a peculiar situation," Harry said, turning to the subject that had brought him to Tucker's in the first place.

"By my count you've got at least a baker's dozen," the old farmer said, "but go ahead."

"Do you recall my mentioning Rachel Whittaker?"

"Morrison Perkins' first wife. Didn't she turn up at his funeral?"

"She did, and her daughter just told me she learned that her mother has been making calls to Gwyneth and to call boxes in Avola. I'm waiting to find out if the calls were made before Perez was shot."

"The daughter's a psychiatrist, isn't she?"

"Yes."

"Isn't the mother of unsound mind?" Tucker asked, showing surprise.

"Well, how unsound is the question I need answered. Before Rosamund, a whole case study herself if you ask me, told me what her mother had been doing, I thought the woman was so incapacitated that she needed a minder twenty-four seven. Now, I don't know what to think."

"Although I can probably guess, you haven't said what the phone calls mean or might mean," Tucker said.

"Rachel Whittaker has been keeping an album of newspaper clippings, tracing Gwyneth's life from her marriage to Perkins to the present," Harry said, noting Tucker's quickness. "Her daughter says it means nothing more than that her mother's obsession with Perkins includes anyone who has had an intimate relationship with him."

"Do you think it likely that she shot Gwyneth Benbow?"

"It entered my mind that, unlikely as it sounds, she may have been the instigating intelligence behind the shootings of Perez,

Gwyneth, and me."

"Cleaning the plate, so to speak."

"Removing the stains that have sullied her husband's memory, yes."

"Acknowledging the strangeness of human behavior, I still find it a very long stretch," Tucker said. "Do you suppose that cider is chilled enough to sample?"

"There's only one way to find out," Harry said, finishing his lemonade and holding out the empty glass toward Tucker, who was already on his feet.

"I've got two mugs in the freezer, ready and waiting," he said, taking Harry's glass and disappearing into the kitchen.

Harry leaned his head against the back of the rocker and lost himself in thought. But his mind had reverted to Holly and not Rachel Whittaker. It was not an altogether pleasant reverie. Yes, he had put a patch of flowers and love-making on their quarrel, but the issues that had led to it were being carefully avoided.

Because of that, thinking about her brought on the kind of heartache he had hoped not to have to endure again. In fact, he recalled all too clearly that, having lost two wives and a lover, he had sworn on a mentally accumulated stack of Bibles that he would never expose himself to that agony again.

Now look where he was! In love with Holly Pike and probably incapable of giving her what any woman in her position had every right to expect. Wouldn't it make sense, be fairer to her, to sever the connection now, endure the pain, then seal himself off permanently from this kind of torment?

Tucker, shouldering open the screen door that had a squeaky hinge, announced bravely, "This will be the test that counts. On your feet."

Harry made it to his feet—relieved at being delivered from his thoughts—and took the proffered mug. The mugs were sparkling with frost, and the amber liquid that Harry could glimpse through the melted spots on the sides glinted like very old gold.

"Here's to the girl's sister," Tucker said, raising his mug.

"To the sister," Harry said, deciding not to recite the couplet.

A quiet moment followed while both men drank, watched with interest by Oh, Brother! and Sanchez from a sanctuary of shady grass just beyond the stoop.

"When did you drive in the bung on this?" Harry asked, staring reverently into his half-empty mug.

"Last October twenty-second," Tucker said quietly as if they were conversing in a cathedral.

"Mark it on your calendar as a day of thanksgiving," Harry said, holding up his mug to the light and staring at it as if it held the answer to all life's questions.

"It must have been the lemon," Tucker said. "Either that or, passing by, Pan brushed the apples with his fingers."

"To Pan," Harry said and both men emptied their mugs.

When Harry reached home, he found a message from Rosamund Fairbrother waiting for him.

"Mr. Brock," she said, "I had hoped to find you at home. If you receive this before seven this evening, please call me. I have the information you requested, but I prefer to give it to you in person."

Harry glanced at his watch, then picked up the phone.

"Perhaps you will wish to write these dates down," she said, having answered and heard his voice.

"Go ahead," Harry said and began writing.

"That is all the calls my mother made to Avola," she said when she reached the end of the list, "so far as the company can tell."

Harry saw at once that they had, in fact, all been made after the date on which Gwyneth's affair with Perez was reported by the media and ended just before the divorce decree was issued.

There were thirteen calls in all, half a dozen made to Gwyneth and the remainder, Harry assumed, to public telephones. But he intended to have them chased down by Jim's people.

"Do you know whether or not your mother made any calls, following the date of Ms. Benbow's divorce, to a Dallas, Texas, number?"

"*Dallas!* My mother knows no one in Dallas," Fairbrother responded, obviously offended.

"It's Eric Scartole's home. He returned to Dallas soon after the divorce."

"Mr. Brock, it is becoming tiresome to reassure you that my mother has had no contact with Mr. Scartole," Fairbrother said, making her irritation evident.

"Dr. Fairbrother, forgive my reminding you, but you were equally sure your mother had not been calling anyone in Avola."

There was a lengthy silence.

"I must admit, Mr. Brock, that I was exceedingly troubled to learn she had been making calls without my being aware of what she was doing as well as deeply troubled by her refusal to admit that she had made them."

"I'm sorry. If it's any comfort, Gwyneth Benbow insists the calls were harmless. She has not told me their exact content, but I gather they focused on her relationship with your father."

"That is of some help. Thank you for sharing the information with me."

There was another pause. Then she said, "But what else has she been doing and why?"

"Would you be willing to ask the phone company to check for Dallas calls?"

"To what end?"

It was Harry's turn to hesitate. "I can't say much about that because it is part of the Tequesta County's ongoing investigation into the death of Henrico Perez and the Gwyneth Benbow shooting." He decided to leave himself out of the equation for the moment.

"Yes, I understand. Do I have your assurance that my mother's name will continue to be kept away from the press?"

"I can give you a qualified yes, but in the end the unfolding of the investigation will determine the answer."

"Very well, I'll make the call."

"And about the album," Harry said, as mildly as possible.

"Ah, yes, the album. Yes, she has some clippings from your local paper that refer to Ms. Benbow's marriage to Mr. Scartole and some later dealing with her affair as well as a report on the issuance of the divorce decree. And there is an entry in my mother's hand, which reads, 'A disgraceful end to an unworthy relationship.' "

"And that's it?"

"That's it, as you put it. And I hope that our business in now concluded."

"It may be, but as I said earlier, Dr. Fairbrother, the investigation is not yet over."

CHAPTER 27

Harry spent a restless night, having picked up again the miserable theme of leaving Holly that degenerated into an unsatisfactory debate with himself, hampered by the cynical audience of one, seated in the shadows at the rear of the auditorium, who kept breaking in to remind both sides that in all probability Holly had already severed the connection and was even now seeking a replacement.

Never had the dawn been more welcome to Harry than this one, and at its first graying, he flung himself to his feet as if escaping from a bed of nails. In the end, the cynic had won, and Harry decided he had to find out whether or not he had been consigned to the rubbish heap.

Punishing himself further, Harry made a pot of coffee in the half-light with the dawn chorus ringing in his ears and drank a cup. When he had come downstairs, his eyes felt as if they were full of sand and his mouth tasted like a slit trench. The coffee did nothing for his eyes, but it scoured his mouth and crushed all thoughts of breakfast.

Taking his twelve gauge pump gun out of its closet, Harry checked to see if there was a shell in the chamber and if the safety was on. Because it was far too early to call Holly, he decided to put in an hour or two walking the Hammock. The walk would kill some time, but it also was part of his warden's responsibilities to make sure orchid and other poachers were staying clear of the Hammock. The only way to do that was to make frequent checks.

Sore leg or not, Harry looked forward to the walk. He enjoyed keeping up with the teeming life on the Hammock, and early morning was one of his favorite times of the day to be outside, provided that he was equipped with insect repellent, a long-sleeved shirt, and full-length trousers, tied at the ankles, to frustrate ticks and other creeping and crawling blood and meat eaters.

His plan was to walk the sand road to its end at the flooded cypress forest of the Stickpen Preserve, then turn west and slowly make his way in a long arc back to the house. For the most part he would be on trails of his own making, but if something interested him, he would leave the trail and steer by the sun. In this part of Florida, the sun was nearly a constant companion. His walk beside the creek was pleasant but uneventful, and when he reached the spot where the remains of the cabin were located and where Tucker had found the carcass of the deer the monitor lizard had been scavenging, he did what he often did when coming this way.

He stopped and allowed himself to remember Katherine Trachey, who had moved into this cabin with her two children after the death of her husband, who had abandoned her. She had traced him as far as the Hammock and stopped at Harry's place to ask directions. She was too late. Will Trachey had been killed. The upshot of it all was that Harry married her and adopted her children, and then she and Harry had a child of their own. But after several years, she left him because she could no longer bear the strain of living with a man frequently in danger of being killed, and he would not give up his work.

He stood for a few minutes, staring at the destroyed cabin, remembering the half-starved young woman with two worn children in tow, who had appeared at his door that long-ago morning.

A sudden clamor of a small raft of outraged mottled ducks, rising wildly from the water and scattering as they rose, jumped him out of his musings. He turned toward the creek in time to see a very large red-tailed hawk strike down a Louisiana heron in an explosion of feathers. The heron, which had been wading in the creek's shallows, was killed instantly by the force of the hawk's plunge, one of its talons, Harry guessed, having been driven all the way to the heron's heart.

Trampling the already dead bird, the hawk gave a scream of defiance as if daring Harry to try to take away its prey. Its broad and powerful wings beating heavily, the bird rose slowly from the creek and bore the heron away, leaving a scattering of white and gray feathers on the slowly moving black water, to briefly memorialize the event.

Harry had lived far too long in close contact with the natural world to be distressed by the scene he had just witnessed, but the suddenness of the attack and the ducks' wild cries had set his heart hammering. There was a moment on seeing the end of the hawk's stoop when his impulse was to shoot the attacker. But it was over in a moment, and he slipped the gun back into the bend of his left arm and even smiled at his response to the sudden burst of rapidly fading adrenalin that had exploded through his system.

His walk was uneventful until he was moving through a quiet grassy opening in the woods about three-quarters of the way along the arc of his return. The grassy space had probably been caused by the collapse of at least two of the huge hardwoods making up this section of the Hammock. Their fall, either due to lightning strikes or a storm burst, must have occurred many years ago because there were no remaining traces of the once towering giants.

The glade was one of Harry's favorite spots along this path, and he paused to look around and wonder why the opening had not grown over and why there was no bird or cricket song. A moment later he heard something heavy thrashing in the bushes that marked the edge of the clearing to his right. Moving slowly in that direction, he no longer had to wonder why it was so quiet, but he very much wanted to know what was causing the disturbance.

It seemed likely, he thought, that whatever was creating the racket had heard him and stopped long enough to decide he was not an object of interest. The grass around him was chest high, and the new growth, concealing whatever was going on, was dense and another ten feet in height. He carefully backed out of the clearing and into the shade of the tall trees and began to walk slowly around the clearing so as to come up on the dense growth from the forest side.

He had not gone far before he located the disturbance and approached it slowly. The slashing and thrashing sounds had picked up again, and now he could see the tops of the saplings in one area swaying and crashing into one another as if they were being violently shaken. But Harry still could not see far enough into the trees to discover what was happening there.

Wise or not, he decided he was going to solve the mystery or . . . He chose not to complete that thought and went forward slowly and quietly. The air under the large trees was scarcely moving, except for erratic puffs of wind rattling twigs and leaves in the dense canopy. He had worked his way to within about thirty feet of the densest section when one of the vagrant breezes swept around him from behind and bent the saplings in its passing.

For a moment, the sounds in front of him ceased, and then something large and in a hurry began crashing toward him. Harry backed away, to give himself as much distance as possible from whatever was coming, wondering if his curiosity had gotten ahead of his judgment. But he didn't have time to think about that because in the next instant a very large monitor, its head and neck drenched with blood, broke through the last of the screening shrubs, its long, twisting body coming straight at Harry.

Firmly resisting the inclination to just get the hell out of there, Harry raised the shotgun almost to his shoulder and watched the appalling creature plunge toward him, jaws agape. Harry's purpose in waiting was not to test his mettle but to concentrate the buckshot as much as possible. When the monitor was within fifteen feet, he raised the gun's butt to his shoulder and fired.

The racing lizard ran straight into the charge, killing it instantly, but, as with the first one, the animal's body, somersaulting toward Harry and smashing to the ground almost at his feet, continued to writhe and buck as if possessed of a life of its own.

Just like a snake, Harry thought with revulsion as he moved around the dead animal and followed its trail into the thick growth. Another breeze rattled the leaves, bringing with it an unmistakable stench, but Harry went ahead and found the remains of a doe hanging in a wire noose, surrounded by a humming and buzzing cloud of flies. She had been pregnant and very close to delivery. The monitor had torn open her stomach, and the remains of the unborn fawns were scattered on the ground, along with a twisted coil of her intestines.

Having used his cell to photograph the dead deer and the scene, he turned his attention to the spring snare that had caught the deer and strangled her. His rising fury was not directed at the monitor, which had been doing what it was born to do, but at whoever had set this wretched device and then gone away and not come back to check on it. One end of the wire was around the deer's neck and the other end attached to a three-inch-thick sapling that been bent down, trimmed of its branches and fastened with a second wire to a notch cut into the trunk of another tree in such a way that the deer's struggle would free the second wire, allowing the sapling to spring up and at least partially lift the deer off the ground.

Lacking an axe, Harry placed the barrel of his shotgun a few inches from the sapling and blew it in half. Then he unfastened the choke wire at both ends, rolled it up, and laid it on the ground. He took several more pictures, two of the now quiescent monitor. That done, he picked up the roll of wire, slid it over his arm, and left.

Once home, Harry phoned his contact at the Fish and Game Department, made his report, forwarded the pictures, and said that he would mail the wire. That done, he cleaned the shotgun and then took a second shower, dressed, and with a great deal of misgiving, drove to The Oaks.

"The more civilized element in this community calls before making a visit," Holly said without looking at him. She was dressed in her work clothes, jodhpurs, riding boots, short-sleeved white shirt, and dark glasses, watching Sunday River as Buster led him around the exercise yard. Because he was still saddled, Harry guessed Holly had just finished riding him.

"Is anything wrong with him?" he asked when he grew tired of being ignored.

"Does he look sick to you?" she demanded, finally looking at him, an action that brought Harry no comfort.

"If he lies down and won't or can't get up, you should worry."

"Buster," she said sharply, "that's enough. Wash him, then walk him, dry, and box him."

Turning to Harry, she said, "You come with me," and strode away toward the shaded part of the drive leading to the house, slapping her riding crop against her leg as she went, forcing Harry to consider the possibility that things might soon become much worse than they already were.

"Running isn't currently in my tool kit," he called after her.

"Who cares?" she said without looking back or slackening her pace.

Then, stepping into the shade, she spun on her heels, planted her fists on her hips, and said loudly, "Where the hell have you been?"

"On the Hammock, mostly," he said. "Earlier this morning I was running a check on the back part . . ."

"I don't want to hear it. I thought we'd made up!"

"Well, yes, I guess we did."

"Don't you know?"

What Harry did know, was the nature of the country ahead. It was dry, desolate, populated with biting insects. All that grew there were thorn bushes, and under them were poisonous snakes.

"You said we needed a time-out," he said somewhat feebly, aware that no answer would be the right one.

"Road apples! There are protocols covering these situations, goddamn it! Is it any damned wonder your women leave you?"

"I don't think protocols had even a minor role in those troubles," he said.

"Don't get smart with me, Harry!"

She had moved up so that her face, which was very red, was about a foot from his. The smell of her warm body, heated from riding, filled his nostrils, seriously upsetting the stability of his system.

"You've made a mistake," Harry said, only half his mind on what he was saying. "Buster's giving Sandy River a bath, and then he's going to rub him down, and after that . . ."

She snapped off her glasses, glared at him, and said, "Why do you think I'm standing this close to you?"

In the midst of their wrangling, Nip had trotted up, alert and with his ears cocked. He was not wagging his tail and he was watching Harry closely.

"We have company," Harry said.

"Don't try to change the subject."

"Okay, I was going to pull you against me just hard enough not to hurt you or, maybe, only a little, to convince you of how aroused I've become being so close to you, but now Nip's arrived, and I feel confident that were I to grab you, I would get my good leg torn off."

"What if I told him to sit down?"

"He can leap from a sitting position. I've seen him do it."

"If I promised to call him off?"

"Forget it."

"Plan B: Assault me slowly. Pretend we're both naked in a bath of #50 oil."

"I keep thinking about the dog."

"Harry," she said, her voice dropping in pitch and friendliness.

A growl began to rumble in Nip's chest.

"All right, all right, I'm starting," he said, looking into her eyes and trying not to think of the dog.

When he had pulled her against him, she very slowly raised her arms and folded them around his neck. With nightmare slowness he tipped his head forward and pressed his lips against hers. By this point in the negotiations, Harry had forgotten about Nip because Holly was pressed against him from knees to mouth, and he was experiencing no difficulty in imagining the oil bath.

The kiss went on so long that when they broke apart, they both gasped like divers breaking into the air at the last possible moment.

They were greeted by loud whistles and cheering from the staff of Number One Barn.

"You told me they weren't watching," Harry said when he found he could speak.

"I lied," she said calmly, breaking into a wide smile. "Let's give them a bow."

Grasping him by his right hand, she spun him around, doing his bad leg no good. "On the count of three," she said. "Three."

And they very slowly, maintaining the spirit of the thing, gave their audience a deep bow, which earned them a round of applause.

Walking back to the house, her arm linked through his and with Nip leading the way, Harry said, "It was thinking of you in an oil bath that gave me the courage to carry it off."

"You were lucky, you know. Nip was trained to protect me," Holly said, smiling sweetly at him.

"I thought you knew what you were doing," Harry said.

"Well, I knew I wanted you to kiss me."

"Do you think we'll do this often?"

"Which of three possible antecedents for *this* do you have in mind?"

"My thinking hasn't taken me that far."

"Then assuming we'll make it to all three, the answer is, 'More than likely.' "

"Am I getting a little old for it?"

"You'll be a lot older when I'm done with you."

CHAPTER 28

It was Thahn who gave Harry the best advice he had to date as to his situation. He had finished having a long lunch with Holly and was leaving. Thahn met him at the foot of the stairs and did what he had never done before. He stopped Harry and put a comforting hand on his shoulder. "Harry," he said in a serious voice, "if you are to have a life worth living, you must cultivate inner peace."

"Easily said, Thahn," Harry said, slightly puzzled, but also wondering if Thahn was making a joke.

"True. Begin by accepting that she will outlive you."

"Do I look ill?" Harry asked, more suspicious.

"No, perhaps a bit fatigued, but before going into combat, you must accept all that may happen to you. That done, anticipation of pain and death can then be put out of your mind, allowing you to go forward, prepared for battle."

With that, Thahn, who was a man of indefinite age but, Harry knew, much older than he, gave Harry's shoulder a squeeze and a slight shake and walked away.

"Thahn . . ." Harry said, but the man kept walking and was soon out of sight.

Harry experienced several fairly strong responses in rapid succession but, a moment later, they were all swept away by his sudden understanding of what Thahn had told him.

"What was that all about?" Holly called down from the gallery.

Harry looked up at her, leaning over the railing, held in place by her sudden radiance.

"You're going to outlive me," he said.

Harry was inclined to go on pursuing Rachel Whittaker's calls to Gwyneth and people unknown in that critical period between the exposure of Gwyneth's affair and her being shot. He had thought the matter through enough to feel almost certain that Whittaker was somehow involved in that shooting. But there was the troubling matter of the unidentified numbers that she had called. Jim had sent them to the investigating team, but the results had not yet come back—for all the usual delays plaguing an understaffed, underfunded department.

Until he had the names attached to those numbers, he was stymied.

"Complaining is not going to help," Tucker had told him.

He had received the same sympathetic response from Holly, who was now out of reach at another breeders meeting, this one in Bozeman. "Bozeman!" Harry had protested.

"Have you ever been there?"

"No."

"Then don't knock it. The mountains are wonderful and the Absarokas are spectacular."

"What kind of name is Absaroka?" he demanded, sulking because he wasn't going with her, and was already seeing tall, lean, wind-burned men in ten gallon hats converging on her in a barroom. She was wearing a white deerskin shirt, cut deeply in front, standing at the bar with one foot on the rail, drinking whiskey out of a shot glass. A man in a striped shirt with black armbands was playing the piano . . .

"Native American people from that area," she told him in a superior tone of voice, dispersing his fantasy. "People like you, who haven't been there, probably know them as the Crow Nation. Is that name familiar to you?"

Well, he had asked for it.

After that stimulating experience, he decided to take a trip of his own, this one to Kevin Mulvane's boatyard. Mulvane greeted him in a friendly manner by offering him a slice of the Gala apple he was eating, holding it out to him between his thumb and the blade of his jackknife, which he was using to cut up the apple.

"Not bad for a store apple," he said, chewing while he spoke. "Usually, they taste like a drugstore by this time of year."

"Thanks," Harry said, thinking it was wiser to eat the slice than to ask what the knife had been used for—scraping out dirt from under dirty fingernails had occurred to him—or to turn down the offer.

"You worry about what's sprayed on apples nowadays?" Mulvane asked while chewing and beaming down on Harry.

"I usually peel mine," Harry said.

"No use, Harry," Mulvane said, shaking his head and frowning. "What's going to get you is going to get you. What brings you out here?"

"I've got some more questions to ask Hank Tolliver. All right if I go over there and talk to him?"

Mulvane had given up on the knife and bitten into the apple. "Too late," he said, wiping his chin with the back of his hand.

"What's happened to him?" Harry asked, alarmed by the news.

"Nothing, so far as I know, but a few days ago he came by and gave his notice. I put one of my nephews in the boathouse. He'll do until school opens. Then I'll have to think about someone permanent. You know anybody sober daytimes who might be interested?" He stopped chewing to grin and say, "It would help if he had a little duck in him."

"Did Tolliver find another job?"

"Not to my knowledge. Course, he's tight-mouthed as a cat about his doings."

"Is it possible that he's persuaded his wife to let him stop working so they can qualify for Medicaid or some other federal health program for the destitute?"

Mulvane shook his head. "I know Myra Emily Tolliver fairly well from back when she had her health," he said. "She's got a poker in her back and a head hard as blue rock. She'd never back off."

Harry shook hands with Mulvane and left, determined to chase Hank Tolliver down. He still had questions to ask him, and he recalled something Tolliver had said the last time they talked, something he had let pass at the time, thinking it was of no relevance to the inquiry.

"Then I guess you really meant it when you said you and your wife were expecting an improvement soon," Harry said although Tolliver was still glowering at him.

They were standing on Tolliver's unpainted front steps. Harry's reception at the house had not been gracious.

Tolliver ignored the gambit. Stepping out onto the landing and pulling the door shut behind him, he demanded, "What the fuck do you want?"

"Five or ten minutes of your time if you can spare them?" Harry had backed down two steps to keep from being pushed.

"You want some more hospital time?"

"Not hardly, Mr. Tolliver," Harry said, "but counting myself, three people have been shot by what may be the same person. It's been very difficult, however, to find any connection among the three of us that would lead anyone to want to kill us."

"Why are you telling me this?" Tolliver asked, his scowl deepening. "Do you think I've got something to do with your being shot?"

"No. But because he kept his boat in Mulvane's boat storage, you had more contact with Eric Scartole during the period when his wife's affair with Henrico Perez broke into the news than almost anyone else I know of, aside from his friends at the club."

"Then you do think he killed Perez and tried to kill his wife," Tolliver said, showing some interest.

"Right now, what I'm trying to do is to establish as best I can that he couldn't have shot them, and I'm making some progress."

"Where do I come in?"

"If I can prove he was not in Avola when the shootings occurred, I will pretty well lay to rest any suspicion that he was involved in the attacks on his wife and Perez."

Tolliver stared at Harry, chewing on his bottom lip, apparently thinking.

"What about you?" he said finally.

"What reason," Harry asked, "would he have for shooting me?"

Tolliver's eyes narrowed and his lips widened in an unpleasant smile. "Maybe whoever done it was laying a false trail. You think of that?"

"No, but it's a big risk . . ."

"I'm moving on, Brock," he said, "might be best if you did too."

"All right," Harry said, backing awkwardly down the remaining steps to the cinder path. "I hope you and your wife find a way to help her."

Tolliver was halfway back in the house when he stopped and turned, his face dark and contorted in a spasm of emotion that, whatever its source, chilled Harry with its intensity. "My wife is my business, Brock."

★ ★ ★ ★ ★

Four days later, Harry was sitting in Jim Snyder's office, reviewing the progress or lack of it in the three shootings. It was turning into a glum meeting. Even Hodges hadn't found anything to
laugh at.

"Am I the only one who thinks it odd that Hank Tolliver's
quit his job with Kevin Mulvane but hasn't applied for food
stamps? Because Mulvane said he quit, I'm assuming he doesn't
qualify for unemployment insurance."

"That's right," Hodges said at once. "I've got a nephew who
had a beef with a supervisor and got huffy and quit. Now, in
this job market, goodbye paycheck, goodbye compensation, and
goodbye chances for getting another job."

"Why should we find anything Hank Tolliver does interesting," Jim demanded, kicking back his chair from the desk. He
got up and began pacing, rubbing his head vigorously.

"Be careful, Captain," Hodges said, grinning at Harry, his
round face beaming, "you might set your hair on fire."

"Not funny, Frank," Jim said. "Put your mind to work on
these assaults, will you?"

Hodges' face fell, but not far. It was too round and cheerful
to express remorse with any conviction.

"He's got a very sick wife in need of an organ transplant they
can't afford," Harry said in response to Jim's dismissive question. "Why is he quitting now? According to Mulvane, Mrs. Tolliver would never agree to their going into complete financial
dependency in order to get the transplant."

"Harry," Jim said, halting in front of him and frowning down
from his considerable height, "the Tollivers are people you don't
know anything about. You may think you know them, but you
don't. I do. I grew up amongst them, and something I learned
early on is that trying to figure out why they do things is a
waste of time. Something else I learned is that it's no good ask-

281

ing them because they won't tell you."

"Jim, I can't bring myself to believe," Harry said, trying to conceal his irritation, "that Hank Tolliver quit work for no reason or that he suddenly made up his mind to sit in his house and starve to death when his credit ran out."

"I can understand that," Hodges said, "but I also know what the Captain's talking about. My people came from somewhere up in those mountains. And there was a story in our family that I heard from my grandmother. It went like this: The Griswold family had lived alongside my Gramma's folk for twenty years that she knew about. They was good neighbors, minded their own business, and helped out when called on. Then one day just after harvesting their corn and with no explanation to anyone, they pulled their house down, loaded the boards onto a wagon, herded up their pigs, whistled in their dogs, put their cat and belongings in the other wagon, counted the kids, and moved 'round onto the other side of the mountain."

Harry started to say something, then didn't. There are situations in which there is no contending. Harry thought this was one of them.

"But there's no need to become discouraged, Harry," Jim said quickly in an upbeat voice. "You've got an interesting lead in those phone calls Rachel Whittaker made to Avola, even if we still don't know who she was calling."

"Aside from Gwyneth Benbow, of course," Hodges put in, "or Mrs. Perez."

Both men were looking at Harry with concerned expressions.

"When are we going to have that information?" Harry asked, uncomfortable with their scrutiny. *Why are they looking at me like that? A stranger in a strange land,* he thought. Who said that? He had said it about Samia Perez.

"They're promised but they're not here," Jim said in a resigned voice.

"Let me know, will you, when they do arrive?" Harry asked. Thinking of Samia had jiggled something in his mind, and he left Jim's office planning to call her.

More thought led him to the conclusion that he would probably get more information from either Alex or Basma—if he talked to them separately—than he would from Samia, who might even resent further questioning.

A maid answered his call and told him that Alex had returned to the university but that Basma was still at home. He asked to speak to her.

"Mr. Brock," she said, "how can I help?"

"Have the police talked with you?"

"Oh, not the question I expected. Yes, they have."

"Would you be willing to talk with me again?"

"Of course. I enjoyed our last conversation. Don't expect, however, to learn anything new. I don't have anything new to tell. Would this afternoon work for you?"

Harry said it would, and they settled on a time.

When he reached the Perez house, Basma and not the maid answered the door. He had expected another version of Samia, but Basma, aside from the black hair, which she wore short, was quite different in appearance from her mother, taller and more athletic. She had her mother's arresting eyes, and following her into a living room, Harry saw that she moved with her mother's grace.

"This is a very nice room," Harry said when he was seated, "but it doesn't hold a candle to your mother's."

Basma laughed and looked around at the pastel-colored furniture, the silk flowers in a tall vase on the glass coffee table, tile floor beyond the area rug, and the white Bermuda shutters.

"Florida blah," she said, turning back to Harry with a smile. "As for my mother's room, I haven't decided whether it's a museum, a shrine, or a mausoleum."

"It is a beautiful room," Harry said, surprised at feeling defensive, "but it's only complete when your mother's in it."

"Oh, ho!" Basma said, sitting forward in her chair, "Look out, Mr. Brock, or I will think you are falling in love with my mother."

All this gaiety, Harry thought. *In benefit of what? Drawing boundaries? Marking territory?*

"It would be very easy to do," he said mildly. "She's a beautiful and extremely interesting woman."

"Yes, isn't she?" Basma said, settling back, the smile fading.

"Have you ever met Eric Scartole?" Harry asked.

"What makes you think I might have?"

"It was a question, not an accusation. Have you?"

"No."

Harry noted that another Basma was emerging. "But you do know who he is."

"Yes."

"Did he confront your father and threaten to kill him?"

"What makes you think such a thing?"

"Not an answer, Ms. Perez."

"No," she said, leaning forward again, serious this time, hands folded, her forearms resting on her knees. "My father is dead, Mr. Brock. Nothing can change that, not arresting and punishing the perpetrator of the crime, nothing."

"That's true," Harry said, "and your refusal to answer my question has something to do with your determination to protect your mother. Am I right?"

"Yes."

"And where your mother is concerned, you consider yourself to be the best judge of what she wants?"

"Be careful, Mr. Brock. I am not an Algerian displaced person. One single step too far, and I will have your license."

"Neither is your mother," Harry said, unperturbed. "She is not either defined or contained by any trivializing category. As for threats, empty or otherwise, they are not worthy of your intelligence."

"And poking around in the wreckage of this family is scarcely worthy of a self-respecting man."

"Very quick, Basma. What did he do?"

The quick shift in approach seemed to rattle Basma. She sat staring at him, silent.

"I'm on your side in this," he told her quietly.

"Mr. Brock," she began, but Harry interrupted her.

"Call me Harry," he said. "The less clutter, the better."

"All right," she said. "And if I tell you?"

"It will advance the investigation substantially."

"And if the media gets hold of it, it will become one more public humiliation for my mother."

Harry could not stifle a sigh. "There's no question, Basma," he said, "that if it's what I think it is, and if the information is leaked, it will be milked for all they can get out of it. No question at all, but . . ." He extended his hand toward her in an abbreviated pushing motion. "But Captain Snyder and his team have a compelling reason for keeping the information secret."

"And that is?" she asked.

Harry made a decision and said, "You must not breathe a word of what I'm going to tell you to anyone, not even your brother. If you do, you will seriously jeopardize the investigation. It will reveal the direction the investigation is taking to those who up until now have been considering themselves safe."

"Do you mean, Harry, that all of these shootings are connected?"

"Almost certainly. He did confront your father, didn't he?" In for a nickel, in for a dollar, he decided, thinking he would get more from Basma if he persuaded her that he trusted her and was making her part of the process he had been describing.

"Why do you think that?"

"Because for much less incentive than he had regarding your father, he flew all the way from Dallas to Avola after I telephoned his mother and tried to take my head off."

"All the evidence suggests he failed or else you stitched it back on," she said, unable to stifle a smile.

Harry laughed, then said, "How did your father come out of his encounter?"

The smile vanished.

"My father was sitting at his desk in his study when Mr. Scartole arrived. Mother said she heard Mr. Scartole shouting obscenities at him, and as she was approaching the door, it burst open and Mr. Scartole was backing out of it, followed by my father, holding his service revolver.

"Mother said it was the first time she had ever seen it. Mr. Scartole left, obviously still very angry."

"Your mother told me guns were not allowed in her house, that she had seen enough of guns in Algeria."

Basma actually laughed. "From what Mother told me, I gather that before she was done with him, Father probably wished he was still confronting Mr. Scartole."

"That was the only encounter between your father and Scartole?"

"As far as I know."

"I suppose you didn't tell the investigating team about this event."

"No."

"Were you asked specifically if Scartole had confronted your father?"

Basma frowned. "I don't think so."

"Good, but if you were, you must tell them the truth. There are very severe penalties for withholding relevant information in a murder investigation."

"Who decides what is and what isn't relevant?"

"In this case Harley Dillon, the assistant state attorney for Florida's 21ˢᵗ district."

"Sounds impressive."

"He's an impressive individual. Don't let your schooling go to your head."

"Now you sound like my mother."

"I'll take that as a compliment."

"Harry, I don't want her hurt any more than she has been already," Basma said.

"Neither do I. But she wants whoever killed your father found. Can you accept that?"

"Can I?"

"I think so because, in all fairness to your mother, you must."

CHAPTER 29

After leaving Basma, Harry called Holly.

"Can you take off a couple of hours?" he said when she answered. "There's something I want to show you."

His reason for calling really was that he wanted to talk to someone he could safely open up to about where he was in the investigation. He could have talked to Tucker, but Tucker wasn't Holly.

"I've already seen it," Holly said in a way that made her sound as if she was throwing a javelin. There was pause while Holly did something accompanied by the squeaking of leather being stressed, followed by a loud, "Oof," followed an even louder, "Idiot!"

"Would you like some privacy?" he asked, baffled by what he was hearing.

"It's Scotsman," she said between gasps for breath, "he's been walking on his hind legs for the last five minutes, and I've been half out of my stirrups because I thought the damned fool might fall on me. He's on four feet at the moment."

Harry repeated his question.

"I'll need half an hour."

It was more like fifty-five minutes, but Harry spent the time with Nip, playing tug of war under the oaks with six feet of very thick nylon rope, knotted at each end. By the time Holly appeared in a white sundress and matching sandals and hat, Harry was certain his arms had been stretched an inch.

"He beats me every time," she said, getting into the Rover, "usually by pulling me off my feet. Where are we going?"

"Tern State Park and you are lovely."

"Thank you, where is it?"

"On the coast."

"That narrows the spot to about two thousand miles."

"It's in the northwest corner of Tequesta County, and about ten miles above Avola."

"Why are we going there?"

"The tide will have been turned for about half an hour. The rest is a secret."

They left their sandals in the Rover and walked down a winding, sandy trail through a mixture of sea oats, cabbage palms—their fronds clattering in the breeze off the water—saw palmetto, sea grapes, and the occasional tall spike of white-flowering Spanish sword.

"I forget how beautiful this is," Holly said, pausing to look through the thin screen of palms and brush at the sweep of brilliant white sand and blue-green water. There was a moderate chop, creating waves enough to draw an ever-shifting boundary of white surf between the sea and shore.

"Once I'm here, I love it, but I don't come nearly often enough," Harry said. "Keep walking. It gets better."

When they reached the end of the path, they were confronted abruptly by a sparse meadow of sea oats and wire grass, beyond which a fifty-yard tongue of rushing water was surging from the sea into the gap in the beach and rioting under an arched steel pedestrian bridge, planked with wood, spanning the water.

"This isn't big enough for the Okalatchee," Holly said in surprise.

"No, it's the South Branch, but it carries a lot of water." As Harry expected, the incoming tide was surging east under the bridge. "Onto the bridge," Harry said, "and run. The sand is hot."

It was and Holly shouted "Ouch!" at every step as they raced for the wooden planking. Harry sucked in his breath and tried to keep up with her. Once on the bridge and closer to the water, Harry found what he hoped to see, a pod of dolphins leaping and cavorting in the racing water.

"Is this your surprise?" Holly asked when they reached the center of the bridge and were leaning over the wooden railing, watching the dolphins.

"Part one," Harry said, delighted that Holly was pleased.

As both Holly and Harry could see from their perches on the bridge, what had appeared from the end of the path to be dolphins leaping and charging through the water for the sheer joy of it, was in reality the serious business of the animals feeding on schools of mullet and catfish, and large snook riding the tide inland in search of food. But as with almost all of their activities, they turned it into play. Knifing in and out of the water, they tossed their catches into the air, leaped clear, and snapped them up again before they reached the safety of the churning water.

Gradually the pace of the feeding slowed, and the two watchers left the bridge in favor of the relative coolness of the path.

"I enjoyed that," Holly said, pulling off her hat.

Harry did the same and used that much-abused item to mop his face. "So did I."

"What is part two?" Holly said, stopping to study the surround scrub, "I really don't see . . ."

Harry laughed. "No," he said, "this place wasn't made for much more than holding hands."

"Too bad."

"I think it's time I told you what I've been doing out of your sight."

"Who is she?"

"One of the strangest murder cases I've ever worked on."

"You mean Henrico Perez's shooting, don't you, Harry," Holly said, stopping to look at him, "then Gwyneth's and yours? I know about them. Are you going a little weird?"

He looked at her and thought how much he enjoyed being with her.

"I haven't told you about Rachel Whittaker," he said, "or her psychiatrist daughter or about Hank Tolliver and his dying wife, or about Samia Perez and her college-aged son and daughter."

"No. Do you want to?"

"Yes."

They had begun walking again, only now, as Harry began describing Whittaker and the others and their circumstances, they had slowed to a stroll, frequently interrupted by Holly's questions.

"Fascinating," she said when he was finished. "Why have you waited until now to tell me this?"

This was several minutes after they had reached the Rover, which was parked in a bamboo grove, giving shade and a strange musical accompaniment in the form of hollow-sounding ticks and tocks as the breeze blowing off the water sent their swaying stems clattering into one another.

"Holding back? Maintaining distance? I'm not sure," Harry said, responding to a sudden urge to say something he hadn't taken sufficient time to consider properly, "but I don't want to hold back any longer. It's an important part of my life with you and I want to share it—the way you have shared your life at The Oaks with me."

They had been standing side by side, leaning against the Rover with a partially screened view of the Gulf in front of them. But now Holly moved away from the Rover and took several quick steps toward the water before stopping abruptly.

"I'm not sure I understand what you mean, Harry," she said in a strained voice.

"Have I offended you in some way?" he said, disturbed by her response.

"No, but you've frightened me," she said, turning to face him, wearing a troubled expression.

"Okay," Harry said, knowing exactly what he had stepped in and angry with both of them—himself for having been so careless and her for not warning him—"let's forget I said that. You're busy and so am I."

He pulled open the door to the rider's seat and stood back, holding it for her. She hesitated for a moment, then, still white-faced, strode past him and clambered into the Rover. The walk around the rear of the SUV was one of the longest and least pleasant journeys Harry had taken in some time, but it did give the red glaze on his eyes time to clear.

"I could have handled that better," he said once he had buckled himself in.

"So could I," she said.

At this point neither had looked at the other.

"Harry," she burst out, snapping herself around in the seat. "I'm sorry. I should have known—No! I did know. I wanted it to happen, but then, when it did, I was terrified and then furious with you for saying what you did."

Harry stopped the Rover. He released his safety belt and turned to face her. Those simple actions gave him time to think. "I'm sorry too for being angry, with myself first and then you. But that doesn't address the question, does it?"

Holly regarded him in silence, wearing an expression that seemed to Harry remote, as if she was seeing him from a great distance.

"We lost people we love," she said, "at nearly the same time. My gunshot wound healed quicker than the one that came with losing Brandon and then learning that he was sleeping with another woman when he married me and had gone on sleeping with her until his death. Then, when she committed suicide, I developed the insane conviction that she had done it to be with him and that they were together."

"And you were angry with me because . . . ?"

"Harry," she said quietly but with intense feeling, "please don't ever ask me to marry you."

"Because you don't love me."

"No, because I do."

When Harry reached home, he found a message from Jim on his answering machine. "Call me," was all he said.

In ordinary circumstances, Harry would have complained to Heaven about having to chase Jim all over Tequesta County trying to reach him. But after leaving Holly, he had drifted into a state of mind somewhere between joy and dread in which he alternated between the happiness that Holly's saying she loved him had engendered and a deepening concern over what the consequences would be for each of them over time resulting from her refusal to marry him. No answer presented itself. With considerable relief, Harry called Jim.

Jim was in his office and answered in his usual harassed office voice. Harry easily visualized him rubbing his head in frustration.

"I have the results of the department's query on the Rachel Whittaker phone calls," Jim said at once. "They were made, as far the company providing her cell phone service can tell, to public phones in downtown Avola. The dates of the calls correspond to those given you by Dr. Fairbrother."

"Then the calls were made between the publication of Gwyneth's divorce decree and the time of Scartole's moving to Dallas," Harry said.

"Which does not necessarily mean that Rachel Whittaker was conspiring with Scartole to kill Ms. Benbow, Perez, and you," Jim said in a minatory tone.

"Do you have enough evidential leverage to persuade a judge to issue a warrant to examine Whittaker's bank transactions over the period in question?"

"I doubt it," Jim said. "More to the point, I don't have enough evidence to persuade Sheriff Fisher to spring for the costs of the search."

"Are we agreed that we're not talking about a professional behind that gun?"

"He'd have starved to death by now," Jim said.

Jim had made a joke. Harry laughed, mostly in support of the effort. He was not himself in a jolly mood.

"At least we can be grateful no more complications have surfaced," Harry said.

"We haven't been very impressive so far," Jim said, sounding depressed.

"Don't go glum on me. You know success in this business is ninety percent showing up every day. And speaking of daily things, how are Clara and Kathleen?" He was hoping to cheer Jim up a little.

"Things could be better. There's a boy in Clara's class who's a bully, but up until this incident he's left Clara alone. A couple of days ago, he pushed her into the wall on the way to art class, making her drop her painting gear.

"He made a bad mistake in staying to scuff around in the things she had dropped. Clara is going to have some of my height, and she has her mother's temper. She caught her balance, turned, balled her fist, and punched him on the nose hard enough to set him on his can. He bled pretty profusely and howled. Now, the kid's parents are trying to have Clara expelled from school."

"They'll fail," Harry said. "Katherine and I had something like that happen with Minna, only she tangled with an upper-class girl who liked twisting the arms of kids smaller than she was. She tried it on Minna, who stamped her heel into the girl's foot. When the girl released her arm, Minna kicked her in the stomach. She went down with all the wind knocked out of her. Her parents threatened to sue the school, me, the state."

"Did you tell Minna she overreacted?" Jim asked.

"No, that Saturday I took her in town for a vanilla and strawberry sundae. Katherine was not pleased."

"I gave Clara three extra dollars in her allowance. Her mother was not pleased."

"Somehow, we all survive these things," Harry said. "On our race card, which horse looks most promising?"

"Frankly, Harry, none looks very impressive."

"How about Scartole?"

"Thanks to you, we know for sure he wasn't in Avola when any of the shootings took place," Jim responded, "and his phone records don't show any calls to Avola since he left for Dallas."

"And we can't get a warrant to open his bank accounts."

"Not a chance."

"Well," Harry said, "here's some more confirmation of Scartole's violence. I've had another talk with Basma Perez that resulted in her telling me that Scartole came to the house to see Perez right after the news of his affair with Gwyneth broke. He began shouting at Perez, cursing him, and possibly threatening him with a beating. Perez took a revolver out of his desk drawer and forced Scartole out of the house at gunpoint."

"But as Harley keeps telling me when I go in asking for money," Jim said bitterly, "he wasn't in town at the time of any of the shootings, and we don't have squat when it comes to identifying whoever did the shooting for him—if the shooter was doing it for him."

"Okay," Harry said, "but I've got the feeling there's something right under our noses."

Once in Jim's office, he looked over the reports on Whittaker's phone calls, and with more help from Jim got the locations of the call boxes. They were scattered over Avola and suggested nothing other than random dialing.

Once out of Jim's office, he sat for a while sorting through the pieces of the puzzle but failed again to see how they fitted together. Rather than grind his teeth over that failure, he decided to give another puzzle a try and called Fairbrother at the same time she had asked him to call before, counting on her routine to find her in.

"Mr. Brock," she said, expressing surprise. "I find myself repeating that it was my understanding that our business was concluded."

"I have a favor to ask of you," he said.

"Of me?" she asked in a rising voice, fortunately free from anger. "I can't think . . . Oh, does this have anything to do with my mother?"

"Yes."

"Oh dear, what is it?"

"First let me give you a pair of dates. They bracket the period shortly before the death of Henrico Perez and the time when Scartole returned to Dallas to stay."

"Very well," she said after writing them down. "Now what?"

"Would you be willing to ask your accountant to examine your mother's banking accounts, to see if any significant sums of money have been transferred from them to an account in Avola or Dallas?"

"A name?"

"Yes, if possible, but I will gratefully settle for only the date or dates and amounts of the transactions, if there are any, and the account numbers to which the money was transferred."

"I am astounded, Mr. Brock," Fairbrother said, sounding as if she might break out laughing. "The only person in Avola whom she knows is Gwyneth Benbow, and it's my understanding that Ms. Benbow has a great deal of money already. Why would my mother have any reason to give her more?"

Even knowing it was a mess of his own making, Harry really did not want to tell her but had nowhere else to go.

"It now appears to be a real possibility that the person or persons who planned the attacks hired someone else to do the actual shooting."

"Ridiculous!" Fairbrother protested.

"I'm afraid not," Harry said. "Many professional killers have a waiting list."

"Please do not condescend, Mr. Brock," Fairbrother said, her voice dropping an octave.

"I assure you, Dr. Fairbrother," Harry said, "I thought you did not realize that crimes of the sort we are discussing are often hired out."

"And I meant, Mr. Brock, it is ridiculous even to think that my mother could have done such a thing. She may be slightly gaga, to speak colloquially, but she's not a killer. Jackson! Stop that. Stop it at once."

"What was he doing?"

"Attempting to have sexual intercourse with the cat."

"I imagined him to be a much larger dog."

"He is a large dog, making his efforts all the more ludicrous."

Harry found the event and Fairbrother's humorless commentary hilarious.

"Was that why," he asked, desperately wanting to laugh, "the last time we talked, she took refuge on the top of the refrigerator?"

"I hadn't thought of that, but quite possibly. Now, can we

put this nonsense concerning my mother behind us?"

"I'm trying to do just that, but until someone with access to her financial records can assure me that in the recent past substantial sums of money have not been transferred out of her accounts, I'm not going to be satisfied."

"Do you realize that any such transactions would be handled by our accounting firm?" Fairbrother asked.

"And the reports are mailed to you on a quarterly basis?"

"Yes."

"Have you looked at the June numbers?"

"They haven't arrived yet."

"Those numbers are all entered in the electronic record," Harry said, becoming a little impatient. "Men with green visors are not sitting on tall stools entering them in ledgers with quill pens."

"Satire does not become you, Mr. Brock."

"Please forgive me, but your pretending to me that your mother is simply a little 'gaga' when in fact she's a potentially dangerous and obsessive maniac who believes it is her duty in life to keep the memory of her husband, a minor deity in her view, free from contamination is equally unbecoming."

Harry had taken a deliberately dangerous chance, based for the most part on his conviction that Gwyneth, as she had done before, had lied about the nature of the phone calls Rachel Whittaker had made to her.

"Are you angry with me, Mr. Brock?" Fairbrother asked calmly.

"No, but I ought to be because I think you know perfectly well what your mother's condition really is. Otherwise, why does she have a male minder?"

"Because her mood shifts are erratic and occasionally extreme. She is also unaware of her condition, but in some areas nearly normal. And, yes, she is given to outbursts of verbal abuse when crossed, obsessive, and irrationally protective of Morrison Perkins' memory. But that does not make her a murderer."

"You may be justified in assuming she is not, but in this particular situation, there is a way not based on assumptions to find out."

There was a pause, then Fairbrother said in a hard voice, "If you were to be right, Mr. Brock, do you realize how hideous the consequences would be for this family?"

"Yes, I do. It is already hideous for the Perez family. Gwyneth Benbow is still plagued by night terrors and facing more surgery to repair the damage done to her by the would-be assassin's bullet, and I will be limping for some time."

"I did not mean to suggest that the harm already done was not extensive and dire but was only thinking more locally, for the moment."

"I understand, but do you think you might have the accountants take a look and get this behind us?"

"I suppose I must, and upon reflection, yes, I will—and apprise you of the results. Jackson, what are . . . Jackson, get off me. Get off! Goodbye, Mr. Brock. Oh! This goddamned dog!"

CHAPTER 30

"I found I wasn't very pleased with myself," Harry said, clambering up from his knees to ease his back and wipe the sweat out of his eyes.

Using Tucker's crosscut saw, a devilish instrument of torture in Harry's view, he and Tucker had just cut down an old pear tree in the orchard that had stopped bearing fruit. His leg was loudly protesting what had just been done to it, and he wanted to limp around for a few minutes, seeking relief, but he didn't dare to for fear Tucker would make some derogatory comment on his fitness or, more likely, lack of it.

"Was it a clean kill?" Tucker asked, still kneeling and sprinkling kerosene on the saw blade, preparatory to cleaning it with a tattered blue rag.

"Yes."

"Was it attacking?"

"I now doubt that," Harry said. "Although at the time it felt that way, just as it did when we shot that first one. But in both cases, I now think it's likely they were just trying to reach water."

"It's true," Tucker said, "that you and I were less than a hundred yards from the edge of the Hammock and the Stickpen Preserve."

"And I was closer than that with this second one, and both times we were between those monitors and the water."

Tucker picked up his axe and began clipping the limbs off

the fallen pear. Harry, still sore, reluctantly picked up the second axe and set to work. They worked in silence until the job was done.

"Let's just drag these branches out of the grove and declare victory," Tucker said. "Tomorrow or the next day, I'll harness Oh, Brother!, put a chain on the stump, and he'll snake it out of here before you can say, 'Jack Robinson.' "

The big mule had been supervising the operation while Sanchez was sleeping in the grass under a nearby tree, and at the mention of his name he pricked his ears and moved toward the men.

"Yes, we're talking about you," Tucker said, stroking the mule's shiny black neck before gathering together some of the branches and dragging them away.

A short time later they were seated at the table in Tucker's kitchen, sharing a potato salad containing chopped cucumber pickles, hard-boiled eggs, celery, mayonnaise, a sprinkling of grated Parmesan cheese, and a splash of garlic vinegar.

"Then what's your answer to the monitor problem?" Tucker asked, tucking his napkin into his collar. "Is it a problem?"

"Only if we say it is, I suppose," Harry replied.

"Let me remind you, there won't be a ground nesting bird— that includes the nightjars, will's-widows, and burrowing owls— left on the Hammock. Seems a lot to lose," Tucker said.

"Add bobwhites and wild turkeys to the list and probably rabbits."

"What about our foxed Bonnie and Clyde and our pair of coyotes?" Tucker said, putting his fork down in alarm. "The gray fox dens aren't very deep, can't be or they'd fill with water. Same thing for the coyotes."

"Before we get too worked up here," Harry said, returning to his salad, "both monitors had been lured inland by the smell of rotting meat, and the owl nest you lost was less than an eighth of a mile from the creek."

Tucker had also resumed eating and now appeared to be weighing Harry's comment in silence.

"I'm one with those," he said at last, wiping his mouth with the bottom half of his napkin, "who say a sepulcher is a sepulcher, whited or not, but in this case you might be right. I guess we'll just have to wait and see."

"I intend to keep a close watch on the Hammock, and if I find evidence of their depredations extending inland, we might want to keep on killing them. But you probably should go ahead with your plans to strengthen the henhouse and its run."

From that, they moved to Harry's investigation, a subject very much on Harry's mind, and he began bringing Tucker up to date by describing his attempts to persuade Rosamund Fairbrother to open her mother's bank accounts for scrutiny. Tucker then asked if there was any real possibility that Rachel Whittaker had hired someone to kill Perez, Gwyneth Benbow, and Harry. "And why you three in particular?" he said.

"It's easy to make a case for Gwyneth, given Whittaker's obsession," Harry said, "less simple to see why Perez had to die although he was linked to Gwyneth's adultery, and a real stretch to make a case for killing me."

"Then your efforts to get access to Mrs. Whittaker's bank records are more a matter of making certain you have followed every lead than expecting that there will be a positive outcome."

The two men began clearing the table and continued talking.

"I'm not sure," Harry said and laughed ruefully. "My only other suspect is Eric Scartole, and it has been established that he was not in Avola when any of the shootings occurred. Jim says he doesn't have a glimmer of hope that either Harley Dillon or Sheriff Fisher will take on the cost of such a search, even if Jim could persuade a judge to issue a warrant, which he can't."

"Do you want any coffee?" Tucker asked, passing Harry a red and white checked dishcloth.

"Too hot," Harry said.

"My thoughts as well. What are the risks that this shooter, whoever it is, will have another go at you and Ms. Benbow?"

"I'd have to say fifty-fifty, but I don't have enough information to make a guess with any conviction."

"I suppose," Tucker said, leading the way out to the stoop, "that because Perez was killed, it might be logical to assume you were all supposed to die."

"Probably, but it's a conclusion that gives me no comfort at all," Harry replied.

Harry had arranged to meet Gwyneth at two, and after a short stint at his desk, writing insurance company surveillance reports, he drove into town. Tucker's reminder that he and Gwyneth were still in danger had sharpened Harry's awareness of their exposure. Not that he had forgotten it, but the slipping away of the days had dampened his concern. When Gwyneth left the hospital, she had, of course, lost her police protection, and Jim had told Harry there was no money to extend it.

Harry had given up trying to explain to her what to do and what not to do to protect herself, but she was not really ready emotionally for a serious talk on that subject. And he doubted that she would listen now. By the time he had come through the gate and parked the Rover in the now-deserted parking area, he still hadn't decided on a strategy for broaching the subject.

After he had negotiated the outside steps, a smiling Margarita answered the door and greeted him with a smile but he was scarcely inside before Gabrielle, blushing slightly, came hurrying from her office to meet him.

"Don't worry, Mr. Brock," she said, a bit too cheerfully, as if getting them past an awkward moment. "No fitness tests today.

We'll use the elevator. How are you feeling?"

"Better than I was," Harry said. "Thanks for asking. I see the workers have left."

"At last," she said with a compelling show of sincerity.

She paused to have a brief conversation with Margarita in rapid-fire Spanish, then put an arm through his and led him across the foyer to the elevator, describing briefly the repairs that had been made.

After that, she asked him about the investigation, but just before reaching Gwyneth's office, she interrupted his answer to say, "I'm glad you've come, Mr. Brock. She gets a little blue rattling around in this big house. Since the workers left, we've been mostly on our own, and only she and I and Margarita and her husband, Joseph, the maintenance man, are here at night."

The news disturbed Harry, possibly because he had not given serious thought to the staffing arrangements in the house or where everyone slept.

"There's no easy way to say this, Gwyneth," Harry told her as soon as they were settled in front of the bay windows, which no longer wore the shreds of leaves and shattered branches the storm had plastered there, "but I've put off saying this too long. Living as you do in this isolated house, you are putting yourself at serious risk, especially at night with only a few servants scattered through the staff quarters."

"Are you trying to frighten me, Harry?" she demanded, coloring slightly. She was wearing her heavy black hair in a gold circlet and draped over her left shoulder, the way he recalled she wore it the first day they met, and in black slacks and a maroon silk blouse, she was just as striking.

"Try not to be angry with me," Harry said, "but I think you should seriously consider leaving Florida, possibly the country, for a year or so, or until this killer is caught."

"I will do no such thing," she said, bouncing to her feet, her blue eyes boring into his.

"First, consider this: I'm almost certain that the same person who shot Perez shot you and me, Gwyneth. Also, I think the person is a hired shooter, paid to kill all three of us, and he's not going to be paid until we're dead. So he's coming back."

Harry had risen with her and was now facing an angry woman, and was not surprised. It was the way she had responded when he first broached the subject, but she was now far stronger physically and emotionally, and he thought she could stand a little pressure.

"What about you, Harry?" she demanded, her fists doubled.

"Being shot at now and then goes with my work," he said.

He did not say that there was no way to protect yourself from someone who wanted you dead except to put yourself where the killer couldn't find you. But he intended to if nothing else could persuade her.

"I don't think that's funny," she said, nursing her shoulder.

"I didn't mean it to be. I probably should have been more forceful about this the first time I mentioned it."

"You don't know that the same person shot all three of us," she responded in an angry voice. "I think it's more likely some maniac shot me. Why would anyone want me dead? It doesn't make sense, especially your crazy idea that Eric might be stalking me with a gun." She paused and Harry tried to speak, but she cut him off. "How many people have gone to jail because of you? You must have an enemy list longer than your leg."

"Which one?" Harry asked. "It feels now as if the right one is shorter than the left."

"Will you please be serious! I'm not leaving my house, my friends, everything and everyone meaning anything to me, to enter into something resembling a witness protection program. I might as well die and get it over with."

The moment had come as Harry feared it would.

"Denial won't change what's real, Gwyneth," he said quietly. "There is ballistic proof that the same gun was used in two of the three shootings, which suggests that it was the same person shooting in each case. You are in serious danger. And you're not being asked to change your identity. I'm asking you to slip quietly out of town, then get on a plane in another state, and stay away from here until we catch whoever shot us."

"Okay," she replied, dropping back into her chair. "This is what I'm willing to do. I'll hire a private security firm to put this house under twenty-four-hour surveillance. How's that?"

Groaning silently, Harry sat down. He leaned forward, elbows on his knees, and, dreading what was going to follow, said, "Gwyneth, listen to me carefully. No one can protect you from someone who wants to kill you and has access to a knife or a gun. What is accomplished by having a guard walking beside you when neither of you knows what your assailant looks like? The only safe course is to go where this person can't find you."

"I can't go away now," Gwyneth said calmly, her anger appearing to have abated. "I have skin grafting and other procedures still to complete."

"All right," Harry said, "will you promise to hire the security people and have at least two men patrolling the grounds?"

"Why two?"

"In case one gets shot."

"What in God's name does Holly Pike see in you?"

"It's a mystery."

CHAPTER 31

Later that day Harry received a call from Rosamond Fairbrother.

"Mr. Brock," she said, "while it might be argued that what I have to tell you is none of your business and, in all probability, of very little interest to you, I feel, nevertheless, that I should share this information with you in order to relieve your mind of any lingering doubts as to whether or not my mother has been in any way involved in recent events concerning the shooting of Ms. Gwyneth Benbow."

Several seconds passed after she stopped speaking before it dawned on Harry that she was actually finished. He had become slightly mesmerized by the flow of her words.

"I'm very grateful, Dr. Fairbrother," he said, a little more heartily than necessary in an effort to dispel any suspicion that he had stopped listening . . . *Dear God,* he thought, I'm *doing it.* "I'm interested in anything you have to tell me."

"Very well. To my surprise and chagrin," she began bravely or so Harry thought, "I have learned that my mother has been playing poker, a game I can scarcely believe she had ever heard of, on the Internet, wagering and losing substantial sums of money. Apparently, although she refuses to confirm or deny the accusation, she was introduced to the practice by the chauffeur whom we dismissed.

" 'It's where the action is,' has been her only comment on the subject."

Harry laughed. "She has, or had, a secret life," he said. "Have you ended it?"

"Not entirely, but she has been limited to a fixed number of losses in any given week."

"And no money has been transferred to southern Florida?"

"None."

"What about the phone calls?"

"I have had my law firm pursue that issue with the telephone companies—I thought I owed you that courtesy—and the answer appears to be that the calls to Ms. Benbow went through and were taken by her, the remaining calls were not answered by anyone, and their purpose, if there was one, must remain a mystery."

"You know," Harry said, "I'm relieved. Thanks to you, we have closure."

"I suspect you must feel relieved that Ms. Benbow is now out from under the shadow of suspicion, at least regarding Mr. Perez's death."

"Actually, it was her ex-husband who has had some of the shadow you mentioned," Harry said, picking his way through that thicket with care. "That is not to say that I think he killed Perez. What you have told me makes it clear that your mother was not involved in planning a murder with anyone connected with the shootings."

"Then I take it your relationship with Ms. Benbow is entirely professional."

"If you have a spare fifty minutes, perhaps we could discuss that in more depth than I can indicate in answering your question. But my interim answer is yes."

"Life and our relationships generally are more nuanced than yes and no reveal. Have you found that to be true, Mr. Brock?"

"Increasingly, and seldom has the knowledge increased my peace of mind."

Dr. Fairbrother actually laughed. She had a good, rich laugh, and Harry experienced a faint stirring of arousal. He smiled, pleased.

"How is Jackson?" he asked.

"He is much better and under far less stress. He's been to the vet."

Harry's stirrings vanished.

"And?"

"He's fully recovered, and the cat and I have ceased to be objects of sexual interest."

Rosamund Fairbrother's call had removed one line of inquiry for Harry and the sheriff's department, but it intensified a second. It was, Harry recognized, one thing to theorize that the shooter was a hired gun but quite another to prove it.

"And what if there ain't no hired gun?" Hodges demanded.

He and Harry were standing in the broiling sun fifteen miles east of Avola on the gravel shoulder of the east-bound lanes of I-75, better known as Alligator Alley, connecting Avola on the west coast with Weston and greater Miami on the east. As they talked, they were watching a very large tow truck, backed half of its considerable length down the embankment that lifted the road bed above the surrounding swamp. The truck's engine was roaring and a heavy steel winch cable, running out from the truck and plunged into the green tangle of saw grass, stunted palms, cattails, saw palmetto, and other scrub growth, was vibrating with tension as it rolled slowly onto the black metal storage barrel, dragging something still buried in the green mass of the swamp out of the undergrowth.

"Then I'm not hopeful we will ever solve this mess," Harry shouted back. "How did you ever discover the car was out here?"

Very early that morning, the sheriff's department had received a call telling them there was a car with a dead body in it

off the south side of the Alley about a hundred and fifty yards
east of the fifteen-mile marker.

"We already traced the call to an all-night diner in the reser-
vation rest stop," Hodges said, "but nobody we could find remembers seeing anyone using the phone. Of course, they ain't
the most talkative people you'll find."

"How did whoever called you find it?" Harry asked, assuming the answer was either an orchid poacher, an alligator hide
hunter, or a poor, enslaved graduate student from the University of Miami, doing research for his dissertation.

But before Hodges could reply, a man spattered with mud,
soaked to his armpits and draped with water lily stems, came
thrashing and splashing out of the tangle of trees, grass, and
water. He shouted at the man handling the winch, "Keep it
coming! Keep it coming! Don't for Christ's sake let it stop!"

Whatever else he said was drowned in the roar of the truck's
engine as the winch man advanced the lever controlling the
winch, which, loud before, began howling like a devil in sight of
its prey. Harry and Hodges gave up talking and watched a battered sedan, nearly buried under trailing branches, vines, and
mephitic mud, the smell of which blew up the bank and made
Harry wrinkle his nose, wallowing and heaving as it was dragged
tail first slowly but steadily onto the bank and draining water
like a shipwreck being hoisted from the sea.

Once it had been dragged its full length up the bank and well
clear of the churned mud and water, the winch operator cut the
motor.

"That's a relief," Hodges said, starting down the bank and
waving the troopers out of their cruisers parked along the road
behind him.

"There's more than snakes and muck in that car," Harry
said, slowly following Hodges while moving closer to death and
its corruption.

"Smells that way," Hodges agreed, beginning to study the vehicle. "This car had a rough ride getting to where it was found."

Harry thought that was no exaggeration. The windshield was shattered. One of the passenger-side windows was missing, and both headlights were all but torn out.

"It's all yours," Hodges shouted to the detectives from the crime scene division, who were pulling on plastic gloves as they edged gingerly down the bank, notebooks and other gear tucked under their arms, and showing no enthusiasm for the work ahead.

"What's left of whoever it was is still behind the front wheel," Hodges shouted, having made a quick circuit of the car. "Watch out for water moccasins," he added, grinning broadly.

The detectives, two men and a woman, gave no indication of having heard him.

"Snooty bastards," Hodges grumbled to Harry, who was finding the climb more of a challenge than the descent as they scrambled back up the bank.

"You know anything about this?" Harry asked.

"I'm afraid so," Hodges said, breathing heavily and mopping his streaming face and bald pate with a damp red bandana. "I checked the tags. Unless the coroner tells me different, there's an elderly man, or what's left of him, in there, who went missing about five months ago. Vanished without a trace."

"Lincoln A. Rutherford," Harry said. "The name stuck because I thought somebody liked the names of presidents. And I'll wager that A stands for either Adams or Arthur."

"That's the man," Hodges agreed. "And I'll bet he died behind the wheel, shoved the pedal on that big Buick to the metal, shot off the bank back there where's there's no fence, and plowed a hundred yards or so into the undergrowth before hitting the I-75 barrier fence and coming to a stop."

"That would have been four or five months into the dry season," Harry said.

"That's the answer," Hodges agreed, with a dramatic wave of his hat before putting it back on his head. "Nobody noticed the hole in the jungle, and in no time at all it filled in. The rains came, the water rose, and goodbye Lincoln A. Rutherford."

Throughout their conversation, Jim had been in his cruiser, dealing by phone with a call from Harley Dillon's office regarding a grand larceny case that Dillon was prosecuting.

"The thing is," Jim complained, rejoining Harry and Hodges, "that whenever Harley is handling a case that originated in our department and it begins to go south, it's suddenly our fault."

"Sometimes it is," Hodges said, "but not this time. You told him, Captain, there were problems with at least one of the witnesses, but he was sure he could take the jury with him."

"Is this Rutherford?" Jim asked, nodding toward the car. Harry knew Jim was already regretting having criticized a superior officer and wanted to change the subject.

"The tags on the Buick say so," Hodges replied.

"Then, if the coroner agrees, we'll notify the family. They'll be relieved."

"Goes two ways, don't it?" Hodges said. "They won't have to worry any more about what happened to him, but they won't have any hope left he might still be alive."

The three men stood looking at the car with its grisly contents and the detectives busy at work. Two had put on face masks, but Harry knew from experience that they wouldn't lessen the stench.

"Finish what you were starting to tell me," Jim said, addressing Harry.

"Rosamund Fairbrother cleared up the mystery of her mother's phone calls," Harry said and then repeated what he had already told Hodges.

"Then we're down to Scartole," Jim said glumly. "By the

way, have you talked with Ms. Benbow about what Dr. Fairbrother told you?"

"No," Harry said. "Do you want me to?"

"No. I'll take care of it. Have you any suggestions for making the interview go well?"

"Oh, yes," Harry said and gave Jim instructions on how best to approach Gwyneth. "But you know," he added, "for all Fairbrother's oddities, I have come to like her, and I think she's a person of integrity, and God knows she's bright as the evening star."

"I thought you had a thing going with Holly Pike!" Hodges said loudly, displaying wide-eyed surprise at what he had just heard.

"Sergeant!" Jim said, his ears reddening. "You ought to know better than to say something like that to Harry or anybody else."

"It's okay," Harry said, actually stepping between the two men and holding up his hands. "I know what Frank means, Jim. I'm not offended. He's just expressing concern. And Frank, I have no romantic interest in Dr. Fairbrother. I just admire her. And she's got a husband, not to mention her mother."

"Are we going to have to push for cooperation over those phone records?" Jim asked.

"No, not if whoever talks with Dr. Fairbrother listens carefully and keeps the questioning low-key and, above all, assures her that her mother's name is not going to be given to the media. Oh, make sure the questioning doesn't run over fifty minutes."

"Fifty minutes?" Hodges asked.

"Once upon a time, psychiatrists scheduled talking therapy sessions for fifty minutes," Harry said. "Now it's more like ten minutes and a prescription for pills. She's still got a thing about time."

"As I've already said, if you're right about the calls," Jim said, "we're stuck with Eric Scartole, who couldn't have been the shooter."

"Aren't we lucky?" Harry said. "By the way, are you going to find out who phoned in the information about the car with the dead man in it? I'm curious about what he could have been doing out in that swamp."

"Very funny, Harry," Jim said.

Hodges laughed for him.

Having grown tired of waiting for news about Jennifer from Sarah, Harry called the hospital and asked for Jennifer's room number and telephone.

"She's no longer with us, Mr. Brock. She was discharged three days ago."

"Discharged!" Harry said. "Is that a new euphemism for dying?"

"Oh no, Mr. Brock. She's gone home."

He shouldered the risk of having Clive answer the phone and dialed Jennifer's house.

Sarah answered.

"Why did Jennifer leave the hospital?" Harry asked, trying not to sound agitated.

"And hello to you," Sarah answered. "She said, 'I'm going home,' and here she is. Hospice has taken over from the hospital's palliative care unit and is doing a fabulous job. I'm really impressed. Why did you call? Were you intending to speak with Jennifer?"

"I see the gatekeeper has her hand firmly on the latch," Harry retorted, deciding too late that he was dumping his adrenaline jump on his daughter.

"I thought you'd be glad to hear that she's well enough to express her wants," Sarah replied.

"I'm angry with you, I think, for not having told me you'd made the change. Let's start over. How is she?"

"Okay," Sarah said with a sigh, "it's been a little weird, to be honest. Physically, she's extremely fragile. But everyone who should know about these things has stopped trying to predict when the end will come. The nurse who's checking in with her on a daily basis has told me several times to let go of that worry. 'It's a useless waste of time and energy,' she says, 'When it's time,' has become my mantra."

"Is she out of pain?"

"Yes, they're particularly good with pain management. And when she's awake, which is intermittently and has nothing to do with whether it's daylight or dark, she's remarkably lucid and very much Jennifer. Are you still thinking about coming to see her?"

"Yes. I suppose you're no happier now about my coming than you were the last time I called."

"I'm at least ambivalent," Sarah said, "and still concerned that your coming might upset her."

Harry made a mistake and knew it as soon as the words were out of his mouth. "Does she ever mention me? No," he said instantly. "Don't answer that. I'm sorry I asked. It wasn't fair to Jennifer and it wasn't fair to you and not to me either, for that matter. Answer this instead: How are you bearing up?"

"Better now than before," she said, with relief in her voice. "All that running back and forth to the hospital was beginning to wear me down."

"Is Clive still with you?"

"No, he's missed a lot of work, and Lillian finally said they had to go home. He resisted—he's stubborn. I wonder where he got that?—but Lillian told him that refusal was not an option, and they left yesterday. I have to tell you, Harry, it's also a relief. Being around Clive right now is a downer."

"What's the baby's name?" Harry asked, thinking how pathetic it was that he didn't know. Momentary anger, old and—he'd thought—burned out, flared up. Its seeds were hot coals under the ashes, and his question had breathed them into flames. But he stamped them out. He was done with his anger over Jennifer's actions after the separation. If he couldn't extinguish it, he could bury it. And he did. Again, or so he thought.

"Joel," Sarah said and did not elaborate.

"Someone in Lillian's family?" he asked.

"I don't know. Ever since my divorce Clive hasn't had much to do with me. I wasn't invited to the wedding."

"Have you been building bridges in the last weeks?"

"I'm inclined to say, a bridge too far."

"Don't give up."

"How about you lending a hand?"

"We'll see."

That's where they left it—like, Harry thought, so much else in their mutilated family relationships that had been buried over the years.

CHAPTER 32

It took Harry a few hours of concentrated desk work, followed by a long evening walk to the end of the sandy Hammock road with the sounds of the early frog choruses and the high, wild calls and beating wings of hundreds of herons, ibises, and wood storks passing over his head, returning to their roosts, to cleanse his mind of the wretched and pointless bitterness that had come flaming out of its ashes as soon as the call ended.

Laying out his solitary meal and wishing he was sharing it with Holly, he recalled by some odd chemistry of memory, something Tucker had said to him soon after his arrival on the Hammock. "A two-hour walk on Bartram's Hammock has more healing power than a bucket full of the balm of Gilead."

At the time, Harry thought Tucker LaBeau must be a bit touched, but taking the cover off his slow cooker and smelling the aroma of his sweet potato, chicken, sausage, carrots, onions, roasted peppers, and garlic casserole reminded him how much he owed to the wisdom and gentle guidance of his old friend.

By the following morning, Harry's head was filled again with the problem of solving the mystery of the unknown shooter and finally deciding to have a go at persuading Gwyneth to carry a gun.

"You must be crazy," she said to him, getting to her feet as if words were an insufficient rejection of the suggestion.

They had been sitting in striped canvas deck chairs in the shade of a large fichus tree on the ocean side of her house, looking out across an Olympic-sized swimming pool and beyond it to the blue Gulf, sprinkled with white sails. Gwyneth was wearing a red bikini and a white pool jacket. The temperature was in the mid-eighties, but a brisk breeze off the water made it feel much cooler.

It took Harry a little longer than she had taken to get to his feet. "It's not at all crazy," he insisted. "Have you ever fired a handgun?"

"Wait," she said, shedding her wrapper, "I want your opinion on something." She turned to face him and slipped her jacket off her shoulders. Her bikini top didn't leave much to speculate about, but Harry thought he'd better not mention that.

"What do you think?" she asked, moving a bit nervously and frowning at him.

"About what?" Harry asked uneasily.

"What you were just staring at," she said.

"I think it's very becoming," he said.

"What?"

"Your swimsuit."

"Cut it out, Harry," she said, her voice rising shakily. "Come right out with it. What's wrong with them?"

The cloud lifted from Harry's mind, revealing his mistake.

"Nothing's wrong with them," he told her with an ardent honesty. "Your breasts are beautiful."

She looked at him as if she didn't believe him. "No bullshit, Harry?"

"Honor bright," he said, allowing himself to smile, mischief entering. "Want me to check your bottom? I remember that in the hospital you were concerned about it."

"Good idea," she said quickly. "My back still looks awful," she added, turning and pulling her jacket up to her waist. "Now you can look."

"Perfect," said as enthusiastically as he could.

"Oh, good," she said, turning again to face him. "I've been using my stair machine and walking."

"There's just one thing," Harry said. "There's no charge for the evaluations, but I expect to be invited to the showing when all the repairs are finished."

She sat down, leaned back a little gingerly in the chair, looked up, mischief of her own in her smile, and said, "Of course. Would you prefer a private showing?"

"Thank you. How is the work progressing?"

"Oh, a slick finesse, Harry," she protested. "Well, who wants a repair job when you get a new one?"

"If you only knew," Harry said, bringing her smile back.

"Good. As for the repair, it's progressing damned slowly, and it hurts like hell. Worse still, nobody will tell me when it will be over. Sometimes, I feel worn out by it all, but then I stop feeling sorry for myself and say, 'Just get on with it.' "

"Does it help?"

"Yes, in some strange way it does."

"Speaking of getting on with it," Harry said. "I'm serious about your getting a gun."

"I don't like guns."

"Irrelevant. If you won't leave Avola, having the security people on the grounds and being armed are the next best things. By the way, I didn't see anyone when I drove in."

"They arrive about sundown and leave when the sun comes up," she said, her distaste for the arrangement showing.

"Okay," Harry said, quite sure it would be a mistake to ask for more coverage, at least not until he had persuaded her to carry a gun. "Now, I know a man who will have you scoring tens on paper targets within a week. Every night, he forgets more about guns than I will ever know, and not only is he one of the top handgun marksmen in the state, but he's also the best teacher. He's a man who makes you feel safer just being near him."

"Who is this paragon?" Gwyneth asked, showing some interest.

"His name, get ready, is Bubba Miller. You have never met anyone like him, and I doubt that you ever will again."

She leaned her head back and laughed one of her good laughs that always made Harry grin in appreciation.

"Can you imagine anyone christening a child Bubba?" she asked.

"When you see Bubba, you may change your mind."

"What makes you think I'm ever going to see this man, much less let him try to teach me to shoot a gun?"

Harry glanced at his watch. "I'm going to introduce you to him in about forty minutes. If you start getting ready now, I think we'll just make it."

"Am I going to like this man?" Gwyneth asked as she got into the Rover twenty-five minutes later.

"I think so," Harry answered, getting them under way. "He takes a little getting used to. And I want to warn you not to take personally the fact he doesn't smile at you. It won't be because he doesn't like you, it's because no one has ever seen him smile. When I first met him, his not smiling was a little intimidating. But I soon got over it, as I'm sure you will."

When they turned into the dirt front yard of the low, tin-roofed, unpainted wooden building with the battered sign over the door that read, "Bubba Miller's Gun Shop," Gwyneth leaned forward, staring at the sign, and groaned, a sound that expressed an emotion several degrees beyond despair.

"Don't be alarmed," Harry said. "Wait until you see what's inside."

"You mean it will be worse?"

"No. This is the time to suspend disbelief."

"Jesus, Harry," she said, letting her nervousness show, "this is no time to be quoting Coleridge."

The screen on the door was badly rusted and made a dolorous sound when Harry pulled it open for her, at which she rolled her eyes, frightening Harry, who for a moment feared she was going to faint.

A mountain of a man came through a door behind the nearest counter and stepped quickly around the counter to reach them. Gwyneth drew in her breath and stepped back, treading on Harry's sandal, causing him to swear.

"You must be Gwyneth Benbow," the man said in a voice that belonged in the bass section of a Russian Orthodox choir. He was almost seven feet tall and filled a door when he stood in it. "I'm Bubba Miller."

He came to a stop in front of Gwyneth and extended a hand the size of an iron frying pan, glowering down at her in grim concentration.

"Yes," she said, as if she wanted to deny it, "I'm pleased to meet you."

"You always associate with riffraff like the feller trying to hide behind you?"

"He forced himself on me," she said.

Harry let his breath go in relief. She hadn't run out of the shop screaming.

"Well, he's way out of his league with you, but I admire his courage."

While he was saying this he reached over Gwyneth, grasped Harry's shoulder, and pulled him out from behind Gwyneth as if he had been moving a child to where he could get a better look at him.

"How's that leg coming?" he asked.

"Slower than I'd like, but it's mending. You're looking well." By now they were shaking hands.

"Doing fine. By the way, Ms. Benbow, I'm Bubba to the world. I may as well be to you."

"Oh, good. I'm Gwyneth. Harry says I should learn to shoot a gun. Do you think I could learn to do that?"

Bubba stepped back and surveyed her. "Two eyes, two hands, two legs. You're not crippled or blind. I don't see why not."

"Would you be willing to try to teach me?" Gwyneth asked in a much more confident voice but not smiling.

"I suppose Harry said I would, so I'll have to say yes. When do you want to begin?"

On the way back into town, Gwyneth at first sat beside Harry without speaking. He thought he knew what was going on and let the silence stand. When she broke it, it was to say, "I don't believe I did that," as if she had not been staring out the windshield for the past five minutes.

"What do you think of his shop?"

"I didn't know there were so many kinds of guns in the world," she replied, still staring out the window as if not wholly recovered. "They covered the walls, the shelves in all those glass-front cases, and Bubba said he had more in another shed. Will I have the courage to go back there alone?"

"I don't know. Did he frighten you?"

"At first, but when we shook hands that all went away. It was like being with a talking horse."

"Why a horse?" Harry asked, surprised by the comparison.

"Because they're big and they don't smile either, but you can tell right away whether or not they're dangerous."

"And Bubba's not."

"No, and I think I'll keep my appointment."

Harry limited himself to, "Good," but he felt like cheering.

★　★　★　★　★

In his quiet moments, Harry found he was thinking more and more frequently of Jennifer and remembering in no coherent order events in their life together. A few times, Holly had caught him during a pause in their conversation. "Are you feeling all right?" she asked him the first time it happened.

"Oh, sorry, I was a bit distracted," he said and picked up the conversation again.

But it kept happening, and she finally called him on it. "Harry," she said, "are you growing tired of me?"

On this occasion they were taking Nip for his evening walk on one of the several shaded rides on the estate. Harry had begged off their usual routine of riding with the excuse that it was easier to talk when they were walking, which was not true but not quite a lie.

"What?" he asked, then caught himself and protested that nothing could be further from the truth.

"Then tell me what keeps taking you away from me and don't fabricate," she said with genuine concern.

Harry was quiet for a moment and extended that pause by pointing to a gopher tortoise that Nip had nosed out of the grass and into the trail. That distraction was further extended by Holly's scolding the dog that had been trained to leave the wildlife alone but frequently fell from grace.

Harry was not sure how to respond to Holly's demand. The last time Jennifer had come into their conversation, the encounter ended in a quarrel. But he did not like lying to her about anything that involved their relationship.

"It's bad enough," she protested, "that I have to hear Gwyneth describe at length the body check you gave her and how wonderful it is that she can feel free to ask you to do something like that without being jumped on. Don't look smug and don't believe a word of it. She's just putting a burr under my saddle."

"Why?"

"She's jealous. I've got something she hasn't, you. Now stop stalling and answer the question."

"I don't know why," Harry said, "but I've been thinking about Jennifer. Out of thin air, scenes from those years when we were together, suddenly appear in my mind—the cabin we lived in, the children swimming in the lake, a bull moose putting his head underwater to eat the water lily bulbs and making the kids laugh."

"Are the memories painful?" Holly asked, taking his hand.

"I don't know, not exactly," he said, his answer shaping itself as he talked. "They're intensely evocative of a place, people, and a time that are long gone but still vividly present."

"Have you made up your mind yet whether or not to go see her?"

"No, and I think it was probably my most recent conversation with Sarah that has triggered this slideshow of the past. I'd like to stop talking about this if we could."

"I think it's interesting that you left Jennifer out of your line-up of scenes," Holly said with a supporting smile that looked strained to Harry. "Are you thinking of her?"

"Yes."

"And you don't want to share those scenes with me."

"No."

"I understand that, Harry," she said, giving his hand a squeeze. "I don't want to talk with you or anyone about my memories of Brandon. Does that bother you?"

"It hurts when I think of your loving another man, Holly, but I don't believe that love is a zero-sum game. Your love for Brandon doesn't diminish your love for me—at least, I hope it doesn't. Whatever love I still have for Jennifer certainly doesn't diminish my love for you."

By now they were standing with their arms around one another, and Nip came running and sat down, pressing against them while they were kissing. Whining pitifully and not getting a response, he leaned harder against them until they staggered to the side to keep from falling over, their kiss degenerating into laughter.

"Which one of us is going to kiss him?" Holly asked.

" 'Not I,' said the cat."

"It's disappointing, Captain," Lieutenant Millard Jones said, leaning forward in his chair to ease the crease in a trouser leg. Jones was a small, neat man with a thin, closely trimmed mustache and thick black hair. Slightly overweight, he looked more like the president of a bank than the head of the department's criminal investigation division.

A dedicated bachelor in his early fifties, he was a legend in the department, a subject of constant envy among the male half of the force that regarded him with awed resentment. Women said nothing at all about him, but blushed whenever his name was mentioned. It was rumored that he had made love to every woman in the department at least once. If he passed close to a strange woman on the sidewalk, there was a ninety percent chance that she would turn to look at him. The remaining ten percent turned to look at women.

He was also a dedicated and very effective detective and an outstanding division leader. Jim invariably gave him one of the highest performance ratings in the yearly staff reviews. He was not presently, however, enjoying one of his shining hours.

"You're sure, Lieutenant," Jim said, dropping his feet off the desk with a crash when they struck the floor. "Not one?"

"I'm afraid not, Captain," Jones said, beginning to shift uneasily in his chair.

Harry was stunned by the news, and Hodges for once had nothing to say. He simply gaped at Jones with disbelief.

"Millard," Harry said, forcing himself to speak—Jim was so chagrined that he had resorted to tipping back in his chair and staring at the ceiling—"there must have been thirty names of people on that list who were sitting close enough to our man with the sack to have identified him."

"That's right, Harry, but I and my people talked to every single one of them, and none of us got any more in the way of a description than you got from Peter Rahn. If I recall, he described the man as 'of medium height, wearing dungarees, a baseball cap, and a long-sleeved shirt, buttoned at the wrists.' Is that about right?"

"I think so. He added that the man was carrying a sack."

"And Rahn did not think he would recognize the man if he saw him again?"

"That's right."

"He was very observant. Most of the people we questioned got only two of Rahn's identifying details. No one thought they would recognize him."

The room went quiet for an extended period of time, except for the tiresome creak of the ceiling fan as it slowly revolved one creak per revolution.

Millard Jones finally sighed and said, "There's one bright spot. A drunk in the holding pen a few nights back identified Jack O'Lanton. He's a bootlegger of corn whiskey who passes through Night Town every now and then. The drunk was threatening him with violence for having spiked his last batch of white lightning with epsom salts, leaving devastation in its wake."

Only Hodges laughed and started to tell a story about spiked cider but was instantly squashed by Jim, who had shifted his attention away from the ceiling to glare at Jones.

"All those man hours," he said, "and what have we got?"

"Nothing!" Hodges crowed.

"That's right," Jim said. "Nothing."

Harry had stopped following the conversation, to think about Jack O'Lanton. "What would a man who calls himself Jack O'Lanton, runs a whiskey still, and peddles his wares in Night Town be doing in a conservancy lecture on Nile monitor lizards?" he asked no one in particular.

"I asked myself the same question," Jones said in a hopeful voice, probably having seen a glimmer of light in the encompassing darkness enclosing him.

"And?" Jim demanded.

"I didn't find an answer, and finally stopped looking for one."

"I don't think it was Jack O'Lanton in that hall," Harry said to Jones. "Didn't you say you had interviewed every person on the guest list except O'Lanton and concluded that none of the people in that hall had any connection with Perez, Gwyneth, or me?"

"That's right," Jones said. "Then we interviewed a second time the thirty-two who might have been close enough to the mystery man to identify him."

"But not Jack O'Lanton," Harry said.

"Oh, we ran him down finally, but he wasn't in Avola on any of the times Harry and the other two were shot."

"Then I think," Harry said, "the man with the sack was the man who signed in as Jack O'Lanton."

"Who outside of the police would know Jack O'Lanton?" Hodges demanded in a loud voice.

"Probably not anyone who made it a practice of attending Conservation Club lectures," Jim observed.

"And what would lead such a person to shoot Perez, Gwyneth Benbow, and me?" Harry asked.

"Someone who hired him to do it," Hodges said, "then told him where to look."

"And who would want all three of you dead?" Jones asked.

"Make a guess," Harry said.

"Eric Scartole," Jones said without hesitation, "that is, assuming our shooter hasn't got three separate clients and decided to kill the three of you in the order he was hired."

"I think we can rule that out," Jim said dryly. "And if we do, where does that leave us?"

"The person we're looking for must be right under our nose," Harry said, avoiding Jim's question.

"Whoever he is, Captain," Jones said, "he's familiar with Jack O'Lanton and, ergo, probably not a member of the leisure class."

Jim stood up and began gathering the papers and folders on his desk. "I've got a meeting," he said, "and Lieutenant, I'd appreciate a little evidence of deep thinking on this before we lose Ms. Benbow or Harry, for that matter."

Hodges laughed. Jones did not, and Harry made a face getting to his feet. Putting any extra weight on the leg still hurt.

"I'll put the stick in, Captain," Jones said, following Jim out the door.

"You taking any extra precautions?" Hodges asked Harry, looking at him as if he didn't think he was.

"Frank," Harry said, pulling on his hat, "you and I both know there's damned little one can do beyond not sitting at night in a lighted window."

CHAPTER 33

It didn't happen in a lighted window or across a crowded room, but just before dark while Harry was turning off County Road 19 onto the Hammock Road, there were two very loud bangs, followed by the Rover's sudden slump to the left, throwing his shoulder against the door.

Shotgun, he thought as he freed his seatbelt and threw himself to the right, getting his head out of the window. The Rover, with two flat tires and no acceleration, thumped to a stop.

An instant later, another blast took out the driver's window, covering him with glass pellets. *Buckshot,* Harry thought coolly as he twisted his feet out from under the wheel. The windshield went in two more blasts. Reluctantly abandoning the safety provided by the dashboard, Harry scrambled between the seats and rolled onto the rear floor, just as the space where he had been lying was ripped with lead, turning the driver's door into a sieve.

That's six, Harry thought. *Time to reload, I hope.* He eased open the back door, slithered headfirst onto the sand, and rolled over to look under the Rover toward the bridge. But he saw only sand and weeds at the edge of the road.

All right, he thought, *I know where you are—the same place you were before.* Inching into a crouch, he raised his head just enough to peer through the windows toward the wooded bank at the edge of the bridge. The sky was still bright in the west, but at

329

ground level the light had faded to the point where all cats are gray.

Harry saw only the shapes of trees, weeds, and stopper bushes.

"Then let's do it," he said. With a very brief prayer that his leg wouldn't give out, he dashed across CR 19 in a hobbling sprint. Squeezing his eyes shut, he gripped his CZ in both hands over his head and dove headfirst into a tall patch of Queen Anne's lace. Spitting out sand and leaves as quietly as he could, he wriggled deeper into the flowers and then turned and eased himself back to the edge of the road, his leg howling in protest at what had been done to it.

Danger sharpened Harry's responses but it also calmed him, a gift that had saved his life a number of times. Now, lying on his stomach with nothing but a thin screen of wildflower stems between him and a twelve gauge shotgun in the hands of someone who wanted very much to kill him, Harry was entirely concentrated on trying to anticipate what the man was going to do next, but time ran out before he did much thinking.

Slightly to the left of the patch of trees and shrubs on the creek bank, a blurred figure rose out of the bushes and began blasting the spot where Harry had dived into the Queen Anne's lace. The first blast tore through the flowers and ripped into the sand, sending up a cloud of dust. Harry waited to see where the next charge was going. It struck an instant later three feet closer to Harry.

"Right," Harry whispered and began rolling away from the advancing blasts as fast as he could. He did not worry that the shooter was going to hear him with the gun roaring as it was. He was also counting as he rolled and saw that the buckshot would be raking him before the shooter emptied his chamber. By now he had rolled into a tangle of taller weeds. He stopped rolling, rose onto his knees, and fired four times through the intervening bushes at what he hoped was the shooter, then pitched down to his left and scuttled away as fast as he could scramble.

Silence.

Harry stopped and swung himself toward the road, squinting through the grass, hoping for a target.

Nothing.

There was no sound, none, not even the whine of a mosquito. Then, one by one, the frogs began to bell, and in the next five minutes colony frogs began to sing in chorus, the nightjars boomed overhead, the insects began fiddling, and the midges found Harry.

"I'd as soon be shot," he muttered.

With some trepidation he slowly rose to his feet. The light was gone now, and he guessed he would be invisible against the wall of trees behind him. Nevertheless, he moved across the road very slowly, scanning the creek bank as carefully as he could. When he got to the edge of the road and could see the faint glimmer of the water, he stopped.

To the north, he heard an engine start and gradually fade away.

"I missed," Harry told the moon, just making an appearance through the trees. Then he had another unpleasant thought.

"Shit," he said. "I've got to trade for another Rover, and the new insurance premiums will be a horror show."

"By God," Hodges said, in obvious admiration, pushing his hat back with his thumb and staring at where Harry had been lying, "you was close enough to feel the wind of that last charge."

Hodges, Jim, Harry, and half a dozen detectives and crime scene people with chalk, cameras, measuring tape, and plastic sample bags were combing both sides of the road for anything that might lead toward the shooter.

"It was closer than I wanted it to be," Harry admitted.

Jim stepped back onto the macadam after being shown the

place where the shooter had been crouching.

"Slim pickings," he complained. "Three cigarette butts and that's it."

"It's something," Hodges said. "There's DNA on them cigarette butts—and we've got the casings. If we ever find that shotgun, we'll be able to match the spent shells to the firing pin."

"Maybe," was as far as Jim was going toward optimism. "Lord, Harry, how I wish you'd taken him down. Don't mistake me," he added hastily, "I don't wish for anyone's death, but at least there's this. You may have nicked him. The team found a few drops of what could be blood on the tree that was nearest to him."

"I hope you're right," Harry said. "I walked Jones up the road to where I thought the man's car was parked. Neither of us saw any blood on the road, meaning I didn't do any serious damage."

Actually, Harry had been out on the road and along the shoulders since dawn, searching for blood or tracks, but he didn't want Jim thinking he'd been tramping over the area ahead of the crime scene crew.

"I don't get it," Jim said with exasperation sharpening his voice. "This man doesn't know the first thing about how to go about killing people. Everything he did here was wrong. A professional would have killed you in an instant."

The observation ruffled Harry a little, but he had to agree that Jim was right. "And there's something else," he added, having been prodded by Jim's remarks into revisiting the event, "he ran away much too quickly."

"Scared?" Jim asked.

"Possibly, but whatever it was, he left in a hurry. I don't think that nick he got is the answer."

"Those two factors might add up to something in time," Jim said without conviction.

"Actually," Harry said, changing the subject, "I'm worried about Gwyneth."

"I thought she had armed security on site," Jim said, showing mild alarm.

"A couple of sleepy retired cops from the city police department," Hodges said with a gleeful grin, "who never shot anything but a paper target in their lives."

"That's no way to talk about fellow law enforcement officers," Jim protested without denting Hodges' grin.

"They'll find a spot," the sergeant continued, "to sit down where the dew won't settle on them, then break out the coffee and tuna salad sandwiches and spend the night lying to each other about the fish they've caught and their poker winnings."

Jim started to protest, but Harry spoke first. "Frank may be having fun with this, Jim, but there's some truth in what he's saying. Is there any chance of your department providing some backup for our two heroes?"

"Not one in a million," Jim said, while Hodges stood with his thumbs hooked in his belt, glumly shaking his head.

"This man is dangerous," Harry said. "He's no marksman, but by switching to that pump gun, he's improved his odds. And there's something else. He moves like an Indian. You can see how dry the sand and the brush are here. Last night when he left, I never heard so much as a dry leaf crackle until he started his car.

"Even if those security men are on their feet and moving around, he could walk past them and they'd never see him."

"Then he's spent time in the woods," Hodges said.

"Wait a minute," Jim said. "Harry, you heard him drive away?"

"I'm assuming he was the one. I didn't see the car or whatever it was. I was nailed down here for a while because, as I said, I didn't hear him leave, and I had to assume he was trying to outwait me and hoping I'd get up and step into the road.

The moon was rising, and I would have made a fine target, one even he couldn't miss."

"I think Sergeant Robbins was filling in for a deputy in this area last night. Frank, call Corporal Banks. Ask her to get Sergeant Robbins on the line and switch the call to me when she's got him."

"He's probably going to be sleeping, Captain," Hodges said.

"I know that, Sergeant. Make the call."

"Sorry to wake you, Sergeant," Jim said a few minutes later. "Were you on CR 19 last night around seven o'clock or a little later?"

Jim listened, then said, "Thanks, Sergeant. Go back to sleep."

"Well," Jim said to Harry, Hodges having been called away by Jones, "he met only three vehicles on 19 in the time period that concerns us—a large Airstream RV, a truck loaded with green tomatoes, and a white Ford pickup at least ten years old with what he thought was a male driver but couldn't be sure. The tomato truck was traveling five miles over the SL, but he let it go."

"Will that be a black mark on his record?" Harry asked.

"Very funny. Your shooter could have been driving any one or none of the three vehicles," Jim said.

"Let's keep the white Ford pickup in mind," Harry said. "By the way, can you find out who in the county owns one?"

"That depends on who answers the phone at the Florida Department of Highway Safety and Motor Vehicles when Sergeant O'Reilly calls. Sorry, I mean Corporal Banks. Speaking of Maureen, weren't you and she . . . ?"

"Yes," Harry said quietly, "we were, but it was never going to work. We both knew it, but for a while . . . You might not believe it, Jim, but she's a kind, loving, and gentle woman."

"Tell it not in Gath," Jim said. "She's a force to be reckoned with."

"Once in a while," Harry said, obviously lost in a memory, "just for a joke, I'd sit on her lap. Not much did, but that made her laugh, and then she'd hug me. When Maureen O'Reilly hugged you, there was always a risk of having your back broken, but if that didn't happen, all the worry and meanness in you would be squeezed out. And if she kissed you, it was a touch of heaven."

"She's a captain now," Jim said, grinning at Harry's expression. "Now then, Lieutenant Jones with Hodges in tow is headed this way. We're going to close this down. When I know what we've got, Harry, I'll give you a call."

Harry walked back over the bridge and to his house with the wisps of memory of Maureen O'Reilly slowly fading and being replaced by concern for Gwyneth. It wasn't until he had laid out for Jim his certainty that she was not being adequately protected that he'd admitted to himself the seriousness of her exposure.

True, she had, according to Bubba, taken to her Smith & Wesson 642, "like a coon to peaches," but Harry thought a .38 caliber revolver in Gwyneth's hands would not prove to be much of a match for a surprise attack by someone armed with a twelve gauge shotgun.

No one, he thought, was likely to get into Holly's house unnoticed with Nip on guard, but Gwyneth had no dog, and this man would slip through her outside guards like smoke through a screen. In addition, being convinced that Scartole was behind the shooter, Harry had no trouble thinking that his killer would know where Gwyneth's bedroom was located and how to get there.

The real problem, he told himself, stepping into the lanai's welcome shade, was that he had no idea how to protect her from what he felt sure was coming—unless, of course, he spent the next few nights in her house.

"I suppose," he said to Gwyneth that afternoon, "if you tell me to leave, I'll have to go, but that's the only way you're getting rid of me."

They were sitting in her second floor living room. The two ceiling fans were turning slowly and silently, stirring the air and giving it, Harry thought, the feeling of being alive. Very pleasant.

"Why did you convince me to go to all the trouble and expense of learning to use my 642, which, by the way, Bubba says I handle like a natural? I'm now in the ten ring ninety percent of the time."

"You know what comes after pride," Harry said, actually very proud of her but not willing to let her know it, at least not until he'd persuaded her to let him stay in the house for the next few nights.

"Yes, I know what followeth! God, you're a pain sometimes," she complained, twisting in her chair so she wouldn't have to look at him.

"The answer to your question is that I'm not going to be with you during the day, and you'd better not carry that gun at the bottom of your handbag. Has Bubba talked to you yet about holsters?"

"Out of the house, I'm wearing a back holster and a sleeveless jacket to cover it, like this," she said, plucking at a lapel.

"Excellent. By the way, it might take two of us, and I'll feel a lot better knowing you've got my back."

She turned back, blushing slightly. "Thank you," she said.

"In advance," he said, "there are two kinds of people in the world, those who can shoot other people and those who can't. Those who can't tend to be the more intelligent half but the less reliable. I tell you this, just in case you can't, and then blame yourself in case he shoots me and then you."

Before Harry could say anything else, Gwyneth was on her feet with the .38 in her hand, pointed at his head.

"How about I shoot you now and put you out of your misery?" she shouted, giving every indication that she might.

"Not with the safety still on and no shells in the cylinder," he told her.

"Bubba would kick my butt if he saw me do that," she said, returning the gun to its holster in a single, smooth motion.

"I'm tempted to do the same thing," he said.

"Would you stop there or do other things to me?" she asked hopefully, laughing when he turned red. "You are so busted," she said, wagging a finger at him.

"Why are you carrying that gun around when it's not loaded?" he demanded, trying to save face.

"I'm having a little trouble loading it and then putting it in the holster. Actually, it frightens me. So I'm practicing with it empty."

"Are you afraid you'll accidently fire it?"

"Yes."

"Okay, here's what you do. You load it, you go to a room in the house where even if you fired it, no one would be hurt. Then you start by slowly drawing the gun and holding it out in front of you, leaving the safety on. Do you think you can do that?"

"I think so."

"Keep doing that until it gets to be boring. Then draw it, slide off the safety, keep your finger off the trigger, and point it at something on the wall. Do that until you're tired."

"And then I draw it, put my finger on the trigger, slide off the safety, and shoot myself in the foot."

"A guarantee, you will only make that mistake once," Harry told her.

"Could I practice the final routine in Bubba's firing range?"

"Check with him, and if he's agreeable, start shooting at your target. And wear that gun loaded just as soon as you can. Put it under your pillow at night loaded. It will soon feel like a part of you."

"What about having you in the house?" she asked in a serious voice that made Harry uneasy. "Will I grow accustomed to that too?"

"I snore. You'll be glad to get rid of me."

"Are you planning to sleep in my bed?"

"No, but I want a connecting room."

"Will the door be locked from your side?"

"No, and not on yours either."

"All right," she said, "but don't forget it was your idea."

CHAPTER 34

"Let's run over this again," Holly said the following afternoon as they were riding together toward the Black Angus pasture where Holly intended to check on a couple of cows that were due to calve. "You spent last night with Gwyneth Benbow and will be sleeping there, not here with me, until the man who tried to kill you is caught. Make any alterations in the summary that you think appropriate."

Her voice was deceptively friendly but the accompanying smile was false as hell. Harry was not deceived. "As I said, I have my own room."

"That's nice. The bedroom next to Gwyneth's with a connecting door."

"Well, yes. In case—"

"She needs a body check in the night?"

"Holly, please, someone is trying to kill her. The men she has on the grounds are duffers. Jim can't scrape up the money to put any of his people on guard duty. She has a gun she's learned to use, but she's not you. And I don't think she . . ."

"Bullshit!" Holly exploded, making Scotsman shy and begin dancing until she reined him in with savage efficiency. Aisha, ever protective of her rider, cocked her ears and put some distance between herself and the hubbub and nearly dumped Harry doing it.

"Bullshit!" Holly repeated, forgoing a chance to laugh at Harry, who had lost a stirrup and was pulling himself with both hands on the pommel back into the saddle. "Gwyneth has been showing you her breasts and her ass for a while now. What does this tell you?"

"Never look a gift horse in the mouth?" Harry asked, slightly winded from his exertions and not giving the gravity of his situation sufficient attention.

"Oh! A joke! You're within a whisker of having me break your other leg or pull a Bobbitt on you, and you're making a joke."

While she said this, Scotsman, registering Holly's upset state, was pirouetting, throwing up his head, squealing and giving every indication of a nervous collapse. Harry, meanwhile, was leaning over Aisha's neck, trying with poor luck to retrieve his reins. Even Aisha was beginning to show the whites of her eyes.

"Holly, I'm sorry," Harry gasped, with the pommel jabbing him in the stomach. Aisha, losing patience, lifted her head enough to let Harry grasp the reins and sit back. "I don't know what to say. I have no intention of making love to Gwyneth, and I'm sure she'd shoot me if I tried. So what's all this about?"

"How do you think it makes me feel," Holly shouted, "knowing you are sleeping night after night with only an unlocked door between you and a drop-dead gorgeous woman, who keeps showing you her top of the line personal equipment?"

Harry's dismounts were not things of beauty, and this one with a game leg was so ridiculous that even Aisha looked away, but he didn't fall down, which was the very most that could be said in defense of it.

"Stand!" Holly said in a voice that brooked no contradiction. Scotsman's front feet struck the earth and stayed there.

"When are you going to spend a night with me on the Hammock?" Harry asked with equal firmness.

"What about tonight?" she answered, coming out of her saddle like a winged bird. She landed squarely in front of Harry without a quiver and planted her fists on her hips.

"It's about time," he said and pulled her to him and kissed her.

"That was wicked," Holly said when they were capable of speech.

"The kiss?"

"No, that strategy to change the subject."

"I was under intense fire from a superior force," Harry said. "Why has it taken you so long to agree to sleep on the Hammock?"

"Your bedroom is a stage where a cast of thousands have auditioned. I thought I probably wouldn't make the cut."

"Now who's being silly?"

"I can't spend tonight with you, Harry," she said becoming serious and leaning back in his arms. "You've got to be with Gwyneth, and for God's sake take care of yourself as well as her."

"Okay, but it's a long time before dark."

"Yes, and looking over the cows will be thirsty and tiring work. When we're back at the house we'll wet our whistles and then have some down time."

"I suppose we might consider a practice run . . ." Harry said, looking at the surrounding ground.

"Do you think?" she asked, also looking.

"Sand, fire ants, chiggers, ticks, snakes in the ferns, poison ivy," he recited.

"Biting flies," she added, slapping at the back of her neck, "and horse manure."

"Let's get the cow thing behind us," Harry said.

"Does it mean we're getting old, Harry?"

"Certainly not," he said, struggling into the saddle. "It just means we're delaying gratification in order to increase desire."

341

"Was that Aisha who laughed?" Holly asked, having found her seat in a single, swift leap.

"Is it possible that whoever was shooting at you was more seriously wounded than you thought?" Tucker asked.

It was three days after his dust-up with Holly, and Harry was struggling to understand why Holly hadn't been attacked.

"I don't think that's possible," he said. "My CZ 75 is a 9 mm, and the bullet weight I use is 115 grams. If I had hit any part of the shooter solidly, he either would have dropped in his tracks or left a blood trail escaping."

Tucker and Harry were sitting on the split log seat on the edge of Tucker's citrus grove, watching a doe with twin fawns slowly drifting through the trees. The deers' coats changed constantly with the play of the morning sun and dappled shade on them as they fed on the heavy grass under the trees. Sanchez was lying beside Tucker, having a nap while Oh, Brother! grazed a short distance away.

"Then your best guess is . . . ?" Tucker said, watching the fawns trying to find the courage to approach the big mule, who was paying no attention to them.

"Do you think that doe knows Oh, Brother!?" Harry inquired.

"Yes, and so do the fawns, but they also know their mother doesn't want them fraternizing and especially not with Sanchez, who would like nothing better than to have a good run around with them."

"She's not that trusting."

"No. As long as he's lying down, she won't be troubled, but if he gets up and starts toward them, up goes her tail and away they go. Why hasn't he attacked Gwyneth?"

"That's a question I can't answer. In fact, there doesn't seem to be any discernible strategy in how he's gone about this whole enterprise. If I didn't have to, I couldn't believe he's the same person who killed Perez."

"Do you suppose he scared himself killing Perez? Did something happen there that made him so skittish?"

"I don't think so, but maybe it was his shooting Gwyneth that did it. If it hadn't been raining so hard, he almost certainly would have been identified."

"Unless if it hadn't been raining he wouldn't have done it."

"I'm fairly credulous, but I can't believe he knew it was going to be raining when the talk was finished, or that his being at that talk and his carrying a gun, and deciding to kill Gwyneth were coincidental."

"Neither can I. Do you think it was the man with the sack who shot her?"

"He's our only suspect, which doesn't answer your question, but I can't do better."

"There's something that bothers me about the assumption that he was the shooter," Tucker said, then fell silent.

Harry sat watching the deer for a moment, waiting for Tucker to finish the thought. When he didn't, Harry turned to his old friend and said, "Because?"

"He left the hall early, was wearing workman's clothes, and needed a shower. What's the term I'm searching for?"

"Stereotyping," Harry said.

"Classifying by irrelevant factors."

"That's right. But the hard part is that all too often those factors are valid indicators," Harry said. "In this case, the man stands out because men like him almost never appear in that venue."

"All the more reason to double your doubts about your conclusion that he's under suspicion," Tucker insisted.

Harry walked home, turning over Tucker's adjurations concerning the man with the sack and finally admitting that none of the information he had about the man linked him directly to Gwyneth's being shot. After all, someone else in the hall could have waited for Gwyneth to leave, followed her to her car, and shot her. In that low level of visibility the risk of being seen was almost nil. Even the sound of the gun was masked by the thunder.

It was, Harry admitted, a depressing conclusion, but not a new one, and in his work, he reminded himself, you were obliged to work with what you had, not what you would like to have.

"The answer to this particular riddle," Harry paused to tell a large yellow rat snake hanging in the branches of a young buttonwood tree beside the road, "is here somewhere. It's just a matter of finding it."

The snake, being deaf, made no response other than sticking its tongue out at Harry and lifting itself onto a higher branch, continuing its search for lizards.

"I wasn't very impressed with that bit of wisdom either," Harry said before resuming his walk.

Once he was home, Harry called Sarah.

"I was just wondering whether or not I should call you, Harry," she said. "There's been a change."

Harry had detected a change in his daughter's voice, but he did not think that was what Sarah was talking about.

"Jennifer?" Harry asked.

"Of course," she said, "what else?"

"I'm sorry," Harry said, "I don't keep in the front of my mind as much as I should how much of the weight of your mother's illness you're bearing and have been. What's happened?"

"She's grown quiet," Sarah said, the dullness returning to her voice.

"Can you say more?" Harry asked quietly into the silence

that followed her remark.

"Not a lot. She's not reading much either, but she's not, as far as any of us can tell, in any discomfort or any weaker physically or mentally than she was."

There was another pause. Harry waited it out, sensing that Sarah was struggling with something.

When it came, Harry understood at once. She was barely able to control her voice. "Yesterday afternoon she asked me if I remembered the time we were coming home through the woods with our Christmas tree you had cut and tied to the toboggan. 'Your father was ahead of us a little way,' she said, 'pulling the toboggan, and you and I, carrying Clive, had fallen behind because the snow was deeper on that part of the trail, and suddenly an enormous bull moose stepped into the trail in front of us.'

"I was knocked back on my heels, but I gathered myself enough to say that I did and that I remembered how startled I was by his sudden appearance and by how big he was. 'I couldn't see your father because the moose was between us,' she continued, 'and was afraid he had not seen the moose because it appeared without making a sound.'

"Then I said you fired your rifle, and the moose laid his antlers back on his shoulders and ran into the woods.

" 'He was a beautiful animal,' Jennifer said, 'and I remember being so glad Harry hadn't shot him.'

"That was all she said. Harry, do you realize that it's the first time I've heard her speak your name since she left you?"

For a few moments Harry didn't trust himself to speak, struggling as he was with the sudden flood of conflicting emotions washing over him. In no order, he experienced grateful relief that at long last Jennifer could say his name, an upwelling of love for her, mingled with equally strong anger and regret for the wasted years, the stupidity of it all, the folly, the pain—

which was not yet over and, he thought bitterly, might not ever be as long as they drew breath.

"Somewhere the longest river winds safely to the sea," he said, unable to give voice to any of the surging thoughts and feelings churning in him.

"That's it?"

"No, Sarah, it damned well isn't, but it's all I can say right now."

"I walked out of her room," Sarah said as if Harry had not spoken, "and when I was in my room, I fell face down across my bed like a kid and cried my eyes out. She's giving up, Harry. She's letting go."

"Or maybe she's making peace with herself. I hope that's what it is."

"If you're coming, Harry, I don't think you should wait much longer."

"No, neither do I," he said.

And there it was again, the conflict between his work and the needs of those people who had the claim of family, regardless of how shattered by time. Seeing the choice this clearly did nothing to ease Harry's onset of guilt, which no amount of rationalizing had ever cured.

Standing in the kitchen beside the table, he stared down a long corridor of time, stretching from that cabin in the Maine woods that had been his and Jennifer's first real home and the house in which he was standing on Bartram's Hammock, searching for something that would tell him what he was going to do, go or stay.

But the answer was never in doubt. Would he step back from Gwyneth when without him she would almost certainly be killed?

"I can't leave at once, Sarah," he said. "Someone I'm responsible for is in grave danger."

Sarah broke the connection. Harry punched in her number, but she did not answer.

"Just like your mother," he heard himself say. Which he knew as soon as he spoke wasn't true.

What, then? he asked himself, trying to gain some distance. *It's clear enough,* his inner Jiminy Cricket told him. *Once again, you're probably not going to be there when she needs you, and you've put someone else's needs before hers.*

Harry had very little time to brood over this latest failure because Jim called him. "Do you know where Hank Tolliver lives?" Jim asked.

"Yes."

"You'd better get over here. Both Tolliver and his wife have been murdered."

"If this don't beat a blue moon, I'll eat raw dog," Hodges said as soon as Harry stepped across the threshold of the Tollivers' house, crowded with crime scene people.

Jim was standing near a single bed pushed against the wall in what Harry guessed was the living room. Bedclothes were thrown half over the foot of the bed, a ripped-open mattress was leaning against the wall, and a woman's body lay on the floor, looking as if it had been dumped out of the bed. Jim's wife, Kathleen, the M.E. for the 21st district, along with Jim and Lieutenant Jones, were standing over the body, listening to what Kathleen was saying.

"Is that Mrs. Tolliver?" Harry asked as Hodges strode toward him, the unpainted floorboards under his feet creaking as he advanced.

"It was," Hodges replied. "Come back here with me, and I'll show you the other half of the romance."

"Was she shot?" Harry asked.

"Nope, and we'll have to wait for Kathleen to give us the cause of death. When she finds out, that is. For now she'll only say it might have been the fall onto the floor."

It was a short walk from the living room into the kitchen, furnished with an ancient oil stove, a sink, a bare wooden counter under the room's only window, and a rickety wooden table that might once, like the cupboards above the sink, have been painted green, and two spindle-backed chairs.

Commanding the space between the living room door and table was the sprawled figure of Hank Tolliver, outlined in yellow chalk, wearing a pair of ragged pants and an A-shirt with three bloodstained holes in its front. He appeared to have fallen backward and in his right hand was still gripping a twelve gauge shotgun with a pump action. His left hand was flung out to the side. The gun's barrel lay across his stomach.

"Did you notice the bruises on his face?" Harry asked, dropping onto his heels for a close look. "His nose appears to have been bleeding, and that left eye is swollen almost shut."

"I figure he was standing in the door we just come through when he was shot," Hodges said. "He probably was having some kind of altercation and had come out here to pick up that shotgun, and got back as far as the door before being knocked down."

Harry was still staring at the shotgun, his mind catching up with what he was looking at.

"Remington 870," he said.

"Expensive gun," Hodges said. "New, too. Give you any ideas?"

"Where would Tolliver have gotten the money to buy a gun like that?" Harry asked, not wanting to answer the question directly because he knew where it was leading.

"There's a new Ford F-150 sitting in the yard," Hodges replied, "still got its cardboard tag."

"When can you get your hands on that shotgun?"

Hodges grinned. "You're thinking the same thing I am. It will take a while. Millard's people are going over this place with a magnifying glass in one hand and a pair of tweezers in the other. Kathleen's been out there with Myra Emily for about half an hour."

"Frank," Harry said, turning away from the body. "Have you looked to see which dealer that truck came from?"

"Not yet."

Harry nodded and went out into the yard. He opened his cell phone and punched in a number. A man with a heavy voice answered.

"Mr. Mulvane, it's Harry Brock. What kind of truck does Hank Tolliver drive?"

"You ask the most damned fool questions," Mulvane replied and followed that comment with a chuckle. "Let's see. If I remember right, it's a white Ford that's older than my grandmother. Why the hell would you care?"

"I'll explain the whole thing to you later," Harry said, elated. "Thanks for the help."

Then he walked back into the house as fast as his leg would allow and interrupted the conference beside the bed by greeting Kathleen.

"Hello, Harry," she said, "not exactly a pleasant social moment. I understand you know something about this mess."

"Not as much as I need to, and no it isn't. How's Clara?"

"She's fine, but if you don't see her pretty soon, she's going to be all grown up."

"I promise to do something about that. Can I borrow Jim and Millard for a minute?"

"I think I can spare them," she said, trying to swallow her smile as she looked at Millard but grew pink anyway.

Jim scowled at that display, and Harry hurried the two men

toward the door and away from the centers of the detectives' activity.

"Have you noticed the new truck in the yard?" Harry asked, pointing at the white Ford.

"So?" Jim said, and Millard, obviously trying to avoid being noticed, only nodded.

"I'm almost certain that Tolliver's trade-in will be an old white version of this one."

"How do you know?" Jim asked, coming out of his sulk.

"Kevin Mulvane told me not five minutes ago."

"Millard," Jim said, "get on this and find out if Harry's right."

"Right now," Jones said and almost ran out of the house.

"It's not his fault, you know," Harry said, grasping Jim's arm and managing not to grin.

"I know," Jim said, his face falling, "but . . ."

"You don't have to explain. I already know. And by the way, that's a new Remington 870 Tolliver's holding. Where did all the money come from?"

"Harry's right, Captain," Jones said, coming through the door. "The trade-in is a ninety-three Ford. The one in the yard was sold to Tolliver two days ago. There are indications here that Tolliver came into some money. If you're finished with me, Captain, I'd like to look into that."

Jim nodded, and Jones left.

"Must be a burden," Harry said as he watched Jones go.

"Are you out of your mind?" Jim shouted.

Kathleen, who was bent over Mrs. Tolliver's body, looked up, registering alarm. All the detectives in the room turned to look at Jim.

"You're frightening the help," Harry said, almost sorry for what he had done.

"What do you think we're looking at here?" Jim said, having reined in his voice.

"From what I've seen of it, the house has been tossed," Harry said. "That suggests robbery with an object in mind."

"Money?" Jim asked.

"Probably. This isn't Avola's most upscale neighborhood. The new truck was making a statement."

"Is it time for you to consult Ernesto Piedra?"

"I'm not sure his contacts reach out here," Harry said. "There aren't many Hispanics in this area. I don't think they'd be very welcome."

"Maybe not," Jim said with obvious reluctance.

"I'll give him a call," Harry said quickly. "Now, what if this robbery didn't originate here?"

"Doesn't it make sense to ask that question when we have to?"

"Let me come at it another way," Harry said. "What if we find Tolliver's shotgun was the one used in the shootings?"

"Then we take a long step forward, but how likely is that?"

Harry nodded toward Kathleen, still bent over Mrs. Tolliver's body, and asked, "Are you forgetting something?"

Jim stood frowning at Harry for a moment. Then his eyebrows shot up and he said, "Lord, Lord, it had gone entirely out of my mind." He pulled off his cap and rubbed his head. "She was dying for want of a liver."

"And Tolliver quit work a short time ago and apparently bought a new shotgun and a new Ford 150. I don't usually predict the future, but I'm not going to be surprised if Jones learns that truck was bought with cash."

"And you and Gwyneth Benbow are still above ground."

"And Tolliver looks as if he'd been punched out before he was shot. Someone looking for money?"

CHAPTER 35

"There should be a pistol around here somewhere if what we're thinking is right," Hodges said, scratching his chin and looking around at the tossed remains of the room, "but I don't see how we could have missed it."

He and Harry were standing in the center of one of the two upstairs bedrooms, both as time-worn as the rooms downstairs.

"Neither do I," Harry said, disgust evident in his voice. "There's no cellar and no evidence of digging anywhere around the house."

"I wonder if he might have traded it in when he bought the shotgun?" Hodges asked.

"Maybe," Harry said, "but I've got another idea. I think we might find he was shot with his own gun."

"How do you figure?" Hodges asked.

"Setting aside the possibility Tolliver was being robbed," Harry said, thinking his way into the explanation, "who would have a motive to kill him?"

Jim came into the room, his boots ringing hollowly on the worn hard pine flooring.

"The medical examiner is finished with the bodies," he said, wearing a gloomy expression. "Jones and his crew are wrapping up. I guess we can leave."

"Harry thinks we can't find the handgun we've been hoping for," Hodges said, "because Tolliver was shot with it, and his killer took it away."

"We've got a long way to go, Harry," Jim said, looking even gloomier, "before we can even establish a connection between Tolliver and whoever killed Perez and wounded you and Gwyneth Benbow."

"Are you going to see if there's a match between the slugs in Tolliver and those you've recovered from the other shootings?" Harry asked, being careful to keep any impatience out of his voice.

"I'll talk to Lieutenant Jones, Captain," Hodges said.

"All right," Jim said with a sigh. "We're already so far over budget a few more dollars won't matter."

With that he strode away just as Kathleen called him from the front yard.

"He doesn't like her calling him Jim at a crime scene," Hodges said with a grin as he and Harry watched Jim leave.

Harry managed a response that wouldn't contribute to the department's gossip chain, but his mind was on Gwyneth. He had decided to assume that his hypothesis was right and that Tolliver had been trying to kill him. He was also convinced Eric Scartole was the person who had hired Tolliver to do the killing for him.

"One step at a time," was the Captain's mantra, Harry thought. He would wait out the lab work on the bullets that had killed Tolliver, but he would act as if he already knew the outcome.

That evening on his way to Gwyneth's, he called Jim and got the dispatcher.

"Anything new, Anita, on the Tolliver case?" he asked.

"Nothing, Harry, the lab's jammed up. Sorry, incoming, got to go."

A short while later, he arrived at the house. "*Caos*," Margarita said with one hand pressing a hand against her forehead, having let Harry inside.

"What is it?" Harry asked, instantly alarmed.

"*¡Vaya!*" Margarita said, flinging her hand toward the stairs and hurrying away as fast as she could.

Gwyneth, holding a towel across her front, her hair pinned up in a scrambled pile, ran along the gallery and spun quickly at the stairs. "Harry!" she shouted as if he was on another mountain. "Catastrophe! I've got to be at the Eaton Galleries in half an hour. Either Gabrielle or I screwed up my appointment book. You'll have to eat alone, and don't you dare invite Gabrielle to join you."

At that, she turned and raced back the way she had come, apparently forgetting that the towel had to be held up to do its job. Harry got himself up the stairs as fast as he could and hurried along the landing after her.

"I'm going with you," he said, bursting into her room, "and don't argue. Things have heated up, and I'm not letting you out of my sight."

Hearing the door open, Gwyneth had jumped to her feet and turned to face him. She had been sitting at her vanity table and didn't have a stitch on.

"You are not to look at my back," she shouted.

"I've already seen your back," he said, "while you were running along the gallery. And you're standing with your back to your mirror. It doesn't look too bad. How formal is this event?"

"Shirt, jacket, trousers, stockings, shoes," she said, walking sideways while she talked until she reached the bed and pulled on a blue silk robe but didn't tie the belt.

"I can handle it. Put your gun in your bag and don't even think of moving away from my side."

Overcoming considerable inner resistance, he turned around and hobbled toward the door.

"I think we have a little time to spare," she said.

"Stop it," he said, trying to walk faster.

Fifteen minutes later he was at her door again, but this time he knocked.

"Come in," she said, turning away from her vanity table and snapping shut her evening bag. It bulged a little. She was dressed in a long, dark red, black and gold cheongsam and a very short-sleeved, matching red jacket, just long enough to cover the upper half of her back. Her black hair was gathered in a gold ring and draped over her left breast.

"You clean up pretty well for a hermit," she said a little briskly and without smiling.

Harry hardly heard her.

"What's wrong?" she said, showing instant concern.

" 'Made he a woman,' " Harry said reverently, rooted to the spot, staring at her.

Gwyneth came forward, her face lit up with a smile. "You're forgiven." She hooked his arm with hers and turned him gently toward the door. "All we lack is a pea-green boat, Harry," she said, "and I could buy us one of those."

It was Harry's turn to smile. "You don't know," he said, "how close you are to setting off for the land where the Bong tree grows."

"The night's just getting under way," she said, treating him to a dazzling smile.

Going down the stairs, she stopped him and said, "I just realized what it is, Harry. You make me feel good to be me. You can't imagine how long it's been, if ever, since I felt like that."

"Don't stop, Gwyneth," he said, leaning forward and lightly kissing her cheek. "Now, I'm going to spoil everything by asking you a question."

"If you must."

"Does Eric Scartole gain financially from your death?"

"You've learned something, haven't you?"

"My question first."

"Yes. I bought my freedom."

"Okay, now I'll answer yours." From the bottom of the stairs to the Eaton Gallery, he told her about the Tolliver murders.

"So, you think Eric hired that man to kill Henrico and us and killed the Tollivers for failing," Gwyneth said as they walked up the red carpet from the curb and into Eaton Gallery.

"I don't know who killed them, but the house was torn to pieces. Every cupboard, every drawer was turned out, every mattress was ransacked. Loose boards in the floor had been pulled up."

"What was he looking for?"

"Money."

"What money?"

"My guess is the money Tolliver had been given to kill us. What is this event?"

"A money raiser—don't worry, the check I'll put in the purple sack will cover both of us. The money's for a youth center the Friends of St. Lazarus is building in Immokalee."

"Bravo," Harry said, "I'll put on my party face," which appeared to be the same as his everyday face.

This turned out, Harry discovered, not to be the usual open bar affair. The booze was nowhere in sight, but young men and women in black and white circulated constantly offering food and drink. Harry was not sure whether to be pleased or insulted by the way the men and women whom Gwyneth chose to talk with treated him. Everyone smiled, shook his hand, said how glad they were to meet him, a few even said they recognized his name, then ignored him.

"How's the leg?" Gwyneth asked as they waited at the curb for her car, speaking to him for the second time since plunging into the tangle of guests, the first being at the end of what Harry had begun to think a very long evening when she said,

"Cinderella is about to turn into a pumpkin. Find the door."

"It hurts. What about your back?"

"A misery. Look, Harry, I'm certain you're wrong. Eric is not the person who paid Tolliver to shoot Henrico and us. He hasn't got it in him."

The car arrived and Harry waited until they were seated with Gwyneth behind the wheel before responding to what she had said. "You may be right, but he tried to hammer me, and he was pretty rough with you."

"Yes, I'll admit that, but in the settlement I made it possible for Eric to live the rest of his life without working unless he wants to."

"How much better off would he be if you died?"

"A lot, but I didn't and still don't expect him to collect, or if he does he will be too old for it to make any difference."

Harry thought over her reply and decided not to argue. If, as it seemed from what she had just said, she was in denial where Scartole was concerned, what would be gained by trying to tell her so? At the very least, he would upset her and probably anger her. It was unlikely he would change her mind, and he thought that sooner rather than later they were going to find out who had killed the Tollivers.

"Gun under your pillow," Harry said as they were going into their rooms.

"Want to come and check?" she asked, her hand on the door-knob.

"I trust you," Harry said. "Try not to worry," he added, step-ping into his room.

"Coward," she called after him.

He paused for a couple of moments, then shook his head and closed the door.

★ ★ ★ ★ ★

There was an instant during which Harry tried to incorporate the sounds into his dream. Then he was kicking off the sheet and grasping his CZ. By the time Gwyneth yelled his name again, the shooting had started, and he was on his feet, hurrying toward the door separating their rooms.

When he opened it, he thought he was stepping into the O.K. Corral. There were two guns blazing away in there. The drapes covering the windows left the room devoid of light, leading Harry to doubt that either could see anything to shoot at unless one of them was wearing night goggles.

"Harry!" Gwyneth shouted, sounding more angry than frightened, "where the hell are you?"

He was lying on the floor in his bedroom, peering into her room with the left side of his face pressed against the carpet, wishing his head was a flounder. Not thinking it made a lot of sense to answer, he slid backward, trying to make as little sound as possible, and groped around in the darkness in search of a sandal. Success, now what? He was on his stomach with a sandal in one hand and the CZ in the other. Feeling good, he started back for the door, trying to hitch himself along with his elbows, which he learned almost at once was a very bad idea. Although seals make it look easy, it proved not to be.

At that moment, shooting broke out again. Harry swore under his breath, struggled to his feet, and ran forward, misjudging the distance. He slammed into the door, clicking it shut and knocking himself over backwards. Which was a good thing because a moment after the collision, both guns opened up. Harry heard the door being reduced to splinters and the unmistakable snipping sounds of bullets zipping over his head.

"Goddamn it, Harry, get in here!" Gwyneth shouted.

Orienting himself toward the sound of her voice, Harry went carefully on all fours until his head came in contact with the door. Then he eased himself to the floor again, reached up, and turned the doorknob, praying it wouldn't click. He opened the door wide enough to throw the sandal across the room and shouted, "Coming in!" then pitched it. The sandal struck the wall with a satisfying thump, giving rise to a blazing response from the shooter to his right.

Having seen the muzzle blast, Harry raised the CZ and fired. The scream and the report of his gun were nearly simultaneous. Keeping himself just inside his door, he reached around and flicked the light switch. A hooded figure, lying on the floor by the hall door, was groaning and clutching his left leg above the knee, rocking back and forth with pain. The upper part of Gwyneth's body was flat on the bed, her arms stretched in front of her with both hands gripping her revolver.

"Are you all right, Gwyneth?" Harry asked with some alarm, seeing her head pressed facedown between her arms.

"You took your time," she said in a muffled voice.

"You're welcome," he said, stepping around the fallen man and picking up his pistol while keeping his own weapon on their assailant. "Colt M1911," Harry said admiringly, "a classic," and tossed it into a nearby chair.

Gwyneth clambered across the bed and walked up to the fallen man, still holding her revolver. "Who is he?"

Harry reached down and pulled off the hood.

"You ungrateful bastard!" Gwyneth shouted and pointed her gun at the shooter's head.

Harry flung himself against her, and she shot the floor instead of Eric Scartole, who yelled loud enough to be heard over the sound of her .38.

"He's got a new part in his hair," Harry said, standing Gwyneth upright again and taking the gun out of her hands as she tried to catch her balance. Now he had a gun in each hand. There was the sound of feet pounding on the stairs.

"Harry," Gwyneth said in a tight voice, "we're both bare-assed. How's that going to look?"

"I'm dying!" Scartole yelled. "I demand attention."

Gabrielle was the first person through the door, followed by Margarita. Both were wearing wrappers.

"Oh," Gabrielle said, taking in the full frontals and the groaning man on the floor.

"*Jesús,*" Margarita breathed, wide-eyed.

Downstairs, someone began pounding on the front door.

"The goon squad," Gwyneth muttered, then shouted, her face flaming, "Will one of you get the goddamned door!"

Both of the women fled.

"Maybe you'll want to get some clothes on," Harry said.

"Right," Gwyneth said. She ran for her closet and disappeared inside, slamming the door behind her.

The first of two heavy men charged into the room. "We heard shots," he gasped. The second man, leaning against the door frame, seemed too winded to speak and looked as if he might pass out.

"He's Eric Scartole," Harry said. "He needs an ambulance. His leg's probably broken, but nothing hit the femoral so he probably won't bleed out."

Scartole said nothing, having fainted after Harry mentioned bleeding out.

"Gentlemen," Gwyneth said briskly, striding out of her closet, wearing a black skirt, a purple blouse, black loafers, and a purple ribbon holding back her hair, "my name is Gwyneth Benbow. This is Harry Brock, my bodyguard and the man who just saved my life. Harry, perhaps you would like to dress. I'm sure these men are capable of watching our silent friend on the floor."

Harry spent what was left of the night dealing with Jones and his people, answering questions and filling out reports. Jim and a sleepy Hodges showed up at five and shook hands with Harry, congratulating him and asking to hear what he thought had happened.

"What I don't get," Hodges said later after having looked over the bedroom. "is how those two managed to miss each other."

"I refer that question to a Higher Power," Harry said, "and while that's being pondered, offer up thanks they were amateurs. You should have heard it. It was like the landing at Normandy."

Jim was glancing through some papers Jones had given him. "Filo says the front door was locked. How did Scartole get inside?"

"Whoever looks through his pockets will find a key," Harry said, assuming Filo was one of the men from the security agency.

"She didn't have the locks changed after dumping him?" Hodges asked, sounding dumbfounded.

"Apparently not," Jim said. "It would save us a lot of work if women would remember to do that when they're breaking up with someone."

"Anybody found out why he wanted her dead?" Hodges asked.

Jim shook his head, still reading.

"It was the will," Harry said. "He was going to inherit money. I gather a lot of it."

"That doesn't make sense," Jim protested.

"No, but Gwyneth was ready to do whatever it took to be done with him," Harry said. "And when he demanded to be included in her will, she gave it to him, never for a moment, I guess, thinking that she was signing her own death warrant. Until tonight, she's refused to admit he had anything to gain from her death."

"Lord, Lord," Jim said, raising his eyes to the ceiling.

"Yes," Harry said. "And he had Perez shot out of jealousy and me to stop my pursuit of him."

CHAPTER 36

"So," Tucker said, "Scartole will be charged with murder and attempted murder."

He handed Harry a glass of plum brandy and sat down in his bentwood rocker, watching the evening light fading in the trees.

"That's right," Harry said. "The sentence will probably be stiffened by his demand to be included in her will as a condition for her getting the divorce quickly."

"What will that get him, life?" Tucker asked, sipping his brandy.

"Unless the judge asks for the death sentence," Harry said, "but if he does, there's a good chance it will be rescinded on appeal. After all, he wasn't trying to rape her, he'd already had a go at that, only kill her."

"Once acquired, bitterness is an unquenchable thirst," Tucker said, glancing at Harry with a concerned expression. "How's Gwyneth?"

"I don't really know," Harry said, staring at the woods without seeing them. "She put more than clothes on in that closet. Two days after Scartole was formally charged, I got a check in the mail, no note. I haven't seen her since I left her place, which was the morning after the shooting. She hasn't returned my calls. I did my job, was paid, and I should be satisfied."

"Bad reactions to the shoot-out?" Tucker asked.

"Possibly."

"Did you and she quarrel over anything?" Tucker asked.

Harry winced. Count on Tucker to find the soft spot. "Not really, but there's a chance we were together too much while waiting for Scartole to show up."

"But you said she wasn't expecting Scartole," Tucker observed. "Sometimes, shared stress can create an artificial intimacy. Could her reaction have anything to do with those two things? Was there anything like that between you?"

"No," Harry said with too much emphasis, seeing her standing at her bedroom door, hearing her ask if he wanted to check on her revolver, and when he did not accept the invitation, calling him a coward.

It stung then and still did.

"Well, we don't have to talk about that," the old farmer said quickly.

"No," Harry said and took a long pull on his drink.

"Are you going to call her again?" Holly asked as she and Harry stood side by side, looking over the gate into the Barn Two paddock, watching Aisha grazing quietly on the lush grass and calmly swishing her tail. Aisha was coming into heat, and Holly had decided to breed her to Sunday River.

Harry and she were resting their forearms on the top of the gate, their right feet on the bottom plank, but their resemblance ended there. Holly was turned out in spotless riding gear. Even Harry was looking suspiciously spruce.

"Tough question and an unwelcome one," Harry said, "but I think I'm going to leave well enough alone."

"I thought you said you wanted to discuss the situation with me," Holly said.

"I did, do, but only because if I don't tell you, you could read it in the paper or get a call from one of your women friends, asking how you feel about it. You would say, 'What?' and she would tell you."

"Then just tell me. I dislike fishing."

"You weren't . . ."

"Harry, get on with it."

"As you know, Gwyneth and I had adjoining rooms. I was awakened by gunshots and Gwyneth shouting at me to help her. My room was dark, and when I opened the door to her room, there was no light there either. I tossed a sandal against the wall across from the door. Scartole fired at the wall. I saw the muzzle blast from his gun and shot him. I stepped into the room and switched on the light, then picked up Scartole's gun just before Gabrielle and Margarita came running and found both Gwyneth and me with no clothes on."

"Where had she been?"

"Kneeling on the floor on the far side of her bed, firing across it. How they both managed to miss each other in that fusillade, I don't know. If you had heard it. . . ."

"Don't change the subject. So the first people into the room after you were Gabrielle and Margarita?"

"That's right."

"And that was the first time you and Gwyneth had been to-gether since you both went to bed in separate rooms."

"Yes."

There was a long pause, and then she said, "I can see why you didn't want to tell me. How did she look in the altogether— I'm assuming that up to then you hadn't seen the whole pack-age?"

"I don't know, Holly," Harry said, "and no I hadn't. Look, only moments before, that room was a hornets' nest of bullets. I had just shot Scartole. He was yelling his head off. I wasn't thinking about . . ."

"All right," she said, "it was my fault for asking. No, wait, one more question. Do you have any idea why she's angry with you?"

It took Harry a while to say, "Yes," but he finally did.

"Are you going to tell me why?"

"No."

"I already know," she said. "She asked you to sleep with her."

"Holly, I didn't . . ."

"I know that," Holly said, turning him to face her and putting her arms around his neck. "It's why she's not returning your calls."

"I've got something more to tell you," he said when they stopped kissing. "I've got the date for Scartole's trial and permission from Harley Dillon to leave town. I'm going to see Jennifer."

"Have you talked with Sarah?"

"No."

"Are you going to?" Holly asked, frowning.

"When I get there."

"How do you know Jennifer's still alive?"

"I called the hospice. She is. Now don't go all judgmental on me," he said, "I've decided to go without consulting the gate-keeper."

"Good. When are you leaving?" Holly asked, losing the frown.

He glanced at his watch. "Right now," he said, pushing away from the gate.

"I'll drive you to the airport."

"No. I have to do this alone, all of it."

"That sounds moderately grim, but I wish you well."

"Thanks."

They kissed again and held one another for a few moments. Then Harry walked toward the driveway. Holly leaned her back against the gate and watched him go.

"Harry," she called.

He stopped and turned around.

"What?" he asked.

"If you pick up Gwyneth on the way to the airport, I'll hunt you down and kill you both."

"I love you, too," he said, then turned and continued walking toward the Rover.

ABOUT THE AUTHOR

Kinley Roby lives in Virginia with his wife, author and editor Mary Linn Roby.